Figure You Out

THE RED STRING SERIES
BOOK ONE

HANNAH DANIELLE

K.F. STARFELL

Sensitivity read conducted by Marilu Moser
Line/Copy edits by K.F. Starfell
Internal art by @kovalenko.arty
Cover design by Hannah Danielle
Cover character art by S. Renea

HD Publishing

For **VOILÀ** *(Gus and Luke)*

and

*For everyone who has been obsessed with that party scene in the '96
Romeo and Juliet film for the past 25 years. Because same.*

Content Warnings

Gun Violence
Kidnapping
Sexually Explicit Content
Explicit Language
Domenstic Violence
Domestic Abuse
Speculation of Drug Facilitated SA
Underage Drinking (Relived in a Memory)

Voila Songs That Inspired This

Water
Cruel
Pull the plug
Table for One
Hush Now
Glass Half Empty
Drinking With Cupid
Falling Asleep at the Wheel
Figure You Out
Therapy
Anyway
Bad For Me
Potion

CHAPTER 1

Cassiopeia

I usually like having men on their knees before me. It thrills me.

Not like this, though. Groveling, crying, begging for forgiveness with their dicks between their knees.

Literally.

Anton's dick is between his knees. My soon-to-be ex-boyfriend is naked and blubbering, having just been caught with it in the blonde who is scrambling to find her clothes on the other side of the room.

He's holding on to the hem of my sweater for dear life, tears streaking his pathetically crumpled face as he spews whatever bull-shit he can to get me to stop filling the bag at my shoulder.

"*Get off of me,*" I hiss. The anger as it seethes through my teeth does not do the heat thundering through my veins justice.

I have my gloves on, but I am careful not to be subjected to how *he* is feeling in this moment.

He sure tries to make me, though. Anton tries to slip his hand up to make contact with my stomach, to force me to use my empath magic, but I suck in a breath and flinch away, narrowly avoiding the activation of my abilities.

The Varner family crest across my forehead lights with the flush of anger I feel at his disregard of my physical boundaries.

1

"Baby, *please*. This is a mistake. I didn't mean to. Let me explain—"

"Explain why you've chosen to fuck someone else in *my* bed? Absolutely not. Fuck this. Fuck you. Fuck her. I am leaving," I snarl.

He still has a hold of my sweater.

This is pathetic.

"This is our *home*. You can't just—"

"*My* home. *My* apartment. *My* name on the lease. *My* life. Which I have been altering for years to fit *your* needs. *Let go of my god damned sweater.*"

I rip the hem from his grip, and he sobs. The blonde, who I have never seen before, is dressed; a look of horrified shame twists her expression.

"I am so sorry," she sputters as she crosses the room, her own eyes lined with tears. "If I'd known I—"

My anger is blinding, but the way her eye glitters, the panic that lifts her breath, tells me she had no idea Anton had anyone to hide.

She's pretty, even with her tears. Her round brown eyes are depthless, and her hair is spun of sundried wheat, a golden hue that would be difficult to capture with my paints. She reminds me of one of my exes. She even has the same crease between her brows Elide did.

I sigh, the pressure of anger giving way to disappointment, regret, pain for this woman who also just got her heart broken.

"Do you need a cab?" I ask after a few uncomfortable beats of time with no sound to fill the room outside of Anton's sniveling.

She releases a breath and shakes her head as a tear slips free.

"No, I drove. I'm so sorry," she says with a crack under her tone as she flees from the room.

A weight lifts from my chest, and I find it a little easier to take a full breath. I am grateful for her quick departure. And I intend to follow her lead.

I turn to my dresser and gather another handful of clothing. I am not sure I'm fully aware of what I am grabbing or leaving. I just want to go. I want his pitiful sounds to stop. I want the bleeding of my heart to staunch.

I want the anger to burn this away. But already that fire is fading, giving way to the agony of two years' worth of wasted time.

The rage has weakened enough to make me want to crumple to my knees, and I know if I do that, if I let the emotion go, he will convince me to stay. He will find a way to make it so I am blowing things out of proportion. He always does.

Not this time.

"Baby, please," Anton says, his tone more stable now as he rises to his feet, wrapping his waist with a discarded towel.

"I'll be back for the rest of my things soon. The place is yours until then," I say, keeping my eyes trained down as I move for the door.

He reaches for my arm, but I shirk him off.

I am barreling through the apartment building halls before he has a chance to stop me.

Only when the elevator doors close do I allow the weight of what has happened to flatten what is left of my heart. My knees give way, and I slide to the floor with my back pressed to the cool metal wall, the pain of betrayal forcing hot tears free of their cage.

There is something to be said for having an entire train car to yourself because you were forced into traveling over one hundred miles home in the middle of the night.

The silence is a relief.

It's late. I didn't realize how late when I got to the train station, but I wasn't really thinking.

Now, I look at my phone and see it's already almost eleven, which means that when I get to the station in Brunswick it will be well past two in the morning.

I wish I had thought through my plan, even just a smidge. But I had little ability to control the direction of my impulses. And the train was my only option. With no need for a car in the city, I never got one. So, it was either Uber to a seedy motel or just go home.

The decision is easier than I expected it to be, honestly. It's been a long time since I've been home. As much as I still stand by my decision to flee to the city, I've missed my mom and my friends.

The only convenient thing about Anton's lack of control is that he has chosen to ruin our relationship over winter break. I just finished teaching my first semester at the university, and I won't have to be back on campus until class resumes in six weeks.

The perfect amount of time for him to get all his shit out so I never have to see his miserable face again.

The glowing white numbers on the screen mock me almost as much as the picture of us at the football game we went to last month. His favorite team made the playoffs, and I'd surprised him with tickets.

There we are. Frozen in time on the little five-inch screen in my hand. Me reaching up on my tip toes to kiss his cheek, his blonde waves tousled, both of us decked out in the team colors like I ever cared about that damned sport at all.

A pain lances my heart. It breaks free of the carefully crafted box I placed it in as I made the decision to board the train. I release a frustrated breath as I choke on tears, and my head falls against the cushioned seat. I try to focus my thoughts on the monotonous sound of space as it passes by at an impossible speed.

I can sleep. I need to sleep. I have a few hours to go, but I know I won't be able to. And I have no plans for getting home when I get to Brunswick. There will be no rideshares this late at night, and Mom will be asleep and is most certainly not expecting me.

Not that calling Mom is an option. Asking her for help would probably mean going home, and facing Dad after the way we left things is the last thing I want to do. He's the reason I left in the first place.

I sigh and shift uncomfortably, trying to get my stiff muscles to cooperate enough to relax, but they won't.

There is so much about going home that makes me uncomfortable. I left for a reason. I chose my own life, desperate to get away from the one my father crafted for me—the life as an heiress to unbelievable fortune. According to him, I should be grateful. I never have to lift a finger. Why would I want to struggle alone? Just let whatever wealthy man from the highest bidding magical bloodline he chooses take care of me and run his business and blah blah blah.

Well, no. I have never wanted to be a pawn to be traded for more wealth. I have never wanted to marry another magic user. Fuck, I don't want to marry *at all* if it means my autonomy is owned by someone else.

So, after college, when he tried to close the walls in around me, force me into a shackled life, I left. With Mom's help and support, I fled to the city. And I never returned.

I never offered so much as a brief explanation to Dad or the ex-fiancé I left the night before our wedding.

Though, five years later, I have done damn well on my own.

I got my master's degree. I am working on another. I'm a professor teaching equalities and inequalities at the university in the city, which has always been my dream job. I have my dream apartment. A studio for my art. A partner I chose.

My dream life.

Or so I thought.

The sting of betrayal in my chest is nearly unbearable as I think about how much of my life has been touched by Anton over the past two years. How it *does* feel like a failure to have lost some of that stability, and how I can't stop the creeping regret as it colors my decision to come home for the winter break.

I really don't want to see my father. It's not an option.

Maybe I can just go straight to Yvaine's. Avoid my parents

altogether. They don't need to know I'm home. I can hide there for six weeks straight. Figure shit out on my own.

I lift my phone to text my friend, but those glowing numbers stop me. It's so late. She'll be asleep. And the likelihood of a phone call pulling her into consciousness is slim.

Regret creeps in again. I should call Mom. She'd be discreet; she always has been when it comes to me and my own free will. And she would be so happy to see me. But something stops me. I don't want to bother her, either. I am all of a sudden feeling like a huge burden and probably should have just cooled off in a hotel for a night instead of spontaneously hopping on a train.

Before the regret has much of a chance to take root and change my mind, my thoughts travel to lines of intricate tattoos over warm, tawny skin, bright emerald eyes, snarky one-off comments, and the charming curl of Talien's lips as he chides me for some indiscretion.

He'll be awake. Talien is always awake.

Something near my heart jolts at the thought. The excitement that lifts my mood surprises me, considering the reality of how we left things.

Talien, my best friend. We were inseparable for ten years; joined at the hip. Even despite the insufferable generations-long feud between our families. His family is one of many opposing my father's lifestyle. Not that it ever stopped me from staying close to Tal in secret.

That is, until the night I chose to leave. The night I thought he'd come with me. The night he'd broken my heart and left me at the train station alone; sent me off to stay behind for reasons I've never really had the courage to ask about.

A different, ancient agony lances my heart as I swallow past the thick, painful memories. We haven't seen each other since then. A phone call or a text here and there, sure, but I haven't been back, and he has stayed put.

I want to see him—that much I cannot deny—but the dread of facing that night makes it impossible to be excited or even willing to text him for help after five years of mostly strained silence.

I release a frustrated sigh and unlock my phone to open his text thread with a tight fluttering behind my heart. The last message he sent still waits there, unanswered from months ago. It's a message congratulating me on my position at the university.

Guilt creeps over my breastbone, and I bite down on my lip. I really should have responded to that.

I force my thumbs to move over the screen, pushing past the jittering of my nerves, but the words they type out are a ramble, nonsense, nervous nothingness. A text should be easy. But I cannot get my heart to stop fluttering; make the guilt clear enough to type anything reasonable.

I hate texting. It leaves too much up for interpretation. If he's upset with me for not responding to his "congrats" message or not reaching out more, I'll never know from a text. Or I will assume he was either way and get upset no matter what his reply says.

I huff a frustrated breath and bring the phone to my ear as I press the button to call instead. The phone rings, and the sound does little to calm the fluttering of my nerves. It rings and rings, and I think I might give up before he can answer. But I don't have to. The tenor of his voice sounds through his voicemail.

"You've reached Talien Vale. Leave me a message, and I will return your call as soon as I am available."

Beep.

I hang up without leaving a voicemail and release a sigh as I turn back to the text thread. I bite down on my anxiety and stare at the screen for a moment. He's probably asleep. Or working.

Or fucking.

The intrusive thought causes a sluice of anxiety. It is the most likely case. According to Yvaine's reluctant updates at my nosy questions, Tal's revolving door of men and women over the past years has been...impressive, and it was stupid of me to think he could be alone, available, or even willing to drop whatever he's doing to help me.

I sigh. Anxious frustration almost makes me put my phone down. But the promise of relief, of the bliss I know can be found on the other side of a text message to Tal urges my fingers to the screen.

A text can't hurt. And if he's...occupied, he won't respond. Then, I'll find another way home and deal with whatever awaits me in the morning.

I press send, my nerves tangled into a tight knot behind my breastbone, and quickly turn my phone over in my lap as though I can hide from any possible outcome by pretending my phone doesn't exist and staring out into the void of passing night.

Talien

"You little fuck," I growl, fisting a handful of Paris' blonde curls and yanking his head back across his shoulders. He shudders through waves of pleasure as I dip low enough to allow my lips to brush his ear.

"You know you have to ask for those," I hiss, indicating the mess he's left all over the plush comforter made from silk so fine it undoubtedly cost more than my car.

Good. I was hoping to ruin some things tonight. Well, that's not entirely true. I was hoping to fucking end things with this annoyingly handsome playboy. Unfortunately, I can't say 'no' to wasting the money of an overly privileged asshole like him, and when Paris insisted on one last dinner at Miliano's, well...I may be doing fine for myself, but I'm not about to blow three months' rent on a steak and two bottles of wine. Paris' daddy, on the other hand, won't even notice the charge on his standing tab.

What he *will* notice is the entirety of the staff at his favorite restaurant reporting his boy was seen with 'that damned Vale' again. My reputation precedes me as the heir to the ruined Vale name, the founding family who lost everything in the wake of my stupid mistakes.

Maybe daddy Davenport will be angry enough to actually

fucking do something about his 'problem' of a son this time. Wouldn't that be ideal? If Paris is forbidden from being seen within a few square miles of me, I won't have to bother with another one of his speeches about how he 'doesn't care what his father thinks' and 'we can work through this.'

Fuck that. That's how we ended up here in the first place.

The damned wine was just a little too good tonight, and Paris is a *damn* good fuck.

"Sorry, sir," Paris pants, rolling his hips against me, taking my cock deeper as his mark lights a vibrant white between his brows.

I'd never seen anything so beautiful. Beads of water trail along her perfect, warm bronze skin, shining like crystals in the iridescent light radiating from the gorgeous, curling lines of her crest.

"It won't happen again, I swear," Paris says, pulling me back from the memory.

His pale eyes are hazy with ecstasy, and his magical family crest shifts to a faint, warm white as he rolls through his bliss. My chest feels split in two.

Not again.

Paris shouts in surprise as I land a punishing blow to his ass. My hand stings from the impact.

"What was that?" I hear myself demand, but the chasm behind my ribcage continues to break open.

It takes Paris a moment to recognize his mistake. I am raising my hand to deliver the same treatment again when he finds his words.

"It won't happen again, sir," he says hastily. "I'm sorry, sir."

"It better not," I reply, adjusting my grip on his hair and shoving his pretty face into the plush pillows.

Better to keep that mockery of a glowing mark out of my sight.

I try to tell myself it's so I don't have to see his face anymore, so I can forget who I'm with tonight...again. But I know it's because I can't face the memory of *her* mark lighting for me. I've never been able to face it. I've spent so long trying to drown the image of it with waves of different magical crests and countless partners, but it never helps. The memory always floods to the surface, no matter how desperately I try to let myself drown in the feeling of this moment. This body. Whatever body it is on any given night.

But she's always here. Just the flickers of moments we stole throughout high school and a little in college, never much, but those moments haunt me.

I think they will always haunt me.

Paris moans in approval, his voice muffled by the downy fluff. He likes it rough. Really rough. And I need a distraction before the void filling my veins goes too far. I shove away the thoughts of her and try to pull myself into *this* moment. *This* body. *This* feeling, which I can control.

I have complete control.

Leaning some of my weight on the hand I have on the back of his head, I lift my hips. Paris obediently arches his back, giving me a better angle, and I take him hard, pounding into him as if it can erase everything else. I don't want to feel anything else—just this.

At least, that's what I tell myself.

"I don't think I'll be able to walk tomorrow," Paris chuckles, rolling towards me.

I narrowly dodge his attempt to cuddle as I push off the bed and slip away to the bathroom before he starts his damned pity speech again. Thankfully, he doesn't attempt to join me in the shower as he has in the past. Maybe he really won't be able to walk tomorrow.

Beneath the searing heat of the water, I find no relief from the choice image from my past that has latched on to my mind's eye tonight. The shower actually only compounds the problem. It's too familiar, too similar—the hiss of the water, the beads of it trailing over my arms. I can almost hear her shaking breaths.

I switch the water to cold. It is unbearable, but it does the trick. The memory flickers out.

I use more of Paris' fancy hair and body care products than necessary before wrapping myself in one of the plush towels and reluctantly returning to the bedroom. Paris is right where I left him, looking like the picture of a pillow princess with his golden hair tousled and loose around his soft features. Paris is...scrawny, if I'm being honest.

He's really not even my type.

I can appreciate a pretty face, but I like my men more...masculine. Really adds to the satisfaction when you have them whimpering and begging. Paris, well, I'm pretty sure he whines and begs for just about anything that doesn't go just right. Pretty sure his daddy fixes all his little 'mistakes' for him, too.

The feel of his eyes on me as I move about the room only pricks at the irritation growing at the base of my skull. Even without looking at him, I can sense the pathetic little raise of his brows as I scoop up my boxers and start to dress.

"You're not staying?"

"I never stay," I say, not bothering to look at him. The annoyance has spread, stinging around my temples as I grind my teeth to try and dull the sensation.

"But you could," Paris pleads. "I'll order room service. We—"

"Paris, god damn it, no."

The rustle of sheets catches my attention. Thankfully, he has not moved to stand. Instead, he sits up in the massive king bed and crosses his arms over his chest.

"Are you going to see someone else?" His tone is every bit as accusatory and jealous as it was the last time he asked me that fucking question.

I can't help the exaggerated roll of my eyes.

"For the last fucking time, we are not together." I try to focus on buckling my jeans and turning to search for my shirt.

"I don't care if you are. I just want to know," Paris clarifies.

"We fuck. I leave. That's it. That's all it's ever been."

"I want you to stay. I bought you dinner," he snaps, and the whiny tone saturating his voice makes me want to vomit.

"Technically, your father bought my dinner," I counter, locating the mesh undershirt and crop top beneath a pile of Paris' clothes. "In fact, he bought all our dinners and the tickets to that concert and the flowers and the expensive ties. Maybe I'm fucking the wrong Davenport."

The soft fabric of the crop top obscures my view of the disapproving pursing of Paris' lips as I pull it over my head.

"He's straight," Paris huffs when I refuse to give him the satisfaction of meeting his gaze while finding my shoes.

"Sure."

It doesn't matter. None of this fucking matters. I just want to go home. My head is killing me.

"Are you free tomorrow night?"

"No."

"Why?"

Groaning, I drop my head back on my shoulders before turning to him, glaring.

"How many fucking times do I have to dump your ass before you leave me the fuck alone?"

That damn brat tips his chin, a satisfied smile playing on his lips.

"I don't know. How many times will you agree to fuck me for a fancy dinner and some wine?"

Ice forms over the gaping hole in the depths of my chest. For a while, too long, Paris holds my gaze, looking like he believes he's finally won this little sparring match of ours. Inside, another piece of me crumbles away.

When I finally find my hands again and pull on the other boot, Paris nestles himself deeper into the bed, retrieving his phone from the side table and flicking it open absently.

"Oh, you missed a call while you were in the shower."

With a dismissive wave of his hand, Paris indicates the side table. My phone is lying there, face-up, where I definitely *did not* leave it several hours ago when we left a whirlwind of drunken clothing flung throughout the room. Heat floods my chest and neck at the sheer fucking audacity of this little prick.

"Who was it?" I ask, moving to retrieve the phone.

"I didn't answer." Paris doesn't even look up from his screen as my own opens for me, and I tap the icons for missed calls.

My heart thunders to a halt.

What the fuck?

All I can do is stare at the name on the screen.

"Who's 'Cass?'" Paris asks, still scrolling.

Why the hell is she calling me? It has to be an emergency.

Ignoring Paris, I click open to our texts and find a new message.

> Talien Vale- big time lawyer now. Your voicemail is so formal. Weird. Are you asleep or ignoring me? Because if you choose to ignore my call, I'll have to find someone else to make lunch plans with tomorrow.

She's in town? Why didn't she tell me?

Maybe because we haven't spoken in months, and before that it was little more than meaningless back and forths.

Though, they've never felt meaningless to me.

> Hazards of joining the official "workforce," you know.

> Are you home?

> I knew you'd be awake. Not yet. Three hours' worth of a spontaneous train ride away.

> What the fuck?

. . .

Paris clears his throat and repeats his questions, but honestly, he can fuck off. The dots appear on the screen to indicate she's typing, and I feel like I have to move or the anticipation will drive me mad. Pushing off the chair, I pluck my coat from the back of the adjacent chair and slip my arms inside.

"You can't even bother to answer my questions now?" Paris chides, glaring at me over the edge of his phone.

"No, actually," I say as Cass's next text comes across the screen.

> I'm as surprised as you are.
>
> Are you free for lunch tomorrow or no?

"No?" Paris huffs. "You have a lot of nerve, you know that?"

> Yes.

"I do. And we're done. Don't call me again," I say, turning to go.

"What?!"

Paris sounds like he is scrambling to get out from under all the covers, but I make it to the door before he successfully untangles himself.

> What time?
>
> Do you need a ride?

. . .

"I've already blocked your number. Don't bother texting me," I call over my shoulder as I step into the hallway.

It occurs to me that my rapid-fire text messages might be coming on a little strong, so, of course, I type another.

> You're not getting in until after 3, right? Yvaine hasn't become a night owl in your absence, in case you were wondering.

I'm almost to the elevator, waiting for a response, when Paris catches up to me. His usually pale skin is flushed with anger from the line of his hair to the middle of his chest, visible through the V of his silken robe.

"You think you get to leave like this, *Vale*?"

My tongue slides along my teeth, irritation prickling in my temples again.

"Paris—"

"No, you can't be the one that leaves; you're nothing." Paris thrusts a finger into my face.

Ah, here it comes.

"You're just a fucking Vale. You can't leave me."

A long breath filters through my nose as he speaks.

How long can it possibly take an elevator to climb twenty-six floors?

Too long, it turns out.

"I can."

"You're a piece of shit," he hisses.

"Tell me something I don't already know." I hit the button to call the elevator another half-dozen times, just in case this is the one time in history when that actually works.

"I'll find you again. I know where to find you."

"Great. I look forward to ignoring you the next time we happen upon each other," I drone.

The elevator dings, and as the doors open, I heave a sigh of relief.

"Fuck you." Paris folds his arms as he watches me press the button for the lobby.

I gladly return my attention to my phone as his blonde curls disappear behind the metal doors.

> 2 am is tomorrow. Technically.

I huff a laugh, rolling my eyes.

> Ah. True. But, you sneaky little minx, you said "lunch"

> Who the hell has lunch at 2 am?

> I see. Open up a fancy law firm and you're a stickler for the rules now.

> Technically, I'm just an associate. I didn't open up shit. I just nailed an interview.

> And what in the world do you mean? I have always been a perfect example of righteousness and virtue.

> lol

The elevator doors open again, and for the first time in... I honestly don't even know how long, that ache behind my ribs is bearable again.

CHAPTER 3

Talien

No matter how many times I lift my phone to check the time, it doesn't move any faster. The sliver of a red line indicating my battery is low has only served to magnify the sense that all movement of the clock has ceased.

Through the windows of the station, thick drops fall across the pavement.

I pace across the polished tile floor of the train station for what feels like the hundredth time, watching as the times on the screens overhead update with the latest arrivals: just one. Not many choose to travel so late if they can help it.

It's ridiculous, honestly, the nervous twist pulling at my chest as I trot down the station to the correct platform. It's not like I don't know exactly how it will be the second she steps off the train. It will be just like it always is: easy.

At least, that's what I hope for. I try to assure myself this time will be no different. I can't help but notice the sharp bite of anxiety under my tongue.

This time is *different.*

I don't want to believe that. But it's true. We've gone our separate ways for a while, and for good reason. We've been through rifts before, always due to the canyon of obstacles between us and maintaining a friendship, but even with the cold war between the founding families, we always found each other. Year after year. And it was always easy. Like slipping on your favorite jacket when the air finally cools after the summer heat.

This time *is* different, though. So much has been left unsaid. We've never talked about it: me not showing up. She's never really asked. I guess I couldn't blame her. I owe her more of an explanation. *Any* explanation, rather. But I don't even know where to start. When *did* it all start? The night we made holiday cookies in her family home? When I snuck into her room late at night? Or was it the time...

Her bright mark, lit from within and burning over her forehead, coppery skin flushed from the heat of the moment flickers across my vision again.

I shake it away, adjusting the high collar of my coat to give my hands *something* to do.

I don't know where it all began. It has gotten so tangled in my mind over the years. Maybe Yvaine was right about how harmful my behaviors can be; the particular habit of my ever-revolving sexual partners has arguably had the opposite effect I hoped it would on most occasions. Bringing up some of the things I wish I could forget.

I *do* want to forget, right?

The train rolls in. I try to shake off the thoughts of Yvaine's scalding words from the last time we got into it over how I treated Cass. She was right. An asshole about it, but right, as usual. Not that it had made a difference.

Another image plagues me, this one of Paris's smug face at Miliano's earlier, as I agree to find a 'quieter' place to continue our evening.

My stomach knots.

I owe Cass an explanation. For the way I left things. For the distance I let grow between us. She deserves more than silence. But what good will it do to reopen those wounds? She's moved on. She's happy. Successful. Free.

Isn't that what I've wanted?

The hiss of the train doors centers my focus again. My heart is racing, but I land on a sliver of hope still kindled somewhere in my hollow chest.

Being with Cass, it's as easy as breathing, like coming up for air after drowning. And, god, have I been drowning. Maybe this time will be no different after all. Maybe we can pick up where we left off. Maybe I can slide into the comfortable role of her best friend again, and we can pretend I wasn't such an asshole last time. An asshole with good reasons, sure, but an asshole, nonetheless.

Besides, she could have texted *anyone*, right?

Fiddling with the lining of my pocket, I take a deep breath and set a hip against one of the pillars in the center of the station to wait, trying to ignore the tangle of anxious energy forming under every inch of my skin.

A few strangers filter through the doors, looking drained and exhausted from the late-night journey. Then I spot her. Her hair, rather. The voluminous tips of her curls are unmistakable behind the small group ahead of her, and I feel my lungs finally filling with the first breaths of air as she side-steps the man who stopped directly in her path, almost causing her to crash into him.

She's just as perfect as I remember.

My heart twists violently behind its cage as if trying to remind me not to let myself get carried away in this moment. But she's distracted. She hasn't spotted me yet. I have a moment to just admire. To soak in the bright warmth she inspires in me before I pull away again.

Cassiopeia Varner. Five-foot six-inches of fuck-around-and-find-out attitude with the brains to whip any man who even looks at her the wrong way into shape. I've watched her put six-foot-four jocks in their place in the middle of a college party before—it was hot.

Cass is hot.

I've never tried to deny my attraction to her. She's always

looked as if the gods themselves worked tirelessly to craft her every feature: warm, amber skin that deepens with rich olives and warm copper tones as soon as the spring sun starts peeking out again after hiding all winter. Eyes like pools of honey rimmed with the deep brown of the earth after rain. A smile that's all perfect white teeth and wrinkles along her nose. I used to love watching the cut of her jaw whenever she'd throw her head back and belly-laugh at something Niles said. Those moments in which she actually allowed herself to let go and give in to elation.

Her cropped sweater hangs off one shoulder, revealing the lines of an intricate, floral tattoo along the soft slope of her shoulder. Cass is the perfect blend of strength and soft, full curves.

Honestly, those thighs could kill.

I try to shake the thoughts of just *how* I'd like to be killed as Cass sidesteps the man in front of her a second time. Every bit of her fiery spirit floods to the surface as she glares at the man, who hasn't even noticed the curvy little spitfire he just greatly inconvenienced. A deep pink flushes over her cheeks, and I can already hear her spouting something rapidly under her breath. Likely something absolutely withering, not that the man in front of her hears a word of it. He looks baked out of his mind. Cass has never been one to shy away from putting a man in his place, regardless of his current state of mind, but her rich, honey-brown eyes flick to me.

The room is still.

The group of travelers moves away, and I find my wits enough to rein in the outright grin on my face to my usual smirk.

"Firefly," I say, letting myself savor the way her nickname rolls past my lips.

A smile stretches her expression and lights the space, chasing away the anxious crawl I have endured for the past three hours. It does not hide the shadows under her eyes, though. There is a redness, a slight swelling as though she has been rubbing at tears.

"Tal," she says, a relief in her tone as she trots to close the distance between us.

Her pace picks up to a slight jog as I move to meet her. Before I have time to comment on the evidence of her distress, she throws herself into me, surrounding me in a warm embrace, excitement in the lift of her features as she wraps her arms around my middle. I stumble back a step and hold my arms out to ensure she has no bare skin showing. She looks tired and has always hated having to deal with her magic. But she's got a sweater on, and I can't stop myself from catching her greeting with an arm around her waist. I pull her in for a tight squeeze, a chuckle on my breath.

"It's been a while," I say, pulling back enough to get a look at her to confirm the red on the tip of her strong nose and under the dark curl of her lashes.

"I'm really sorry about that. I have missed you," she says, her tone strained.

Her eyes glitter with regret as her hands fall from my waist, and she moves to tuck a stray curl behind her ear with a gloved finger. We step apart, and I'm unsure what to do with my hands for a moment.

It has been so long. Five years since we've seen each other. Five years to battle regret over pushing her away and making the decision to let her leave town alone. In that time, I have lost any ability I had built before to prepare myself for her presence, her beauty. Her soul reflects the light in the room as though she were the very source of it, capable of chasing off any shadow. Already, I can feel the dark weight that clings to me lifting.

The gold flecks in the deep brown of her eyes glitter as she measures my expression, her full lips thin as she waits for my response. Her chestnut hair is shorter—shoulder length now, and the curling crest on her forehead is mostly concealed with the gentle fringe she's got framing her brow. Her skin is still warm, the color of sun-drenched sand of a depthless desert in the face of the cold winter months.

I reach up to twist one of her many curls between my fingers, letting the silken strands brush over the dark lines of the tattoos on my hands.

"I missed you, too." The words feel heavier than I intended, so I flash a smile before I cock a brow at her. "You look good, Professor."

The corner of her mouth twitches, and her eyes flicker, her gaze roaming the lines of my face. A familiar heat lights under my skin as she trails them further to meet the deep V of my shirt. Cass rocks back slightly on her heels, dragging her eyes away and pulling her sweater closed over her cropped tee to protect her bare skin from the chill. It's more difficult a task than I remember to keep my eyes from mimicking her assessment of me, though the fullness of her hips beneath the cut of her hourglass waist has not escaped my notice.

"We're both fancy professionals now. How strange. Still delinquent enough to be available for a spontaneous train station trip in the middle of the night, though."

Cass adjusts the bag on her shoulder, and I offer to take it for her.

"I have a reputation to keep up with," I admit.

"I've got it, thanks. And thank you for coming to get me. It's been a rough night, if I'm being honest. Are you hungry? I need a drink."

Her words string together as she moves past me, and I am left turning to follow her while she speaks over the curve of her shoulder. Her hips sway with her strides, and I can't help but admire how her jeans hug her in all the right places for a moment before I jog to catch up with her.

God, she's even more *perfect than I remember.*

"*That,* I can help with. Coffee or something stronger?" I ask, dropping an arm around her shoulder as we step out into the rain.

"Definitely stronger."

CHAPTER 4

Cassiopeia

E asy.

It's always easy with Talien. I don't know what I was so worried about.

Despite the dread I have been wrestling over facing that memory—the night we'd parted—it's easy to see him, to hug him, to lose myself in excitement over being in his space again.

God, I've missed him more than I care to admit.

It's always been like this. Ever since that first day of high school. The kind, selfless, magicless Vale boy who never cared that I was a Varner, a magic user, an heiress to her father's fortune, and the enemy of his family name. He always saw me for me. He had always been there.

Of course, it's easy. I feel silly for getting so anxious about texting him. We both have our own lives. He's been busy with law school and the bar exam, and I have been working to get my doctorate, securing my position at the university. And I really should have gotten over the sting of his decision by now. He had every right to choose what was best for him, and the evidence of his new life—his career—proved he made the right choice.

Still, I can't believe it's been five years since we've seen each

25

other in person. He is the same but different. More tattoos, I find I can't help but notice.

God, I always forget how attractive those tattoos are on him.

They're everywhere now: his neck, chest, arms. Beneath the mesh webbing of the under-shirt peeking out from the collar of his coat, intricate designs curl over the lines of his muscles—muscles I've always done a decent job of keeping my wandering eyes from, but I'll be damned if it doesn't look like he's taken up crafting himself into a Greek God as a hobby in my absence.

As though he needs any more assistance in that department.

He's always been beautiful. With eyes the color of springtime maple leaves in the breeze, warm, tawny skin where it peeks out between the art now decorating his flesh, a crooked smile to die for, and charm enough to bring literally anyone to their knees.

He's always been like that. His charm is as sharp as any magical ability.

Being near him is a relief I am not sure I care to admit in the face of the pain I endured only hours ago. It still hurts. The anger still simmers, but I am eager to leave it alone and enjoy the presence of my dearest friend.

I settle into the booth at Rudy's; the cracked red pleather snags my leggings, and the fluorescent lights are harsh on my eyes.

I haven't been to this diner in years. Since senior year of college. It's the preferred late-night stop for hungover or baked students; only a fifteen-minute drive from the campus in town and open twenty-four hours.

Rudy's also happens to be the only diner in town with a complete bar. A two-for-one. Pancakes and cocktails at any hour of the night. What more could a delinquent twenty-two-year-old ask for?

Except we are no longer twenty-two. We graduated college half a decade ago, and I haven't been up past one in the morning in god knows how long.

Tal seems spry, though, like the weight of sleepless nights has never once touched his shoulders. I realize I am staring at those shoulders as he unbuttons his coat and slides it down his arms. He's distracted with flagging down the waitress, so I have a moment to admire that his black, fitted tee stops just under his ribs, giving me a beautiful view of the tattoos snaking over his abs and the sharp V of his hips through his mesh undershirt.

Heat rushes through my veins, but I manage to busy myself as he turns and settles in across from me.

I realize I haven't spoken one time since we parked the car. I've been lost in my thoughts, memories of past lives, versions of us, and now the distraction of his striking appearance. Talien doesn't push, though. That soft smirk he wears so often twists at his lips as he waits for me to find words. It's not unheard of for us to enjoy one another's company with little to no conversation, but there's so much to talk about now.

"You look great. Have you taken to hanging around the gym rats? I thought you hated even the sight of those guys." I clear my throat as I shrug my sweater off to reveal the off-the-shoulder band tee I wore straight from the studio. I remove my gloves and cringe at the state of my skin.

I still have oil paint on my hands, forearms, elbows, every-where. I'm always a mess after an evening disassociating into my art. I feel exposed, underdressed, unclean. He looks like *that*, and I am a mess. A blubbering, red-eyed-from-crying-all-night-covered-in-dried-paints mess.

I'd had no time to clean up, though. Too busy interrupting my now ex-boyfriend's affair.

Talien laughs, splaying his arms along the back of the booth, which tugs his crop top up a little further along his torso.

God, why is he so hot?

"God, no. Niles and I have been training together at their place," he informs me. "I still hate the sight of those guys, believe me."

"Oh, I miss Niles, too. How are they?"

"Opinionated as ever," he says fondly but drops his gaze.

For a moment, the carefree Tal that greeted me at the train

station slips. The smirk warps to the hint of a grimace around the edges of his mouth, and those green eyes go distant. For just a moment, the weight of the world crashes down on our little booth in this crusty old diner in the middle of the night.

And then it passes. Tal's eyes brighten again, life bleeds back into every line of his expression, and he leans forward, folding his tattooed fingers over one another and setting them under his nose. His sharp eyes narrow at me, mischief dancing there in a way I am all too familiar with.

A warmth flushes my chest as his assessing gaze rattles any chance I might have had at holding my resolve steady.

"Why are you looking at me like that?"

"Like what?" His voice curls over the words as that eyebrow of his ticks up. Daring me.

"You know what. Like you expect me to say something." I mimic him, narrowing my eyes as I lean over the edge of the table, supporting my weight on my forearms. "If you have something to say, you should use your words, Talien."

His dark, lined eyes flare.

After a tense moment, he drops his hands to fiddle with the silverware.

"Whose ass is going to get beaten to shit for making you cry? Because you know the second Yvain and Niles hear you're in town, they will demand to know."

I release a tight breath as my chest strains. The battered, bruised heart there knows I have to explain myself. Although, I was hoping to have the opportunity to pretend the past few hours had not happened. To enjoy winter break without having to acknowledge the failure of my poor decision making.

But no. I wasn't able to quell my tears early enough, and now Tal knows something is wrong. Not that he would have been unable to deduce that based on the surprise visit alone.

He watches me. Waits patiently while I wrestle with my thoughts. I swallow a lump in my throat, and my skin crawls under the intensity of his stare.

I shrug one shoulder and lean back in my chair, flicking my gaze to the ceiling in some effort to alleviate the pressure of his attention.

"Tonight was supposed to be a relaxing night—a celebration for completing my first semester as a full-time professor. Anton wanted to stay in, so I spent the evening at the studio. But I decided to come home early because, well...if I'm celebrating anything, it should be with my partner, right? Turns out my surprise early return interrupted a celebration of his own. A twenty-something-year-old, very blonde celebration."

Talien flinches.

"Fuck." He rubs a hand over his forehead as if trying to work out the kink between his brows by force. "That's awful, Cass. I'm so sorry."

"It's fine." I drag out the word with a heavy sigh as I stretch my stiff arms across the table dramatically. "*Es lo que hay*. I don't really want to relive it at the moment, so please tell me about what's been going on with you for a while."

"Understandable. Let's see..." Talien drapes himself across the booth again and feigns trying to think. "I am currently working on a case against the city about the latest housing regulations for low-income areas. It's been exactly as infuriating as it sounds. Niles has been up my ass about a ski trip they are trying to plan this winter at their lodge, which I do not have the time for. What else?"

The waitress finally appears and takes our order. Talien requests water with lemon and one of their famous breakfast plates. I find I am remarkably unhungry, but I order a Washington Apple. I am eager to have something to do with my hands.

"I'm sure that has been infuriating. If anyone can manage to do any good for low-income housing, it will be you."

Talien has always had a kind heart. It comes as no surprise to me that he's dedicating his life and his family name's substantial influence to helping those in need.

"You don't want to go on a ski trip? A ski trip sounds fun. I'd like to go on a ski trip. Is Yvaine going? Maybe we can go tomorrow, and I can avoid having to face anyone else in this godforsaken town."

The waitress returns with our drinks as Talien knits his brow at me, a smile playing over his lips.

He's watching me with an amused expression.

"Though I understand the sentiment and would, quite frankly, not mind skipping town for a few days myself, *tomorrow* seems a little unreasonable, don't you think?"

"Not when you consider having to face my father after years of blatant avoidance and refusal to come home," I grumble after taking a long drag of the cocktail. Talien grimaces dramatically over the brim of his glass.

"Listen, I didn't really consider my plan very carefully before I acted. I just walked into that room and saw what I saw, and I needed to *leave*. And the entire train ride home I tried to justify it with thoughts of how nice it will be to see my friends, my mom, enjoy winter break. But now the adrenaline has worn off, and I'd much rather go sleep in the snow in the mountains than have to take the lecture waiting for me from my father."

The weight of disappointment pulls at my words, dragging them down as my rambling spirals out of control. Something deeper cuts as reality sinks in.

It's more than just a lecture I am dreading. A spike of fear coats my breastbone, and I have to swallow a lump in my throat to move past it.

My father is not a kind or reasonable man.

"Maybe I shouldn't have come home. No one was prepared or expecting me. I could go back. Face the problem like an adult," I continue, but by the end of it, I stick my tongue out and mimic gagging as I roll my eyes to slump back in my seat.

The gesture is dramatic, but damn it, it's been a long night, and I am overall tired of having to keep up appearances, be strong, collected.

I just want to be Cass. I want to be a hot mess of a woman in a diner in the middle of the night with her Washington Apple and her infuriatingly charming best friend and leave behind the woes for a moment.

But try as I might to shove them to the back of my mind, the woes stay and the way Tal is looking at me makes me feel ridiculous, but I've already committed to the drama of it all, so I pout my bottom lip and huff irritably.

That slip happens again. One moment, Tal's watching me with the same cocked brow and tilt to his lips; the next, his eyes darken, and the smirk is gone. His gaze drops from my face to watch his fingers twisting absently at the paper napkin his silverware came in. He's already shredded bits of it into a little pile under his palm.

Anxious. Something has upset him, and a crawl of regret lifts the fine hairs along my arms. What have I said to make him uncomfortable?

"You did the right thing," he assures me. His voice is heavy. Low.

For a moment, I think I can hear my own pain reflected in the timbre of his soft voice. I think it must be that I not only abandoned my relationship with my father when I fled town, but ours had suffered, as well. As much as I hated to admit it, as much as I'd wanted it not to, something changed between us when I left.

And I can feel the weight of the past five years as it pulls the space between us taut, the tension nearly unbearable.

Unanswered questions, unspoken thoughts, every moment we've missed each other for one reason or another seems to hang between us. In my mind, I can almost see the catalog of all those times I felt certain there was a tangible connection between us only to have Talien disappear. Or any time I reached out, only to wait weeks for a response.

My one forgotten reply to his text isn't the sum of all that has passed between us. Hell, it isn't even the tip of the iceberg. But forgotten texts and missed calls happen between friends, right? And it's always fine. It's easy with Tal.

It should be easy with Tal.

So why does it always feel like the easy part is one-sided, and it's not the side I have been privy to for the past fifteen years?

But I have to find a way to make it easy, to brush it off, because the waitress returns with Talien's enormous platter of breakfast foods, and he brightens.

See, it's *easy* for him. One smile from a pretty face, and he seems to have forgotten that he might have been at all disappointed in whatever we were talking about.

He flashes a bright smile at the pretty redhead with a full figure and freckles spattering her nose. She blushes beautifully as he compliments her on something, fully dismissing the cloud of our past transgressions looming over him with a flirty smile and a pretty face. And I'm jealous because friends get through it, but I have been stuck in those moments for so long. And he just... recovers.

As the waitress flits off, a newfound spring in her step, much to my annoyance, Talien clears his throat and begins arranging the plates between us carefully.

"You can't go back, Varner," he says, all hints of that somber tone gone from his voice. "Not without backup. I will never hear the end of it if you don't allow Niles to kick Anton's ass at least once before that fucker is out of everyone's lives for good."

"I feel like you're brushing off a desire to do some ass-kicking yourself on Niles. Don't be shy. You've hated him since high school, too," I say, trying my best to keep a tease under my tone as I bring my drink to my lips again.

"Alright, maybe I hated him just a little bit. How he ended up snagging you in a different city with all those options, I'll never know," Talien admits with a look that says he *very much* hates Anton, shoving a plate stacked high with pancakes across the sticky table towards me.

It's true; the coincidence is odd. Anton got his bachelor's degree in the city and ended up staying out there. We'd met by chance at some bar's karaoke night, and I thought it had been kismet.

What a waste it has all been.

I'm not hungry, but I know if I refuse the offering, he will insist, and we will be locked here for however long it takes me to take a bite of the food he ordered because he probably didn't order it for himself, but with my taste in mind to get me to eat something in the depths of my distress.

So, I sigh, pick up a fork to stab the pancakes, and mutter thanks as I take a bite.

"I know you hated him," I say with a roll of my eyes. "All of you did."

An awkward beat of silence follows, but Talien quickly diverts the conversation to telling me about Nadia's latest girlfriend. His younger sister has a history of getting her heart broken, so Talien is understandably skeptical of this newest addition.

I listen. It's a relief to have something to keep my whirling thoughts centered. I miss Nadia. We have always gotten along so well. And his parents. They are the sweetest. I have always been so jealous of their family dynamic. There's so much love there. They never seemed to care nearly as much about the conflict between our families as Dad did. It made his antics seem ridiculous, and it made me furious, honestly. And Mr. and Mrs. Vale were always discreet about my friendship with their son. They protected us where my father would have ruined us.

I always wished things could be easy with me and my parents like it was with Tal and his.

I love hearing Talien talk about them; he lights up like they are the very reason he breathes. It's magnificent, really.

But eventually the pancakes are gone, and my cup is empty, and there is not much left to do but face the reality of my current circumstances.

Which are not ideal. I could go home and face my father, which makes me want to die on the spot. Or I can check into one of the hotels in town, which happen to be owned by the Varner empire, so he would learn of my arrival by morning anyway. Actually, he'd likely learn of it the minute I checked in and send one of his braincell-less cronies to retrieve me in the dead of the night.

"I think I should get on the train and go back," I sigh, my tone flat as I settle into the regret over my own impulsive decision.

A snort from across the table pulls my attention to catch the singular dark eyebrow arched in clear disapproval over those perfectly lined green eyes. Did he redo his makeup before he picked me up or is it somehow just magically perfect at three o'clock in the morning? I need to ask what brand he uses if that's the case.

"Fuck that," he says. "The next train doesn't leave until six, Firefly, and that jackass doesn't deserve to see your face again, especially not so soon."

"Okay, yes, but I am not going anywhere near the Varner hotels, so I have nowhere to go, anyway. Unless *you* happen to have a spare room for the night, it's either go home or sit here until the café opens so I can try to catch Yvaine on her way to work. And I'll be honest, I don't think I am going to be able to stay awake that long."

I feel like the alcohol and obscene hour of the night have stolen all of my ability to think rationally. There's a drop in the conversation, a dead pause as he considers my words.

Why did I say that? Of course, he doesn't want me taking up space in his home. He probably already has someone there. Waiting for him to get back.

This is a disaster.

I spend the entire two to five seconds he stares at me with that depthless expression trying to muster the strength to get up and start walking back to the train station before he replies.

"Yeah, no, you can stay at my place." The words come out on an exhale like he forgot to breathe for a moment.

I must have misheard him because I think he said I can stay with him. I tilt my head and blink mindlessly as I try to figure out which words I misunderstood.

"No, of course, you can stay as long as you need to," he continues, but I am still just staring.

Another full two to five seconds pass, and some awkward tension pulls taut between us before he continues.

"I should have offered sooner, I just...It's been kind of a weird night, honestly, and I haven't... Well, I haven't been back to my place in a few days."

Why hasn't he been home in a few days? Whoever he's been with will probably have something to say about a strange woman sleeping in his spare room out of nowhere.

"But yeah, no. There's room, well, a bed, it's a studio."

Or bed. Not a spare room. Sleeping in his singular bed.

What is happening?

Talien clears his throat and plucks his hand off the back of the booth where his fingers drums while he speaks.

"You're probably exhausted. I'll just get the check," he says, excusing himself and striding off to find our waitress.

I am left gaping after him with a tangle of excitement, relief, anxiety, and dread through my very unstable resolve.

CHAPTER 5
Talien

This is a disaster.

Yvaine is going to kill me, assuming Mr. Varner doesn't find out first and beat her to it. I have absolutely no misconceptions about exactly how well Cass's father would take the news of his daughter bunking up with me, and yet here I am turning the key to my apartment.

"Sorry if it's a little messy. Like I said, it's been a little while."

On the drive back to my apartment, there had been plenty of time to run through every reason this was one of the worst ideas I have ever had, a fact I was sure Niles and Yvaine would be happy to remind me of for the rest of my life once they found out.

Ushering her inside, I flick on the light. I'm relieved to find the apartment in its usual state of tidiness. The coffee table is clear save for a few stray bits of mail and a small file of paperwork. The bed is made. The kitchen is clean.

Thank god.

I'm generally very tidy, but with how often I've been away the past few months, I honestly wasn't sure what to expect.

Shrugging out of my coat, I turn to hang it in the closet by the door and offer to take Cass's as well.

"The bathroom is just past the kitchen," I inform her, hanging her coat.

She moves past me into the room, and I can't help but notice she's gained almost a whole sleeve of tattoos and then some since I last saw her.

"I like the new ink," I say, trying not to stare at the intriguing lines tracing across her waist under the hem of her top.

"Thank you," she says over her shoulder, still spinning on her heel to take the place in. "You've decorated yourself well, also. And this place. It's very Tal."

Kneeling to untie my boots, I narrow my eyes up at her.

"And what exactly does it mean to be 'very Tal?'"

She narrows her eyes at me and tilts her chin as she folds her hands behind her back to ponder the question. It takes some amount of focus to hold her gaze. The art on the wall behind her, just above the bed, features minimal lines and a perfect use of light to convey the image there. It's a subtle piece, that's why I chose it. You can't quite see what you're looking at until you let your mind relax.

It mirrors my current position just enough to send my mind into a spiral of things I absolutely cannot think about right now. Not with her. Not while she's looking down her nose at me, her perfect lips curled into a smile. Not after the way we left things.

It is difficult to hold Cass's gaze, especially as she draws out the moment, forcing me to wait for her response. Teasing.

Little minx.

"Control," she says finally.

I didn't expect that.

I'm not sure what I expected her to say. But, glancing around my clean, orderly apartment with minimal color, nothing that doesn't serve a purpose, sharp lines, dark accents, and only the barest hints anyone even lives here, I see it.

Control.

That's why I can't stand to leave a dish in the sink. Why there's never more than a few days' worth of laundry in the hamper. Why even those pieces of mail on the coffee table are driving me absolutely insane right now, and I know they are the first things I'll address once I get this damned boot off my foot.

Control.

Because when have I ever actually had any?

Certainly not in the past few months as I bled my nights in the clubs and various beds with different bodies into long days at the office, working until Marguerite insisted I leave, just to do it all over again.

I've been drowning.

Drowning under the responsibilities of the cases I've been working. Drowning under the responsibility of getting Nadia through college. Drowning under keeping my parents afloat after everything. Drowning, just trying to keep myself breathing.

Except here. Here, there is control.

I guess I have found a few other places to gain fragments of control as well. Most often with my bed partners, though it only ever helps for a little while. A band-aid to patch a pierced lung.

It's taken me entirely too long to finish untying my boots. I try to cover the awkwardness I feel in my limbs from Cass taking one look at my apartment and seeing me straight through to the bone by chuckling at her and flashing a grin.

"Control? Is that a compliment or an insult, Varner?" I tease, finally getting through the final knot and setting the boots aside. "As I recall, you have very strong opinions on people who are too 'controlling.'"

Her expression falters, and something flashes through her eye before she pulls her gaze from mine to train her attention on the painting behind her. A muscle ticks in her jaw, and her chest lifts with a shallow breath.

"It's neither. I need to use the bathroom. That door over there?" She pulls her bag up over her shoulder again and nods past the kitchen.

I tip my chin and watch her stride down the hall until the

door clicks closed behind her. Only when she's out of sight, and I don't feel quite so transparent, do I manage to get to my feet.

The mail is mostly junk, so I sort through it and move the file to the small table by the door. I've been meaning to bring this one back to the office anyway.

My mind drifts to the diner and the way Cass picked at her food. Little hints of red kept creeping over the apples of her cheeks and the tip of her nose throughout the night. There are at least a million ways I'd love to fuck up that little prick who had the audacity to make her cry over him.

I've never had a steady relationship, never gotten attached like Cass does. I've always been more of the 'casual' type, the 'it's just sex' type. The majority of my partners have understood that. Cass, on the other hand, gives her heart and soul to her partners even if they wouldn't deserve a fraction of her attention on their best days. But that's just Cass.

She loves hard and fast, with every flame of her fiery soul. And she gets burned for it.

I move to the large closet by the bed and shrug out of my shirt.

Over the years, I watched her pour herself into Charlotte, only to be heartbroken when she left her crying in the bathroom. Or when Bryson dumped her in college, for god knows what reason, just to hook up with her a week later at a party for one night and pretend the whole thing never happened when her father invited him over for dinner six months later. Or when Mikaela moved overseas and never wrote again.

Fuming, I tug on my sweatpants and run a hand through my hair. Anton should be glad I don't live within a reasonable driving distance of his sorry ass.

The door to the bathroom swings open, and her hurried footsteps fall into the kitchen before her voice chimes out. I turn over my shoulder to find her with her arm buried in her bag; her attention focused on finding whatever she's sifting around for.

"Well, in my heartbroken haze, I managed to fill this bag with a sweater, a pair of work slacks, and sixteen pairs of underwear. Not a single suitable article of clothing to sleep in or even wear tomorrow. I don't know what I was thinking. Do you think I could borrow a—oh god, you're changing, so sorry—"

Cass covers her eyes and spins on her heel to focus her attention on the ceiling.

With my hands on my hips, I glance down to ensure I did, in fact, succeed in getting my pants on before I got distracted hating Cass's jackass ex.

I did.

"Don't worry," I tease, reaching into the closet for a spare tee, "I'm decent."

The tee lands over Cass's head, hiding the bright pink lighting up her cheeks.

A laugh cracks her voice, and she pulls the shirt from her face, offering a quick thanks before she takes to the bathroom again.

"There are extra toothbrushes under the sink," I call after her, smirking.

She hollers back her thanks and I busy myself folding down the comforter on the bed, gathering a glass of water from the kitchen to set on the nightstand for her. By the time Cass emerges from the bathroom again, I'm stretched out on the couch, checking my alarm for work.

Getting three hours tonight. I guess that's better than nothing.

"You're welcome to pester Nadia for a ride tomorrow if you don't want to be up at seven—" I say, glancing up.

My words catch in my throat.

This is a fucking disaster.

Cass. Cassiopeia Varner is standing in *my* apartment in nothing but *my shirt*.

I gave her pants, too, didn't I? I didn't. I swear I grabbed sweats...No, no, I definitely only threw a fucking t-shirt at her head.

I'm a fucking idiot.

She looks incredible, of course. The oversized shirt hangs beautifully over her full frame, stopping mid-thigh to highlight the lines of her legs. And my fucking chest echoes the uncomfortable twinge from earlier, reminding me exactly how much I cannot think she looks incredible, nor can I admire the gorgeous florals tattooed down the curve of her thighs, how the neckline is too big, and drapes slightly over one shoulder, or the way the V of the shirt cuts just low enough to peak at the tattoo she got right before graduation.

Holy god, I'm so fucked.

"I very much cannot be awake at seven." She swings her hips across the kitchen while simultaneously twisting her hair into a knot on top of her head.

The hem of the shirt moves with her arms to reveal a peek of the black underwear she has on underneath and every indecent thought I've ever entertained in the silence of this apartment about the one person I cannot get out of my head and cannot under any circumstances think about in that way, makes a wildly untimely resurgence in my mind... and elsewhere. Muffling a moan of frustration between my gritted teeth, I adjust myself under the blanket and try to arrange my limbs so I appear relaxed, though I'm most decidedly not.

When her curls are effectively contained, she drops her arms, and her attention finds me where I lay.

"What are you doing? I'll sleep there."

Given I currently cannot get off this couch without making this whole situation infinitely worse, I adjust myself into the pillows and prop my knee under the blanket to hide the *problem.*

"Absolutely not." I try to distract myself with my phone, but I only succeed in staring blankly at the home screen.

"Why? This is your apartment. I can't take the bed."

"Because it's *my apartment*, I insist."

She stands still for a moment, watching me as some strangled thought passes over her expression.

"There is nothing I can do to get you to the bed, is there?"

I swear, under normal circumstances, I have remarkable control over my composure. Unfortunately, somewhere between being screamed at by Paris in the hallway and ending up with Cass in my apartment wearing nothing but one of my favorite tees and a pair of underwear, I seem to have lost some of my sanity. Enough of it, in fact, that I cannot catch the throaty groan as it escapes at the thought of the very many things she could do to get me to that bed.

My entire body flushes with horror. If there was a way to melt straight through the couch and floor, for that matter, or just disappear entirely, I would gladly do so.

Her eyes stretch wide, and she sucks in a sharp breath as her neck flushes red.

"Okay, listen," she groans, exasperated, as she turns, crawls into the bed, and tugs the covers up over herself, "Never mind. It's late. And considering the absolutely unreasonable series of events I have found myself in this evening, I have clearly lost my mind. I'll message Nadia in the morning and get out of your hair."

She finishes her frustrated, frantic ramble as she pulls the comforter up and plops herself into the pillows.

"Kay," is all I manage while still trying to become one with the couch.

Biting my lip, I reach overhead and flick off the lamp.

Honestly, of all the nights that I have spent regretting the way we left things and running through imaginary scenarios which, in some distant universe, may have led us to a similar place, this was arguably the worst outcome.

CHAPTER 6

Cassiopeia

I have not been able to make sense of anything that happened last night. I have tried. I spent hours awake, doing my best to appear to be asleep while I worked to calm the racing of my heart and the buzzing of my anxiety.

How the fuck did I end up in Talien Vale's bed?

And not at all in the way I had fantasized about a thousand times over.

I woke up to a note from him saying he didn't need me out of his hair, and I was welcome to stay as long as I needed.

Another thing I absolutely did not expect after the embarrassment that was last night.

I don't really know what to do about it, if I am being honest. Neither one of us so much as acknowledged what happened between us five years ago—that he was supposed to meet me at the train station, run away to the city with me, start a life that we chose, make something of ourselves away from this town, away from the influence of my father.

Neither one of us seemed willing to touch the emotion around the reality that he never showed up, that he never once offered me any kind of explanation.

The memory hurt. More than I wanted to admit to myself. I

43

buried that pain away a long time ago, locked it in a cage somewhere safe where it couldn't continue tearing at my mangled heart.

As we got to his apartment, I wanted it to stay that way. It was easy to set it aside. The magnitude of how much I have missed him far outweighs my willingness to ruin our likely limited time.

That fact does not make my current circumstances any less frustrating. I am home, in my father's town, with my estranged best friend, whom I have never been able to wrangle my feelings for despite his countless rejections.

And my life in the city is in shambles. Although the sting of Anton's betrayal seems far off now, somehow, I am far less affected by the pain today than I thought I would be.

I have surely lost my mind.

And now I am dressed in Nadia's clothes, having not had any brain cells available to gather anything useful from my own wardrobe. I called her when I woke up, and she was thrilled to learn of my return. Talien's sister lent me some clothes she claimed she wouldn't miss before she drove me to town to drop me off at the cafe before leaving for work.

I am headed for the bookstore with two lattes in hand. One for me and one as a peace offering to Yvaine, who I have not yet called or texted to make her aware of my sudden appearance in town.

She is going to be pissed. Yvaine hates surprises.

I swing open the door to the romance-only bookshop she owns, and the bell chimes overhead as a strong waft of warm lavender overcomes my senses. It's from a candle Yvaine has lit on the counter, where she leans over with her nose pinned to the book she's reading.

She doesn't look up as I move to the counter, too engrossed in whatever erotica novel has her interest.

"Whatcha reading?" I ask, my tone light as I rock on my toes near the counter.

Her deep brown eyes shoot up from the pages and lock on

mine. An expression of shock lifts her striking features as she tries to make sense of my presence, as though I might be a ghost.

It has only been about six months since I've seen Yvaine. She visits me in the city often, but I am never quite prepared for the intensity of her beauty. Her hair is in twists that fall to her hips, and the ones around her face frame its heart shape well. Her intricate family crest stands out on her forehead against her umber skin, which looks lovely in the wash of late morning light from the display window.

"What the hell?" she exclaims, her tone stern as she snaps her book shut.

Her surprised and frustrated demeanor is more than expected.

"I brought you a latte," I say with a terse smile, holding out the drink for her to take, hopeful this small gift will erase the potential for a scolding I am about to receive.

I know it won't. Yvaine is the most opinionated person I have ever known.

She snatches the drink from my grip and sets it down on the counter with a forceful thud. I release a sigh and prepare myself for the onslaught. I should have texted her.

"What are you doing here, and why was I not made aware of it?"

"Sorry, I would have called, but it's been a weird twelve hours," I reply.

It's true, and I am not sure when my brain will start functioning again, but any time now would be nice.

"When did you get in?" she asks, her tone still firm.

"About two a.m."

She raises a brow in surprise. "And you didn't call me?"

"You were sleeping."

"Your mom came to get you?"

"No."

"Niles?"

"Nope."

I shrug a shoulder and take a breath, thinning my lips as I rock back on my heels and avert my gaze.

"Cassiopeia," Yvaine scolds. The use of my full name lands heavy, and her brow drops as she crosses her arms over her chest.

She's pissed. My anxiety flutters, and irritation stretches my chest as I make an attempt to get ahead of what I know she is about to say.

"I don't want to hear it. He's the only night owl I know, and I needed a ride."

It's true, and it only sounds twenty percent like an excuse.

"Why did you even need a ride? And where did you stay? I know it wasn't one of your father's hotels, and Talien doesn't have anything in his apartment but a bed."

I shrug one shoulder and the corner of my mouth twitches as I fail to contain my emotions on the matter.

"That is where I stayed, yes," I say with a curt nod, trying my best to keep my tone casual despite the wild tumble my heart does in my chest.

"In his bed?" she asked with a dangerously raised brow.

"He slept on the couch."

Yvaine's eyes darken, and her expression falls into one of frustrated anger as she rolls her neck and calmly reaches under the counter for her phone, her movements entirely controlled.

"What are you doing?" I ask, anxiety a flutter in my chest as I try to peer over the counter at her phone.

"Texting him," she says, her tone still leveled with aggravation.

"*Why*? It's not a big deal," I groan. That anxiety is piercing now as I try to imagine what she could possibly be texting him.

"It is a big deal! What the fuck do you mean?" Yvaine clicks the send button and slams her phone on the counter to meet my gaze again.

My heart has lodged in my throat, but I do my best to remain light, casual.

It's not a big deal.

I can convince myself of that.

"Why? I feel like it definitely doesn't need to be a big deal."

"*Why*? You've been in love with that man for over a decade, and he's done nothing but fuck with your emotions, that's why." Her tone lifts with anger, and I know it's out of love, a concern for my wellbeing, but the blow doesn't hurt any less for it.

In fact, all it does is cut fresh wounds across the surface of my heart; forces me to relive some of the pain from five years ago. The very pain I have done so well at keeping tucked away.

"Okay...but it doesn't *have* to be a big deal."

"Cassiopeia Varner. Why are you here fucking around with Talien Vale? You have a boyfriend. A life. You better have a good explanation. Like 'we've-all-been-portaled-through-time-and-are-now-stuck-in-the-past' good."

"Well, I regret to inform you that we are very much in the present. But I do *not* have a boyfriend. He chose to fuck someone else in my bed last night. So, in a fit of blind rage, I blacked out and ended up standing here getting yelled at by you. Who I happened to miss very much. I did imagine a lot less yelling, if I am being honest."

"Oh, fuck, Cass," she says with a groan, "Anton was a dick and didn't deserve you. But you can't stay with Tal."

"It's fine," I say, dragging out the vowel of the word dramatically. "I am a grown woman with autonomy over my own emotions."

I think.

"And five years is a long time. I just want to relax, forget Anton, and enjoy winter break with my friends. Can we do that? I love the holidays. And I miss you. And Niles. And I have *also* missed Tal. Let's just let what happened rest and move on."

She measures me for a moment, the air between us thick as she decides on her next words.

"Did you guys even talk about it a little bit?"

"No."

"Good God," she groans and turns her eyes to the ceiling.

"I don't want to. I don't want to know why he didn't show

up. I don't want to relive the heartbreak. I just want to exist. For a little while. I want to forget about my responsibilities and just...enjoy."

"Fine. But I am warning you right now: when this goes poorly, I am going to kill him this time."

"Fair." I shrug a shoulder and reach for my phone, which buzzes in my pocket. The name across the screen with a message waiting to be read sucks the air from my lungs.

"No," I gasp, my eyes stretched wide as a panicked kind of shock pierces my resolve.

"What?" Yvaine's tone lifts with concern.

I can't answer her. I am in a state of shock.

I hear you're back in town, finally. I would love to see you while you're here. Meet at our old spot?

"It's Bryson."

"No!" Yvaine shrieks.

"Yes," I sigh.

"How is that possible? Haven't you been here for seventeen seconds?"

"I have."

My father. Somehow the eyes he has all over the city have spotted me. It's the only explanation for this text from my ex-fiancé twelve hours after I return to town.

Another problem I had no intention of dealing with any time soon.

"Ignore it," Yvaine instructs.

"Already done."

"What are you going to do?"

I think for a moment, and a very significant part of me thinks about getting back on the train again. But I don't want to. I want everything I just told Yvaine I am hoping for out of this. I want a break, a step back in time, a few weeks with friends I thought I might never get to see long-term again.

I want to feel like I have control over my life. I want to stop hiding from my father, if only for a few weeks. And, if that's the case, I know what I need to do. There is only one person who has the ability to wrangle the out-of-control power trip that is Lionel Varner.

"I'm going to call my mom."

CHAPTER 7

Talien

A s it turns out, the situation could, in fact, get worse.

Staring down at the file on my desk, I cannot believe the level of my bad luck. There must be a very petty god out there somewhere feeling entirely too pleased with themselves for raining so much hell on my life at once. And for what reason? I'll be the first to admit I am the farthest thing from perfect. But this just seems cruel.

I only got two hours of sleep, as it turns out. After the lights went out last night, I spent the better part of an hour staring up at the ceiling, trying not to breathe too loudly while my mind turned over every opportunity I had over the course of the evening to *not* make a gigantic fool of myself. Eventually, I managed to find the key to keeping my resolve, the thing that kept me centered every time my heart tried to run away with these feelings.

Cass is off-limits.

She has to be. That's all there is to it.

We've been friends for so long, but that's all it can ever be. I know that. My *brain* knows it, anyway. It just takes a little scolding, a little reminding of all the reasons we can never be more than that, to get my heart on board. Or, at the very least, get it out

50

of the driver's seat so I can fucking function for a goddamn minute.

I need a drink.

That vice is one of the many reasons she should want nothing to do with me.

My coffee is bitter and only room temperature at this point, but I savor it as my ears finally tune back into what Marguerite is saying.

"—can't be more than a few days since they filed. We can work with that, but I need you down there today. Get some statements from the tenants and see if anyone is willing to testify."

"How is he stupid enough to try this?" Flipping through the file, I check the addresses of the buildings set for demolition.

"He's got a dick." Marguerite crosses her arms over her chest and checks the gold watch on her delicate wrist. "For a lot of men, that's enough of a reason to do whatever the fuck they want; coming from old money only adds to the problem."

The head of the firm straightens. Her crisp violet suit has a wide collar that complements the softer tones in her hijab, and both accent the rich umber hue of her skin magnificently. Marguerite is the very picture of power and composure. She's a force within this city, and I've never been so proud as the day she interviewed me personally and hired me on the spot. The work she's done for this city inspired me to pursue law school in the first place. She worked her way up from the bottom, earned every scrap of success in her empire through hard work and determination.

Her sharp eyes land on me for a moment.

"You won't mind reminding him that ours is bigger, will you?"

"After the last settlement, I have to wonder if he gets off knowing how severely you fucked him last time."

Marquerite smirks. She flips closed her own file and moves towards the door.

"I look forward to hearing what Mr. Varner has to say about

getting in the ring with us again. I have to leave the office early today; my daughter has a recital across town, but I'll keep my ringer on. I want an update as soon as you have one."

The moment the door closes, I rub furiously at the ache in my forehead. Maybe if I press hard enough against my thick fucking skull, I'll magically wake up back in my apartment, and this will have all just been a very unfortunate stress dream.

Mr. Varner. Lionel fucking Varner, shark of the hotel business in Brunswick, an absolute titan in this city, and Cass's fucking father is the newest case I've been assigned. More specifically, he got involved in the case I was already working on dealing with the regulations for low-income housing in Southside by filing to rezone the entire district. He proposed a plan for three new hotels, a mall, and upscale restaurants. Of course, all of that would be at the expense of the families currently living in the apartments there, not to mention the community park and homeless shelter in that part of town. All those families will be displaced if he gets his way.

Of fucking course, he would come across my desk the fucking second Cass comes back into my life.

Downing the rest of the cold coffee, I drop into my chair and retrieve my phone from my pocket. There are six new messages in the group text with Yvaine and Niles.

Yvaine:

Good morning. Would you like to tell me why in the ever-loving fuck Cassiopeia slept in your bed last night??

Niles:

•••••••••••

Niles:

OMW

Yvaine:

To the bookshop?

Niles:

Fuck no Tal

Yvaine:

LOL

Dear god, I'm so fucking fucked.

Before I can even get a reply formed on the screen to explain myself, Niles bursts through the door.

They have managed to look the same for the past fifteen years despite their firm line against using their family magic. It makes me think they do still use a bit of their ability to change their appearance at will, even if it's only enough to keep them looking youthful. Shaggy blonde hair frames their face in a slightly more modern version of exactly the haircut I remember from high school, and their perpetual grin hasn't shifted a fraction. The only major difference from our childhood is the black tattoo covering their forehead and the family crest underneath.

"So, I guess this means Paris took the breakup well," they say by way of greeting.

A pit forms in my stomach. I hoped to have time to find a way to paint last night as a reasonable progression of decisions, but the pace of the day has yet to give me a moment's rest.

"He did not, in fact," I grumble, deciding to busy myself with organizing my already tidy desk. "But he wasn't outside my apartment this morning, so maybe I'm in the clear."

"He knows where you live?"

"Unfortunately."

Niles bares their bottom teeth in a comical grimace before

settling a shoulder against the wall and leveling a smug smile at me.

Groaning, I drop my head back on my shoulders and vow to track down and kick some godly ass if I can ever figure out which one of those pricks has orchestrated all of this.

"Out with it," I demand, knowing full well what their next words will be.

"So, you and Cass...?"

Their question hangs in the air until I can stand it no longer, and I roll my head to cast them a withering look. Niles has pursed their lips over an obvious smile, which they are directing down their nose at me.

Sighing, I right myself in my chair and run a hand through my hair. This is ridiculous.

"Get that smug look off your damn face, Sinclair," I growl at them.

Their expression cracks and melts into a different, equally arrogant smile.

"She needed a place to stay," I say. It comes out more defensive than I intended.

Nothing happened. I don't owe them an explanation. They wouldn't give me one had she ended up at their place last night instead of mine.

Niles pushes off the wall and saunters over, flipping the edges of their button-up out of the way so they can half-sit on the edge of my desk and narrow their eyes at me.

"You reek of self-loathing, Vale," they say brightly.

"What's new?"

"What I don't understand," they announce, addressing the room as if we aren't the only two in here, "is why you don't just fucking do something about it for once."

"Don't start."

I push to my feet and skirt around the edge of my desk to pluck my jacket off the hanger by the door. Niles practically bounces after me as we head into the hall.

"Why not? You fucking hated Paris, but how many times did you two fuck? Six times? Or was last night seven?"

The new intern, a pretty young woman who just started a week ago, glances up from her desk as we pass. She stumbles over the words she's trying to say to whoever is on the other end of the phone as Niles' comment rightfully catches her entirely off guard. Red stains her cheeks as I flash her an apologetic smile and shove Niles on ahead of me.

"I'd rather not talk about that at work, thank you," I scold them as we get to the elevator. "And what's your fucking point?"

"You know my fucking point," Niles challenges, folding their arms over their chest and meeting my gaze with the same annoying confidence they do everything with.

I do. But it's not an option. It's never been, no matter how often I've thought about it.

"You know, Niles," I say as we step into the elevator and the doors slide closed, "I think we'd both be a lot happier if you spent more time worried about your own love life."

Their face scrunches up in disgust as they make a dramatic show of gagging.

"Absolutely not."

"You spend a surprising amount of your time worried about who I'm fucking, you know," I observe. "Are you jealous?"

Niles snorts and gags again, this time more genuinely.

"Oh god, no," they assure me, waving a hand.

"Then why the hell are you always in my business, Sinclair? I can't even remember the last time you even went on a date."

"I haven't dated since college," they confirm. "Not really my thing."

That makes sense. They've always been content just being themself, having the space to exist as they see fit without the drive to find another person to latch onto. Niles has, somehow, always felt complete to me. Like they have never had a reason to search for someone to complete them because they've already found that wholeness within themselves.

I'd be lying if I said I wasn't a little jealous of that contentment.

That's not to say they haven't enjoyed friendships. Yvaine, Niles, Cass, and I were inseparable at one point. Since Cass left, the three of us have stayed close, but Niles has never needed more than friendship with anyone the way the rest of us do. I admire them for it. It takes an inner strength I do not have to be that content with oneself.

"Ok," I say as we arrive in the lobby and head towards the doors, "but that still doesn't explain why you're always so concerned about who *I'm* fucking."

The air is cold as we step onto the street, and the ambient noise from the passing cars makes my head pound from lack of sleep.

"I'm only concerned about who you're fucking when you're self-destructing, Talien," Niles says, their tone uncharacteristically serious. The shift is enough to pull my attention to them.

Their ink-black brow is low over their hazel eyes as they meet my gaze. Even the lines of their lips are pulled straight instead of curled in that cocky grin. An icy chill pricks over my skin that has nothing to do with the wintery air.

Words fail me.

They're only concerned when I'm self-destructing? Has it ever been anything but?

For a moment longer, Niles just lets their words sting. Then some of the humor returns to their face, and they rock back on their heels.

"I'm glad Cass stayed with you," they say.

That comes as no surprise; they've been trying to get us to hook up since high school. I roll my eyes.

"Nothing happened," I insist.

"I believe you," they say. "You've been too much a chicken shit to be honest about how you feel about her for the past ten years. I'd be more surprised if you said you had finally hooked up, honestly. And a little hurt, too; as your best friend, I expect to be the first to know when you two finally get over yourselves and put us all out of our misery. And the fact that Yvaine knew before I did is just unacceptable. You know I'll come for your ass if she hears about it before me, Vale."

Ah. There we are. No matter how many times it comes up, no matter how often I tell them nothing will ever happen with me and Cass, Niles has always been our "biggest supporter." I admire them for their tenacity, but god, it gets annoying sometimes.

It would be easier to convince myself to let it go if they would.

"Nothing is going to happen," I say evenly. "Cass is—"

"Just a friend. I *fucking know*," they cut me off, brushing passed me to strut towards my car. "I look forward to the day you stop spouting that shit-ass excuse."

"I look forward to the day you stop crawling up my ass every time Cass is even remotely in the vicinity."

Niles grins toothily at me over the hood of my car, waiting for me to unlock the door.

"Never. Where are we headed?"

Fucking hell, don't remind me.

I unlock the door, and we both slide inside.

"We need to go by the shelter."

"On Southside? Why?"

We pull out onto the street.

"Well, as luck would have it, there's a petition started trying to tear it down for new structures and I've been tasked with finding some people willing to testify in opposition."

"Ah, didn't they try that a couple of years ago?"

"They did. We blew them out of the water."

"So why do you seem more out of sorts about it than normal?"

"Because," I say over a heavy sigh, "this time, a very prom-inent hotel mogul has thrown his hat in the ring."

That comical upside-down grin reappears on Niles' face, but this time, it's laced with genuine concern.

"And does this prominent hotel mogul and member of the mob—"

"Just because you wrote a paper on his shady dealings in college does not make it fact, Niles."

"I was compelling."

"You were."

"Does he know that his daughter spent last night on your couch?"

Again, with that pit in my stomach.

"Bed, actually."

Niles whistles. "I assumed Yvaine was exaggerating that part. Vale, what the hell were you thinking?"

"Nothing happened." I reiterate. "I stayed on the couch."

If Niles could drill holes into the side of my head with their eyes, I believe they would. They let the discomfort from their pointed attention wear on me as I wind my way through the city streets toward the shelter in Southside.

"No," I admit. "Lionel does not know. Cass texted me last night—late—and needed a place to stay. That asshole fucked some girl in her bed, and she caught them."

"Oh, fucking hell, poor Cass!"

"I know. She didn't want to face her parents. What was I supposed to do?"

Niles sits in uncharacteristic silence for a time before blowing a breath through their lips in exasperation.

"The fates must have decided to cash in on a few of your fuck-ups all at once, huh?"

"No shit," I agree, unbuckling and getting out of the car.

CHAPTER 8

Cassiopeia

I'm sure my ribs are going to snap if Mom doesn't let go of me soon. She's been holding on for at least a full five minutes while Yvaine busies herself with organizing some new indie author Omegaverse for its release tomorrow. She is using her magic, curling the tendrils of invisible energy around books to lift them to the highest shelves. The intricate mark on her forehead glows beautifully.

"*Mami*," I wheeze, and she finally releases her grip to step back and get a look at me.

"Sorry," she says with a slight sniffle, but it does nothing to take away from the strength of the remarkable woman before me, "¡Ay, hija! Te he extrañado muchísimo."

"¡También, Mami!"

It's only been a couple of months since I saw her last. She visited me in the city for my birthday in the spring and again over fall break. But she's like this every time. She's always so sentimental.

She looks the same as she always has, honestly not a day over thirty-five, which is incredible. I need to make sure I am better about sticking to the facecare routine she's been pushing on me for the past fifteen years. Her hair is similar to mine in color, and it would also be full and curly if she didn't brush it through to keep it twisted into a claw clip at the base of her neck all the time. Her eyes are warm, a golden brown, and my likeness overall is very similar to hers.

Thank god.

"I'm sorry—" I begin, but she waves me off.

"No, don't. I understand. We're just lucky your father is out of town until next week."

Relief settles over me, and my muscles relax from holding a tension I hadn't known was there.

"But how did Bryson know she was here already, then," Yvaine calls as she flicks her wrist to send a book flying to the highest shelf.

"Oh, Lionel is aware; just not here to do anything about it himself," Mom says with a heavy sigh. "No matter, I'll handle it. I brought the clothes you asked for, Mija, but you can stay at home while he's away."

I shake my head, anxiety spiking at even the mention of being confined within those walls again. That prison.

"No, I'm sorry, Mami," I say with a regretful shake of my head.

"Where will you stay then?"

"With Talien," Yvaine chimes in, her tone flat.

"What? That Vale boy? I thought you two were no longer friends." Mom's tone carries a cautious lift.

That Vale boy.

The use of his name like an insult burns hot over my resolve. I have never cared about the founding family's conflict, and neither has mom. I never really got a clear explanation as to why the Varners, Vales, Sinclairs, and other founding families have always had such friction between them. Not one that made the strife make sense to me anyway. I knew generations ago the Varners broke off on their own to begin building the empire my father has today. A few founding families supported them. From my father's perspective, the other families were in the wrong for trying to throttle the Varners' ambition.

But from the other perspective, the Varners have abused magic for personal gain, which is a strict violation of the code of conduct established at the town's founding.

From *my* perspective, it's all ancient bullshit that should have no effect on anyone anymore. But to Lionel Varner, the Vales and Sinclairs are as good as poison; potential obstacles to his success.

I know Mom thinks it's ridiculous, too. She doesn't mean to use his name the same way my father does, but the clarification is still irritating.

"Talien. Just Talien. We're friends, Ma. We always have been."

"Mija," her tone holds a hint of warning, but honestly, I am not interested in any more scolding.

"*No te preocupes por eso.* Tell me about the winter festival. You're in charge this year, yeah?" I deflect, changing the subject before she can say something to irritate me more than she already has.

She measures me for a moment, and I can tell she is thinking about protesting again, but to my relief, she keeps her thoughts to herself and takes a drink of the iced lavender latte she's brought with her.

"It's coming along swimmingly, of course. It should be the most extravagant I've ever organized. You'll come, sí?"

"Will Dad be there?"

"Sí, but like I said, I will handle him. Don't worry," she says with a casual shrug of one shoulder like it's nothing to her to have to face Lionel Varner.

I admire her for that. A very real part of me wishes I had that strength, that confidence. I can fake it, sure. But when it actually comes to my father, having to deal with the consequences of my decisions, I am scared. I would honestly rather hide than deal with whatever waits for me at the other end of that tunnel.

"Cassiopeia, you don't need to be so worried. It's been a long time," she assures me after seeing the shift in my expression.

Anxiety crawls over my chest. Mom has always been one to compartmentalize, turn a blind eye when she can. She helped me get free of this city. She knows why I left. But it's easy for her to fall into the mindset of playing pretend. It's easier for her.

It makes me sad, and I wish she didn't have to play pretend like that, but no amount of pleading with her has ever gotten her to consider coming to the city with me.

"For you and me, maybe. We see each other a few times a year. But I haven't spoken to Dad in half a decade. I don't know that I can see him."

She looks sad, and her eyes glimmer in a way that tells me she has more to say, but I know she won't. She's always respected my decision. She understands it in a way that most others don't. She herself was married off to the most worthy suitor to keep control over money and power within the same circle. She's been trapped her whole life. She's made the most out of it, but she never wanted that for me.

So, she understands. As sad as it makes her to know that our family will never be the same, will never be able to withstand the façade of a happy, unbothered unit of three, she supports me. I trust her to look out for what *I* think is in my best interest, not my *father*.

"I'll come to the festival," I sigh. "I wanted to go, anyway. When is it?"

"In a week," Mom says with a bright smile and opens her mouth to say something else, excitement lifting her breath, but the chime of the bell at the door pulls her attention.

She looks to whoever entered, and her expression shifts. Her brows lift with a surprise I find rare on her features. She is so infrequently caught off guard.

"Bryson, what a surprise," she says, her tone strained with false politeness as she moves to step between us. The subtle gesture tells me she does remember how severe that evening had been.

My heart seizes, and my first instinct is to disappear. Like, on the spot gather the ability to phase from existence. But sadly, even if I were privy to using my family magic, invisibility is not one of the talents I am blessed with.

Instead, my breath catches, and I whip my attention to find my ex-fiancé standing at the door, an equally shocked look stretching his pristine features.

"Mrs. Varner, Cass—" he sputters, his expression twisting with what I can only assume to be genuine surprise.

He awkwardly shoves his hands in the pockets of his slacks. He looks like he's just left the office, dressed in a perfectly pressed suit, his sandy brown hair slicked back, looking perfectly proper.

"What are you doing here, Westfield?" Yvaine's tone is sharp as she drops what she's doing to storm ahead and cut him off before he can make it any farther into the room.

I am paralyzed. I don't know that I have ever been any less sure of what to do with a set of circumstances in my life. The last time I saw Bryson was the day before our wedding, only hours before I got on that train to skip town without warning.

I'd done well to suppress the memories of that night over the years. I had no interest in reliving any of them.

"I just thought I'd stop by to see if you'd heard from Cass yet, and I see that you have," he says to Yvaine before turning his attention to me. "You look good, Cass. How are you?"

"No," is all Yvaine says as she moves to shuffle him out the door.

I can see the line of Bryson's brow pinch, and worry tugs at my core. I don't want him to get upset. Not here.

"No, wait," I say, my tone a catch in my throat. "It's fine, Yvaine."

"Mija," Mom says, surprised.

Bryson stumbles before he regains his balance after being shoved at by Yvaine but looks to me with a raised brow and surprise in his eye.

"Really, it's fine," I say to Mom, who still looks concerned. "I can't hide from everyone forever.

He looks pleased with himself. My stomach turns over on itself.

"I just thought if there was a chance you were back in town, I didn't want to miss the opportunity. I can't stay now, though. I'm on the clock. We should get dinner, though."

"She has plans," Yvaine shoots.

"She does?" Bryson asks with a raised brow. "If I know anything about Cass, it's that she prefers to speak for herself."

"I do," I sigh. "Not tonight. But soon. I'll text you."

I hope that's enough to get him to leave. He nods with a small smile.

"I'll look forward to it."

And with that, he turns to the door, leaving me standing between my mother's assessing stare and Yvaine's disapproving glare.

It all feels like too much. I still want to disappear. But I don't want to have to explain myself to them. With any luck, Bryson will wait on my text all winter, and I'll leave town without having to deal with him again.

"It's fine," I urge, in an attempt to get the both of them to stop glaring at me. "Let's just go get my clothes out of your car."

To my surprise, Mom follows me without another word from the bookshop.

CHAPTER 9

Talien

"Talien Vale, to what do I owe this unexpected pleasure?" Charlie greets as Niles, and I find him stocking the kitchen.

"Business, unfortunately."

The two boxes of paper cups Charlie is juggling start slipping from his grip, and I move to catch them, helping him get them to the counter. Niles asks if there are more in the back to grab, but Charlie shakes his head.

"No, this was the last of 'em. We're going to need more donations soon."

"I'm on it," Niles announces, whipping out their phone and strutting off to make some calls.

Charlie smiles, the expression not quite touching the thick crow's feet around his cloudy eyes.

"I like that kid," he says, watching Niles skirt around a cot on their way out the door, phone pressed to their ear.

"They're bearable," I admit, leaning against the counter beside him. "So long as you're not doing anything they don't approve of, then they turn into the biggest pain in the ass you've ever met."

"You haven't met my mother-in-law," Charlie groans. "Vince

65

may have learned to deal with her, being her kid and everything, but I swear if that woman comments on another one of my ties—"

A bright bloom of laughter bubbles through the thick smog settled over my chest at the weight of the news I've come to deliver. I hate to trouble Charlie with this, especially after how hard we all fought to keep this place afloat a couple of years ago, but here we are.

"You come for business?" Charlie clarifies, moving to the industrial refrigerator on the far side of the kitchen. He must have sensed the weight on my shoulders.

"I do."

As we gather a few ingredients and prepare the nightly meal for the shelter's residents, I explain the situation to Charlie. That little flicker of brightness smothers in my chest as I watch his brow get heavier with every word.

"Why *this* spot?" he asks finally, tossing another can of corn into the pot and stirring vigorously. "Why *here?* There's plenty of space anywhere else in the city."

"You know why," I sigh, dodging past Charlie's frantic whirling to add garlic powder and paprika to the mix.

Charlie's shoulders curl forward. Defeated.

"I know why. But it doesn't make it sting any less."

"It doesn't," I agree. "But we can beat them. We did it once. We'll do it again."

"For how long?"

"Until it sticks?"

The line of Charlie's mouth tells me all I need to know about how much longer he believes we can continue to fight this fight. How long before they finally win.

"Just talk to them," I say. "Anyone you can send my way is helpful."

"Your folks?" Charlie lifts a fluffy white brow to eye me.

"I'm headed there next."

Charlie nods in approval. "Tell them I said 'hi.' Saw your

mom last week, but your dad's been a little scarce since he fixed that AC unit for us over the summer."

I grimace. "He's been working some late nights."

That was putting it lightly. Dad...well, he didn't take everything well. Nothing ever phases Mom; she's the type that can find the best in everything. But Dad, well, I guess he's a little more like me—the weight of the world and all that shit.

"Vale, you think we can fit five cases of cups, a case of bowls, and three disposable silverware cases in your car?" Niles asks, popping their head into the kitchen.

"Do *you* think we can fit all that in my car?" I ask, narrowing my eyes at them.

Niles squints and draws their lips into a long line before Charlie chimes in.

"I've got a truck. Where do I need to pick them up?"

"Over on 15th and Oak," Niles replies, phone still pressed to their ear as they lean further into the kitchen without stepping inside.

How they move their body in the ways they do is beyond me.

"Stacey's Diner?"

"Yep, I'm on with the owner now. She had a shipment come in with the old logo and hasn't had time to drop them off yet."

Charlie gathers his keys and informs Niles he'll head over straight away. It takes a few minutes to locate another staff member and ask them to watch the pot on the stove, and then he's out the door with a quick thank you tossed over his shoulder. Watching Charlie's rickety blue pickup pull around the street corner, I feel heavy.

This place is a home for so many. So many who were eaten by the system. Caught in the tidal wave only the rich and prosperous had the means to escape. Hell, not even all of us *with the means* escaped it. Sometimes, the cards are just stacked against you. Sometimes, the game is rigged.

An arm around my shoulder pulls me out of my thoughts as Niles casts me a curious look. Not feeling particularly keen on dwelling on the past, I draw a long breath through my nose and shrug them off.

"Come on, Mom would kill me if she knew I was in the neighborhood and didn't stop by."

Much to my annoyance, the very first thing out of Niles' annoyingly loose lips is a very practiced announcement about Cass being back in town, having stayed at my place last night, and 'no, you needn't worry, nothing nefarious happened, your son is a perfect gentleman,' to which my mother *groaned* and *rolled her eyes*.

That is how I got stuck, snacking on a fresh cucumber salad at my parent's dining room table while my mother recounts the numerous texts she and Nadia swapped all day, speculating on the exact scenario that must have occured to get Cassiopeia Varner all the way from Rensfield to my bed in the middle of the god damned night. The most horrifying of the texts involve both my mother and sister's opinions of why it was that nothing "nefarious" happened between us.

I would like to die. Right now. At this table, please.

If looks could kill, Niles would be dead a few times over. Unfortunately, they cannot, so I'm stuck glaring daggers at their smug face across the table as they pop another tomato in their mouth and chew over a wide smile.

"No, I assure you," Niles says, cutting Mom off from reading a text from Nadia that clearly was about to imply that I might be having 'problems.' "Everything works just fine. Just before Cass—"

Their words are cut off by a very well-aimed dinner roll.

"Hey!"

Mother scolds me, popping my arm gently with the flat of her hand after she nearly drops her phone from being startled. I set a hand on top of hers and squeeze as she tsks her tongue at me, a clear sign of her disapproval at my behavior, but also one that tells me she'll let it slide.

With her glasses perched on the tip of her nose like this, she reminds me of Yiayá.

"Hi, can we *not* discuss whether or not I'm functional in the bedroom with my *mother*, Sinclair?"

Mom slips her hand out from under mine and gestures.

"Why? We talk about it a lot," she says as if that's the most natural thing in the world.

I nearly choke.

"*What?*" I turned to Niles for some explanation, but they are just grinning that same stupid grin and looking very pleased with themselves.

"Well, not whether or not your 'functional,'" she clarifies. "Just who you're with. It's not like you tell me who you're dating. You haven't brought anyone home to meet me and your father in years. A mother worries."

"A mother worries. But a mother shouldn't be discussing who is or isn't in my *bed* with my *best friend*."

Niles just bobbles their head happily before biting into the roll they've recovered from their lap.

"Oh, you act like I don't know what kind of boy grew up in my house. You honestly think Niles could tell me anything that would surprise me after all the shit I put up with after you hit puberty?"

I can think of a few things that might still surprise her, yes.

But my mother is not one to lose an argument, and I know better than to continue to push; it will just encourage her to look closer at my life. No, thank you.

"You're right," I agree, shooting a silencing glare at Niles, who, for once, mimes sealing their lips and tossing an imaginary key over their shoulder.

Mom is, unfortunately, still speaking.

"Listen, your father and I did a lot of experimenting when we were younger. We were both pretty wild, but that's okay.

Everyone goes through those urges. You have to find what you like. I mean, there was one time before I met your father that I hooked up with this—"

"*Mom!*"

"What!?"

"Stop," I say over a very flustered laugh. "Please. God."

"Fine. Alright. I'll stop." She throws her hands up defensively, all of her silver rings jingling as she folds her fingers in her lap and tries to hold her tongue despite the obvious pressure her unspoken words are putting on the seam of her lips.

There are a few spare moments of silence before she can contain it no longer.

"I just wanted you to know that you come by it honestly, and it's perfectly natural," she says in a single rushed breath.

Vasiliki Vale is nothing if not honest. I love her honesty, even if it makes me want to crawl under this table and yank out my hair one by one sometimes. Instead of sitting in the discomfort a moment longer, I decide to check my phone.

No new messages. Nadia sent me a long line of scolding texts the second Cass messaged her this morning, so I knew the two of them had coordinated, but a sinking feeling sets into the pit of my stomach.

Clicking open the screen, I pull up her thread and stare, trying to think of anything to say. It's almost five o'clock in the evening, and I haven't even checked on her.

Something prods at the back of my phone, pulling my attention up as the message sends. Niles is peering at me, their head bowed forward like some strange bird as they give me a toothless grin.

Over their shoulder, Mom is trying very hard not to look excited and succeeding in biting down a smile only barely.

"Who's that?" Niles asks in a singsong.

Shifting my eyes between the two of them again, I drop the phone back into my pocket.

"You two are insufferable, you know that?"

They both laugh. And, although I keep the scowl on my brow, I can't help but feel grateful—maybe jealous?—at how simply the two of them see this whole situation. How both of them believe with their full chests that every jest, every poke about Cass and me eventually getting over this little thing between us is just them pushing us closer or opening my eyes. That we'll see eventually we're meant to be together. It's simple.

Except, my eyes have been open for so long, and it's the farthest thing from simple.

It always has been.

CHAPTER 10

Cassiopeia

"D r. Ruth is a *dick*," Nadia rolls her hazel eyes at me as she flips her thick black hair over her olive-toned shoulder.

I crack a smile at her flippant attitude and pop the cork on my second bottle of wine as Nadia complains about the Religion in Society professor at the university in town.

"Yes, that has always been true," I agree. "Tal's wine glasses?"

"Cabinet above the sink. I mean, I don't think any of us came even close to passing with an A."

"At least it's over. You get to enjoy the break now. Speaking of which, tell me about Sophia," I say with a teasing eyebrow wiggle as I pull myself from my comfortable seat nestled into Tal's couch to make my way to the kitchen.

Nadia's expression changes from frustrated irritation to one of straight swooning. It's like I am talking to a lovesick cartoon character. Her girlfriend is staying with her over winter break, which I have learned is a very big step in their relatively new relationship.

Nadia's heart-shaped face tilts as she pulls her knees under her to sit on her feet so she can see me better over the bar top, separating the kitchen from the rest of the studio.

Tal's sister is older now, of course. She wasn't going to remain

72

that bright-eyed seventeen-year-old forever. But knowing that doesn't make seeing her now any less strange.

I remember sneaking around to hang out with my friends behind my parent's backs. Nadia wasn't much younger than us and had often been there. When we were in college, I taught her how to make bongs out of household objects, cover hickeys, and get away with midnight makeouts with forbidden girlfriends in the middle of the night as any respectable older sister-type mentor would.

But now she's responsible, in her junior year of college. She told me she's worked hard to pay her own way, taking a two-year break after graduation to work before applying to the university. She wants to be a politician now, not a famous romance author like I remember. Although I have learned she still posts her work on fan fiction sites as a hobby.

And she's strong. *So* strong. I envy the stability she radiates, the power. She is beauty and strength and everything I hoped she would be.

"Sophia is....she's incredible. I really want you to meet her. She'll just love you."

My phone buzzes on the counter, and I flip it over as I pour my glass of blueberry lemon wine from the local winery into Tal's iridescent wine glass. My anxiety is high now that the town has started to catch wind of my arrival, and I really don't want to deal with another surprise greeting from a past ghost.

Tal:

Tell Nadia I didn't get her anything.

Relief flushes me and I release a breath as I try to corral the excitement fluttering at the mere sight of his name across my phone screen.

"Who are you smiling at?" Nadia asks, and I look up from my phone; said smile I had no control over falls from my expression.

"I'm not smiling."

"You were. What, is he hung up at the office?" she asks with a coy tilt of her eye.

"Why do you think it's Tal?" I ask with a narrowed eye.

Nadia flattens her stare and thins her lips in lieu of a response. I roll my eyes irritably.

"He said he didn't get you anything for dinner," I concede, bringing my drink to my lips.

"Lies," she huffs playfully.

I peel my gloves off to reply.

She thinks that's a lie.

Keys rattle in the lock of the front door, and Talien steps in, a bag of take-out weighing heavy in his grasp alongside a black gift bag. He looks good. Tired. But perfect, just like he always does.

A few dark strands of his thick hair, the same shade as Nadia's, frame his sharp features as they fall forward from its otherwise perfect style. The chill apparently didn't warrant a coat today since he is just in fitted slacks, a pressed white button-up with the sleeves rolled to his elbows, and a thick black leather harness wrapped over both shoulders to buckle across his ribs. The button-up's wear from the day and the ring of smudged eyeliner under his eyes are the only indications he hasn't just finished polishing his appearance.

"Guess she doesn't know me as well as she thinks," Tal greets us, setting the takeout on the small side table and kneeling to remove his boots—another piece of his attire that pushes the boundaries of "business casual" to the edge.

"Bull shit," Nadia chimes.

"Mom's pissed that you haven't been by with the new fling," Talien counters.

The scowl Nadia sends his way is one I wouldn't want to find directed at me, but he barely seems to notice as he tucks his shoes away in the closet and stands.

"For the last time, Sophia is *not* a fling."

"We'll see," he says, shooting a look at his sister on his way to the kitchen.

I'm still just watching them when Talien stops in front of me. He smells like bergamot, cedar, and cinnamon, like the first breeze of winter after the last leaf falls. Just like I remember. And those eyes...

Talien's lips twitch in that familiar crooked grin. I'm already one bottle in, and the wine must be hitting me because I am having a difficult time controlling my train of thought.

"Hi," he says, vibrant eyes flitting to the glass in my hand.

"It's been a long day." I lift it in acknowledgment.

The breath he blows through his nose tells me he has had a similarly long day, and I can't help but notice the flick of his attention to where my lips meet the rim of the glass as I take a drink.

God, has he always been this hot, or was I just that horrifically unattracted to Anton? I know I have always been more attracted to women, and I easily brushed my disinterest in sleeping with Anton off on that....but god damn, I don't know that I have ever found it quite so difficult to control the curl of heat low in my core at just the mere existence of someone in a space.

Hell. God damned wine.

Rolling the inside of his cheek through his teeth, Talien shifts on one foot and shuffles the bags in his hands. He lifts the black gift bag between us and smiles.

"I picked up some things for you."

"You did?" I ask with a pinched brow.

"I did." He drops the bag into my hesitantly outstretched hand.

"What? Why?" I ask with a huff of a laugh. My heart is a pinch in my chest as my cheeks warm.

Tal shrugs and slips past me into the kitchen to set the takeout on the counter.

"You weren't exactly an expert packer last night, so I figured you'd need some essentials."

"Oh," I manage before turning my gaze to the gift, unable to hold the intensity of his attention any longer.

Once I have removed the tissue paper, I reach in to find a new toothbrush, a satin bonnet, a pair of the fluffiest socks I've never had the pleasure of holding in my hand, and a single-use sheet face mask.

"Oh, wow," I say, genuinely a little stunned at the level of consideration he put into the care package.

Though I shouldn't be, Tal has always been more aware than most men when it comes to self-care.

"My unfortunately frizzy hair and I thank you very much." I look back at him with a tip of my chin and a soft dip of my shoulder.

Talien's eyes spark. His attention flicks over me in a way that makes my cheeks heat. He smiles.

"You're both very welcome."

I have trouble containing the giddy grin before it spreads over my expression, so I turn to the bonnet to fiddle with it on the counter, breaking his gaze. My attention snags on the smug look plastered to Nadia's expression as she gawks at me from the couch.

I roll my eyes and turn away to take another drink, busying myself with examining the lack of anything adorning his fridge. Behind me, the bag rustles as he unpacks it. I try to ignore the way my mind follows the sounds of his footsteps across the tiles as he picks a set of plates from one of the cabinets.

"No kung pao?" Nadia asks, sounding disappointed.

A low chuckle rumbles from Talien. It sounds close, reminding me just how small this space is.

"I told you," he teases, "I didn't get you anything. If you had texted to let me know—"

"Shut up. You know Sophia works tonight. Where have you been, anyway? You haven't bought groceries in almost two weeks."

"So, *that's* where all my ciders went." Talien sounds as if he already knew about his sister's theft.

"There were only two."

I can almost hear the roll of his eyes. Turning back to the pair, I find him lifting a plate piled with steaming lo mien and orange chicken. He extends it to me. Nadia is on her knees on the couch, leaning her elbows on the counter to watch her brother with full lips pouted looking pitiful.

"You can eat on the couch with the thief," he informs me, nodding.

"Hey!" Nadia protests, slinking back down in the cushions. "You said to come over any time when I moved in! How was I supposed to know that only meant as long as you were home?"

Talien shakes his head at her and moves to brush past me for the fridge.

"Thank you," I say with a chuckle as I take the plate and move to the couch, grateful for a reasonable excuse to make my feet put some distance between us.

I can't keep my eyes from tracing the planes of his chest over her shoulder as I settle in. He, *for sure,* was not that hot five years ago. Beautiful, yes. But still hanging onto a boyish kind of appearance then, in his early to mid-twenties. Not now.

Holy hell.

Nadia kicks out at my shin, and I start with a chortle.

"Hey! I'm not the one starving you. Here," I say, offering my plate to Nadia. Tal gave me far too much anyway.

"Don't."

The authority in his tone causes another curl of heat I try my best to ignore, but my efforts ultimately fail. Nadia turns to give her brother the full force of her feelings on his cruelty, and I follow her gaze.

Tal's leaning both hands on the counter, looking down his angled nose at his sister with a quirk to his lips.

Good god.

I put my glass of wine down as I peel my heated attention to look at anything else. Nadia's cider, the crushed velvet comforter. The book on the nightstand. The abstract linework painting above the bed. Yeah, that will do.

Except it's not abstract. As my eyes relax on the image, I can make out the lines of what appears to be a man on his knees before a woman, her leg over his shoulder and his face...

Oh god, help me. I am too tipsy for this.

I can't figure out what to do with my thoughts, so I turn to my phone.

> I have something to say.

It is not even a fraction of a second before Yvaine begins typing.

> ??

> He's hotter right?

> I am not attracted to men

> Okay but...he's hotter.

> .....

"Talien!" Nadia snaps with the exact same inflection I've heard their mother use, pulling my attention back to reality as I turn my phone back over in my lap.

Tal scoffs, pulling my gaze back to him. He casually pushes open the discarded bag on the counter to reveal another container cleverly disguised in the folds.

"So dramatic," he chides, setting the entire thing on the edge of the counter just in time for Nadia to snatch it up. He tosses a set of the takeout chopsticks to her and picks up his plate.

"I knew you were lying," Nadia says over the first bite of kung pao chicken.

"Sure." Talien cuts his eyes to me, looking very pleased with himself.

Oh god, I do not have enough control over my thoughts to be able to sort the flurry of knots in my core.

I turn my attention to my food and cannot contain the sound that leaves my throat as I get a taste of the best takeout Chinese food in the country. Hands down. Not a single spot in the city beats this.

"Oh, my god, I forgot how good Jade Dragon is," I say with a dramatic roll of my eyes as I settle deeper into my seat on the couch.

"Talien used to get it for us every week after I moved in to this complex last summer," Nadia informs me. "Then he fell off the face of the earth for a while, and we haven't had it since." She echoes a similar groan and taps her feet happily against the cushions.

"Do you two need a moment?" Talien chuckles over a bite of his own food with a tick of his brow.

"Fuck off," Nadia growls, mouth still somehow full. "You still haven't answered my question."

"What question?"

"About where you've been."

Talien shrugs. "Out."

"*Out*," Nadia mocks. "I know that. But *where*? Niles and Yvaine won't tell me shit."

"Good," he mumbles into another bite of lo mien.

Some pit deep within my core does not want to know where Talien has been spending his nights. I know it wasn't here; he told me as much last night. But images of tangled limbs, men, women, flushes a heat over my chest. I shift uncomfortably in my seat.

"You said you saw your mom today? How is she?" I ask, trying to divert the topic of conversation even slightly.

"She's good—nosy as ever—but good. She wanted me to tell you that she hopes your first semester went well," he says. "She said she'd like to see you before you go back if you have time."

"I'd love to. I have nothing *but* time. Maybe tomorrow?"

"No, we have Niles's holiday party tomorrow," Nadia chimes in.

"Oh? I was unaware of a party. What time? I could just swing by before," I say before taking another unreasonably large bite of orange chicken.

"Eight, I think," Nadia says, glancing at Tal for confirmation. He nods. "I work tomorrow, but I could drop you off before. Does mom work, too?"

"She does." Tal busies himself examining his plate with more focus than it deserves.

"Okay, maybe not, then. Do you have her number?" Nadia turns her attention to me and pulls out her phone. "I'll send it to you. The two of you can just coordinate."

"I'm stuck running errands for Niles tomorrow," Tal says.

"Yeah, I'll just call her," I tell Nadia, and I am about to ask where Vas works because she didn't used to work at all, but my phone buzzes again, pulling my attention.

I look at it, thinking I am going to have to convince Yvaine to turn her car around, but the name across my screen sinks a stone of dread in my core.

> Bryson:
>
> Hi. So, about that dinner. Miliano's didn't have a reservation open for the evening, but they did have a spot for lunch tomorrow. Pick you up at 1?

Tal and Nadia continue their conversation about the party. Something about having to pick up a cake or something, but I can't really hear them. The giddy, buzzed feeling I had moments ago is replaced by a weighted coil of anxiety. A part of me expected this, but most of me is honestly stunned at the audacity of Bryson's blatant disregard of my instruction to wait for a text from me.

"Hey, you okay, Varner?" Tal's voice finally cuts through the haze.

"What?" I look up from my phone to see concern lining his expression. "Yeah, sorry. It's just Bryson."

I turn my nose back to my phone and try to decide if I am going to ignore my ex-fiancé again or deal with the problem because it doesn't seem like he's going to let me take my own time with it. Twenty-four hours, and he's already found a way to contact me three times.

"How the hell did he find out you were back?"

"Be nice," Nadia hisses through her teeth at her brother, who looks like a storm on the verge of breaking behind the counter.

"Why? That asshole is the whole reason she left in the first place," Tal protests. "Why would he think she wants him to text her the second she's back in town?"

Something in my chest pinches as I am reminded of that unfortunate series of events, and my mood sours further. It wasn't just Bryson. It had a lot to do with the idea of Bryson—my lack of choice.

But the choice I made did not choose me back. And I am sitting on his couch, drunk on a bottle of wine, as though nothing has passed between us. What am I doing?

"He wants to talk." I heave a sigh, suddenly unwilling to look at anything but my phone screen.

"Oh, fuck that."

"Talien!" There's that scolding tone again, the one that sounds so much like her mother.

"What? Cass knows what he's going to say. Hell, *I* know what that asshole is going to say. He's said it all before—"

"Talien. Shut. Up." Nadia surges up from the couch, takeout in hand, and turns on her brother.

"It's fine." It's not really, but their verbal tug-of-war is coiling my nerves. I shift in my seat. "He just wants an explanation. I *did* leave him basically at the altar without another word in five years."

The words have more bite than I intended and do not encompass the entirety of what happened, and Tal knows that. He's the only one I went to that night. He saw what Bryson is capable of, and his protests are reasonable. But I am feeling out of control, and I know Bryson won't stop until I concede in some way. And, if I am being honest, I don't feel like Talien, of all people, gets to have an opinion on how I choose to handle the situation.

A bruised cheek took a matter of days to heal. The broken heart I suffered in the wake of Tal's abandonment took years.

I miraculously find the strength to meet Talien's eye as a nagging pain in my chest pulls at my good sense.

He's the first to turn away. A muscle in his jaw ticks as my words land right where I thought they would, and the silence builds. Beside me, Nadia shifts on her feet. Talien just breathes quietly into his almost untouched food.

"I'm gonna go," Nadia informs us after the moment has stretched longer than any of us are comfortable with.

I want to ask her to stay, and the way Talien's eyes lift to follow her as she flees the apartment tells me he echoes the dread in my chest.

The door closes, and the air stiffens. I can almost feel it as the silence stretches between us. I don't want to speak first. I don't want to ask the question because I am not sure I want to hear the answer.

But I can't ignore the weight on my breastbone, the way every one of my senses prickles, remains aware of even the rise and fall of his chest as he stands still, trapped in thought.

His voice breaks the tension, relieving me of the impossible decision tangled through my thoughts.

"I'm sorry, Cass," he says, and, for a moment, that weight lifts. "I'm just stressed about the case I'm working on."

I am dazed as I look back up at him, and it takes me a moment to figure out where his words land. I cannot explain why, despite the apology, that twinge of pain only worsens. It flares a heated irritation in my core.

But I don't know if I am capable of having this conversation at all, let alone drunk on wine and already close to tears.

"Yeah, I get it. I'm sure having me here isn't helping with stress levels. I can find somewhere else," I say, turning to my phone.

"That's not—" Talien cuts himself off with a heavy breath and runs a hand through his hair. "I'm—It's not—God. I'm sorry. You can stay if you want to. Really. You being here isn't the problem."

His stumbling manifests in him trying to dispel the energy by tidying the remains of his unfinished dinner.

"Do you want me to stay?" I ask, because I genuinely cannot get a read on whether or not that is the case.

I can't even decide if I want to be here right now. What I want is for it to be like it used to be. Easy. And it felt like it could be, but maybe that's a delusion. Maybe it can't be like it was until we hash out what happened five years ago.

Maybe it can't be like it was at all.

"Yes."

The weight behind that word hits me in the chest.

I lift my eyes to find him with his back to me, fussing with putting the leftovers in the fridge. I pull myself to my feet, my vision spinning slightly as I round the couch to stand at the bar top. An urge to reach out to him pulls at me. It startles me. Quickens my pulse.

I want to touch him.

It's rare I feel a spark to use my near-dormant magic, but it feels like I need to. Just one brush of my fingers over his cheekbone, one flutter of my knuckles over his forearm, and I would feel everything. I'm not wearing my gloves, and I think I might do it. The drive is insatiable, but I manage to keep myself still, keep some distance between us.

Now is not the time. Not with my inhibitions lowered like this. Not without his consent. An emotional read is the most intimate thing I can share with someone. I can't just take it. I don't want to. I want him to tell me what's on his mind. I want him to be honest.

"Tal," I say in an attempt to get his attention again.

He finishes stuffing the leftovers away and turns to lean his hips against the counter across from me. The line of his jaw is hard, clenched, but he meets my gaze.

"I want you to stay," he reiterates, his voice clearer than I expected. I wonder if the confidence in his tone is meant for himself or me. "But I understand if you don't want to."

I release a short, strained breath and meet his eye, measuring it as best I can.

Do I want to stay? I think about it for a moment, as much as my clouded thoughts will allow me. I imagine going to Yvaine's, and something sharp pings in my core. I do that, and when do I see him? When do I have time to make up for the last five years of radio silence? If there is one thing I know for certain, it is how much it hurts to miss him. And right now, I don't have to do that.

"I want to stay."

His chest softens like he has been holding his breath, waiting for my answer. Shifting his hips against the counter, he crosses his heels over one another and folds his arms over his chest.

"Okay."

I wait for more, but he just searches my face. His jaw is still tight, but his brow has relaxed.

"Okay," I repeat.

And although some of the tension in the air has lifted, something is still strained. My phone buzzes in my hand again and I sigh as I turn it over to see Bryson has texted again.

I can call them about dinner again if lunch doesn't work.

"He's not going to leave me alone until I talk to him," I mutter.

1 is fine. I'll meet you there.

"I should have kept my mouth shut earlier." Tal clears his throat and pushes off the counter. "You don't owe me an explanation."

He moves past me to the closet near his bed and pulls out some clothes and a towel, leaving me at the counter. He doesn't speak again as he makes his way to the bathroom, and the door snaps closed.

I struggle to categorize where any of my emotions sit at the moment. I am still close to tears and I don't know how to get myself out of it. But I need to by the time he is out of the shower. So, I get myself a glass of water, quickly change into some sleep clothes Nadia loaned me, pile my hair into the bonnet, and pop some pain medication for the headache I will surely have in the morning before I settle into the couch and do my best to will myself to sleep before he returns.

CHAPTER 11

Talien

Her soft sighs are music to my ears. Again, I trace my fingers over the curve of her thighs, following the gorgeous outline of the tattoos as her fingers tangle in my hair, pulling me closer, demanding more, and I give it willingly.

She tastes amazing. I groan as her sweet scent fills my nose and coats my tongue. Her hips roll.

"Tal!"

God, yes. Keep saying my name like that.

I look up to watch her head drop back against her shoulders. Full curls flow over her arms and cascade along her moonlit curves. It drives me wild seeing her come undone for me.

"Like that," she gasps as my lips move against her, tongue teasing with slow, agonizing strokes. "Yes, use that beautiful mouth of yours for me."

I groan against her. My fingers dig into her hips as she rocks onto my tongue, taking what she needs from me. Her intensity grows, her movements turn frantic, and my head spins with the ecstasy of watching her. My mouth traces from her clit lower, pulling a gasp from her, and a sharp tug on my hair directs my attention back.

"I didn't say you could stop," she says.

Her voice, her hand fisted in my hair, the command she has over me causes my head to spin, tumbling over the edge into that hazy space where I am nothing but hers. Only hers.

Eager to please, I adjust my weight on my knees, trying to find a spot where the kitchen tiles don't cut into me while I refocus my tongue on her. She adjusts on the counter, tipping her hips, setting a calf on my shoulder to give me better access, and leans back on a hand to watch me.

The heat in her caramel and honey eyes lights me on fire. Her breathing quickens. Her lips part. Her body starts to shake.

I am hers.

"Cass," I groan against her as she comes apart for me.

The sunlight filters in beneath the curtain.

I'm still breathing heavily from the intensity of that goddamn dream. Every inch of my body is poised, hungry, desperate. I can't even remember the last time I was so worked up.

Thick dread coats my chest. I hope to all god that I stayed quiet, at least. Things have been awkward enough without me calling her name in my sleep.

Mustering the courage to start the day, I sit up on the bed, tucking the blanket over my lap carefully. If Cass hadn't been asleep by the time I was done in the bathroom last night, I would have put up a fuss about her taking the couch, but she looked so peaceful. I settled for draping an extra blanket over her and resigned myself to bed.

The blanket is folded and placed over the back of the couch.

The bathroom light is off.

Cass is gone.

A confusing mix of disappointment and relief fills the space where dread had been as I relax into the pillows and take another moment to calm my racing heart.

Reaching for my phone, I find it's well past noon, and I have twenty new messages from Niles and a dozen missed calls.

Oops.

Pushing off the bed, I hit the call button and put the phone to my ear as I head to the closet for clean clothes.

"Oh, my fucking god, where the hell have you been? Don't answer that, because if your next words aren't 'I'm sorry, Niles, Cass and I finally talked about our feelings, and we just lost track of time, but I already have your cake, and I'll be there in five minutes,' I don't want to fucking hear it."

Funny. That's almost exactly the greeting I anticipated.

I keep quiet as I shuck off my sweatpants and start to get dressed, knowing the silence is the opposite of what Niles actually wants, despite so much insistence otherwise.

"Talien Adonis Vale, if you don't answer me this instant, I'm going to come through this phone and beat your tattooed, moody ass," Niles huffs.

"I overslept," I say, buckling my favorite calf-length half-skirt over the top of my pants.

The heavy sigh on the other end of the line tells me Niles is less-than-thrilled with how mundane of an excuse I have for them. Slipping a wide-knit, artfully tattered, cropped sweater over my head, I trot to the bathroom to finish getting ready.

Starting my day behind is a great way to keep from letting that dream catch up with me.

By the time I make it to Niles' with the cake, they are a whirl-wind of anxiety flitting around their elaborate, pristinely deco-rated family home. Niles is the sole heir to one of the founding families in Brunswick, a founding family on the Varner side of the conflict, until after their mother died in an accident in high school. Niles took over the family fortune and has been working tirelessly since to undo damage from decades of using magic for personal gain. The proceeds from these parties go to local chari-ties; they work with the community every chance they get, and they even went so far as to tattoo over their family crest, wanting to be as far removed from the old Sinclair legacy as possible.

For most, the whole process of grieving while simultaneously rewriting history would have been overwhelming; for Niles, it had been therapeutic. They thrived in the intensity of running the family business and enjoyed doing away with the less-than-ethical policies their mother had allowed in favor of humanitarian practices.

Now, almost eight years later, they are one of the youngest, most influential magic users in the city. Funny. Considering they seem to think they can't throw a holiday party without me there to boss around.

"For the love of god, there you are!"

Niles trots down the stairs, taking them two by two and leaping down the last four without a care. One of the nearby staff clutches their chest in concern as their employer rights themselves and straightens their elaborately colored peacock-toned suit as they strut towards me.

"My cake? Why aren't you dressed yet?" Niles asks, glancing around me as if I might somehow be hiding a three-foot, tiered cake with massive sugar snowflakes behind my back.

"It's in the van, and what do you mean? I am dressed?" It comes out as a question as I look down at myself. I rather liked my fitted black jeans, the heavy combat boots, the skirt that drapes from my right hip, around the back of my waist, and stops behind my left leg. Paired with the thick sweater, I thought I looked rather presentable. No less so than I normally do, at least.

"What do you mean, 'what do you mean'? It's a masquerade." Niles flails their arms in a wild display.

"You did not tell me it was a masquerade."

"I *did*. It isn't my fault you don't listen. Never mind, I'll fix it later." They wave me off, dismissing the thought. "My cake?"

I roll my eyes and turn to lead them outside.

"I didn't realize you have absolutely no concept of space until

I got to Kiki's, although I guess I should have been concerned when you asked about the boxes yesterday."

The bakery had to lend me one of their delivery vans, which led me to question why Niles sent me to get the cake in the first place since it was clearly an option to have the damned thing delivered.

As I pull open the back doors to the van, Niles cheers and claps giddily.

"Oh, it's *perfect*! Mom would have loved those colors."

I can't help but smile as they direct a few of the nearby staff to help us get it inside. For all their antics, Niles has always known how to hold onto the good things. Even when they were at their lowest, they had found bright spots. I admire them for that.

As we head back inside, I can't help but reflect on how much things have changed since the last time we had all attended one of these lavish parties. The time just slips away.

I'm not allowed to stay lost in my own thoughts for long. Niles has a long list of tasks that should have been completed hours ago, and even with a full staff at their disposal, we'll be lucky if we're not still hanging garlands when the guests arrive this evening.

CHAPTER 12

Cassiopeia

I adjust the elaborately decorated napkin in my lap and pick up my phone to check the time for the hundredth time. It's 12:46. Only two minutes later than the last time I checked.

I hate Miliano's. It's one of those spots that won't say it's exclusive, but they turn their noses up at anyone who isn't from a wealthy family. Of course, when I arrived early and asked for the Westfield reservation, the host knew exactly who I was and showed me on without hesitation, exactly like they might have years ago. Like no time has passed at all.

Although the host looked judgmentally on my attire. I got ready quietly this morning to avoid waking a still-sleeping Tal and chose to stay underdressed in Nadia's low-cut cargo pants, cropped band tee, and open cardigan. I refuse to dress up for this place or adhere to the rules of fine dining etiquette for people who don't even have a solid definition for the word "respect."

Bryson would have to take this Cass or no Cass at all.

None at all would have been preferable, but that hope is far-fetched. I need to deal with this so I can get past it. Move on. Get him to let me be so I can enjoy the rest of my winter break in peace.

"Cass," Bryson's low baritone rings out over my shoulder, and I jump in start as I rise from my chair.

I wish my nerves would take a back seat for just a while, but that seems to be an unreasonable hope. My heart is already hammering against my chest.

"Sorry, didn't mean to startle you," he says with a perfect smile and perfect teeth to compliment his perfect face and perfectly groomed hair.

Irritating, really. He looks like a Ken doll plucked straight from the shelves and dressed for an overly formal meal in the middle of a Saturday.

"It's alright." I smile, and to my surprise, he moves to pull me into an embrace.

I am not expecting the contact. Dread coats my breastbone, and my entire body tenses as I suck in a breath, trying to prepare for an onslaught of magic. To my relief, it doesn't come. I am sufficiently covered. I keep my arms out to the sides and hold my breath until he loosens his grip and steps back to look at me. I shrug out of his hold and settle back into my seat.

My anxiety is absolutely through the roof, the flutter in my chest nearly unmanageable. It's not a good start to the less-than-pleasant conversation we have ahead of us.

He follows suit and settles into his seat across the table.

"You look amazing. God, it's been so long," he says.

"Yeah, it has. Look, Bryson, I don't want this to be weird. I'm really just here to tell you—"

"Whoa, Cass, slow down," he interjects with a furrow of his brow. My irritation pricks at the interruption. "We have time. I don't need you to start throwing excuses at me. Just relax. I want to enjoy this time with you."

Excuses.

Anger flares in my chest and a flash of a memory from that night saps the breath from my lungs.

Excuses my ass.

I no longer have the physical evidence of what he's capable of.

But it's already been proven emotional wounds don't heal as easily as bruises. The uptick in my pulse, the nervous slick of my palms, and the way my thoughts cloud over as I try to maintain my composure solidify that for me.

"No, see," I say with a tight release of breath, straightening my spine, "we aren't going to do the thing where you take control of the conversation and get whatever you want anymore. I am not here to enjoy time with you. I don't really know why you'd think that after what you did. I am here for closure."

Even as the word falls from my tongue, I know it's a mistake. I don't know why I thought this was the right thing to do. I know I felt like he wouldn't leave me alone until I talked to him, but now I wish I had just stayed firm. Stayed away. Why is this always such a tangle?

"Closure?" he asks with a raised brow. The terse lift in his tone raises the hairs along my neck. "You think I need closure?"

I lose my train of thought as fear coils in my core. I don't want him to get angry.

"Well, I assumed—"

"You assumed I was left sniveling after you when you left? That would have been likely had your father not offered me a position at headquarters, anyway. He made good on the promise to take care of my family despite your irresponsible decision to throw your life away. No, I asked you here because I thought you might want a chance to start over. See what you've left behind."

He opens his palms to the restaurant around him, presenting himself as a prize, and my stomach turns. I can see nothing but his dangerous temper, his arrogance, and the crest to go with the pair.

It takes me a moment to center myself, but soon, my irritation simmers quickly to a boiling rage, and I'm not sure I have the patience to sit here to even blow him off. I am not the same woman he was engaged to, easily molded, pushed around. I *have* healed since then—despite the involuntary response my body has to this man. I have grown. I am, at the very least, stronger than his ability to bulldoze a conversation.

"You thought I came home to get a second chance with you?" I ask, incredulous.

The words almost feel like Styrofoam in my mouth, they're so unbelievable.

"Tell me that's not even a little bit of the reason," he scoffs.

"Bryson Westfield," I fume, "I left for a reason. One I don't really feel like I should have to explain to you. I'd like for you to know that I made the right choice, and I prefer the life I have now. Without you. I hope you have a good holiday."

I rise from my seat, tossing my napkin on the plate. I am impressed with my resolve. It's stable and confident despite the way my heart hammers against my ribs, even though it feels a little like my lungs have forgotten how to accept oxygen.

"Wait, you're not staying to eat. It cost me a fortune to get this reservation," he barks, rising.

His spike in anger causes my spine to tense, but I am already leaving. I turn over my shoulder and take a few steps backward to answer.

"I hope you enjoy your lunch," I call as I turn back around to make my way onto the street.

I am proud of myself, but the weight of half a decade's worth of trying to forget why I was afraid of Bryson Westfield hangs from my shoulders like a dark cloak of dread as I make my way toward Yvaine's bookshop.

CHAPTER 13

Talien

SENIOR YEAR OF COLLEGE

*T*hese parties are always the same. Just a bunch of fucking creeps waiting for one of the girls to get "drunk enough." I usually enjoy my fair share of alcohol, but I know when to quit. The hungry way the entire overgrown collection of testosterone that is the football team is watching the girls in the middle of the cleared-out living room as they dance makes me sick.

Cass looks just as breathtaking as ever in her fitted black baby-doll tee, a pair of tight-fitted jeans, and her magic shielding gloves up to her elbows. The black material only barely covers the peak of paint splatters over her arms. She must have spent today in the studio. She's always such a messy painter. It makes me smile. Cass stumbles out of the kitchen with Yvaine on her heels, a new drink in hand.

So, she did forget she gave me her last drink to watch over.

Sighing, I take a sip of her discarded beverage as she moves this way and fix my best, lighthearted grin over my expression.

Bryson, the current boyfriend and perpetual itch under my skin, intersects her at the couch. Yvaine curls her lip in disgust at West-field but quickly gets distracted when a very pretty, very curvy cheer-

96

leader bumps into her, spilling her drink, and proceeds to apologize profusely while patting down Yvaine's now-soaked tube top.

Well, I know what she'll be doing later.

Bryson says something, and Cass apparently forgets where she is going and lets him remove her drink from her hands to lead her onto the dance floor.

Typical.

I edge around the pulsing bodies to retrieve that *drink from the crowded shelf by the hall. I decide to finish off the forgotten cocktail and lean a shoulder against the wall. That idiot she's with is barely coordinated enough to dance, so he settles for grinding against her. Downing the rest of the contents in the plastic red cup, I wander to the sink and dump the remainder of the one Bryson had his hands all over. I'm not taking any chances with him, not with his reputation.*

Moving back into the main room, I lean against the doorframe to watch. Cass is lost in the music, head tipped back against Bryson's shoulder, eyes closed, hips swaying as the beat pulses through the speakers. The music is loud enough it thumps in my chest. Normally, I'd be in the sea, lost on the same waves, the same press of bodies, the same heady drunken haze.

But not tonight. Cass showed up an hour ago. She stormed into the room like a tornado and went straight for the booze. I checked on her, but she'd brushed me off, pulled me to the dance floor just long enough to make Bryson livid, and then stormed off again.

I wanted to punch him. Whatever she was upset about, it was his fault. But somehow, we'd still ended up with her in his arms and me watching from the sidelines.

It's not like I had another option. It has to be this way.

For the past forty-five minutes, I've been trying to sober up. Try something new for a change.

Bryson moves to whisper in Cass's ear, and her eyes snap open. Caught under her gaze, I can barely breathe. I've been staring.

She looks furious.

Wheeling on Bryson, she bats his hands away from her waist and snaps something I can't hear over the music. He follows her to the table in the corner, where she gets another drink. He promptly snatches it from her, causing more rage to boil out of her. He smiles, like getting her mad at him was the whole point, and hands it back. Cass gulps it down.

The oaf leads her back to the dance floor, but it's not long before he says something else to anger her. Cass teeters out of his arms and shoves past him to storm off down one of the halls.

Bryson moves across the room to down the rest of his drink, then skirts the dance floor and follows.

When I come around the corner, he is jiggling the handle to the bathroom. He lifts a fist to pound on the door, but despite his efforts, it remains closed and locked.

"I doubt she needs your help taking a piss, Westfield. Give the girl some space," I say, sauntering up.

His attention snaps to me, and his expression twists into something feral.

"Fuck off, Vale. I can handle my girlfriend," he snips.

Rage boils under my skin. This motherfucker has been asking to get the shit beaten out of him for years.

"You okay, Varner?" I call, choosing to focus on Cass instead of this idiot.

"Tal!" Her voice answers from inside the bathroom.

Bryson's expression lifts in surprise. "I'm out here, Cass," he shouts into the door.

"No," she slurs, her voice barely audible over the noise of the party, "not you. Where's Talien?"

"Hey, Firefly," I call back, meeting Bryson's glare, "everything okay in there?"

"I can't stand," she answers.

"Open the door," Bryson interjects before I can reply.

Concern replaces the irritation bristling under my skin as the idiot bangs on the door, and I put a gentle hand on his shoulder.

"Hang on, Westfield," I say. "She's going to need water and something to eat. Go get a bottle from the fridge and food."

"I said fuck off," he snarls.

The bathroom door clicks and swings open. Cass is leaning against the door with all her weight, and her half-closed eyes fall to my face immediately.

"I want to go," she mutters, tipping forward.

I elbow past Bryson to catch her before her knees hit the floor. I don't have time to make sure my skin doesn't meet hers, and she winces as her hands tangle in my shirt. Her crest flashes, and I adjust my grip away from her bare midriff.

"Okay, yeah, sorry. We'll go."

Her head falls against my chest, and she manages to get her feet under her.

"Stop," Bryson demands.

He reaches out to grab her forearm, and she flinches. Her fingers twist tighter in my shirt, and she tries to pull her arm back.

"No, Bryson," her words slur.

He pulls at her again, and the rage in me snaps loose. I jab a pressure point in his shoulder with a finger, causing him to yelp and step back as he shakes out his arm. Stepping between him and Cass, I lean her against the doorframe and close the distance. Bryson retreats a step before we're nose to nose. Hatred flickers in his eyes, and his crest lights. I don't have magic to back me up, but I don't need it. I've been wanting a reason to beat the shit out of this guy.

"Do it," I dare him. "Hit me. Light me up. I'll even give you the first shot."

"Talien, no."

Cass's voice is clearer, and her gloved fingers wrap around my elbow as she tries to pull herself from the wall.

Bryson is frozen in shock. His expression is lined with anger. His wide eyes flit between me and Cass.

"Let's go," she whispers.

"If you go with him, we're done," Bryson snarls.

I slip my arm around her waist, keeping my hands tucked in my sleeves to avoid touching her while I help her stumble along. She twists both fists into the fabric at my side and struggles to keep her head up. It falls against my shoulder, and she closes her eyes as she mutters something incomprehensible. Bryson doesn't move as I practically drag Cass back down the hall. He knows the Dean's stance on violence especially involving magic, and with Cass as the only witness, we both know he'd be fucked trying to get another scholarship if he dared release even a lick of magic on me on school grounds. I imagine I'll have hell to pay later, but that's a problem for another day.

I catch Niles' eye on the way to the door and nod back down the hall. They seem unsurprised and go to buy us some time, their crest lighting as they step into the hall to intersect Bryson.

The plan is to haul Cass down the three flights of stairs and out to my car so I can take her home, but we are not even to the stairwell when she starts complaining she's going to throw up.

Cursing, I fumble for my keys and get us back to my door as fast as possible. We barely make it to the bathroom before she's sick.

"I'm so sorry," she groans.

She sits on her feet and rests her head on her arm as she slumps against the toilet. Her cheeks are tear-stained, and her neck is speckled with red patches.

"No, don't be," I say, wetting a cloth and dabbing it against her forehead. "I wanted to leave anyway."

"You can leave me here if you want to go back."

I fill the cup on the counter with a splash of mouthwash and offer it to her. She swishes and spits, returning the cup for me to discard and taking the water bottle I offer instead.

"You're in no condition to be alone, and I don't want you puking all over my stuff."

She drinks and leans her head against the wall before taking a breath. Her eyes are still glossy, and her skin has a sickly pallor to it, but I am glad to see she can at least keep her head up.

"I won't throw up on your stuff," she promises.

I narrow my eyes at her.

"I don't believe you," I tease.

Cass, very stubbornly, struggles to her feet and looks pleased with herself. She smiles down at me and sets a hip against the wall.

Oh god. *How many times have I dreamed about being right here, on my knees, for this woman?*

She measures me, and her gaze drops to my lips. Her own part over a sharp intake of breath, and my heartbeat quickens. The whole world seems to still around us in this moment, and then her eyes lift to mine again.

"I'd like to shower, I think. Everything is spinning," she mutters.

Panic floods my veins before my common sense claws its way back in: she means she *needs a shower. Her. Alone.*

I exhale heavily through my nose and rise to my feet, trying to shake off the rush of heat fucking everywhere inside me.

Cass moves to take a step, stumbles over her feet, and trips. I manage to snap myself out of my spiraling thoughts in time to catch her with my hands carefully placed over her shirt. She grips my arms, giving herself a chance to stabilize.

"Fuck," she hisses, "I did not have this much to drink."

I choose not to give my opinion as to what exactly happened with her drinks. Instead, I help her back to the floor, step over her, and reach in to start the shower.

"Maybe I didn't eat enough today."

She rolls her head back to rest against the wall.

"I don't think that's the problem," I say, setting my hands on my hips.

I stare down at her momentarily, trying to decide if I should help or leave her to it. She's barely able to stand, so leaving her doesn't seem like the best option.

"Okay, Varner, come on." Just act. Don't think too hard about it. *"Let's get you cleaned up and into bed. You're going to feel like shit for a few hours, but it'll pass."*

"I think you should maybe just leave me here to die."

Cass waves dramatically at me, her long curls falling over her face.

"Sorry, no, dying is not on the table, I'm afraid."

I stoop to brush the hair from her forehead with a careful touch. I manage to avoid direct contact, but the gesture reveals her Varner family crest—the very symbol of everything that stands between us.

"Up." My tone is terse as a weight sinks over my breastbone.

She groans miserably and glares at me from the corner of her eye.

"I don't want to do that. The room is spinning with my eyes closed."

"Fucking shit," I sigh. "Alright."

I squat down and slip my hands under her shoulders, hauling her up; I set her on the toilet and take a steadying breath.

This is a fucking disaster.

"You can undress, or I can dump you in fully clothed. Which is it?"

She thinks for a moment with squinted eyes and fumbles with the hem of her shirt. She manages to get a few fingers under the edge but makes no progress on getting it over her head before I can stand it no longer.

"God, the water is going to be cold at this rate," I growl, setting my teeth, "Do you want me to help you?"

She considers for a moment, a tangle in her eyes as she bites down on her bottom lip. I know she cannot be touched. I don't quite understand it, but I know she can sense emotion, and physical touch sparks her magic, which tends to make her panic. I've never really pried; she doesn't like to talk about it. I just know not to touch her. Outside of accidental brushes, she's only ever allowed me to touch her a few times. And I wouldn't ask, but she can't seem to make her fingers work properly for longer than a few seconds.

A part of me wishes I could take the offer back. I have no idea how much emotion she can sense or really how it works at all. If there's a chance she can feel even a fraction of this spiral I am locked in, I shouldn't go anywhere near her.

Before I can come up with a solution, she nods. I suck in a breath to calm the flutter of my nerves.

Shit.

I release that terse breath and nod.

"Arms up," I order, and Cass obeys.

I move quickly to avoid a full-on magical episode, and, in one swift motion, I yank the top up over her head. My knuckles barely graze the bare flesh of her midriff, and she tenses but relaxes as her black lace bra is exposed. A tattoo pokes out under the thin material and curls between her breasts.

She didn't have that in high school.

The way it accentuates her form is mesmerizing. I shake the thought and set the shirt on the counter. Cass leans back against the tank of the toilet and pulls her gloves off before she rests her hands in her lap, lolling her head back to look at me and sighs.

"I need you to help me with my pants." Her words are slow, like she's trying desperately not to sound slurred.

"Oh, dear god," I mumble under my breath, "This is not how I imagined this."

"What?"

"Nothing. Let's do this."

My heartbeat thunders between my ears. It's all I can do to keep my breathing steady as I kneel to remove her shoes before returning my gaze to hers. Her eyes are focused on mine, clear and bright. Her chest rises, and her lips part as she holds my stare.

I've done this so many times before. Undressing someone should not matter this much. I tell myself it doesn't matter.

So why the fuck are my hands shaking?

"Are you ready?" My fingers flutter over her hips.

I need to control the torrent of my emotions. Quickly.

She draws her bottom lip further between her teeth and nods with a glittering gaze, which doesn't help the thin leash I have on these wild emotions in the least.

Forging ahead, I take her by the waistband and carefully snap open the clasp. She leans back, and I yank them off her in as swift a motion as I can manage. Despite my efforts, my fingers graze the length of her thighs, and she gasps. The intricate crest over her forehead flashes a cool toned glow and something in my chest clenches.

How the fuck did we get here?

Cassiopeia Varner is sitting in my bathroom, clothed only in a matching black lace set. And, no, I have not missed the way she keeps biting her bottom lip.

Fuck me.

"Oh, fuck me," she echoes my sentiment, leaning forward and steadying herself with a grip on my shoulders.

"Don't say that," I grind out, dropping the jeans on the ground at her feet. "Alright, in the shower."

"Can you carry me?" she asks, her tone sounds far more steady than mine somehow.

"You want me to pick you up?"

I need to get my emotions in check. Immediately. It would probably be easier to spontaneously learn how to fly.

"Yes, Talien."

The sound of my name on her tongue is solid, a corporeal thing that locks itself around my heart like a vice. There's a weight to the confirmation. A deeper intention. She is giving me permission to touch her.

The significance of it is not lost on me.

Without allowing my nerves to keep me locked in place for long, I scoop my arms under her back and knees to support her, and she slings her arms around my neck. I am vibrantly aware of every point our skin meets. Cass bites down so hard on her lip I think she might make it bleed. Her mark surges with another flow of color, and she hangs her head back, a look of ecstasy over her expression.

How did we get here? I'm not sure. It's been a very confusing few minutes.

I'm so fucked.

As the water hits me in the face and soaks into my shoes, I feel like an idiot. I'd been too wrapped up in the moment to remove them.

When the water hits her skin, she lifts her head and sucks in a sharp breath.

"*Your clothes,*" she exclaims, her tone bright with surprise. "*What are you doing?*"

"*Listen, you were taking for-fucking-ever to get in this damn shower, and I panicked.*"

I set her down, help her sit on the shower floor, and release her to run a hand over my drenched face to clear some of the water. She keeps a hold of my shirt collar.

Her crest goes dormant.

"*You are a fucking nightmare, Varner,*" I chuckle, flicking some of the water from my fingers in her face.

Beneath my breastbone, my heart thunders like a wild animal. I try to assess the tidal wave of emotions coiling through me. Maybe she didn't sense too much. I wasn't touching her long.

Cass tugs on the fabric at my neck. I think she might be trying to keep her balance again, but her gaze is stable and sure.

"*Do you want to take your clothes off?*" she asks, and the entire world goes silent. The only sound accompanying my racing thoughts is the thundering of my heart as it rages in my chest.

There is still a tilt to her voice, her words blending into each other at times as she fades in and out of focus.

I start to speak over the pounding in my chest, which I'm certain she can hear, but I stop myself. I don't know what I was going to say.

She and Bryson are on the rocks again, and she wants something easy. Pointless. A distraction. Just like everyone else.

I am always the distraction.

I narrow my eyes at her.

"*You are drunk, Cass.*"

The clear flash of disappointment passes through her eyes, and she swallows.

"*Talien,*" she leans in, her grip on my shirt tighter, using it to pull herself closer.

I'm frozen.

"*Cass,*" I whisper, my gaze catching on her parted lips, causing the rest of the thought to dissipate.

Instead, a breath escapes me, and my chest tightens at what

closing that distance would mean. Damned if I don't want to, though.

She waits only a heartbeat longer before she pulls me in, and our noses brush; the falling water steals some of my ability to see, but the glow of her crest brightens the space.

"Cass," I want her name to come out like a warning, but it doesn't. It sounds desperate, like a plea, and her grip on my sopping shirt tightens as she sucks in a breath.

The glow brightens and catches my attention, spinning my already clouded thoughts.

"Tal," she breathes, tipping her chin to brush her lips to mine.

The sensation is maddening, and I lose all sense of control. My heated thoughts spin into a wild frenzy. Before I can think or gather my senses, she catches my mouth with hers, and her hands tangle in my hair.

I know I shouldn't. I should stop this. Nothing good will come of this. But for a moment, just a fraction of time in the miserable past few years, I let myself feel something.

My hands find her face and hold her to me. She groans into my mouth. The sound is bliss in my ears. Quickly, with feather-light touches, I allow my tongue to trail over her bottom lip. A soft whimper escapes her throat, and she parts for me, scrambling closer to press her chest to mine. Her movements are uncoordinated, and on the slick floor, she knocks me back against the shower wall.

I chuckle, feeling her echoing smile against my lips.

"Sorry," she pulls back only to whisper before diving back into the feverish way she drinks from me beneath the falling water.

Her mark is vibrant now as she drags her hands to trail along the planes of my chest. Her touch lights my skin on fire. For the first time in years, I feel alive. My fingers trace her frame to settle against her hips; I dig my nails into her soft curves as my tongue sweeps over hers again.

She manages to shift herself so her knees are around my hips. Cass groans as she settles herself against me, her heat only building the growing ache in my pants as she arches into me. I moan against her lips, fingers digging into her rolling hips. She mutters my name again between kisses, and her fingers grapple for the hem of my shirt as she moves against me. The desperation in her movements washes over me, stealing the breath from my lungs.

I can feel the last threads of my resolve fraying. I have wanted this for so long. Wanted her. I wanted her to feel safe enough with me to touch me. To reciprocate this feeling that has been bleeding me out for so many years. I have wanted her to take me, claim me, make me hers. I want to forget why I've pushed her away, why I've only allowed myself to dream of moments like this. I want to let go. I want this to be the beginning. Our beginning.

You will not taint my daughter.

My senses snap back into place as she grinds against me again. Her voice is husky in my ears, still panting my name. Lost in the moment.

I press the heels of my palms to her hips and push; a gentle but firm movement to call her back from this drunken mess.

"Cass, wait..."

CHAPTER 14

Talien

"I look fucking ridiculous."

"Don't be silly," Niles chides, barely sparing me a glance as they adjust the final touches on their feather cuffs and fluff a hand through their teal blue hair.

"A knight?" I detest absurd display of false virtue looking back at me from the mirror.

"You look dashing."

"There has to be another option," I groan, turning to get a side view of the slightly too-small suit of chainmail Niles dug from their storage room of previous costumes from what I can only guess is every occasion they've ever worn a costume.

"There are plenty of options," Niles chirps, carefully setting their peacock mask in place before turning to me. "But you're going to be a knight because it's your own fault for never listening to me, and beggars can't be choosers. And also, your ass looks amazing in that, so you're welcome."

My ass does *look amazing in it.*

Niles hands me the very shiny metal pauldrons and bracers with leather buckles while pointing the beak of their mask high.

"I said, 'you're welcome,' asshat," they sing-song at me.

Not even being forced into this ridiculous costume can keep me from chuckling at their ridiculousness.

"Fine! Thank you!" I snatch the rest of the costume from them and buckle myself in.

"How am I supposed to dance in this?" I call as Niles disappears across the hall to their bathroom.

"You'll figure it out," they sing back.

"Cass! You look amazing!"

Niles' cheery tone pulls my attention up from adjusting the bracer on my right arm for what feels like the tenth time since I put it on. They're only a few steps ahead of me on the stairs, and below us, standing in the center of the foyer, are Cass, Yvaine, and her long-term girlfriend, Seti.

"Yvaine, Seti, you both look incredible, as well!" Niles practically flies down the rest of the stairs and bounces up to the group. "Seti, how is your mother? I heard she had to cut her trip abroad short?"

I don't hear the rest of the conversation. Nothing could have prepared me for the way Cassiopeia looks—amazing is putting it lightly. She is staring up at the flickering decorative snowflakes overhead, her curls perfectly pinned over one ear. A simple but decorative silver mask glitters over the top half of her face. It does nothing to hide even a fraction of her beauty, though.

She has her bottom lip between her teeth as she takes in the decorations. A flush of heat pulses through me as the sight summons images of the dream from this morning and pairs it beautifully with the memory of how intoxicatingly soft her full lips felt against mine.

Shaking away the sinful thoughts and trying very hard not to pay attention to the way my body reacts to the reminder, I remind my feet how to move and trot down the rest of the staircase. A hostess comes to take their coats, and a second wave of heat flushes my skin as Cass's jacket falls from her shoulders.

Cass has always been shapely, but over the past five years, she has filled out beautifully. The silky white dress she wears spills over her curves and falls to her knees. One side of the silken fabric cuts up to reveal the slope of her bronze thigh. My breath catches at the exposed dip of her hip and the flowery tattoos adorning her flawless skin. She adjusts her silver gloves up to her elbows and turns to thank the hostess with a stunning smile. Yvaine hands her a delicate set of white feathered wings, helping her to shrug her arms into them.

She's an angel.

I almost stumble over my feet. The costume is stunning on her and I couldn't agree with the choice more.

Of all the days to wake up from that *dream...*

As she turns over her shoulder to peek in at the ballroom, I get a clear view of the back of the dress, which drapes precariously low along her hips, leaving room for the wings between her shoulders but highlighting the gorgeous lines of her back and the curling phoenix tattoo flowing along her spine. Wings and feathers of flames curl out across her shoulders beneath the thin silver chain straps of the dress. I know every line. Every flame. Every feather.

That's my *phoenix.*

I had no idea she'd kept the sketch, let alone gotten it tattooed *across her entire back.* Cass never shows so much skin, not for lack of confidence but to deter people from touching her without her consent. My mind is a swirl of chaos and nothing all at once.

I'm still just standing in the middle of the foyer, feet seemingly frozen in place, when her eyes finally scan the room and land on me. Her attention calls me back from my spiraling thoughts, and I'm able to catch my breath.

Forcing my feet forward, I move to stand beside Niles.

"Hey," I manage to choke out, still caught in the intensity of Cass's presence.

"Hi," she says, the corner of her red-painted mouth twitching as her gaze trails down the armor.

I tell myself I can't actually *feel* her eyes tracing over the lines of my body, but that does little to curb the heat curling in my core.

Why hadn't she told me about the phoenix?

"A knight? In shining armor and everything?" she asks with a coy half smile, "I peg you for more of the mischievous, morally grey thief type."

You can peg me any way you like.

God, get ahold of yourself.

I cough a laugh, trying to cover up the heat flushing through me at my idiotic brain. I'm grateful for the mask hiding at least half of my surely bright red face.

What else did she even say?

"Ah...yeah...I missed the memo, actually."

"You did nothing of the sort," Niles bites, barely turning from their conversation with Seti.

"It was all they had," I admit, pointing out the slightly too-small sleeves that barely reach my wrists.

"Ah." Cass tips her chin in acknowledgement.

Her attention does not linger long before her chest rises with a short breath, and she turns her attention to Niles.

"What can I help with?" she asks.

Niles spends the next forty-five minutes flitting around the ballroom and terrace, ushering in last-minute arrivals for the snack bar like a panicking canary, and I don't have many more thoughts to spare on the significance or lack-there-of of the tattoo. I take every moment Cass has her back to me to study the lines and ensure I'm not imagining things. But it's identical to the one in my memory, sketched on the back of a set of history notes in homeroom senior year.

It *is* my phoenix.

Yvaine and her girlfriend are quickly sent off to help organize the seating areas scattered around the ballroom, while Cass and I are tasked with twining faux crystal snowflakes on a string of fairy lights around every banister visible and a few I'm certain none of the guests will be anywhere near. A sharp look passes from Yvaine to Niles as our assignments are dished out, which tells me she not only disapproves of Niles leaving Cass in my care but will have words with them on the matter later. Niles shrugs her off with a smile and disappears to attend to a very poorly placed ice statue.

Cass and I are busy wrapping the fragile garland around the banister on the terrace when the first guests arrive. Magic users and otherwise arrive wearing full ball gowns, tuxedos, and costumes of all kinds. Some wear slight masks to highlight their crests, with intricate hairstyles to frame their faces. Others have masks to cover them from forehead to chin. Each costume is extravagant and intricately designed.

It's been some time of me just watching the guests filter in before Cass clears her throat, waiting for me to hand her my end of the garland.

"Sorry." I quickly fall back into our comfortable rhythm on this final stretch of banister.

"You're fine," she breathes a chuckle. "Do you think we will ever be released from the role of decoration slaves, or will we have to enjoy the party from the sidelines?"

"Oh, no. This is a life sentence," I assure her.

She huffs a laugh and looks up at me from under her lashes. A beautiful rose color highlights the apples of her cheeks just under the silver mask.

I want to ask about the phoenix. She definitely didn't have it done before she left—the backless dress her parents had purchased for her wedding made me certain of that. But I couldn't imagine that she kept that sketch, not after everything. And yet...

Once the last of the lights are in place and I've talked myself out of a hundred different reasons to bring it up, Niles flits back outside to beckon wildly at us. It's not long before we're standing near the base of the stairs, champagne in hand, while Niles makes their way up the stairs and turns to clink their glass. The now full ballroom turns their attention to our host, who soaks up every gaze and flashes the brightest of smiles. It's always striking to me how they manage to look so warm and inviting beneath the darkness of that tattoo across their entire forehead, blotting out their crest.

"Ladies, theys, he/hims and gays," Niles begins, raising their glass, "I want to start by thanking all of you for your generous donations. As many of you know, all of the proceeds collected tonight will be donated to Brunswick Elementary and Brunswick High School to help fund the upcoming cafeteria renovations. So, again, thank you."

We all applaud. Niles turned these balls into charity events years ago. Many prominent families who had a standing invitation before Niles took over the family fortune were booted from the invite list and replaced with private families. A pang of hurt echoes under my chest as I scan the room.

Mom and Dad haven't come for years despite Niles' insistence.

"Enough housekeeping, though," Niles says, waving their free hand. "Let's get this party started; what do you say?"

The entire ballroom erupts with cheers. They certainly know how to work a crowd. On cue, the lights cut out, and the snowflakes overhead bathe the room in flowing waves of colored light. Music floods in, loud, pulsing, and it's exactly the song I expected Niles to kick off their winter party with. The latest remix of holiday classics spun into an intricate web of lyrics and melodies that blends the entire season into a single, pounding song.

Niles hops down the stairs and flounces up next to me to offer a hand to Nadia's girlfriend with a bow.

"Care to dance?" they say with a wink at Nadia, who huffs, blowing the feathers around her black mask about. She seems to be dressed as a black swan to compliment her girlfriend's white variation of the costume.

"You know I always get the first dance, asshole," Nadia complains.

Niles laughs brightly and offers an arm to my sister instead.

"Oh, alright. Tradition. You're such a stickler."

The two of them fade into the crowd. Sophia awkwardly excuses herself in search of a drink while Yvaine and her girlfriend head out onto the dance floor, leaving Cass and me alone at the bottom of the stairs.

I am wildly aware of the way she shifts next to me, swirling her drink in her hand and watching the guests moving to the music—anxiety knots in my stomach. *I know* I'm treading a very fine line. *I know* how things have to be for me and Cass. *I know* I'm balancing on the edge after everything. But right now, with the pulsing lights and the music...I don't care. Another problem for another day. Tonight, I want to tempt fate.

Setting my lemonade on the nearby table, I lean down, my lips almost brushing over the shell of her ear. My whole body is aware of the distance separating us—that fine line of air heats between her skin and mine.

"May I have this dance?"

Her chest rises, and she turns to meet my eye. There is a glimmer there, a playful sheen, as she considers for a moment. The corner of her full mouth quirks, and she extends her hand with a slight tip of her chin.

We wind our way through the crowd until we find a place far enough from the outer ring of bystanders, where the music drowns all else, and the lights send waves of purples, blues, and greens rippling over Cass's exposed skin, much more than I am used to seeing on her. My chest is tight. Every limb feels taut with anxious muscles, but I force the pounding of my heart away and allow my body to relax into the rhythm of the music. I spin her with my grip on her gloved hand, and her curls fan out around her face. She lands sure-footed again with a smile, and the beat changes, the song fading out of its tempo and into the string of notes for a new one. Her expression lights with excitement, and she jumps as the rhythm settles into one of her favorite songs. A sultry tempo pulls her hips into tight circles, her hands move to the hair at the base of her neck, and she lifts her locks as she stretches her arm above her head with her face to the side as the music takes control of her body.

She is breathtaking.

It takes me a moment to remember to move along with her, but when I do the fluid dance is easy and mindless. I've spent so many hours under lights just like these, with music just like this, trying to numb everything, to drown it out. Trying not to feel.

But I want to feel this. I want to remember this.

Cass and I, we don't have many moments. Flickers here and there. Nothing more. Fractions of a life that I have been trying desperately to let go of, only to pull myself further under in a matter of forty-eight hours. Those moments have become the only bright spots in my life. Like the phoenix, just a gift passed between "friends" when we were supposed to be studying.

It feels dramatic. I have a wonderful family. A good job. Friends.

But I never recovered from Cass. In my soul, I know I never will.

Maybe once, long ago, we had a chance if things had been just a little different. If I hadn't ruined things and then continued to ruin myself in the wake of it all. Perhaps things could have been different once. But they aren't now, no matter how badly I want them to be.

I told you to stay away from her, boy.

Those haunting words, that horrific memory, threaten to plague my temporary bliss. I know this can't last long. It won't. But I can allow myself to savor this moment. To collect one more flickering memory to hold close when she's gone again.

Cass twists a little further from me, and I reach out. My arms hover around her waist, and she offers a coy smile as she takes my wrists in her gloved hands. She sways into me with the music and guides my hands to her hips as our bodies collide.

She bites her lip and hangs her head back as her eyelids flutter closed. She curls away, spinning out on the beat, and I yank her back, using her momentum to spin her into my chest. Her eyes flare dangerously.

"Don't wander off," I tease, trying to focus on the way the lights dance in her eyes instead of the feel of her pressed against me or the slight parting of her lips.

I know I wanted to tempt fate...but I'm already losing this battle.

The lines of her body relax into mine as the rhythm flows through her, and she flashes me a crooked tilt of her lip as a devilish glint lights her eyes.

"No?" she asks as she moves her arms to rest on either side of my head. "You don't have a dozen people here waiting to get a piece of you?"

An echo of that hollow feeling reverberates through my chest, but I silence it by focusing on the tilt of her lips and the feel of her hips swaying under my fingers.

"What makes you think it's *me* they're waiting to get a piece of?" I lean back enough to get a view of the way the dress accentuates her every curve.

"You like the dress, then?"

More than you know, Firefly.

I dip my nose to almost brush hers and narrow my brow at her, a smile curling my lips.

"There's not a damn soul in here who *doesn't* like that dress on you."

Before I can allow my gaze to drop to her mouth or let my mind wander to the memory of those lips against mine, I take her hand from my shoulder and spin her again, pulling her back against me with a grip on her hip.

"Go ahead," I whisper against her ear. "Let them admire you."

She releases a laugh and throws her head back, but the music takes her body anyway. She sways to the beat, her hips melting into the heady rhythm.

I am lost. Beneath the thrum of the music and the feel of Cass against me, I lose myself. My resolve slips just a little more as I let my body move against her, allowing myself to breathe in this moment, to pretend this is simple. Easy. It's always easy with Cass. It should be, anyway.

CHAPTER 15

Talien

"I had no idea you could dance like that, Vale," Cass says with a raised brow before leaning across the bar to catch the bartender's attention. The very handsome masc with a clean fade and a sharp jaw, who I've seen at one of the many high-end clubs throughout the city, eyes Cass in a way that heats my skin. It shouldn't bother me. But it does.

"I've had a lot of practice since you've been gone," I say.

Leaning against the bar beside her, I watch past Cass's pristine profile as the bartender finishes her current orders with a dramatic flourish and saunters over.

"Don't tell me," she starts, narrowing perfect blue eyes at Cass as if trying to read her. "Macau with an extra cherry?"

I huff through my nose.

"Close," I grumble, rolling my eyes at her forwardness, not that I should mind.

Cass flashes her a winning smile and touches her gloved fingers to her chin as she leans over the bar.

"A sex on the beach."

The words sound sinful as they fall from her lips. Heat rushes through me, and I have to bite back the sound boiling up my throat.

118

"Coming right up," the bartender says, taking her error in stride.

She winks at Cass and moves to start the drink as Cass turns her attention back to me. I manage to snap my jaw closed before her eyes land on me, I think.

"I guess I'm invisible," I say, displaying my hands in dismay.

"Hm," she muses, tilting her attention to me with playful heat in her eye. "Maybe she's not into the hero knight-looking type. Or maybe she just likes me."

I'm helpless to stop the huff of amusement—and a little more jealousy than I intended—from escaping my lips.

"Oh, she *definitely* likes you." I tip back on my elbows enough to glance down the bar.

The bartender is almost finished with Cass's drink and is only idly listening as another guest tells her their order.

"Oh, what's the matter? Can't handle a tad bit of attention strayed from you?" Cass croons in a teasing, lilting tone.

Every nerve lights under the fire in her eyes. That hooded gaze could damn near get me to do anything she wanted.

God, I'm so fucked.

Turning to lean on one elbow, I offer her a crooked grin. I drop my voice to a low rumble in my chest.

"Is that what you want?"

Her lips part slightly, and her eyes flare as she sucks in a quick breath. It's a tense moment before her lips part to indicate any response, but it is not her voice that cuts the thrum of the party.

"What are you two up to?" Yvaine's judgmental tone perks my ears before she cuts between me and Cass, shooting me a poignant glare as Cass moves to make space for her.

Yvaine is dressed as the devil to Cass's angel. She wears a skintight red dress that stops mid-thigh, the color pops against her dark skin. Her crimson mask is adorned with an intricate, swirling, black pattern. The mask splits across her forehead to reveal her crest and arches up to meet the two small red horns clipped into her twists at the crown of her head. I admit I had no space to notice the pair's matching costume set as they arrived; all my attention had been focused on Cass.

"Don't you look like a terror," I tease, unable to hide my disdain for the interruption. Yvaine wrinkles her nose in response. "Drinking, dancing, the usual."

The bartender returns with Cass's drink.

"Enjoy that, love," she says with a wink before turning her attention to Yvaine. "Another whiskey sours?"

"Invisible," I say under my breath, shooting an incredulous look at Cass.

She laughs, and Yvaine turns to lean her back against the bar, propping her weight on her elbows.

"Cass, Niles needed your help in the dining room; they sent me to find you."

"With what?" she asks, taking a sip.

"I have no idea, but if you don't hurry, they'll likely combust."

Cass nods and rolls her eyes but meets my gaze with a half-smile before she turns to make her way toward the dining room. She's not a few feet away before Yvaine turns on me with a furious glare.

"Enjoying yourself tonight? Seti looks stunning in that armor. I'm afraid if she's dressed as a knight, I'll have to ask her to change. Only room for one Lancelot in these halls. How embarrassing." I gesture at my costume and smile despite the frost in her mood.

"What do you think you're doing, Vale?" Her words come out on a spiteful accusation.

Okay, I guess we're feeling bitey tonight.

I shift myself off the counter and fold my arms over my chest.

"Well, I *was* just trying to get a drink, but I can't even get the bartender to acknowledge my existence thanks to you and Cass," I quip, but Yvaine's jaw ticks, so I roll my eyes and reroute. "Calm down, we're just having fun."

"Yes, you always have fun. All the way to a broken heart for both of you. Are you going to get your head out of your ass this time, or do I need to preemptively beat you bloody?"

Damn.

Yvaine has always been a straight shooter, but sometimes, her words cut more than usual. Sighing, I moved to lean against the counter beside her again and busy myself twisting the rings on my fingers one by one.

"I'm not going to let it get that far," I assure her. "We're just enjoying the party."

"You better be," she warns, "Believe it or not, I *am* looking out for both of you. You're the one I have to watch wallow through the pain when she leaves. I don't like when you're like that."

She takes the drink the bartender sets beside her, and by the end of it, her voice is softer, with a tone of worry under it I did not expect.

It takes me a moment to find my voice again. Any words seem to catch in my throat. They're sour on my tongue. I chew the inside of my cheek for a moment before the bartender finally deigns to ask what I'd like.

"Water," I say with an annoyed grin. She nods, looking equally irritated about our exchange, and moves to fulfill my request.

"You're not the only one," I tell Yvaine over a heavy breath, unable to lift my gaze to hers.

When my water arrives, I turn to set my hips against the bar. The air feels heavy. I wish I had a stronger drink, but I can't tempt fate *that* much tonight. No. My wits need to stay intact.

Movement catches my eye over the heads of the other guests —a shock of blonde curls. Rage boils up, drowning out the other swirling emotions beneath the surface.

"Excuse me," I say to Yvaine, returning my glass to the bar and skirting through the crowd towards him.

"What the fuck are you doing here?" I growl, snatching him by the arm.

"Hello, Talien," Paris greets.

I use my grip on his arm to direct him through the nearest set of doors and out onto one of the terraces overlooking the courtyard. Once we're a good distance from the door, Paris breaks my grip on him and straightens his suit.

He scans me with a sour look.

"I like you better when you dress like a slut."

"I know this may come as a shock, but I didn't dress up for you. What the hell are you doing here." My breath plumes in the cold air, a reflection of the steam building under my skin.

How dare he show his face here after everything. I want to shove him off this damned balcony. It's only a short drop to the courtyard, where other costumed guests are strolling arm in arm.

I'm sure the rosebushes would break his fall.

"I was invited," Paris says, crossing his arms over his chest and sticking his rounded nose in the air.

"You weren't." I let him hear every drop of venom brewing in my throat.

"My family has connections."

"Not these connections."

"How would you know?" Paris's posture shifts.

He thinks he has the upper hand. My instincts tell me to proceed with caution.

"Why are you here," I growl, glancing at the nearby couple who have decided to join us. They're too caught up nibbling each other's ears to pay us much attention.

"Honestly, Vale. Did you really leave me just to jump in bed with Westfield's girl?"

I cannot mask the cold fury that hardens my jaw. Pain shoots through my palm as my nails bite into it.

"*What?*"

"You left me just hook up with Cassiopeia Varner? That's fucking ballsy considering what her father did to your family, isn't it?"

Paris' blue eyes flash with a dangerous light. My jaw is clenched so tightly I can hear my teeth grinding together.

"Tread carefully," I warn.

"Or what, Vale?"

My threat hangs empty between us. There's nothing I can say. No threat I can follow through on if he continues, and he knows it. For once, Paris actually has the upper hand.

Again, I consider how little effort it would take to tip him over the railing and fill his stubborn ass with thorns.

Niles would skin me alive.

"What do you think Bryson would have to say if he saw how you were dancing with his girl?" Paris asks, smiling.

"She's *not* his girl." The bite in my tone tears at my throat.

Paris's smile widens. "Oh, you don't have to convince me," he coos, setting a hip against the railing.

Maybe he'll just lose his balance.

"We all know you're the reason the wedding was called off in the first place, Vale. Little Varner whore."

My self-control snaps. Without a second's hesitation, my fists are tangled in the collar of his tailored suit. Paris yelps as I shove him precariously over the railing. His hands latch onto the damned buckles of my costume, clinging to me desperately.

"Fuck you," I growl.

"Woah, woah! Don't drop me! Don't you dare drop me!" Paris shrieks.

"Hey!" Someone calls behind me.

"Take it back."

"Okay, okay! She's not a whore. I didn't mean it!"

Begrudgingly, I pull Paris back to his feet and step away, shooting a look at the couple standing nearby, who look worried.

"We're fine," Paris says, smiling. "Just a misunderstanding. Nothing to worry about."

The pair eye us suspiciously before turning to leave. Paris straightens his shirt, huffing as color returns to his cheeks.

"You're going to regret this, Vale," Paris hisses, calmly, adjusting his cuffs.

"Get out." My voice is cold.

As his footsteps fade, I can't feel the chill on my skin anymore or hear the distant sounds of the music drifting out onto the terrace. The only feeling is that broken part of me splitting wide, swallowing me whole.

CHAPTER 16

Cassiopeia

"Hi, hello, I am here to ask you why in the fuck you made up some story to send me to Niles."

My voice cuts over the music, and Yvaine turns over her shoulder, her expression still stretched in laughter from talking to the handsome bartender. Talien is gone, and I cannot stop the slight sinking disappointment at the realization.

"I don't know what you're talking about," she says, her tone dripping false innocence as she flips her twists over her shoulder.

"Oh? Should I go and get Niles, then?" I ask, pointing over my shoulder as I retreat a step.

"No," she sighs and rolls her eyes. "I don't want to deal with their attitude at the moment. I made it up."

"Why?"

"You know why, Cassiopeia. You've been back for ten seconds. And you had a boyfriend fifteen seconds ago."

I narrow my eyes at her.

"I am here to have fun with my friends at a party. Don't be an asshole."

"I'm not! I am actually trying very hard to hold back on the asshole, thank you very much. Look. You know where I stand. You also know I will scrape your heart out of the gutters every single time. No matter what. I would just prefer not to for once. I also just want to have fun with my friends at a party. But the two of you looked close to taking to the closet out there, and I will not have my night ruined so quickly."

"We did not!"

"You're delusional. I want to dance. Will you come?"

I scoff a laugh at her ability to brush off a conversation the second she is done with it. I don't know if my eyes could roll any harder. But before I have a chance to offer a retort, she has her hand on my wrist and drags me past moving bodies back to the center of the crowd to meet her partner.

We laugh and dance away an impossible number of songs. Somewhere along the way Nadia and Sophia join, then Niles. All of us lose our stress to the rhythm, laughing, drinking, all without a care in the world.

All of us except for Talien, who I have not seen since I left the bar. It's been a long time, and I keep the corner of my eyes on the crowd, then to the edges of the room, but cannot find any trace of him. Until finally, between songs, I see a flash of his shining armor as he storms off around the edge of the dancefloor, past the bar, and straight to the balcony. His shoulders are tense, his brow is pulled together, his jaw ticking with some writing emotion. Niles sees, too, and their attention flits around the room before they squeeze between Nadia and Yvaine to follow him.

Worry pricks at me, and I watch until Niles closes the door behind them, and I can only see the outline of the two of them through the frosted glass. They disappear to the edge of the balcony, out of sight by the end of the next song.

I can no longer control the urge to follow, to see if Tal's alright. I lean over to Yvaine to tell her I am refilling my drink before I slink through moving bodies to get to the door.

I hesitate, a catch of anxiety in my chest as my hand meets glass, but it's too late. I've already started to push it open, and it is only another second of misguided, alcohol-fueled confidence before I am closing the door behind me, the cold night air sharp as it rests against my bare skin.

"—it's not that simple," Talien groans. His voice is heavy, slurred a little. When did he have time to get drunk?

"The fuck it's not," Niles bites back, sounding firmer than I've ever heard them. "I'm tired of you suffering because you're too damn proud to accept help."

"It's not that *simple*."

"Why didn't you tell me? Five years? And you didn't tell *me*? I'm your best friend."

"I know."

The sound of heavy footsteps along the balcony stops, and I heard a boot shuffle against the stone floor.

"When were you going to tell me Charlie knows you because your family fucking *lived* there. All this time, I thought it was just because you volunteer there so much. Oh my god, I want to kick that bastard's ass—"

My anxiety spikes. I should move, make my presence known. But I can't. My feet have turned to leave, and my heart lurches in my chest as Talien's voice falls.

"Niles." His voice has taken on a dangerous tone.

"What, Vale?" Niles snaps, their shoes squeaking to a halt.

"Don't go picking fights you can't win," Talien says, sounding heavy. Niles scoffs. "I mean it. Leave it alone. We're past it now."

"You think *he's* going to be 'past it' when he finds out where Cass is staying?"

My chest seizes as my mind races. I've had too much to drink to make sense of much, but I know the only "he" they could be talking about is Lionel Varner. But we shouldn't have to worry about him for a week. I should be able to enjoy one party without having to think about his influence.

But he's here. Somehow, he's always fucking here. Suffocating me, closing the walls in on me. And this time, he's done something to the Vales. Something Tal felt he needed to hide, something he didn't tell me about—or even Niles.

A thick silence follows those words. I hear the sounds of Talien moving. His voice drops low—low enough that even through my strain, I can't make out the words. And then there are footsteps. Heavy boots headed for the door. The door I'm still right in front of. My feet are still frozen. Why won't they move?

Talien rounds the thick stone column, making for the balcony entrance, and freezes. He stops so abruptly, Niles only narrowly dodges running into him, and dances into view around his shoulder. Their eyes go wide, their lips dropping into an almost comical 'O'. But I can't tear my eyes away from the look of horror on Tal's face. His brow is heavy and pinched over wide eyes; his jaw is clenched so tight the muscle flickers.

"I'm…just gonna give you two some privacy," Niles says, drawing the start of their sentence out for far too long as they slide past the both of us to sneak through the door behind me, leaving me trapped under the intensity of those eyes.

It's difficult to clear the cloud of my thoughts enough to force any sound into my voice, but I manage.

"I assume I was not meant to hear that," I say, my tone relatively neutral considering the flourish of my pulse.

The muscle in Talien's jaw flexes again.

"*What* did you hear?" he asks, searching my face.

"Enough to know you've been hiding something."

Talien huffs, looking away.

A knot behind my breastbone twists as I consider the possibilities. A million scenarios play behind my eyes. All horrific. There are no limits to what my father is capable of. I thought I'd shielded my friends from his crueler dealings, but apparently not.

"Your family. Are they alright?" My tone wobbles this time.

I am losing control; the crawl of anxiety is too thick under the haze of alcohol. I take a breath and shake out my hand at my hip.

"They're fine," Talien assures me. He moves to set a shoulder against the pillar and crosses his arms over his chest. "Since when did you start listening in on private conversations?"

"It wasn't my intention," I say, though a flicker of heat rises at the accusation.

Talien lifts a hand to scratch at his jaw, tipping his gaze away from me as he props an ankle over the other.

My attention snags on the shift of his posture, the severity in his eye, the darkened timber of his tone. I know I should have left. I know I should not have listened. But in this moment, I am not certain I will be able to think about anything outside of those endless, horrific possibilities.

"I froze. What could be so bad you needed to hide it from even Niles?" My tone is softer than I expect, I am not sure I want to hear the answer, but I need to. I'll lose my mind imagining all the ways Lionel could have tortured them.

His gaze falters. Dragging his bottom lip through his teeth. Talien takes a deep breath.

"Despite what they think, I don't tell Niles *everything*," he says.

"What happened, Tal?"

For a moment, his eyes soften. Behind the green, pain pulses through them. My heart lurches, and the need to reach out to him overwhelms me. A wire pulls taut in my chest. I clench my fists at my sides.

Just before I think he's going to speak, to tell me everything, to finally give me answers that might start to untangle this web spun around us, the mask slips back into place. That cocky grin twists his lips, and he pushes off the column to move towards me.

"It's awfully cheeky of you to demand answers about a conversation that doesn't concern you," he says, slipping his hands into his pockets and dipping forward enough at the hips to look me in the eyes.

My blood boils as I tip my chin in defiance, gritting my teeth.

"It doesn't? I'm not stupid, Talien. As far as I'm aware, there is really only one person who would be concerned about where I'm sleeping, and he doesn't take kindly to those who have crossed him. What. Happened?"

That pain flashes through his eyes again, and Talien's gaze drops to my lips. His breathing hitches, causing the barest lift of his chest, but it's enough to send a new kind of fire coursing through me.

And then he straightens, stepping away from me. Turning, he waltzes to the balcony railing and leans his hands against it, looking out across the estate.

"It was a long time ago," he says, as if that explains anything. "Let's leave it at that."

"Leave it at that?" I follow him with a march in my step, my heels clicking against the cobblestoned balcony.

"Talien, look at me." My demand is severe as I reach the banister.

"*Fuck me*," Talien groans under his breath, but he obeys, laying his head back against his shoulders and rolling it sideways to look at me.

There's a heat in his gaze. I try to tell myself it is just because we're in the middle of an argument.

I open my mouth to speak, to demand answers, to do anything but stare at him the way I am, with lips parted and a warmth crawling up my chest, curling low in my core.

My thoughts scramble as my eyes get lost in his deep emerald coves. They're darkened with the weight of unknown burdens.

I have lost my voice.

He waits, watching me as the chill pricks against my flushed skin. After an awkward amount of silence has passed between us, Talien's dark brow ticks up. A smirk curls at his lips.

"How long am I supposed to look?" he purrs.

Good god.

My pulse spikes, and I have to fight an intake of breath.

"As long as it takes," the words come out low, on a heated breath, and I can't help but shift closer.

The cocky expression on his sharp features falters. Those eyes flare again as a heated breath escapes his lips in a puff against the frosty air.

"As long as it takes for what?" he asks, his voice low, softer now.

God, anything.

But I can't speak. Can't think. Every fiber of my being wants him to be closer. A vibrating in my chest pulls the minimal space between us taught. I manage to control my hands enough to reach up and push a lock of fallen hair from his tense brow. The silvery satin glove stands out against the dimmed evening light.

"Talien..." His name is a whisper on my lips, a plea bearing more weight than I know how to express.

I don't know if it's the gesture or the need in my voice as I say his name, but something breaks the spell between us. Talien's eyes close, and then he shifts, drawing in an unstable breath as he straightens out of my reach.

"It's fucking cold out here." The words are shaky as he flexes his fingers to bring warmth back into them.

I have not noticed the chill. Not until that heated band between us snaps as he steps away. I haven't been cold. Not with the fire in his gaze lighting my soul ablaze.

If there is frigid air, it was placed there when he disconnected.

Just like he always does.

The sting of rejection bites at the backs of my eyes, and I can feel my limited control slipping.

"Yeah," I say, my tone flat as I release a breath, "colder than I expected."

I turn on my heel, headed for the entrance to the ballroom before I can misread any more of his hooded gazes and heat-dripped words.

CHAPTER 17

Cassiopeia

"Maybe you should just let it go," Yvaine says as she takes a bite of the chocolate croissant I brought her from the Café.

I pretend to flip through a graphic novel I pulled from one of the shelves. An unsuccessful attempt at a distraction in the face of my distress over the previous night's argument with Tal. Irritation flares in my chest at her dismissal, likely aided by the throb of a hangover headache.

"*You* let it go," I bite as I snap the book closed and look up to meet her assessing stare from where she stocks her shelves.

She snorts a laugh and rolls her deep sandalwood eyes.

"Don't laugh at me. This is serious. If my father has had his hands in Tal's life, I need to know about it."

She heaves a sigh and shelves her last book before she turns to give me her full attention, her arms crossed over her chest in clear disapproval.

"Why? I thought you wanted as far away from Lionel's shit as possible."

Yvaine knows better than anyone else exactly what *shit* it is I tried so desperately to get away from. I've confided in her about

132

the underlying foundation of my father's hotel empire, the less legal dealings. She's never so much as batted an eye at the fact.

Honestly, if anyone would be capable of taking on Lionel Varner, it's Yvaine.

"I do. But this is Talien we're talking about. Nadia. I can't let my friends suffer because I chose to run away."

The words sink a heavier stone in my chest than I expect. After the stiff silence hangs between us for a moment, I place the weighted feeling as guilt. I am reluctant to admit I had not thought once about any potential repercussions my leaving would have on my friends. I never thought Talien had been close enough to Lionel to get caught in any crossfire. I thought I'd protected him well enough.

If I'd been home, I could have stopped it. I could have helped.

Although, it's hard to imagine exactly what steps I would have taken to prevent anything, considering I have had absolutely no luck in uncovering any information in the hours since the party.

No one will talk. Whatever happened had been bad enough to keep everyone wanting me in the dark. It wasn't just Tal. I called my mom, Nadia, even Vasiliki. No one had anything to tell me.

It's killing me to not know what happened.

"You tried Nadia? And Vas?" Yvaine asked, her tone softer as she watches me deteriorate into my thoughts.

"Neither one of them offered any insight," I answer with a weighted disappointment pulling at the edge of my tone.

"And Niles?" Yvaine asks, glancing down at her phone before setting it aside again.

"Refuses to answer their phone and I got a ramble of a text about letting us work this out on our own."

Irritating, insufferable individual. Niles is always the first one to talk. Now, of all times, they decide to keep things close to their chest.

"Okay. So, remind me again why you are snooping around trying to find information no one seems keen on giving up?"

"I *need* to know," I say, my voice stretching on a dramatic groan as I stretch my arms out over the counter.

"Then talk to Tal," she says with a roll of her eyes.

"He's mad at me."

I can't stop the shiver as it snakes my spine at the memory of that silent simmer behind his emerald eye. I wish I could say I regret overhearing his conversation with Niles, but I do not. My heart aches over it, but not with regret. It's more like remorse for the illusion I held of the trust I thought we held between us.

"He's not mad at you," Yvaine insists, checking her phone again. She types a quick response before tucking it away again.

"You didn't see the look on his face," I say with a heavy sigh, that pang near my heart twisting.

"No. But I have seen the way he looks at you ninety-nine percent of the time. He's not mad at you. If he was, he's over it."

"Okay, well, you weren't there. I tried to ask him, and he was mad at me."

"I don't know what to tell you, Cassiopeia. I warned you things would get messy, and you didn't listen *so...*" A sharp cut of irritation lifts her voice as she turns over her shoulder to get back to her task.

I open my mouth to offer a retort, but the bell on the bookshop door sounds across the empty space, pulling my attention from our conversation with a furrowed brow to see who entered with the "closed-for-lunch" sign hung clearly on the door.

To my horrific dismay, Bryson saunters through with an annoyingly bright smile on his face.

"That damned door should have been locked," Yvaine grumbles as she rises to a stand, her gaze flicking to the dull crest on Bryson's forehead before she storms over to meet him. "Get out."

"Nice to see you, too, Miss DuPont. Funny way to treat your potential customers," he replies with a cocky twitch of one brow.

He turns his attention from Yvaine and steps farther into the room. The set of his shoulders and the tense line to his jaw set the hair along my arms on edge, and a familiar knot of unwanted dread twists in my core.

"We all know damned well you have no interest in anything in this store. We are closed for lunch. Leave," Yvaine repeats herself, her voice echoing more dominance this time.

"It's okay," I sigh, mostly in hopes of shaking off the unsettling wave of nerves his presence has instilled, and rise to my feet.

"It's not," she insists.

Bryson opens his mouth to speak, but I cut him off with a curt tone.

"What do you want, Bryson?"

"I just came by to tell you about a set of concert tickets I bought when you got into town. The Vellas. The show is this weekend, and I thought you'd want to join me."

A spike of furious anxiety pierces my chest as I process his words. It quickly settles into confusion. I furrow my brow and cross my arms over my chest. First of all, the Vellas have never been a band I enjoyed. The folk group is *his* favorite and we saw them regularly as a couple, but it had never been my thing. Secondly, I am entirely unsure which part of our "date" yesterday left him thinking I would want to go out with him.

"I don't think so." My voice settles into an uncertain cadence as I turn over the conversation we had over lunch in my mind.

"I already have the tickets. They're non-refundable. C'mon, for old time's sake."

The smile on his face insinuates a carefree attitude, but I know better. I recognize that edge to his voice; he's already decided for me.

My pulse thrums against my temple, and I release a stiff breath as I try to reconcile with the wave of emotion that has overcome my senses. A decade's worth of memories I've locked away threaten to break the seal of my composure, and I cast a fleeting glance to Yvaine, a plea in my eye. She catches my attention and nods almost imperceptibly as she looks back to Bryson.

"She said no," Yvaine snaps as she steps toward him to intercept any advances he might make.

"Cass." My name falls from Bryson's lips on an incredulous breath, like he can't believe the dismissal.

I finally manage to gather enough words to speak. "I thought I made myself pretty clear yesterday. I don't think doing anything for 'old times sake' is the right move."

Bryson's expression shifts, a dangerous line settling over his brow, and an angry heat replaces his previously light demeanor. The sudden change curls a tension of unease under my already unstable resolve.

"What will your dad think when he hears what you've been up to since you've been back?" he asks, his tone simmering.

"Are you threatening me?" The heat under my words is fueled only by the spike of anxiety his insinuation causes.

He can't mean anything other than Tal. He'd always had a problem with our friendship. And now, knowing Lionel has done something to the Vales, I can't help the flutter of fear his anger causes. I am not the only one at risk here.

"I will not tell you again, shithole. Get. Out. Or I will remove you myself," Yvaine demands before he has a chance to elaborate on his remark.

Bryson steps back on his heel with a smug expression stretching his features and a huff of a laugh.

"Send Talien my regards."

His words land like a hammer to my chest. The air is sapped from my lungs, and my eyes stretch wide as my fears are confirmed.

Yvaine waves her arm with a furious flourish, and the crest on her forehead lights as her magic sends the door snapping open. The gesture radiates only a fraction of the anger across Yvaine's expression. Bryson turns on his heel and leaves the shop without another word.

I turn to Yvaine with my eyes stretched wide, unable to shake the dread coursing through my veins. Tears prick the backs of my eyes, and I shrug helplessly as I shake my head in disbelief.

"Okay," Yvain sighs, a rare hint of anxiety under her tone. "Maybe we *do* need to get to the bottom of the Vale situation before your father gets home."

CHAPTER 18
Talien

Tink. Tink. Tink.

The sound of someone tapping on glass pulls me from a very warm, very nice dream that I was rather enjoying. Here, it's cold. Fucking freezing, actually.

Blinking, I lift my head, which I immediately regret as pain lances through my skull.

Hung over. Great.

The massive twinge in my neck from sleeping with it slumped against my steering wheel is arguably just as bad as the hangover.

Tink. Tink. Tink.

I can't see who it is through the foggy windows, but the silhouette of a toboggan with a giant puff in the middle and a parka is much too bright to be anyone but Niles.

My fingers are practically frozen, and Niles continues tapping incessantly while I stiffly search for my keys. It takes a moment before I'm able to very painfully retrieve them from my pocket, my fingers burning from the scratch of my pants against the dry, frigid skin.

Once the car is on, I roll down the window and glare up at Niles, who smiles.

"It went that bad, huh?" they ask, their brow dipping with concern.

Rubbing my cold hands together for warmth, I gingerly set my head back against the headrest.

"I guess so; I can't really remember." The steam from my breath billows above me in little clouds.

Niles gives an exceptionally heavy sigh and retrieves a coffee from the roof of the car. As I take the steaming cup from them and savor the way it heats my fingertips, a vivid flash of the dream I'd been having washes over me; a very different heat flooding over my fingers, lust-filled moans falling from crimson-painted lips... and then it's gone. Just the barest hints of the memory remain.

Suddenly, I'm very awake.

"What time is it?" The forgotten clock on my dash is only remembered as the words pass my lips.

"Eleven thirty," Niles informs me just as I find the numbers myself.

"Shit, I'm late for my shift at the shelter."

"I know," Niles says. They tap the roof of the car and move around to the passenger side to slide in.

"Charlie called about an hour ago and asked if I knew where you were," they inform me as I pull out of the bakery parking lot, noting the delivery van I'd borrowed yesterday parked very neatly beneath the sign. "I told him you'd skipped out on my event, called a ride-share, and I assumed went home. I'm surprised no one else woke you. The bakery was so busy this morning they called to ask me to return the van before noon."

That's some relief, at least. I'd never driven drunk, but I hadn't been in my right mind after Cass left last night. I guess I'd made it to my car and decided to wait in the cold to sober up a bit. Not the first time that's happened.

"Can you drop me off at home? I have some calls to make today." Niles twirls their phone in their long fingers before clicking open their messages and beginning to type.

"Sure."

I twist my head again, trying to loosen the screaming muscles along my neck as I pull into the busy street.

"That makes two hundred and eighty-three names, most of which are willing to write letters or make a statement against the buyout," Charlie says, chewing the edge of the pen in his hand. "I don't know, Vale. That's not enough."

"I know," I groan, gathering the last of the loads of laundry—residents' clothing in separate labeled bags, bedsheets, kitchen towels, etc—into the back of Charlie's pickup. "I'll do some interviews this week. My mom said a few of the tenants in their building would be willing to talk to me."

When I turn to take another bag from Charlie, he hasn't picked it up from the cart; he's still just staring at the small list of names on the clipboard.

"Hey," I say, putting a firm hand on his shoulder, "we're going to beat him. People need this place. We won't let them tear it down."

"Yeah," Charlie agrees, but his voice is hollow, eyes distant.

The drive to the laundromat would have been silent, except that Charlie's pickup has needed thousands in repairs over the last ten years, but he and Vince poured every penny they had into the shelter instead of themselves. The engine roars as I pull into a space in the parking lot of the laundromat, throw it into park, and drop my head against the steering wheel.

"This hangover might just be the one that does me in," I moan, taking a blessed moment of silence before I venture back into the screaming world around me.

Staring at the backs of my eyelids, I try to pull the image hovering in the back of my mind into focus. Whatever dream Niles woke me from this morning was gone in an instant, but a shadow of it has been flitting around the hazy, throbbing mess of my brain all day.

It's no use, though. Without food and a lot more water, I'm barely functioning.

Heaving open the door, I force myself out into the wretched sunlight and start hauling the laundry inside.

It's going to be a long day.

It was, in fact, an obscenely long day. After dropping off the clean laundry, helping Vince and Charlie get the sheets back on all the mattresses, and playing a quick game of ball with some of the kids, I am, thankfully—finally—on my way home.

Niles managed to get quite a few of their colleagues behind the campaign to save the shelter and low-income housing complex, so that was something, at least. The moguls have been trying to tear down this section of town and rebuild for years, and a part of me is convinced they'll never be able to. We're too resilient. We're outnumbered, but we're not lacking in anything else. They can't possibly win this time.

But Lionel Varner...

He's unpredictable, as I've seen firsthand. Or, rather, extremely predictable in outcome; it's the methods that are the tricky part. I've turned over time and time again how he managed to buy the majority of the stocks from my family's company almost overnight. In less than a week, he wiped out my family's name, took over the company, fired everyone loyal to the Vale name, and blacklisted my father and mother. Not ten weeks later, we were foreclosed on—which my mother could never make sense of—and that was it. In the span of a few months, we went from living the life my parents had always dreamed of to scraping by at the shelter, trying to get enough saved for a place for all of us.

Dad hasn't been the same since.

It killed me to see him so lost. Mom, she bounced back. She had her hand in that company as much as Dad did, but it wasn't her dream. She'd found her way in writing—children's books, mostly—inspirational pieces about diversity and equality. She'd made friends and volunteered at the shelter when she wasn't busy with the thousands of other ways she found to be happy after everything.

But Dad, he fell. Hard. I used to think he was one of those people with the world at their fingertips. He was charismatic, outgoing, charming. Anywhere we went, people knew him, greeted him with a smile, and he remembered them. Always. Their faces, their names, families.

Hell, I had been blessed with my fair share of charm, but Dad wrote the book on it.

It's funny how your opinion of someone can change when you've seen them at their worst. I never wanted that to be the case, but it was. Watching him lie on a cot while the three of us worked multiple jobs each to get us back on our feet...It changed everything.

The car engine cuts out and I breathe a heavy sigh of relief or, what I wish was relief. Instead of feeling the anxiety coiling in my chest release, it has been winding into an entirely new knot for the past hour.

I haven't checked my phone all day. There wasn't a message from Cass when I looked. I don't know if I expected as much, but the lack of contact after the way we left things last night stung. I tried to type something out again but gave up and discarded the phone into my coat pocket, where it weighed on me like an anchor the rest of the day.

Sighing, I determine that the bag of Fuego BBQ chips, the bar of sea salt and caramel chocolate, and a pack of ciders are probably the weakest attempts at an apology I could have devised, but I have little choice at this point. I can't avoid this conversation any longer.

Opening the car door and grabbing the bags, I slide out and

make my way to my apartment, trying to rehearse some semblance of an apology for upsetting her. As my key slides into the lock and begins to turn, the image from the dream that's been eluding me all day finally solidifies.

It was Cass—the same fire in her eyes as last night, the same quirk of her lips. As much as her face captivates me, it is the fact that she's seated naked on my couch, legs folded to one side, curves and tattoos on full display that truly stops me in my tracks.

The chill in the air does nothing to calm the heat rushing over my skin. The idea of her waiting on the other side of this door makes my heart beat like it's running a marathon.

I'm certain my mind is just running away again like it did the night before. The images of her legs spread for me, the outline of her against the moonlit window, and the sounds that bled from her lips haunt me once again, only adding to the slight tremor in my hand.

It's ridiculous.

I know that. I know she's *not* waiting naked for me on the other side of this door. I know I *shouldn't* be dreaming of Cass like that, let alone standing out here replaying all the images my mind sculpted in such detail over the past ten years. I *shouldn't* have spent so long pining after her when nothing could come of it.

I told you to stay away from her.

I told you there would be consequences.

The memory of those words chills some of the nervous heat boiling lower and lower. I know I'm being stupid. Cass is probably just watching TV or reading or in the shower.

Fuck.

I quickly shove away the spiral my mind tries to take in pursuit of that image and scold myself for continuing to entertain these feelings for my friend.

Friend. Nothing more.

It can't be more.

Taking a deep breath, I finish turning the key, wondering how

I'm going to explain why it took me so damn long to open the door as I push through the nervousness and into my apartment.

It's dark. The blankets are still folded neatly over the back of the couch; the TV is off, and there's not even a light peeking out from under the bathroom door on the other side of the room.

Cass isn't here. From the looks of it, she hasn't been back since she left yesterday morning.

A cool breeze reminds me I'm standing with the door wide open, and I find the muscles in my legs to pull myself across the threshold. The bag of snacks feels heavy as I set it on the nearby table and stoop to remove my shoes.

Once I've rid myself of my jacket and set Cass's treats on the kitchen counter, I flick on the light and dig my phone out of my pocket.

Still no messages, but the anxiety poised under my ribs won't allow me to leave it that way any longer.

Not on your way back to the city already,
are you?

I stare at the words. They're wrong. I delete the message and try again.

Hey, I'm sorry about last night

The better part of five minutes is eaten away, rearranging the words to try and find a way to explain how the whole evening went so wrong. All of them feel empty.

Should she have listened in on my conversation with Niles?

No. Am I still angry? Yes. Very. But the anger dulls at the thought of her choosing to leave because of it. I can set aside my feelings, like I always do, for Cass. If choking down the way I feel about her, or the way I feel about this whole god damned situation, lets me continue to keep up this thread of friendship we have left, I'll swallow those feelings again.

If that's what it takes to protect her, to protect my family, I can manage it.

Me too. I didn't mean to upset you.

My heart gives a painful twist. I know Cass. She's never one to shy away from honesty, especially when it comes to her father and his "outdated views." She'd be livid if she knew the extent of his influence over this situation.

I overreacted. Bumped into an ex, a bad one, you know how it is.

I shouldn't have put that on you.

I get it. Exes suck. Mine won't go away either. Are you home?

Yeah.

Should I bring your things by Yvaine's in the morning or...?

> No, I'll be back, if that's okay. Mom just needed some help with festival stuff for a few days. Keep my singular pair of work pants and seventeen pairs of underwear safe for a few days?

My damned heart is drumming wildly again. I can't help but think she's staying away because of me. I know she wants answers. She deserves an explanation for what happened that night. For what changed.

> That seems like a lot of responsibility, but I guess I can manage for you.

She deserves better, but I'm not better. Isn't that the whole point? Isn't that why we're here in the first place?

> Lol I'll be back in a couple of days. I'll bring dinner. Any requests?

The tension I'd been holding in my shoulders relaxes some. My stomach grumbles at the thought of food, but I ignore it and head to the bathroom to wash the day away instead.

> Surprise me

CHAPTER 19
Cassiopeia

SENIOR YEAR OF HIGH SCHOOL

I grumble at the rolling pin that has refused to cooperate as I try to flatten my ball of cookie dough. It keeps sticking. There's flour everywhere. I peer at Tal, who has been using various cookie cutters to make shapes in his perfectly flattened dough since he passed the rolling pin to me.

He seems to feel my gaze and meets my eye. A laugh cracks his chest as he sees the altercation I am having with this uncooked baked good, and I glower, blowing a breath out through flared nostrils.

"The flour is supposed to go on the dough, *not you*," Tal says, flicking some of the white powder at me. "Do you need help? Or are you determined to pound it into submission on your own?"

"You know—don't look at me. I should be able to do this on my own." I try to maintain the glare, but a smile breaks my expression under the heat of his attention.

Tal's lip curls into that smirk he always gives me when he thinks I'm being ridiculous, but he turns back to his dough.

"*Should* being the operative word there..." he mumbles under his breath, though it's loud enough for me to know he meant for me to hear his jibe.

I groan and flick my flour-covered fingers back at him. A room-brightening laugh cracks his chest.

As I roll the pin towards me, more flour is pushed off the table to dust my sweater. I groan again in frustration.

"Fine, yes, okay. Help, please."

"Mrs. Varner, what happened here," he asks Mom, who happily works on her cobbler across the kitchen. "Cass is one of the smartest people I know. How is it your daughter is bested by a rolling pin? You really should let her cook more often."

Mom snorts and almost spits out the wine she's taking a sip of. She doesn't break stride as she sets it on the counter to get bowls down for the icing she will make.

Mom encouraged me to invite Tal over while Dad is away. She wanted to meet him after he asked to take me to winter formal. I am glad she's been so supportive of this. I've needed her here. And she definitely likes him, not that there is literally anything to dislike. He's perfect.

Maybe she can finally convince Dad to let up on his beliefs about the stupid founders' conflict.

Tal moves to take the dough off the counter in front of me, grinning at my mother as she flits about the kitchen.

"Hey." I nudge him in the side with my elbow. "Shut up."

He smirks at me and kneads his dough.

"You really are a dreadful baker, Cassiopeia. Your father's genes ruined that for you," Mom chides.

"Don't worry," Tal says, sprinkling the counter with a thin layer of flour before setting the dough in front of me again. "I think you can be taught."

The way his lip curls over the words makes my heart flutter. He gently removes the rolling pin from my hands, careful to avoid touching me, and coats it in flour before handing it back.

"Okay, now, even pressure, start in the middle. Just rock it back and forth at first."

My heart feels tight, like something is wrapped around it, tugging it toward him, and my eyes linger a moment too long on his face before I put the rolling pin back down.

"I'm just not very good at doing things slowly," I say.

"No shit," he teases, chuckling.

He leans a hand on the counter to watch, and his breath brushes over my ear.

My heart jumps into my throat, the sound of its beating thrums between my ears. I do as he says and take a breath. The dough attempts to cling to the pin, but it starts to flatten out as I work with it a bit.

"Better?"

Tal nods. "Turn the pin. Now, go crossways to flatten it out this way. May I?"

His hands hover over mine, but he waits for me to nod. I wasn't thinking. I should have prepared better for the contact. I suck in a breath as a jolt of heat hits me square in the chest, but I do well to stifle the surge of magic before anything has a chance to settle in. My crest flares, but when my shoulders relax, he moves my hands with the pin, rolling the dough back and forth to offer instruction. I can't contain the fluttering wings of my heart. The sensation of my vivid magic as it works through his wild emotion clears my mind of all thought.

My nerves tangle in my limbs, and I fumble the rolling pin. I move out from under his grip and shake my hands out nervously.

"Maybe you should just do it." My tone is lighter and more sure than I imagined it would be, but he narrows his eyes at me briefly before folding his arms over his chest.

"Absolutely not. You'll never learn if I do everything for you," he says with a wink and moves back to his waiting dough.

Mom is no longer in the room. When did she leave? The air seems to thicken between us, and the fluttering of my heart increases its pace to a steady gallop.

I need to get ahold of myself. I focus on the dough in front of me and try to follow his instructions. After a minute or so of steady progress, it looks about right, and I set the rolling pin to the side.

"Alright," I sigh and brush my flour-covered hands off on my skirt, "I'd like some cookie cutters, please."

Tal passes them to me, all except for the large tree, which he has placed just out of my reach.

"Why can't I have that one?" I ask, pointing to the tree.

Tal looks up from under his brows as he transfers his cookies to the cookie sheet. Mischief is written all over his face.

"I gave you all of those," he says.

"But what if I wanted to make exclusively trees?" I tease.

He finishes transferring the cookie he has on the spatula with one hand so that he can snatch the cutter from the counter. He folds his arm behind his back and smirks.

"Oh, now you're just being rude," I laugh and step around the corner of the island, reaching for my prize.

Chuckling, Tal dodges my attempt and tosses a puff of flour in my face. I yelp in surprise and stretch up on my tiptoes to reach above him for the cookie cutter. I stumble into him, and our chests touch.

"Talien!" I laugh as I grip his forearms, trying to yank them closer to me.

The electric jolt of emotion from the sudden contact catches my breath again. It's bright, and it tangles with my own bliss beautifully.

"You have all of those!" He twists an arm out of my grasp to gesture dramatically at the counter, grinning at me.

"But I want that one," I insist, stretching higher and wiggling my fingers. I am on my toes, the other foot pointed out as I keep my balance with my grip on his arm. His excitement flares against mine, and I can't tell who's wild bliss is more vibrant. It's exhilarating.

"You can't have this one, it's mine."

I jump to snatch the cookie cutter and bump him again, causing us to stumble. His back impacts the edge of the counter, and the cookie cutter goes flying. Tal is belly-laughing with his head tipped back, and his arm wrapped tightly around my waist to steady my fall.

I rest my hand on his chest, and I'm sure the smile on my face radiates the warmth spreading through me. My other hand is still on his arm, and emotion pulses from the contact. My magic pings bright against his excitement. It radiates a color of what I feel blooming within my chest. The radiance sends glittering magic coursing through my veins, causing a heady sensation.

"No!" I protest, throwing my head back dramatically.

"No? You didn't think that pouncing on me would knock the cookie cutter across the fucking room?"

I tilt my head forward again and find his face close, our noses almost touching. My breath stops short, and my heart thunders between my ears.

"No," I breathe, my eyes flit to catch the line of his lips briefly before I fix them determinedly on his eyes.

That familiar look of mischief shifts. The bright bliss I feel radiating from him twists into something deeper, something heated. My pulse spikes. His usual smirk fades, and the guarded look in his eyes clears to something like understanding. Beneath my hand, his breathing stills.

In one fluid motion, Tal's lips are against mine. His arm tightens around my waist, and his hand finds my cheek, holding me to him with a tenderness I wasn't expecting. Every inch of contact sets me on fire. He can't know what it does to me; we haven't really spoken of my power, but, oh god, I cannot contain the roiling emotion as it overwhelms my senses. I can't tell who's feeling more out of control, but it doesn't matter.

All of the tension in my body bleeds away as I part my lips, and Tal sweeps his tongue into my mouth. I wind the fabric of his shirt in my fist and tangle the fingers of my other hand in his hair. My heart is bursting at the seams. I cannot be close enough to him. Tal pulls me tighter against his chest, his fingers curl into the hair behind my ear.

"Cass," he whispers against my lips, breaking away to set his forehead against mine and breathe.

"Wow." The word comes out on a flutter of breath, my chest

heaving in time with the clamoring of my heart, and my eyelids drift closed.

Tal chuckles, and a wave of cool relief drifts from him to settle over me.

"You have no idea how long I've wanted to do that," he says.

A brightness fills my chest and I smile as I reach up to touch my nose to his.

"Yeah," I begin, but the sound of footsteps pulls at my attention.

"Does anyone have cookies ready for the oven yet?" Mom chimes from the doorway. I sink to my heels and drop my hands.

"Oh!" she chimes. "I see you've been busy with other things."

She wiggles her eyebrows and snags her wine from the counter.

"Mami," I scold, but she lifts her brow and turns around with a raised hand as she takes another drink.

Tal is scratching his chin and staring out the window into the garden, his face a vibrant shade of red when I turn back to him. I offer him a smile and reach out to squeeze his forearm.

Taking a short breath, I move around the counter to pick the cookie cutter up off the floor. I am wildly disappointed in the abrupt end to our moment. I am dying to know what's going on in his head. If his thoughts are buzzing as loudly as mine, but I am no longer touching him, and it feels like it would be overstepping to take another glimpse now.

When I turn back, Mom is next to him, cutting cookies out in my dough.

"Hey!" I shout.

"You're too slow," she shrugs a shoulder.

Tal also shrugs at me, his face still red, but that confident smirk starts to reappear as he returns to his scraps of dough and begins to reform it.

I bump Mom with my hip to get her out of my way and begin to cut out my own cookies. Tal shoots me a mischievous half-smile, and I don't need the physical contact to know what he feels about our stolen moment, the promise of more moments just like that is etched in the curve of his lips. For the first time in what feels like maybe my whole life everything feels right.

CHAPTER 20

Cassiopeia

My nerves are out of control. I spent all day hyping myself up for this, but now, with the clock rapidly winding down to five-thirty, I am not sure I have ever known how to take a steady breath. Tal will walk through that door any minute, and I suddenly feel like nothing but a ball of chaos. I haven't seen him since the party, which now feels like a huge mistake.

Mom needed my help painting some decorations to help with the festival, and I got sucked into it. At least, that's what I told myself. Now, with the festival tomorrow, it's difficult to ignore the fact that I'd wanted to avoid this pending conversation with Tal.

I have not had any luck uncovering what happened with the Vales, and it's come down to a matter of just...asking him again.

Not that I think that's going to go well, but I have to. Bryson threatened him. I need to know what's going on before it gets any worse.

Hopefully, the promise of holiday cookies and a hot meal will soften the blow of the inevitable pain in the ass this conversation is going to be. The ghost of that blissful holiday memory in my family home eases my nerves a little, at least. It's one of my favorites.

I am barely able to escape the more heartbreaking feelings that come along with it, though. The aftermath of realizing the kiss, our date to the winter formal had been a mistake. That, for some reason, he changed his mind. He thought it was better we stayed friends.

Of course, *friends* was better than nothing at all. It was safer that way, anyway. At least, I thought it had been. Now, I am not sure he's ever been safe.

How had the time slipped by so quickly? There's flour everywhere; the cookie dough isn't even close to the right consistency, and the Kreatopita smells like it's burning. My apron is a mess, and I clearly have not had enough wine.

I release a frustrated sigh as I wipe my messy hands on my apron and pick up my glass to allow the warmth of the red wine to wash over my wiry resolve.

The soft rustling of keys in the lock spikes my heart rate. I instinctively straighten myself and brush my hands off a second time, but the mess of this frock cannot be saved. I don't have time to reroute before the door opens, and Tal's dark head swings into the room.

His eyes go straight to the mess of my apron, and a smile breaks over his features.

"Smells great." He locks the door behind him and removes his coat.

As he picks a hanger out of the closet and slings his coat over the wires, I can't help but admire the touches of wildness that still cling to this refined, working-professional version of him. The black satin button-down is adorned with a pattern of flowers swirling across his shoulders and chest. The sleeves are rolled to his elbows, and he has a leather harness buckled over one shoulder. It wraps around his waist, bringing attention to the sharp cut of his muscular build.

Once the coat is hung, he props a shoulder against the wall and crosses a boot over his knee to remove it.

Talien lifts his attention to mine. The tension from the past couple days lingers in the glittering green of his eyes, only tempered by the softness I am so familiar with. He tracks his gaze over me quickly and tips his head to peer in at the counter as he removes the second boot.

I manage to tear my stilled attention from where he stands to the oven, where the Vale family recipe I have given my best shot at creating most certainly does not smell great.

"I got the recipe from Nadia," I say on a flutter of breath as I rush to pull the pie to the stovetop. It's black around the edges. "I fussed too long with the cookie dough, and I think I ruined it."

It's difficult to temper the deflated disappointment in my chest as I poke at the crisped edges with a spatula.

Talien pads across the floor and leans over my shoulder to get a look. A soft snort through his nose is all the response I receive before he moves to the sink to wash his hands.

Once he dries his fingers and pulls an apron over his head, Tal inspects the flour on the counter and the unruly wad of dough sitting mangled in the center of it.

"What's this?" he asks, his voice thick with humor.

"My attempt at sugar cookies," I say with a sigh and a roll of my eyes. "I thought it would be a fun thing to do and also that I would be capable of literally anything involving kitchenware, but obviously I am still bested by flour."

A bloom of laughter breaks from him as he pokes at the dough with a finger.

"Have you gotten any better with a rolling pin?" Those green eyes dart to me with mischief dancing behind them.

A heat flushes my cheeks as my mind drifts back to that night ten years ago. Excitement flares in my chest. I'm glad he held onto the memory, too.

"Glad you remember that disaster as well as I do. We can order something out; this thing is a brick," I say, nodding to the failed attempt at a home-cooked meal.

"I'm sure it's not that bad," he chides. "We'll salvage what we can."

"You really don't have to eat it. Let's just order pizza or something," I insist. "You're probably tired. This was silly, let's just relax."

Something shifts across Talien's features, a softening of that hard line always lingering over his expression. The air is tangible between us for a moment.

"You're supposed to chill the dough before you roll it out," he comments as his eyes slide back to the counter.

"Okay, well, I definitely didn't do that," I huff and stare sidelong at the mess of flour.

My nerves urge me to release some of the wiry tension in my bones. I should apologize for the other night, ask if he's okay, anything. But, now that he's in the room, I am not sure I have it in me to unearth the mountain of emotions that is sure to accompany the lingering conversation between us.

I am frustrated—beyond frustrated, actually. I'm a full-grown adult. I should be able to corral my anxieties long enough to have a reasonable, mature conversation.

I move to grab my wine glass again and take a long swig, relishing in that comfortable warmth again. Talien wraps my miserable attempt at cookie dough in plastic and sets it in the freezer while I watch, letting the tart, fruity bite of the wine continue to calm my nerves and center me.

Turning, Talien retrieves his phone from his pocket and flashes a smile at me.

"Gyros? There's a place that delivers just around the corner. Ten minutes tops," he says as he eyes the glass in my hand and turns to retrieve another from the cabinet near him.

"That sounds amazing," I sigh with a significant amount of relief. "I'll get this mess cleaned up."

"Leave it," Talien says with a soft chuckle as he pours himself some wine. "It needs to cool before we try to save the pan."

He takes a long drink, breathes a heavy sigh as if the weight of the day is starting to lift from his shoulders, and turns his attention on me again.

"How was being home?"

"Helping Mom with the festival was fun, but actually being in that house was, honestly, miserable. There's a reason I don't go home ever," I groan against the coil of dread in my core over having to relive being confined within those walls.

Talien laughs, swirling the wine in his glass as he lifts the phone to his ear to order. I remove my apron and fuss with tidying the kitchen as much as possible while we wait for the food to arrive. When we have our gyros in hand, we sit opposite one another on his couch and effortlessly fall into a rhythm of bright conversation. It isn't long before my nerves have completely dissipated. It's either the wine or his ability to force a sturdy kind of stillness under my resolve; I am not sure which. But it doesn't matter. I have never been more content than I am now listening to someone talk about their day.

He's been telling me about his help with the homeless shelter downtown. The passion that comes with every word only lifts that bright feeling in my chest further. I didn't realize he worked so closely with Charlie. I used to, in high school, and I missed it dearly.

It isn't long before we are both glossy-eyed from the excessive amount of wine I brought over, and we are laughing mirthfully as Talien recounts his experience helping Niles prepare for the masquerade.

I have tears in my eyes, and my stomach aches as I double over. I have to set my glass on the bar top behind me to keep from sloshing it on his leather couch. The sound of my laughter is only eclipsed by his, a vibrant chime to echo the light behind my heart.

"I swear, they make me want to pull my hair out sometimes," Talien chuckles before draining the remainder of his wine in a single gulp.

Our laughter mingles as he takes my glass from the bar and gets to his feet.

"Another?"

"Yes," I say, turning to watch him with my chin resting on my arms as I drape them over the counter. The collection of cookie cutters there reminds me of our forgotten plans. "Do you want to make cookies, or was that dumb?"

"Oh, I forgot!"

Talien almost spills the wine as he stops pouring, clangs the bottle down on the counter, and spins on a toe. He's at the freezer in a couple long strides and returns with the bundle of frosty-looking dough.

"It's ready," he announces, prodding it.

"We don't have to if you're enjoying just sitting," I say, but I can't help the smile that creeps over my expression at the sight of Talien moving through the kitchen to pull a spotless apron over his head.

I'd only ruined his spare, thank goodness.

"Don't be a tease," he scolds over his shoulder, tying it neatly around his waist before setting the oven to preheat. "You tempted me with cookies. We're making cookies."

"Okay," I say with a lengthened breath as I pull myself from the couch.

A flutter of nerves pierces my wine-spun haze as I remember why I set up this whole evening. The cookie-making was meant to be an easy way to break the ice of tension lingering over the conversation we need to have.

And now, high on the bliss of spending too long in his orbit, I *really* don't want to have that conversation. It will ruin this heady feeling I am enjoying far too much.

I help Tal set up the cookie cutters along with the rest of the tools we are going to need. He turns on a holiday music playlist before he tops off both of our glasses. I put the flour-covered apron back over my head, and he moves to stand at the counter next to me, just around the corner, so we can still see each other while we work with our own balls of dough.

I take my time rolling mine flat and offer a raised wiggle of a brow as I gesture to my work with a look of pride.

"Oh, very impressive, Varner," Tal chuckles, sprinkling more flour over his rolling pin and rubbing it down with one hand. "And you did it half-drunk."

"Blind confidence, I think," I say. "How well do you remember the last time we did this?"

A soft warmth moves over Talien's cheeks. I would convince myself it's from the wine, but the shade deepens almost instantly. His eyes drop to the neat circle of dough in front of him, but not before they catch on my lips.

"Every detail," he confirms, giving his station one final pass with the pin before setting it aside to select a cookie cutter.

The already unsteady thrum of my heart stumbles as his words land. I stop breathing, and I barely manage to catch the stutter of my hands.

What am I supposed to say now? Better figure it out quick.

"Your cookies were so much prettier than mine." My voice floats out, coated in the ghost of the distant memory. It doesn't sound at all as light and carefree as I hoped it would.

In return, Talien offers a soft, throaty sound of agreement, focusing entirely too much attention on the perfect placement of each of his cookies in the dough. That warmth in my chest inflates as I chance a look at his expression. My eyes snag on the curve of his bottom lip as he bites down in apparent concentration. His hands work the dough with a steady rhythm, his tattooed fore-arms flexing with every turn of his wrist.

A heat flushes my cheeks as he meets my eye; those emerald irises glint with a flicker of mischief as my gaze falters for a moment.

"I am looking forward to kicking your ass this time, though," I say with a quirk of a smile. "I've practiced my icing skills."

"Oh?"

The curl of challenge in his tone slides over me. One perfect brow arches as he eyes my cookies, a pattern of holiday-themed shapes already visible.

"Feeling competitive this evening, I see," he teases before

pushing his sleeves up over his elbows again and refocusing on his work.

The shift draws my eyes back to the lines of his tattoos, but a bright pop of color catches my eye. All of Talien's tattoos are black, except the delicate, perfectly sculpted dahlia draped over his forearm. I recognize those intricate crimson petals blooming over the inky swirls. It's mine. The one I drew for him in exchange for the phoenix now stretching over my shoulders. Curiosity tangles with my significant lack of inhibitions, and I cannot control a flow of excitement as it curls through my awareness.

"What is that?" I ask, nodding to his arm. My tone comes out sharper than I intended.

He glances at the tattoo, then at me, and a smile tugs at the corner of his lips. Crimson floods his cheeks.

"That? It's a tattoo," he says, refocusing on his cookies. "I have a bunch of them, actually. They're kind of subtle, though. I'm a stuffy professional, now, you know? I understand how you missed them."

I roll my eyes at the drip of sarcasm, and a belt of laughter cracks my chest as I wipe some loose hair off my forehead with the back of my flour-covered wrist.

"Yes, until now, I thought you were relatively clean-cut," I tease with pursed lips. "*That one* in particular, isn't like the others, though, is it?"

He stays stooped over his cookies, but those eyes dart to mine under his brow.

"No, it's not," he concedes.

I think he might say more, but he turns back to his cookies and straightens. With nimble fingers, he clears the dough from around the shapes and balls it in his palm.

"I couldn't help but notice that you have the matching piece," he says.

My heart skips a beat as the full force of the memory hits me. It's a vision of a much younger version of both of us sitting in study hall sketching out our fantasy first tattoos. We'd drawn them for each other. I chose a dahlia for him, and he'd spent months working on the phoenix I now have inked over my entire back. We exchanged the images with a promise to someday get them together.

That never happened, but I'd always loved the phoenix he'd worked so hard to bring to life. He has so many tattoos. He's covered in the free-flowing art. I never imagined he would get the little flower I sketched for him so long ago.

"I had it done when I got out to the city. I met a really talented artist at the studio who wanted to work on something for me. Her work was perfect for the phoenix." I try to keep my tone level as I explain, but the beating of my heart betrays my effort to appear unphased.

"She did a beautiful job," he says. A tenderness coats his voice. The loving timber pulls at my heart.

Without waiting for the tension to settle between us, Talien sets aside the ball of dough and moves to retrieve the cookie trays for us.

"I got mine about three years ago," he says as he moves. "Found that sketch when I was moving into this place and went the next day."

He tilts his arm to look at the inked flower before setting the tray on the bar top where we can both reach it.

Am I breathing? I can't tell. I genuinely do not know what to do with this information.

"Why?"

It takes him a moment to consider his words. He stares down at the slew of cookies and flour across the counter, takes a long drink from his glass, and sets it aside before finally meeting my gaze again.

"I missed you." His voice is sure but soft like he's afraid to admit it.

Something near my heart fissures, and I can't help the way my eyebrows pull together. I lose all ability to keep my thoughts trained on the task at hand.

He missed me.

A very significant part of me is happy to hear it. But the ravenous beast of heartbreak left behind after years of sewing my own wounds together keeps me from reaching out the way I want to.

Oh god, I want to. I want to reach across the counter and turn the corner of his mouth up with the pad of my thumb. I want to run my fingers through the thick tresses of his hair, trace the lines of his tattoos below the collar of his button-down.

I want him to know how much I have missed *him*. I want to show him.

God damned wine.

"You missed me?" I ask, my voice barely above a whisper as I abandon my dough and move around the counter to stand closer. My muscles move of their own accord. I have no control, and that terrifies me. But the gravitational pull that is Talien Vale has rendered my good sense useless.

Something that looks like an echo of pain flickers through his eyes.

"Every day," he answers, his voice matching mine. Hushed.

The oven beeps.

Talien breathes, the moment between us shattered by one little sound. He squares his shoulders, and it's like I'm watching him pull the wall between us back into place.

"The dough's going to get too warm to roll if we don't hurry up," he says. His words have their usual lilt to them, but his tone is still heavy as he moves his cookies to the tray.

A part of me is grateful that the tension has released, and I can focus on my own rational thought again, but I can't ignore the slight disappointment as it coats my resolve. Why is it like this with him? It feels like we get pulled together, like we might be on the same page, then something happens. The cord between us snaps. He shuts it down. I don't know why it's so difficult for me to keep my emotions in order with this man.

"Right," I say with a sharp intake of breath and turn back to my station.

Beside me, Talien is already rolling out a second sheet of dough.

I scan the mess of cookie cutters between us for a moment, searching for the one I want. Just as I spot it, Tal's hand shoots to claim it. I gasp and lunge to snatch the tree-shaped cutter, and my reach is a fraction of a second quicker. A triumphant smile stretches my lips as I pull my prize to my chest and meet his attention, where I find an expression of exaggerated shock and disbelief. The way he runs his tongue over his teeth in mock frustration curls a heat low in my core, but a charged laugh breaks my silence.

"Cheeky thing," Talien scolds, drumming his fingers in the flour on the counter, sending little plumes of white into the air. "You don't even have enough space for that one."

"What do you mean?" I ask, my tone lifted with a flirtatious kind of surprise, but I look to my dough to find that he is correct, I haven't left myself space for the tree. "Well, I'll start over."

Talien's eyes flare.

"Start over? What's wrong with all the cookies you've already cut?"

"Well, none of them are the tree!"

"Varner," he warns, a smile teasing the corner of his mouth.

My cheeks warm at the low intensity of his tone, and the heat in my core curls with the glimmer in his clover eyes.

"*Vale,*" I say in a mock impression of his scolding and scrunch my nose as I turn slightly, keeping the tree tucked close to my chest.

With a dramatic sigh, he glides around the edge of the counter.

"Is that how it's going to be, then?"

"I don't have any idea what you're talking about." My voice is thick with false innocence as I slide back, my hip pressed to the countertop to keep the small distance between us.

"Of course, you don't," he chides.

In a flash, his hand darts out and snatches my wrist, yanking me towards him. I gasp at the contact; my eyes stretch wide as a flare of energy radiates from his touch. I haven't been wearing my gloves. A familiar warmth, like the heat of too much cinnamon on your tongue, and a bright burst of something like sunlight welcome me with the contact of his skin.

He seems to realize his mistake almost immediately as he releases me with a regretful expression, but it's too late. I've lost my balance, and he has no choice but to stabilize my fall with a hooked arm around my waist.

I steady myself with a hand on his arm and the spike of wild energy only intensifies. It's a low heat I cannot temper before it has the chance to flood every vein. My own excitement is magnified by the spike of emotion I get from Tal. It overwhelms me, and the tingle of my crest lights my forehead before I have a chance to shut the surge of magic down as more washes into me through the connection.

A lurching feeling in my navel: desperation. A tightness like suffocation pulling my throat closed: longing. Another rush of the heated taste of cinnamon over my tongue: desire.

Beneath that, a raging inferno of lust rooted deep within my soul.

I am not sure if it's mine or his. I am not sure I care.

With our chests pressed together I have to tip my head back to catch his eye. His attention is trained on me with an expression I find difficult to place in the tidal wave of sensation clouding my already unstable ability to steady myself. His lips are parted, brow knitted over wide eyes and fixed on my crest as the light dances over his features.

"Talien," my voice is barely a breath on my lips.

His vibrant eyes flick to my mouth as though tracking every syllable as my voice curls around his name, and his chest expands against my own. Another pulse of desire bleeds from his skin to mine.

"You okay?" His voice is rough, breathless.

My voice has left me, and I can only nod. As if on its own accord, my hand slides from its place to curl over the firm muscles of his arm. My touch follows his carved lines until my fingers find the hair at the base of his neck. My magic spikes again.

There it is. That burning desire. It tugs at that spot beneath my breastbone. I can't breathe. Can't think.

My eyes only leave his long enough to mark the way his lips part as the light over my forehead shimmers through a ripple of iridescence.

"Cass," he whispers. It sounds like a warning. He tenses, but his head tilts back into my touch.

I watch as a shiver snakes his spine, across his shoulders, and then he's drawing a deep breath through his nose as he pulls away. The warm kitchen air feels cool in the space between us. Talien keeps his hands on me as he steadies me against the counter. I don't want him to pull away, but my fingers fall from his hair as he places a distance between us. Something else swirls through the warmth of longing and desire still radiating from him, something dark and cutting.

It pricks at the edge of my awareness. The sensation is sharp. Fear?

"Think you can stand?" he asks, flashing a crooked smile.

"What are you so afraid of?" The question is bold, but it is matched by the vivid sting of disappointment already gnawing at me, threatening to ruin the glowing space carved out between us.

I don't want that to go away again. I want him to stop pulling away.

He withdraws his hands from me.

"You almost cracked your head against my counter," he says, turning back to the scattered cookie cutters and selecting a snowflake. "I'd hate to ruin such a lovely night with a trip to the emergency room."

A heated frustration flares in my chest. It's too late. He's already distanced himself. I am not sure how I keep getting myself tangled up in this exact moment over and over again. It's part of the reason I set up this entire evening in the first place, isn't it? To talk about this.

No. It was to talk about what he's keeping secret. But now it feels like it's about this. About why he gets close enough to trap me in his gravity and then immediately places that wall between us. Why he is on the list of people who have abandoned me.

God, I don't want that to be the case, but it is. It is, and admitting that hurts far more than I will ever allow myself to show.

I am almost able to chalk it up to another misunderstanding, another set of misread signals. I would be able accept that I have overinflated feelings for someone who has only ever seen me as a friend.

If it had not been for that undeniable desire at the flare of my magic. He feels more. I can still taste it. The coursing energy is disorienting. The glow of his lingering emotion is warm. It leaves a brightness behind that most certainly does not belong to me.

My head spins. I will not let him do this again. He will either face me now or...

I'm not sure what lies on the other side of that '*or*,' but my blind confidence is doing a good job of making it so that I don't have much space to worry about that.

"Talien, look at me." My tone is more firm than I expect it to be; a hint of demand lifts my words as I shift closer, closing the distance he's placed between us.

His shoulders stiffen, but when he turns to face me, his expression holds that same searing heat from moments ago. Beneath the fire, there's a softness around his eyes, in the tilt of his brow. I saw it on the balcony the other night when I used those same words to command his attention.

He's in there. Trapped somewhere behind that barrier. I am going to tear it down with my bare hands. That glimmer in his eye begs me to try.

"Cass..." This time, my name sounds like a plea on his lips.

I am done. The wobbling timbre of his voice breaks the last of my resolve. I need answers. I need him to be honest with me. God damn it, I need *anything* from him to make the bleeding of these old wounds staunch.

"Do you want me?"

The words, as they fall, are not delicate or gentile. But there is nothing delicate about the way that I feel. I need him to meet me where I stand or not at all.

There is no air left in the room. I watch for the rise and fall of Talien's chest, but he doesn't appear to be breathing. He just looks at me. His eyes wander across my face, down the length of my neck, over the curves of my chest and hips, and back up. They linger on my lips. The air continues to hang thick and stiff between us.

And then he takes a breath. It's a sharp, almost agonized, exhale as he sets both hands on the counter and drops his head.

"Fucking hell, Varner," he groans, almost doubled over. I can't breathe. My heart is seizing in my chest.

"God damn it, Talien. Either you do or you don't. Which is it?"

I am frustrated. It wasn't the right question to ask, but I am having difficulty hanging on to my very thin resolve. It's the best I can do.

I'm not sure if it's embarrassment, disappointment, or the flare of frustration that is more prominent as he remains silent, but none of the emotions do much to temper the fire urging me on. If having to answer that question causes him this much stress, I should not have asked. That should be enough of the answer I am looking for.

But I can't disengage. Not this time. As much as it feels like my nerves are on fire—like my chest might cave on itself—I hold firm.

I know what I felt from him. I need him to answer me. Just this once.

I move closer with my eyes trained on the line of his jaw, and my fingers flutter over the intricate pattern of the dahlia, just barely hovering over his skin. I watch his reaction, wait for him to stop me, but he doesn't. The magic in my core jumps to life at even the promise of use, and my crest tingles.

I don't touch him, though. I won't take what is not freely given.

"I can feel it if you'd prefer."

A longing deep within the pits of my soul screams for the possibility of breaking this dam between us.

"I don't want—" My heart freezes as he groans again and pushes off the counter to thrust his hands into his hair. "Cass..."

He busies himself with unproductive tidying while his jaw ticks.

"Okay." I release a frustrated, shaking breath. "I'm not sure why I asked. Your clear torment over even the idea is enough."

My cheeks are hot, and I start to untie my apron, urging my fingers to move quickly, begging my feet to carry me away from the pain I know is about to cleave my chest in two.

Before I make it a single step, his hand catches my elbow, only making contact with my sweater, and he spins me back into him. I gasp as my balance is tilted, and my eyes flare as I find our chests close again.

The very hands of the clock seem to stop ticking as he peers down his nose at me, an intensity in his eyes I could not have prepared for.

"Stop," he says, exasperated, a tortured rumble pulling at the edges of his low tone. "Damn it, Cass. I want you. God knows I shouldn't, but I do. More than anything."

God.

Talien chews his cheek, and a storm brews behind his eyes. They flit as though searching for something in mine. My lungs are starved for air. The space between us is stiff, thickened with years' worth of unanswered questions, unrequited feelings.

My heart hammers so viciously against my ribs I am sure he can hear it. There is not a single word that feels good enough in the wake of his confession. My heart is going to bleed out. If he takes a moment longer to decide what he is going to do, I'll die right here in the aftermath of our ruined evening.

"So, take me," I say on a ghost of a heated breath.

Some of the tension in his brow dissolves as my demand lands.

"God damn it, Firefly, when did you get so fucking bossy?" he growls.

Before I have the chance to take a breath, his hands snake into my hair, and his lips crash into mine. I don't have time to prepare myself for the onslaught of emotion as it breaks the seal of my resolve. It's a searing heat, so intense I am not sure where my hunger ends and his begins. Every inch of my body is set aflame as I relax my frame into his, tilting my chin to keep up with the greedy parting of his lips.

I tense and suck in a breath as the curve of his mouth melts against my need, and my crest burns with the overwhelming sensation of his desire tangling with mine.

CHAPTER 21
Talien

I don't know who I thought I was kidding when I let Cassiopeia stay here. We've teetered on the edge of this precipice for so long I've forgotten what it feels like to fall. I don't think I'll be able to recover from it this time. Somehow, that doesn't matter.

The only thing that matters is the feel of her hands twisted in my hair and the hunger of her lips against mine. She moves against my mouth with a fire that lights every vein. I had no idea it was possible to burn for someone the way I do for this woman in my arms.

I meet her hunger with my own, letting my hips drive hers back against the counter. I need to be closer to her. I need to feel her consume me, to feel those hands on me. Claiming me.

As my tongue begs for entrance at her lips, I allow my hands to trace the lines of her waist, finding the brush of her soft skin under the hem of her sweater. Her curves nearly undo me, and I groan against her lips. She sucks in a breath and tangles her fingers in my hair as she arches against me, as though even the mere brush of my fingers against her flesh sends her reeling.

"Talien," she murmurs. Her voice is low in her throat and

strained with an all-consuming need. Her vibrant crest washes an iridescent glow over the space between us.

"Oh god, Cass," I moan, echoing her desire with my own. "Say my name like that, and I'll do whatever you want."

My hands find her waist and hoist her onto the counter. I slide my hips between her knees as visions of that dream flicker through my mind. Flour billows around her thighs, and I capture her mouth again, driving my tongue against hers, swallowing the gasps of delight as they spill from her throat. A heat coils deep within my core at the thought of pulling more of those sounds from her, watching her come undone for me.

Desperate to feel her close, to meld into her, I hook my hands under the backs of her knees and drag her to the edge of the counter to meet my hips. Her heat against the hard ridge of my cock pulls a deep growl from my throat.

This woman will be my undoing.

Even through our clothes, I can feel her pulsing with need as she locks her legs around my waist to roll her hips against mine. It's my turn to gasp at the sensation.

Never have I felt this way. In all my life, nothing has come close to the bliss of kissing her, feeling her desperate for me, even allowing myself to enjoy the sensation of her skin against mine. I can't quite allow myself to believe it's true, that it's not just another dream built from the shattered remains of my broken heart. I've wanted this for so long. Wanted to be hers for *so long*. There are so many reasons we've missed each other, most of them my own stupidity and fear. But now, I don't want to let this moment slip through my fingers. I won't.

Cass's lips part for me, and I am lost in the dance of our tongues. Her grip on my hair is dizzying. I am a slave to her will. Helpless against her commands.

No one has ever taken control of me. I never allowed anyone that privilege, but I want her to. I want to serve her, worship her, to make up for all the time I've wasted wishing I'd done things differently.

My kisses stray from her lips, curling up the line of her jaw to the curve of her ear. She hisses with pleasure as my tongue dances over the sensitive flesh.

"Have you imagined this as much as I have, Firefly?" I ask against the shell of her ear before nipping at its crest.

Cass shudders, and her chest rolls into me as she arches her spine. She releases a mangled sound of desperation and turns her face to catch the soft skin of my earlobe between her teeth. Her lips close around the flesh, and she moves her fervent kisses to the crook of my neck.

"God, yes," she breathes. "Every day."

My nerve lights as her lips trail my skin. I drop my head back on my shoulders to give her access, digging my fingers into the curve of her hips. Her feverish kisses along my neck are maddening. She rolls against me again, and I can't help the mangled sound of frenzied desire as it peels from me.

"Tell me what you want," I groan.

The words sound desperate. Every day I've spent aching for things to be different between us, for her to kiss me like this, touch me like this, every hour I've spent trying to drown out my need to be near her, to be everything to her, is weighted behind those words.

Her fingers flutter to the ties on my apron, and she claims my mouth again.

"I want this off. All of it." The demand in her voice coils that winding need tighter.

"God, impatient, aren't you?" I chuckle against her lips as I move to obey.

Her fingers make quick work of the apron. She releases my lips long enough to get it off my neck and toss it aside. I start on the buckles of the harness around my chest as we meet again. With nimble fingers, she brushes mine aside to take over ridding me of the leather accessory. It's only a few quick moments and a stretch of heated, tangled kisses before she is working to unbutton the length of my shirt as well.

My mind is a blur. I tangle my hands in her curls instead, giving myself over to her, letting this go at her pace—which is furious and frantic.

Thank god.

Cass's touch, the desperation fueling her fingers as she tugs the shirt from my waistband, is enough to leave me breathless, and then her hands are on my chest. She groans, and she slides the fabric from my shoulders.

"God, you're incredible," she breathes.

Her hands move to my belt, and she hooks a finger behind the leather to give a gentle tug as she pulls my bottom lip between her teeth.

"Fuck," I manage over a strangled groan.

I want to feel her skin. I want to strip her bare, but I force myself to focus my attention on her lips, on the feel of her fingers working my belt open and fumbling with the button of my pants. My cock is throbbing, straining to get to her touch.

"Cass," I hiss against her lips as my fingers tighten in her hair.

I know if she touches me, I'll be lost completely. I want to feel her hand around me. I want to drown in the sensation of her touch. But more than that, I want to learn every detail of the fantasies that have played out in her mind. How many were the same as my own? How often have we laid awake at night, miles apart, imagining each other in the same way?

She teases with a feather-light dip of her fingers beneath the line of my boxers; my head spins as her manicured nails trace the line of the V pointing to my hips.

Cass leans back only enough to move her hands to the hem of her shirt. Within a heartbeat, it's over her head and on the ground, exposing a lace bra. The color is a deep burgundy, complimenting the lovely blush over her chest.

"You're gorgeous," I breathe, drinking in her curves.

Her glowing crest snags my attention. My hands ghost over her full thighs, along the dip in her hips, over the curve of her waist. I allow my fingers to brush her skin, but only barely. When I reach the soft lace, I peel my eyes away from her striking amber skin and the beautiful florals scattered across her flesh.

I know Cass can sense emotions, can feel them roiling inside me somehow. The thought thrills me.

"What do you feel?" I ask, watching her honey-gold eyes as they flare.

She huffs a breath of a chuckle. The corner of her full mouth twitches. I can almost see the thoughts turn over behind those molten irises.

"Everything," she breathes but shakes her head slightly as though she wishes to try again. Her fingers move to my hair, and she curls them, playing with the locks at the base of my neck as she contemplates.

"A light. In my chest, it's bright. And warm. I feel a heat. Desire. But it's more than just that; it's rooted deep. I don't know, it's very difficult to explain, especially when everything is so..."

She sucks in a breath, and her eyes flare as I drag my knuckle along the length of her spine. Her eyelids flutter closed, and her head hangs back as she stabilizes herself with her grip on my hair. It sends another rush of need through me.

"Intense?" I ask softly, admiring how her lips part at the sensation of my touch.

"Yes," she breathes. "I can't begin to describe to you what even that does to me."

God, if this simple touch does so much, what will she feel at the mercy of my fingers? My tongue?

My cock throbs with a fresh rush of heat at the thought.

I tease with a fluttering touch over the strap of her bra, slipping my fingers under it and admiring the swell of her chest as her breathing hitches.

"Do you want to slow down?" I ask, watching her face.

"No," her answer is quick, her tone sure.

I trace lower, sliding the strap off, letting my touch dance over the angle of her shoulder, along her collarbone, and down. I hesitate over the swell of her breast, holding her gaze.

"Use your words, Firefly," I purr, letting demand curl over my tongue. I stoop to nip at her ear lobe again, gripping her hips to tip her closer. "Tell me what you've imagined most."

The corners of those maddening lips twitch, and she tilts her head to lock her eyes with mine again. She trails her hands over my chest, along the planes of my abdomen, and leans in to brush her nose to mine. Her sweet breath washes over me, and my head swims as she tugs on my belt, holding me to her.

"I've imagined you on your knees for me most, I'd say," her voice rolls before biting down on her bottom lip.

I groan, unable to contain the flush of lust that roars through me as I roll my hips against hers. The light on her forehead surges, and her eyes flare.

"You think you can handle my tongue, Varner?" I tease, tracing the waistband of her leggings.

"There's only one way to find out, Vale." Her tone holds a hint of a tease, but she is breathless; the words come out on something like hushed disbelief. I feel it echo in my chest.

How did we get here? Does it matter? I can't let this moment slip away. I lean into the spark of mischief I feel every time she gives me an order or looks at me with such...authority.

I want her to take control from me. I've been drowning in it for as long as I can remember. I don't want it anymore; I want to give in to her, to her every desire. I want to watch the spark in her eyes when I make her *work* for that control.

Tipping my chin at her, I allow my fingers to tease lower.

"I want to hear you say it," I tell her over a mischievous grin.

Her mouth quirks a smile and her eyes light as she reaches up to grip my hair again. She gives it a gentle tug to tip my chin and presses a kiss to the corner of my jaw before she moves her lips to my ear.

"I want you on your knees before me, Talien. I want to come undone for you."

I can't breathe. I can't think.

The feel of her hands, the command in her voice, it consumes me. Without waiting for my mind to have a chance to catch up to this moment and fuck everything to shit with worry, as it has every other time Cass and I have come close to breaking down these walls, I move.

My hands slide beneath her leggings, savoring the fullness of her ass and the soft brush of her skin as I peel them off. She lifts her hips to let them slide away, watching me with a heat in her eyes I know I'll never recover from.

I'm not sure I'm breathing as I lower myself to my knees, marveling at how magnificent she looks. Regal, even surrounded by a mess of flour and forgotten cookie dough. The burgundy lace of her bra and panties makes the dark lines of her tattoos stand out against her skin.

Kisses follow my fingers down the length of her leg as I slip her knee over my shoulder. As my fingers reach her hips, I pull her closer to the edge of the counter.

She adjusts herself as I continue to place kisses higher and higher, savoring the little gasps of pleasure my lips pull from hers. Tenderly, I trace down the lace pattern of her panties, teasing closer and closer to her sweet center as my lips focus on a sensitive spot over her thigh.

Her lips part, and her chest hitches as her eyes fill with molten desire.

Watching her face, I draw my finger down the center of her, watching those eyes widen and her skin flush with pleasure. I can't keep my own groan quiet as the evidence of her need meets my fingers.

Slowly, I circle the spot again, moving my mouth up her leg. Cass's hand finds my hair again, gripping it like it's a lifeline.

Her hips rock toward me, begging for my touch. A smile breaks across my lips as I drift closer, teasing her lightly over the lace with gentle circles.

Her sweet scent fills my nose, and my cock floods with pressure again.

God, it takes everything in me to hold back and savor this. I want her to remember every second.

"Use that beautiful voice of yours, Firefly," I say, and close my mouth over her.

The taste of her, even through the barrier of the lace, sends me reeling. I'm ravenous for her. For more. My tongue thrums against the swell of her clit, traces down the center of her, teases at the edges of her panties.

"*Talien*," my name is a strangled breath on her lips as she curls her hips, her body's silent plea for more.

And I give it. I peel aside the panties with one hand, as the other hooks around her thigh, and savor the sight of her. The neatly trimmed curls of dark hair frame her beautifully slick cunt.

I place a kiss to her inner thigh and chuckle at the moan of disapproval from her as Cass rolls her hips toward my mouth again. Her fingers tug at my hair, begging.

"You're beautiful," I whisper against her skin, swiping a finger over her swollen clit.

"Oh god, *please*, Tal."

I want to commit the way her voice sounds to memory. How it strains with desperation, the delicate timber of her tone trembling around my name, but my control is wearing thin.

"Please, what?" I ask, raising a brow as I flick my tongue over her. Teasing.

I wonder if she can sense how close to losing control I am.

"You're such a *tease*," she seethes through clenched teeth, a groan straining her voice, "Please, Talien. Let me have that sweet tongue of yours."

I am undone.

My mouth finds her. Hot, musky, and absolutely intoxicating. Her sweet arousal seeps over my lips, across my tongue, and I let it dance along her, hungry for more.

I drag my tongue over her clit, slowly, savoring every drop of her. She gasps as I reach the peak of her and flick the tip of it until she's breathless.

Once her grip in my hair is vicious, I deny her more, letting her come down from the precipice as my lips work against her. I lose myself, savoring every sensation of her, exploring the pulse of her against me, the grind of her hips as she tries to steal more and more.

I chuckle at her obvious frustration before dipping lower. I watch the heated look on her face, past the swell of her breasts and the slope of her soft, perfect belly, as I drag my tongue through her center. The evidence of her own molten desire drives me wild.

I need more.

My hands lash around her thighs, pulling her closer as I drive deeper. She cries out and bucks against me as her head hangs between her shoulders. Flour stains her skin where my hands have tracked, and that gentle blush over her chest has bloomed a bright, vibrant red.

"That's it, Firefly," I say between flicks of my tongue over her beautiful petals. "You taste amazing."

She lets out another mangled sound as I kiss along her lips, sucking one into my mouth and then the other. Teasing her like this spins my awareness; like the sweet heat between her legs has the ability to instill its own vivid kind of high.

Again, I stoop low, exploring her with long strokes, feeling her grow more and more breathless. My tongue circles lower and lower, following the way her hips buck and roll for me. Letting her lead me.

I have lost control. My thoughts aren't my own anymore. The only thing that exists is Cass—worshipping her like this, pulling those precious sounds from her. My body is nothing but a tool for her pleasure.

"I want you to ride my tongue," I groan. The words are thick and heavy. "Use my mouth. Take what you need."

Without a second to waste, she does as I've asked. She tips her chin to look down at me, and her expression twists with desire.

She strengthens her grip in my hair and curls her hips, rocking against me to get my tongue where she needs it. My name falls from her lips over and over, like a blissful plea; like speaking it will bring her the ecstasy she craves.

My mind is blurred with the bliss of submitting to her, letting her use me. I could stay here for hours, drinking in everything she has to give me. Her hips drive against me as her cries grow more and more frantic. Her heels dig into my back, pinning me against her.

I get a moment to catch my breath between her desperate grindings as she adjusts her legs to give me a different angle, dropping one delicate foot to the tiles beside me while the other stays rested over my shoulder. The rush of air in my lungs is thrilling as she twists her hand in my hair and grinds my mouth against her again.

Her scent is all-encompassing, and I am as desperate to please her as she is to take my admiration. She tips her hips, driving my tongue deep into her core, and I moan against her as the taste of her soaks my palate. My face is slick with her arousal, and I have never been so overcome with bliss.

"Oh, my god, Talien, please," she whines, her tone strangled with need.

I release another moan of approval against her as she tips her chin down to look at me. Fire lights through every vein at the sight of her crest bright and glowing across her forehead.

For me. She's glowing for *me*.

Keeping my eyes trained on her beautiful face, I redouble my efforts, pushing her closer and closer to that edge until I can feel her spilling over it. Her legs tremble and clench, pinning me to her as the waves of pleasure pulse through her. She sags against the counter, shaking as I slowly work my mouth around her. Gentle, caressing, savoring every flicker of pleasure I can still pull from her.

Her chest is heaving, her breaths coming in labored waves as her body trembles through her release. I move my lips to place a tender kiss on her inner thigh and take my time memorizing the lines of her. She adjusts her seat on the counter and leans back on one elbow, her chin tipped to the ceiling as she tries to catch her breath. Her skin glistens with the sheen of ecstasy.

Cass tips her head down at the loss of my mouth. She moves her legs and beckons me to stand with a gentle tug on my hair. I do so without a thought, and she claims me again. Her arms drape over my shoulders, and she arches her body into me, her slick heat grinding against my length.

"I need you," she says between desperate kisses.

"God, yes," I growl against her lips.

My fingers hesitate at her hips, gripping the lace panties still draped over her incredible curves.

"You were pretty adamant earlier," I say, stealing her lips again. "I wasn't under the impression I'm allowed to undress myself."

Her eyes flare, and she reaches between us to make work of unfastening my pants.

"You were *so* good for me," she croons, her voice dripping with the exact timbre of dominance that sends my thoughts reeling through a clouded haze of desire. "Get these off and fuck me, Talien. However, you want me. I can't wait any longer."

"Fucking god, I love how demanding you've gotten," I growl, stripping off my pants and boxers before sliding her panties over her thighs and tossing them away.

I catch her mouth with mine again as my hand slides around to undo the clasp of her bra. As it falls to the floor, I take another moment to drink in how gorgeous the woman before me is. Every inch of her is perfect, from her powerful thighs and full hips to the softness of her stomach and her flawless breasts.

I am stunned. She's a goddess. And I am clearly taking far too long to fulfill her very direct orders.

"Tal," she says turning my gaze back to hers with a gentle tilt of her finger under my chin.

She opens her mouth to speak, but her words get caught. Her

luminous eyes search mine, a torrent of emotion swirling within their depths.

"Sorry," I say, cupping her face in my hands and kissing her tenderly. "I just needed a moment to appreciate how fucking gorgeous you are."

Her lips curl in a smile as she hums with approval.

"So are you," she murmurs.

I chuckle, feeling heat flood my cheeks in a rare moment of embarrassment. I work hard on my appearance, it's true, but hearing it from Cass's lips does something to me. The sensation doubles when I realize she can probably feel the rush of embarrassment through my skin.

My eyes flit to her crest before dropping to her attention again.

"Thank you," I say, kissing the tip of her nose. "I don't know how overwhelming your magic can be like this. Is there anything I need to avoid? Or anything you don't like?"

She takes my hand and moves it to her breastbone, flattening my palm so my fingers spread out over her collarbones. A sharp breath lifts her chest, and her crest flares a vibrant white before it turns back to the iridescent shimmers.

Cass shakes her head, her eyes brimming with emotion. She places her palm over my breastbone, mirroring my contact. It is only a heartbeat or two before a tingling sensation bleeds from her palm. A warmth washes over my chest. Confusion grips me for a moment, but it is quickly replaced with what can only be described as a radiating light. It beams through my heart, lifts any fraction of worry or doubt that might have still clung to my shoulders. It feels like home. Like my soul has been wandering for as long as I can remember, and I've never known how weary I'd become in the journey until now—now that my heart and hers are finally whole.

My veins flood with a vibrant buzzing of electricity, and my heart thunders against the walls of my chest.

"Can you feel that?" she asks. It's all I can do to nod. "It feels like this. Overwhelming, but...oh god, exhilarating. And even the fact that you stopped to ask...just... I trust you, Tal. However, you want me. I mean it." She finishes on a near whisper, her voice is thick with the threat of tears.

I open my mouth to reply, but the words get caught behind my own welling emotion. I am stunned, overwhelmed with the sensation barreling from her touch to the tunnel around my heart.

Another wave of warmth seeps through Cass's hand, followed by a rush of something else, something sweet and fiery. Lust. My own desire sparks to life in answer. Cass flashes me a mischievous look from under her lashes and bites her bottom lip.

This woman...

Another pulse of need sparks through my chest as I trace her collarbone to the hair at the base of her neck. Tangling my fingers in the curls there, I tug her head back and pull her against my chest.

"Now, I believe you had a request. What was it again?"

She smiles, her lips curling in a coy tease as she turns her eyes to the ceiling, feigning thought.

"I believe I asked you to fuck me. I'm yours."

A low growl simmers in my chest as I trace my hand down her cheek, the line of her jaw. The iridescent glow over her crest shimmers in waves.

I claim her mouth with my own again, driving my tongue past her lips. Stooping down, I hook my hands under her ass and lift her. Cass lets out a squeal of delight as she drapes her arms over my shoulders and hooks her ankles behind my back.

My goal is the bed, but with Cass kissing me like I'm the air she needs to breathe while grinding her bare, molten core against my abdomen, I only make it a few feet. Cass's back hits the wall as my mouth breaks from hers to trail kisses over her neck and jawline.

"*So* fucking needy," I growl against her ear. "Was my tongue not good enough for you?"

She groans and tilts her hips against me. "Your tongue was *divine*. But I need to know what you can do with your cock."

"Oh, fuck me," I hiss, adjusting my hold on her to get a hand free. We may not have made it to the bed, but we're close enough I can reach one of the drawers on the nightstand. "I had no idea you had such a dirty mouth, Firefly."

"Do you like it?" she croons, a smile under her tone.

"God, yes. I want to hear every filthy thing you think while I'm fucking you."

Cass grins with approval. I ease her down just long enough to get the thing on before I've hoisted her up again and pinned her to the wall.

I position myself at her entrance. The heat of her against the head of my cock nearly pulls me apart at the seams, but I steel myself and find her gaze.

She's so wet she's dripping, and the sensation almost sends a shock through my cock. I press into her, savoring the way her eyes roll back at the sensation. I want to hear her beg for more. I want to light the same fire I saw in her when I teased up her legs with my mouth, but my resolve is gone.

I press in a little further and swear as her heat envelops me.

"Fuck, Tal," she exclaims on an intake of air. Her nails dig into the flesh at my shoulders.

"That's right. Keep making those sounds," I say, nipping at her neck. "You're being so good, taking me *so* well."

I pulse at her entrance, watching the beautiful flare of her crest as I sink further and the little huffs of disappointment as I retreat. When I press in again, Cass clenches around me. I hiss and drop my forehead to the crook of her neck.

Her fingers tug at the back of my hair, yanking me up to meet her fiery gaze again.

"God, you're such a *tease*," she groans before claiming my mouth with hers.

She nips at my lips, sweeps her tongue through my mouth, all while she tightens her thighs around my waist to tip her hips into me. I meet her need, and she takes the length of me while we do our best to devour one another.

"Yes, Tal," she breathes between kisses. "God, fucking incredible."

"Oh my god, so are you," I breathe out.

Feeling her all around me makes what's left of my crumbling dam break loose. I lock my arms under her knees, tilting her back against the wall as her hips sink lower, opening her for me. Cass moans in approval, and I unleash myself on her. Letting all the pent-up nights I've spent dreaming of her, of this moment, and wishing I could go back in time to fix things between us flow out in a fury where our bodies collide.

I drive into her over and over, loosing myself in her slick heat, the desperate sounds, and the lust-fueled, filthy words that drip from her lips as she encourages me deeper and harder and faster. She is everything. She is the only thing left in the world. Her voice is my only guide, and the pulse of her cunt around my cock lights my soul on fire.

All traces of time are lost to me. All I know is I can feel her nearing that peak again. Her walls close in around me, growing tighter and tighter with each thrust as my cock throbs.

Cass spills over the edge again, dropping her head back against the wall as her body convulses around me, taking me over with her. That radiant light flashes through my chest again, just as it had when Cass's hand was pressed there, and I can feel her. All of her. Her bliss, the shadow of lust fading beneath that ecstasy, the relief. And then I'm falling. Falling through what feels like endless lifetimes, memories of dreams and fantasies, and things that feel more real than those. This moment, held so close to her, wrapped in the aftermath of our passion, over and over again for lifetimes.

My head is on her shoulder, and she releases a heady laugh, her entire body melts against mine.

"God," she says, her chest rising and falling with unsteady breaths. "Are you alright?"

She runs a hand through my hair, and I lift my head to meet

her eye. Her palm finds my cheek and I turn into the touch to press a kiss to the heel of her hand.

"Incredible," is all I can manage through the gasps for air.

I've never felt anything like this. In this moment, I am whole. I am complete. Cass is my home, and my soul is finally finished wandering.

CHAPTER 22

Cassiopeia

Never in my life have I felt anything like this. Tal is beside me, lying on his side with his head propped on the heel of his hand while his other traces circles over my bare back. His comforter is draped over my hips. After everything, Tal helped me clean up, made sure I had enough water and a snack, and fixed the bed with enough pillows to keep me comfortable in any position.

I've never had anyone treat me with such kindness. I am not sure if I am capable of categorizing any of the countless whirring emotions I have after the tidal wave that has been this evening.

I'm afraid to break it, like if I say the wrong thing or move too quickly this dream will shatter. We still have so much to talk about, but I can't start that now. Tomorrow, maybe, after the drunk-spun ecstasy wears off slightly.

For now, I hold onto that feeling with every fiber of my being.

He's watching me. Waiting for me to be comfortable enough to rest. Sleep is close to taking me. My eyelids are heavy, and it's all I can do to keep them open.

But I want to stay awake. I never want to stop looking at him. He's so God damned beautiful. I never want this moment to end.

This blissful, pristine evening has been carved out of a lifetime's worth of heartbreak. It's perfect. Talien is perfect.

187

I want to stay awake.

But the sensation of his touch is so soothing. I know I don't have long.

"You have work tomorrow," I mutter. My voice is heavy with impending sleep and is weighed down with the disappointment of knowing I likely won't wake next to him.

"Unfortunately," he confirms. Exhaustion is heavy in his voice.

"Will I see you at the festival?" My words are a murmur suffocated by slumber as my eyelids flutter closed.

"Absolutely," he replies, leaning down to kiss my forehead.

Talien yawns, then shifts beside me, scooping an arm under me and pulling me against his chest. His legs tangle with mine as he settles his chin in my hair and sighs with contentment.

"You are incredible," he whispers.

I hum with approval as I settle myself into his embrace. With his arms around me, I am fading quickly.

"*You* are," I manage to say as the blissful warmth of his skin against mine coaxes me further away from consciousness.

It is only another few moments before his breathing slows and sleep wraps itself around my mind.

<h1 style="text-align:center">CHAPTER 23</h1>

<h2 style="text-align:center">Talien</h2>

By the third time Niles has to call my attention back to them since getting back to the office, they're onto me. They've been unusually quiet today, lost in their own thoughts as they watched me pick through the interviews they've gathered protesting the new hotel. It wasn't until about an hour ago that they checked their phone and finally brightened again, likely due to the promise of the winter festival tonight.

Niles was nothing if not a sucker for festivities.

Those beady little eyes narrow, and they tip their hawk-like nose to glare at me over the hook of it.

"What happened?" they ask.

"Nothing."

I try to cover the smile tugging at my lips by taking a drink of my coffee, but Niles almost bats the mug out of my hand pointing out the traitorous expression.

"Liar! You fucking liar! What happened?"

Niles nearly topples off the corner of my desk but regains themselves and folds their arms. Over the past hour, they'd been recounting to me the highlights of what they think we could use from the interviews we'd been collecting all day with the tenants of the buildings in the proposed demolition site. I'd paid attention for a while.

But it hadn't taken much to set my mind wandering. Just a lull in the reciting of notes, and I was back in my apartment, thinking of the way the moonlight spilled in through the window, draping her perfect amber skin in a soft glow.

Cass was incredible.

I barely slept after she finally drifted off. Instead, I marveled at the patterns of the phoenix twisting over her curves as the snow drifted down outside my window. I didn't want to fall asleep. I didn't want to wake up and find this was all just another fantasy.

I wasn't sure I would survive that.

I've wasted so much time. I understand that now. I've spent so long letting the past control me. I thought it was what was best for Cass, for my family. I thought I had to let her go. But after last night, after seeing the way she looked at me. Hearing the sounds she made under my touch. After I'd watched her throw herself into this wild thing between us with the same passion I felt burning under my ribs, I knew I'd been a fool.

Everything has changed.

I don't know what that means for us. Cass has to go back to the city in a few weeks, and I'm—well, five years ago, I was supposed to go with her. Start a new life. As friends, then—or that's what we said. We both knew there was something there; we'd been dancing around it for years. The "plan" was to run away "as friends." Get her away from this picture-perfect life her father was carving out for her in vivid detail.

When she asked me to meet her, I knew what was left unsaid. Cass and I could never be "just friends." It was never supposed to be that.

Five years wasted because I was too hot-headed to just fucking run. I saw the bruise, the mark Bryson left her with, I saw her tears, and I let all the hatred that had built in me for so long boil to the surface. I knew it was stupid to go after him. I knew there would be consequences. I *didn't* know how close Westfield was to Lionel Varner, then. I thought he was just a potential son-in-law. I didn't know going after him would lead to the tidal wave that almost wiped my family from Brunswick.

I didn't go with her. I didn't start over somewhere new, and now my whole life was here. Wasn't it?

"Did you kiss her?" Niles hisses over a toothy grin.

Setting the coffee aside, I level an unamused look at them and blow a heavy breath through my nose, determined not to waste another moment of my time on thoughts of past mistakes.

"I think we're about done here," I say, starting to clear my notes from the desk.

Niles barks in protest as I *shoo* them off of one of the folders, and they flit after me, whipping out their phone.

"I'm telling Yvaine," they announce.

"Telling her what?" I ask, flipping through the interview with one of the families living at the shelter. "I didn't say anything."

"Your silence confirmed it."

"My silence didn't do shit."

Something about this interview pulls me back to that night so long ago—the same deep weight of dread tugs at my chest. I can't breathe.

You will not taint my daughter.

I shake off the memory, the chill in the air, the threat in his voice.

Niles is grinning smugly at me over their phone.

"What did she say?" I ask, raising a brow at them and tossing the file onto the desk.

"Nothing yet," Niles sighs, still seeming pleased as we gather our coats and make our way to the car, "but Yvaine is going to kick your ass if you did. I'm just looking forward to the show."

Yvaine is certainly going to have *something* to say when she finds out. But Cass and I have *somewhat* agreed to keep things quiet for a couple of days to let it settle in. Hopefully, we can all enjoy the festival as friends—without any ass-kicking—then Cass and I will be free to spend the rest of the weekend hidden away in my apartment, making up for lost time.

CHAPTER 24

Cassiopeia

"Are you going to seethe in silence all the way to the festival, or do you have something to say?" I ask Yvaine, who is gripping her steering wheel so tightly her knuckles are stretched pale. She flicks her eyes to the rearview mirror to get a look at me in her back seat.

"I am just trying to prepare myself for the inevitable shit show that is on the horizon. Now, let me breathe."

I roll my eyes. "Nothing is going to happen."

"It already has!" Her voice is a high squeal of panic that fades into a shame-weighted whisper as though she cannot fathom the words she is about to say. "You *fucked* him."

Seti snorts a laugh from the passenger seat. Tal and I agreed to let it settle for a few days, but I simply could not control myself. I had to talk about it. It was too big, too bright in my chest.

"Is it so unbelievable?" Seti's honey-toned words drip as she reaches over to give Yvaine's thigh a squeeze.

They're cute together. Seti is the perfect masc to Yvaine's femme, and her very even temper complements Yvaine's opinionated nature well.

"Yes, it is *'so unbelievable,'*" Yvaine hisses. "You went over there to figure out what Lionel did to them. Did you do that? No! Did

193

you talk to him about how horrifically he broke your heart? No! I swear to god, I am going to castrate that man."

"Talien or Lionel?" Seti asks playfully, wiggling her dark brow and turning back to wink at me. The streetlights overhead wash over her light brown complexion, bringing out the blush over her strong cheeks.

"Both," Yvaine seethes.

"I'd rather you left Talien's alone. It was quite nice," I teased.

Yvaine groans miserably with a strangled expression of disdain as she releases an exaggerated gagging sound. The display leaves me suppressing a bout of laughter. Seti's chortles echo mine.

"I want you both to stop speaking to me for the entire remainder of this drive," Yvaine demands.

Seti flashes a teasing look at me over her shoulder and I offer a sheepish smile as I focus my attention on the falling snow out the window.

CHAPTER 25

Talien

If there's one thing the people in this town do not take lightly, it's the holidays. The freshly fallen snow hangs heavy on the roofs and awnings of the buildings lining the main strip. Outside every door is a simple fir tree laced with twinkling white lights topped with a red velvet bow. Each and every window of the shops features a perfect display of holiday cheer.

Candles flicker in all of the second-floor windows of the historical buildings lining the cobbled streets in this part of town and the scent of pine, cinnamon, and hot cocoa drifts throughout the snow-spattered street.

The river rolls nearby. By late-winter it will have frozen to slush, but this afternoon it glitters clear and bright in the sun as barges and ferries travel across the waves.

A band is setting up on the stage adorned with red ribbons and wreaths in front of the old fountain at the center of the roundabout, while vendors selling all kinds of perfect gifts for loved ones put the finishing touches on their booths and chat with the first customers of the weekend.

I adjust the scarf that's crept out of the folds of my coat and try to focus on what Niles is saying instead of scanning the

195

growing crowd for the beautiful set of curls that have consumed my mind all day.

"Honestly, it's not like we have to go any time soon," they're saying, sprawled dramatically against the railing leading down to the walkway near the river. "I just think it would be good for all of us to get away for a bit, you know?"

"I haven't been skiing in years," I say, bringing the hot cocoa to my lips. It stings on the way down, but I barely notice as the rich, sweet yet somehow still bitter flavor as it slides over my tongue; I can't help but scan the heads bobbing around the little tents and shops as the music starts up.

"All the more reason to go!" they insist.

I am about to open my mouth to offer some kind of retort—I'd really rather spend the remainder of this winter in the confines of my apartment alone with Cass—but my thoughts are scrambled as my attention lands on a very pissed off looking Yvaine stomping her way through the crowd toward us. I furrow my brow at her, and before my thoughts have a second to catch up to me, she's reached us, her scowl vicious.

"Aren't you just the picture of joyful tidings," I tease, flashing her a smile.

She crinkles her nose in that way that tells me she doesn't at all appreciate my teasing and raises one hand. With a quick, angry swat, she aims for my hot cocoa. It is thrown to the ground with a disappointing *thwap*. Steam curls up from my sad, empty cup, cracked and lying on its side, bleeding the remains of my cocoa into the snow.

Blinking at the evidence of Yvaine's calculated assassination of my drink, I shake off the steaming remnants from my glove and raise a brow at her.

"What the *fuck* was that for?" I ask, shaking the searing liquid from my glove.

"*That* was because you fucked her." Her words come out on a furious, fuming hiss of hushed words, and she pumps her fists at her sides, her anger evident in every line of her body language.

My stomach drops almost as low as Niles' chin.

"Shit."

"You *WHAT?*" Niles quickly gathers their jaw from the pavement and cackles maniacally. "I fucking *knew* it. You can't lie worth shit, you asshole. WAIT." Their eyes widen in a look of horrified betrayal. "You let her tell *YVAINE FIRST?*"

I'm never going to hear the end of this one.

I'm certain the heat I feel across my entire neck and face is too deep to be explained away by the cold at this point. Groaning, I bat my hand at Niles and level a narrow look at Yvaine.

"Keep it down, please. And, for your information, we weren't going to tell *anyone,*" I grumble.

"Well, that's bullshit. You know I've been waiting for the two of you to get together since fucking high school," Niles huffs.

Glancing around, I notice Seti snickering at the sight of us over Yvaine's shoulder as she approaches, but I find a surprising lack of a certain tattletale.

"Where is Cass?"

"She's getting you more hot cocoa," Seti says, a playful smile in her dark eyes as she tucks her hands into her pockets. "We saw the carnage across the crowd."

Running my tongue over my teeth, I huff a sigh and fight the grin tugging at the corners of my lips. With a hesitant step away from Yvaine, I hook a thumb over my shoulder.

"Is this the part where I run for my life, or did the cocoa satiate your bloodlust?"

Yvaine shoves a finger in my chest, her nostrils flaring dangerously.

"If you so much as *think* about fucking this up this time, Talien Vale, I will gut you myself. Watch yourself."

Her words pierce me. I don't blame her. In fact, my shoulders feel light with relief knowing Cass has people so willing to protect her, even if that means protecting her from *me*. She deserves better, so much better than I've been.

I drop the humor, the part that is relieved to finally be here, with them, with Cass, and free to express how I've felt for so long. I leave behind the raw pieces of me, the pieces Yvaine is all too familiar with. Sure, Niles has always been there for me, always been supportive of whatever there was between Cass and me, always encouraging more, but Yvaine, she was the one who was unafraid to tell me the truths Niles would skirt.

Yvaine's priority was what was best for Cass. It always has been.

I let her in now. Let her see the part of me that is terrified I can't live up to Cass, can't ever be worthy of her, the part of me that knows how badly I've fucked up in the past. I let her hear the reverence in my voice.

"If I fuck this up, I'll bring you the knife."

She measures me, her lips pursed for a moment before she nods. I feel the weight of that promise pull taut between us.

It's only another moment before Cass squeezes through the crowd with two steaming hot chocolates in brown-gloved hands. Her cream-colored parka stands out against the burgundy scarf stuffed into the neck. The red tones bring out the rosy glow of her cheeks. Her curls are coiled into two buns atop her head, and burgundy earmuffs protect her ears from the cold.

She's perfect.

Her vibrant, depthless eyes light when they meet mine. A sheepish smile curls her lips before she steps to stand next to Yvaine, holding out the spare drink for me.

"Hi, please, accept this humble apology-hot-chocolate," she says with a dramatic bow of her head.

Chuckling, I take the cup from her, pointing an accusatory finger at her over the rim. "*You* are a fucking traitor."

"Hi, sorry, no. *You're* the fucking traitor," Niles cuts in, flicking me in the temple. "I spent all day with you. ALL. DAY. And you didn't say a fucking WORD about this to me. Are we even friends?"

"I'm sorry, Niles, really," I say with a shrug, shooting Cass a heated look. "Cass and I *agreed* that we weren't going to tell anyone until *after* the weekend."

"Honestly, fuck you both," Niles grumbles over a half-hearted frown. "Yvaine's my best friend now."

"I accept," Yvaine turns her nose up to the sky and holds her elbow out to Niles, who hooks their arm through hers with a smug expression stretched over their features. "Now, let's get moving or we're going to miss all the fun."

Yvaine and Niles march ahead of us toward the festivities, Yvaine grabbing Seti's hand on the way before I'm left with Cass, who shrugs one shoulder and bites down on her bottom lip, peering up at me through thick, fluttery eyelashes.

"Sorry," she says with a grimace.

The mischief written all over her features pulls every sinful thing we did last night to the forefront of my mind. Wrapping an arm around her waist, I tug her against my chest and glare down at her over a grin.

"*One day*, Firefly. Not even one day?"

She holds her drink close to her chest, and her arms fold between us as she tilts her chin to brush her nose against mine, a glittering smile in her eye.

"*Listen*. It just came out. I couldn't stop it." She stretches up on her tiptoes to press a quick kiss to my lips before breaking from my grip to take my hand in hers.

"We're losing them," she laughs as she pulls me along to follow our friends.

CHAPTER 26

Cassiopeia

I could not have asked for a more perfect picture of holiday bliss. Tal's hand is in mine as we walk the street to inspect the shop's displays for the yearly window decorating competition. Yvaine's is magnificent, decked out with pieces from cultures all over the world. I spot a decorated boat for Tal, figurines of the three kings for me, a minora, a pine tree, a Kinara, Mishumaa Saba, and so many more different decorations adorn her carefully crafted window display. No one else has worked so hard to represent other cultures. My heart glows over it.

We keep circling back to casually take stock of what people think about her display in comparison to others. She's been playing it cool, like she doesn't care who wins the contest this year, but I know how proud she'd be to be named the winner.

I toss a few extra ballots into the shoe box for her bookstore than I am supposed to. Tal does the same. We share a mischievous laugh as we do it.

Niles takes the others to participate in the snowman decorating competition. Tal pulls me into an alcove near the café to steal a kiss. He closes me in, shoulders to the brick wall, and claims my mouth with his. The frigid air is whisked away as heat flushes me. The fairy lights strung above illuminate his features beautifully. The thick tresses of his hair fall over his brow as he pulls back to meet my eye. His breath mists through the air, a personified puff of desperation as my cloud of warm oxygen dusts the icy winter eve.

His nose is cold as he brushes it to mine, and I offer one more quick kiss before I take his hand and drag him back into the crowd to follow our friends at a jog.

He's laughing behind me, and I urge him to keep up. I don't want to miss this; it's my favorite part.

We make it to our friends, and they've already started. They are in the town quad, where the gazebo is decorated with beautiful shining lights and giant glittering snowflakes. They've chosen their spot among a row of other snowman builders. We make it just in time for the whistle to blow to signal the start.

We lose ourselves, all of us, in the sheer bliss that is this evening. It isn't long before we have a structure. It's lopsided and lumpy, much to Niles's dismay, but Seti insists that the magic is in the accessories.

We don't win. Someone who clearly has a background in snow sculptures does. Their snowman looks like it's been carved out of marble, like an actual man. But it doesn't matter. We all take photos with our misshapen snow person, we have a passerby take a picture with all of us, and we are happy.

Really, truly happy. In a way that makes me so homesick I feel it in my bones. I can't help the ache as it takes root. I want to hang on to this bliss, to savor it. But I can't stop the dread of knowing my life hasn't been here in half a decade.

I don't want to think about whether or not I still want that.

I just want to enjoy this. Tal's hand in mine. The free-flowing energy of the holiday festival.

We decide to stop in the café instead of the cocoa stand for another warm drink. We all need to defrost a little. Tal excuses himself to the restroom, Yvaine and Seti go to find us a table, and Niles places an order for all of us. I go to remove my coat and realize my phone isn't with me. I must have left it on the Gazebo.

"I'll be right back," I say.

Yvaine is too love-struck to do more than offer me a brief acknowledgment before she leans in to nibble at Seti's ear, a lust-filled, over-the-moon look in her eye.

I brace myself for the chill again, headed straight for the Gazebo. I can see it from here. I won't be gone long.

I pass a dark alley and a chill snakes over my spine.

A hand is over my mouth, an arm around my waist.

Terror grips me, and I scream, but no one hears through the glove muffling the sound. There aren't many people here, and they're all busy; no one is looking.

I am pulled against a broad chest, and I try to elbow, to break free, but he holds firm. My breath is caught in my throat, my lungs stripped of oxygen.

He pulls me through the alley until we're on the other side, where a parking lot sits. Yvaine's car is right there. My legs are molten; I can't control my limbs. My eyes are wide with horror as I scan the lot for anyone. Anyone to help.

There is no one.

When the light covers us again, I see it's Bryson as he adjusts his grip on my elbow. Fear twists to terror as I try to rip my arm away. Some of that terror curls into blinding rage.

One of Lionel's Cadillacs pulls up. The windows are tinted. Furious does not even begin to describe the emotion coiling hot beneath my breastbone. Before I have a chance to speak, Bryson does.

"Your father wants to speak with you," he says before he opens the door and shoves me inside.

CHAPTER 27

Talien

Yvaine and Seti have confined themselves to a booth in the corner of the crowded café and are very clearly uninterested in being disturbed. Niles, however, is right where I left them, grimacing down at their phone.

I swear I haven't seen them frown so much in the entire time I've known them.

"Hey," I greet them over the din of merry voices.

"Hey," they reply without looking up.

Nadia and Sophia appear in the doorway, and I wave them over.

"Where's Cass?"

"Went to find her phone," Niles grumbles. "She thought she left it by the gazebo. She should be back any minute."

I want to go after her. We've wasted enough time apart, and I don't want to miss a moment. But I talk myself out of it.

She'll be back any minute.

As Nadia and Sophia step up to the little coffee bar, I feel a sharp tug under my breastbone. I *need* to go to her. I've felt this before. The night she left. I swear I could feel the miles growing between us as her train departed and drifted off into the night. It ached worse than the concussion or broken ribs Bryson had given me.

It hasn't been more than a minute since I came out of the bathroom, but I give in.

"I'm just going to see if she needs help finding it," I explain as I slip past Niles.

"If you're gone longer than five minutes, I'm sending Yvaine after the both of you," they chide.

Chuckling, I assure them I won't be long.

The rush of icy air is sharp compared to the warmth of the café. Snow crunches under my feet as I trot across the street, dodging couples snuggled together and giggling children, clutching their parents' hands and tugging them along. From a distance, the gazebo looks abandoned. The cold has clearly driven most of the crowds into the warmth of the shops or around the heaters near the stage, where music twinkles through the night air. The wooden boards creak under my boot as I step into the darkened space.

Cass isn't here.

With a puff of chilled breath, I fish my phone out of my pocket. *I must have missed her on the way.*

It rings to voicemail.

Maybe she ran into her mother. I'd seen Mrs. Ramos-Varner attempt to wave Cass over earlier in the evening, but Yvaine had been on a mission for cinnamon apple scones and tugged us away through the crowds.

I hit redial and scan the bobbing heads and flickering lights for those familiar puffs of curls. A noise behind me pulls my attention from the dwindling crowd. Turning, my eyes scan the dark gazebo. I follow the low, buzzing sound to the far corner, where Cass and I had stolen a moment to ourselves between festivities.

My heart drops to my boots.

The call goes to voicemail a second time as I stoop to pick up Cass's phone off the cold floorboards.

CHAPTER 28
Cassiopeia

I don't need to be brutally escorted to my father's office. I know the way well. Bryson is moving briskly to keep up with me through the halls of the most prestigious Varner hotel, but I've managed to berate him into keeping his hands off me. I can walk on my own.

If Lionel wants a talk, a talk he shall get.

I opt for the stairs. Lionel's office is on the top floor, but I don't want to be alone in an elevator with Bryson. My adrenaline carries my legs with immeasurable strength.

My thighs burn, and my chest is heaving by the time we approach the entrance to his hell cave.

One of his men is standing outside, guarding whatever he's hiding behind those walls today. I tried to stay out of it. I wanted nothing to do with the money laundering, certainly not the more nefarious dealings he's got his fingers in. It's dirty, bloody work covered with the façade of a pristine, marble-and-gold-dusted chain of hotels.

Though, no matter how much I resisted, he made sure I knew what was in store for me if I put up too much of a fight. What he was capable of, what empire waited for me and my *future husband* after he stepped down.

Not a fucking chance did I ever think I'd be setting foot in this office again. Horrors wait behind that door.

But I'm not a meek little girl anymore. I am strong; resilient. I am the woman Mom raised me to be, and I've got the fire he intended me to have. It's just not energy he gets to manipulate anymore.

"He's in a meeting." The man's deep voice rumbles as he holds out a bear paw of a hand to stop me.

You've got to be fucking kidding me.

"I don't give a shit." I swat it away, anger flaring in my chest as I push past him to open the door.

Inside, a man I don't recognize sips on dark liquor from a crystal glass. He's standing in front of Lionel's desk, one hand in a perfectly pressed pocket, not a single wrinkle in his unreasonably expensive suit. His crest is simple, winding under dark curls.

Lionel looks just as carefully crafted. His dark blonde hair is slicked back, his pale face clean-shaven, and his ice-cold blue eyes are piercing as his attention lands on me.

"Cassiopeia?" Lionel's tone lifts with a tinge of surprise, and I am livid. "I expected you to wait outside."

I grit my teeth against fury and close the distance from the door to his desk. My rage takes over as I swipe at a stack of papers. They scatter around the room, the sound only a flutter under my string of curses. The heated words fly freely to cut across his resolve.

"¿De verdad pensaste que iba a esperar después de que me echaste a la calle como si fuera una de tus criminales? No puedes dejarme tener una semana sin lidiar con tus tonterías. Espera a que le cuente a mamá."

Lionel's perfectly structured expression falters, and his eyes darken as my hatred seethes.

"Marcus, I'll have to reschedule. I'll be in touch," he says to the man, who merely nods before setting his glass down to leave.

Bryson shuts the door behind him, closing me in with the two of them. I feel exposed and vulnerable, but I hold my chin high and keep my spine straight.

"You'll forgive me for my inability to excuse that tantrum, Cassiopeia. Mr. Davenport is one of my most important clients, and you forced me to dismiss him so abruptly."

"I don't give a *fuck* about your business. What is it going to take to get you out of my life for good."

"Oh, sweet child," he croons, "Still so naive. Can't say I'm surprised; though, I admit I am disappointed. And I *am* surprised to hear what you've been up to since your return."

He tops off his glass and brings it to his lips as he turns to look out the window over the city. A stone of fear sinks to my core, and my mind scatters. My heart thunders in my chest, and the skin over my shoulders pulls taught with dread.

"Bryson, here, has been feeding me quite extensive reports on your behavior since you returned to town. And here I thought I took care of that Vale boy years ago."

I turn to lock my vicious sights on Bryson, but he seems unaffected. He gets his own glass and plops down on the leather couch near the drink cart, making himself at home.

"*What did you do?*" I hiss.

My asshole of an ex-fiancé shrugs, a smug expression stretching his smile as he takes a drink.

"If you touch him, I'll—"

Lionel interrupts me.

"You'll what? Ruin more paperwork? Throw another tantrum? Make me *feel* about it? You know, I was told your mother's bloodline would sully my own, that her magic was useless, too weak to consider passing on. Though I was *convinced* you'd take after me. An overinflated ego is to blame for that, I fear. But that is one of my greatest disappointments in life: your uselessness is magnanimous."

I swallow a lump in my throat. My heart breaks for Mom. Forever trapped in the hell this man created for us.

"And as though your lack of talent weren't embarrassment

enough, you insist on ruining our name by fraternizing with a Vale. Over and over, Cassiopeia. I truly can't understand it. I thought we'd taken care of it the last time you proved too stubborn for your own good. Your fiancé over there made good work of keeping that boy in the hospital. What was it, two weeks?"

"*What?*" My voice is strangled through despair as I turn on Bryson.

He stands, his height towering over mine, and a familiar, pitted fear roots itself under the façade of strength I carefully locked in place before entering this pit.

I want to duck away, flinch, flee. But I don't. I hold strong. The thought of Tal is the only thing keeping my spine straight, my fists clenched at my sides.

"He deserved it. He came looking for it, actually. Stupid fucking Vale got what he asked for."

A spitfire of curses fly from my tongue. They barrel toward Bryson in both languages with a fire hot enough to singe my knuckles as they hammer against his broad chest.

I don't see his counter coming, and as his fist arcs for my face, I black out enough to avoid having to commit the strike to memory. Pain lances my cheekbone. It's vicious, blinding. Pressure around my eyes swells, and I am sent to the floor. My knees hit the marble as the heels of my hands do, and the room spins.

I should have kept my temper. I know what these men are capable of. But even now, with a ringing in my ears, all I have the space to envision is Talien and what will happen to him if I can't get my shit together.

I can't keep up with my own thoughts; they're too fragmented. Someone is talking, but that ringing in my ear drowns out his voice. My vision blurs around the edges. I lift a shaking hand to find my cheek. It's hot, a trail of blood tracks my jaw from a split in the flesh.

Lionel crouches down, balancing on his leather toes as he tilts my chin up to meet his eye. When he speaks, his tone is understanding, fatherly, but the words are vile. They twist a nausea in my core.

"When will you *learn*, Cassiopeia? I *own* you. I own this entire city. The Vales lost. I made sure of that. Took their empire, too. You either submit, or I will make you."

I can't speak. My tongue has been torn out. My muscles are leaden with years' worth of dread, trauma. This room is a cage; its four walls witness to the many horrors I've had to face in my life.

"I will give you one final chance. You have forty-eight hours to get your things from the city and come home for good. You will marry, as is expected of you, and you will represent this family with dignity and strength. You will not speak to the Vale boy again. Or I'll have him killed this time."

Horror chills my veins, and I choke on a mangled sob.

"Up you get now. No blood on my floors. They've just been cleaned."

He helps me to my feet and turns back to his desk, where he instructs Bryson to clean up the mess I've made.

I turn numbly from the scene, and the brute at the door holds it open for me. My chest is hollow save for the lance of frantic terror straight through my heart.

I can't go back to Tal's. Lionel will have men following me.

With numb feet and a buzzing over my thoughts, I walk to Yvaine's. It takes me so long. She doesn't live close, but the cold does not so much as touch my skin the entire way.

CHAPTER 29

Talien

"Cass can handle herself. She's going to be fine," Nadia is saying as I pace past her for what feels like the thousandth time.

The second I found Cass's phone under the gazebo bench, with her still nowhere in sight, panic seized my chest—that pressure deep within warped from a sharp tugging to a wicked pinch of terror.

"We don't *know* that anything's wrong yet—"

"No one fucking knows where she is, Nadia," I bite back, tracing another path in front of my couch where my sister and her girlfriend are seated.

"I know, but her mom and Niles have it handled."

Yvaine had immediately gone to find Mrs. Ramos-Varner, while the rest of us scoured the festival for any sign of Cass. There was nothing. Not a trace of her anywhere, and no one seemed to have seen anything.

Even after the final song had played and all the vendors began packing up their booths, I kept searching. I'd checked every alley, questioned everyone I ran into, and retraced my path to the gazebo from the café a thousand times.

I lost her. The very second we'd finally decided to give in to

210

this thing between us, she was stolen away. It feels like the ground is opening up beneath me.

"I should be out there looking for her," I snap—the guilt caves in against my chest.

"If she's going to go anywhere, it's here, or Yvaine's; we just need to wait until we know more."

"Fuck that," I growl, prowling back to the door before turning and making my way back into the kitchen.

I can't sit still. I tried. I'm going to come out of my skin if we don't hear something soon. When we left the festival, Yvaine and Niles were adamant that Nadia and I should wait here until they had time to sort a few things out.

Honestly, with the network of contacts Niles has built up throughout this city over the years, I feel confident that they'll be able to track her down faster than any of us could, but doing nothing makes me want to tear out my hair.

"They'll let us know as soon as they know anything," Nadia assures me. Sophia tries to subtly still Nadia's nervous tapping by placing a hand over her knee.

"I know, I know," I seethe in response.

A sound at the door calls my attention just before Niles' dirty-blonde head of curls appears. Relief and panic flood my veins in equal measure as they hurry into the room.

"Hi. We found her," they inform us.

A weight peels off my ribs at those words. I can breathe. They shoulder past me, making straight for my closet.

"I'll explain everything, but we need to go. Now."

"You found her?" Nadia asks her voice tight with emotion.

Niles rips clothes from my closet and shoves them into the duffle bag they yanked off the back of the door.

"Is she ok?" I ask over a swirling nausea of relief and fear.

Niles hesitates, grimacing as they shove another bundle of clothes into the bag.

"She's alive," they assure me. "And mostly unharmed."

"*Mostly?*" I demand. My mind replays all the horrifying scenarios I'd imagined over the past several hours.

Whoever hurt her...

"Like I said," Niles cuts off my thoughts, zipping up the duffle bag and tossing it to me, "I'll explain on the way.

"Nadia, go grab your things, too. We're all going to take a little impromptu vacation."

CHAPTER 30

Talien

Nervousness snakes through me, mimicking the winding roads Niles navigates like they've driven this treacherous path a thousand times. We haven't spoken in almost an hour. After Niles explained Cass's state when she arrived on Yvaine's doorstep and the threat Lionel had leveled on the Vale family, there really wasn't much to say.

Nadia blows a breath through her lips from the backseat and leans forward between Niles and me.

"They just got out of the city," she tells us. "All clear, so far. They're only forty-five minutes behind us."

Sophia had gone to collect our parents. Nadia tried to go with her, but I've learned that once Sophia sets her mind to something, there's no talking her out of it. So, she'd shoved Nadia and her bags into the backseat of Niles' car, kissed her, and sped off into the night to collect the only remaining Vales in Brunswick.

"Good," Niles says, visibly relaxing their grip on the steering wheel. "Yvaine and Cass should be there already."

My leg bounces, teeming with anxious energy as we take another curve.

Cass is okay.

Kidnapped.

Threatened.

Beaten.

But alive and safe now. I could kick myself for not staying closer to her. If I'd just paid closer attention, she wouldn't have had to go back for her phone. If I'd paid closer attention, we'd be headed back to my place now instead of tangled in this mess.

Something in my mind tells me he would've gotten to her either way—that this night was never going to end well now that Lionel is back.

The last thirty minutes of the drive pass in silence; the only sound is the vicious pittering of Nadia's fingers on her phone screen and the occasional muttering from Niles under their breath. We finally pull up the last curved road and turn into the sloped driveway. I'm out of the door before Niles throws the car in park. My heart spirals under my ribs as I sprint up the familiar wooden stairs to the Sinclair family cabin.

"Cass?" I call the second I'm through the door.

She's already on her feet, launched from where she sat next to Yvaine on the plush couch before the fireplace. She sets her mug down and closes the distance to the front door in a few quick strides, her blanket falling from her shoulders on the way. She moves quickly enough to make it difficult to get a good look at her, but I can still see the wicked bruise across her cheek, even under the dimmed lighting.

Her arms are around my waist, and her unmarred cheek is buried in my chest.

"Thank God," she mutters, her voice strangled as her fingers tangle in the fabric at my back.

"Are you okay?" I ask, holding her to me like she'll disappear if I let go. "What happened? Was it Bryson? I'll kill that son of a bitch."

"No, I'm okay." Is all she offers.

"It was Bryson," Yvaine says from where she still stands near the couch. She is folding the blanket with unnecessary aggression, her jaw tensed, and her attention on her task.

I need to see her. Breaking my hold on Cass, I push her back enough to gently cup my hand over the uninjured side of her face. I wait for her to nod, giving me permission to touch her so I can examine the bruising. Her crest flares at the contact. My teeth grind at the sight of the swollen welt on her cheek. The edges are an angry red, and a hint of purple is already forming just under her eye. Her skin is split, and it doesn't look like anyone has cleaned it properly yet.

She tips her chin to turn the bruise away from my inspection, biting down on the inside of her cheek.

"I'm fine," she says, her tone firm but quiet.

"Cass—"

My concerns are cut off by Nadia and Niles coming through the door. My sister pushes me aside and wraps Cass in a tight embrace.

Nadia hisses numerous insults about Bryson, threatens to castrate him, and finishes her tirade with a bit about knocking Lionel's balls up his ass before pulling back to get a look at Cass and huff in frustration.

"There's a first-aid kit in the bathroom," Niles informs us, setting the first of the bags by the door and heading back out to the car with Nadia on their heels.

Taking Cass's hand, I lead her through the expansive living room, down the hall, and into the main bathroom on this floor. While I rummage through the drawers and medicine cabinet for the first-aid kit, Cass wraps her arms around her middle and leans against the counter.

Finally, I find the damned thing tucked in the very back of the cabinet under the sink, and I set it on the counter.

"Come here, Firefly," I say, motioning for her.

She turns slightly toward me and tips her chin to meet my eyes. Hers glitter, a heavy emotion pressing against her stiff expression. In this light, I can see the extent of the wound. The entire left side of her face is battered. It's swollen, and over her cheekbone, her skin is split. It looks like he hit her with a mallet.

My hand shakes with rage, and I clench it at my side. I want to make him pay. I want him to regret ever laying a finger on her.

Some of my temper cools as my eyes roam up to hers—those golden pools of amber twist my heart. More than I want to hurt Bryson for this, I want to make sure Cass is safe. I don't want to let the damage he's done go any further.

Cass is significantly shorter than me, so I help her onto the counter and open the kit.

"Not quite as romantic as last time," I murmur as I slide between her knees and gently tip her chin so I can set a cool rag against her cheek.

She huffs a dark chuckle, and her shoulders curl in as her eyes flutter closed. She turns her face to give me better access and rests her hands on my hips, hooking her fingers through my belt loops.

"I don't know. The *tending to her wounds* trope shows up in a significant number of romantasy books. I'd say we're doing things right by those standards."

I echo her humor and shake my head at her. "This is the part where I'm supposed to ask, 'who did this to you?' and then seek my revenge on anyone who has ever wronged you, right?"

"Except you already know. And you can't do that. Not this time," she says, her tone low again, devoid of any light.

Rolling my lip through my teeth, I set the cloth aside and retrieve the antibiotic ointment from the kit.

"Yeah, that didn't end too well for me last time." I dab the cut along her cheek with the ointment for a moment before my lips twist into a half-hearted smirk. "Although, I saw Westfield a couple of months ago, and I think I could take him now. Man's let himself go..."

"Talien," she says as she grabs my wrist, stilling my hand. The demand in her tone brings my attention to hers. Her eyes are hard, her expression firm. "He said he put you in the hospital."

Those words come out hushed, like she's afraid to utter them.

I grimace. "I forgot you didn't know about that."

Add it to the list I've been trying to catalog of a million things

I need to say, details of my life I need to share with her, things I would have shared if I hadn't let her go five years ago—if I hadn't been stupid enough to go after revenge that night instead of meeting her at the station like I'd promised.

"I don't think you understand how serious this is. I thought you stood me up—this entire time. I've been so upset with you. Heartbroken, really. And I have to find out from my father, from *Bryson Westfield*? They could have killed you, Tal. Then what? God."

She finishes her heated rush of words with a lengthy string of expletives as she turns her attention to the first aid kit to fuss with looking for something. Her neck flushes red.

My face burns hot with shame as I shakily try to replace the cap on the ointment.

"I fucked up," I say, watching her. "I saw what he did to you, and I just lost it."

She releases an angry breath through her nose and shakes her head as she bites down on her lip, still looking down at her hands, but she gives up her fiddling to grip the counter at her hips. Cass shrugs one shoulder and squeezes her eyes shut. A tear tracks her cheek. My heart fissures.

"Cass," I whisper, lifting a hand to gently wipe away the tear, careful not to brush against her injured skin. "I'm sorry. I should have called. I didn't—everything went to such shit after you left, I don't know."

The words are all coming out wrong. I don't know how to explain the mess that kept me tangled and stuck. I don't know how to explain that it wasn't just that I ended up in the hospital but also everything that happened after that night.

I don't know how to tell her about the night I woke up in the ICU with Lionel Varner standing over me or how he ruined my family in the span of a few months because I had the audacity to love his daughter.

My eyes sting.

"I wanted to follow you," is all I manage.

"I know. I don't know that things would have been different if you had, though. I'm so sorry." Her apology comes with more tears, her voice cracks, and when she looks back at me, her eyes meet mine. I can see years' worth of my own heartbreak reflected there, her pain an echo of mine.

"You have nothing to be sorry for."

I sweep her into my arms and pull her tight to my chest as if I can hold her close enough to erase everything that has kept us apart all these years. I want to tell her everything, explain that I typed out numerous emails, wrote more than a few letters, and talked myself through hundreds of apologies, trying to find a way to fix it. I want to tell her about the endless nights I spent wishing I'd done things differently. Wishing my choice had been *her* and not my own damn ego. Wishing my choice had been to ask for her help instead of letting her go.

All the words get caught in my throat. Tears brim, and I tighten my hold around her.

"I'm so sorry, Firefly," I choke. "For everything."

She releases whatever hold she has on her emotions, and her chest caves in as she relaxes into my arms. Tears stain my shirt, and she tangles her fists in the fabric. I hold her there for a long time while she cries.

"Everything is so fucked up," she finally mutters after her tears slow, her good cheek still pressed to my breastbone. "You shouldn't have come here. I should have made Yvaine take me back to the city. You should be safe in your own apartment, in your own town. Your family shouldn't have to worry about any of this. They shouldn't be in the position they're in. I don't know what to do, Tal."

"You know as well as I do that this fucking feud is bigger than you and me," I say. "I thought driving my family into the ground years ago was the end of that bullshit, but it appears Lionel still has a stick up his ass about it."

Fire lights under my skin again. A fresh wave of anger at this ridiculous rivalry that started generations ago over some shit my father only briefly told me about once rolls through me.

She tenses and pulls away to look at me, and her crest ripples with light before she sets her jaw.

"It *is* about us. It's about me, whatever claim he feels like he has on my life. He'll kill you," Her voice cracks, a frantic energy spinning behind her eyes. "He said he'd kill you. I can't let that happen. You can't—"

Her chest is heaving, and her grip on my shirt tightens as she loses her words. Watching the panic overtake her douses my anger instantly.

"Hey, hey, Firefly," I say.

I instinctively reach to take her hand and stop myself. I want her to feel the intensity of what I feel for her, to take comfort in knowing that I will do whatever I can to stay by her side. But she's already been through so much. I don't want to overwhelm her with unexpected contact.

"We're safe," I say, setting my hand against her forearm over the top of her sweater. "Niles knows what they're doing—I wish they'd tell us *exactly* what that is—but I trust them. And Yvaine. She'll fucking tear him to shreds if he so much as gets near either of us again. We're going to be ok."

"I am terrified of losing you again."

I ghost my fingers over the dip of her neck and tuck a stray hair behind her ear. Her gaze is full of uncertainty. Fear. I don't need to be able to sense emotions to see it written clearly in the line of her brow.

Leaning back, I tug down the collar of my sweater to reveal my breastbone, the same place she set her hand just last night when emotion threatened to consume her. Her eyes soften, and tears brim over her lashes again. She lifts a shaking hand and presses her palm to my chest. Her crest lights, and her chest lifts as she fills her lungs.

"May I touch you?" I ask, admiring the beautiful lights dancing under her skin.

She nods, never taking her eyes off mine as I slip my hand under the neck of her sweater and rest it in the center of her sternum. Everything else falls away at the contact. Just this simple touch and everything is whole again. We breathe. Once. Twice. I don't want to disrupt the serenity I see forming in her eyes. I want to allow it to fill her. I never want her to feel fear like this again.

"You will not lose me. I was a fool not to chase you in this lifetime; I won't make that mistake again." I tip my head low and set my forehead against hers, nuzzling the tips of our noses together. "Firefly, I will *always* find my way back to you."

A soft whine escapes her throat, a whimper of a sound, but she doesn't pull away. She leans in to press her lips to mine. The kiss she offers is consuming, and I lean into it. Her free hand moves to my neck, and she pulls me closer as I wrap my arms around her waist.

A knock on the door startles her enough to make her jump. She breaks the kiss, and her eyes stretch wide as she steadies herself with a fist on my collar.

"I'm sorry to interrupt, but Niles is going to combust if they don't get to see Cass soon," Yvaine calls from the other side. "Is everything alright?"

"Yeah." Cass's voice is steady and clear as she answers before turning her attention back to me. "Stay close to me," she says, as though she even has to ask.

CHAPTER 31
Cassiopeia

The sky is light with the first hints of early morning sun. Tal fell asleep over an hour ago. I spent a long time running my fingers through his hair, offering small bursts of serenity through touch to calm him enough for slumber to take him. I wasn't sure he would let it. He was so anxious about losing track of me at the festival. I was sure he had no intention of falling asleep with me next to him.

But my soothing touch worked its magic. Now, I measure the rise and fall of his chest, listen to the thrum of his heart under my ear with my cheek against his heart as I stare at the window, watching as thick flakes of snow collect over the sill. I am not going to be able to sleep; my mind tumbles over the same anxiety-ridden trains of thought a thousand times over, and I can't get them to slow.

You will not speak to the Vale boy again. Or I'll have him killed this time.

I know Lionel means it, and it terrifies me straight to the hollow of my bones. My heart seizes in my chest, and my lungs strip of air as the possibility settles in. According to his demand, I only have two days before he starts looking for me. Will he find me here? Surely not. Niles owns this resort under a different name. They had done well to explain that much after they were satisfied with their inspection of me. They also explained that their personal detail would be patrolling the entrance to the resort and the grounds throughout our stay.

But Lionel is capable of so much more than any of my friends are aware of. I can't risk any of them getting caught harboring me like this, like some kind of runaway in the witness protection program.

He'll ruin them all.

He'll kill Tal.

I can't bear the thought. I don't know what the plan is, but I know it can't end with this, with me and Tal.

My heart fissures, and tears sting my eyes. I finally have him; he's finally being open about how he feels, and now I am forced to distance myself. And god damn it, I tried to do that. I just couldn't. Not with the way those emerald eyes searched mine. Not with how gentle he was with me, how careful he was not to touch me, how he asked for consent, the way he offered his heart to me.

I can feel him now. Even in his sleep, I feel how brightly he glows for me.

My heart cracks further. I can't take it anymore. I need to move. I can't figure out what I'm supposed to do when I'm touching him like this, when I can feel him so vividly.

As slowly as I can manage, I slide out from under his arm, careful not to wake him. He rolls over, reaching to hold on to me, but I shift my pillow to fit within his embrace before he closes it. I hold my breath, balancing on my toes while I wait to see if it is enough to wake him.

It isn't. His eyelids flutter, and he settles further into the mattress.

Gorgeous man. Even in sleep, he looks near angelic.

I release a breath and move to the door. I don my robe and slowly, as quietly as I can manage, sneak to the living room to watch the embers in the fire die out.

Tiptoeing over the threshold, I close the door behind me as gently as I can. I turn my attention to the fireplace, pulling my robe closed over my chest, and I find Niles perched on the couch, their laptop on one knee, an uncharacteristic look of worry over their expression.

Anxiety spikes my nerves. They don't so much as look up to acknowledge me. This steadfast concentration is very unlike them. I move across the room, and there is still no indication that they've so much as noticed my presence.

"Hey. Are you okay?"

"Shit balls!" Niles yelps, almost dumping their laptop onto the floor. "Why don't your feet make any noise?"

"Probably the experience sneaking around in catholic school, mostly." I huff a laugh.

They blow a heavy breath out of their lips and adjust their gangly legs on the couch to make room for me. As I settle in beside them, they shift the checkered blanket around their knees to cover my lap as well.

"Couldn't sleep?"

"No," I groan. "Things are too fucked up. You?"

Niles' lips purse under their nose, and they nod.

"No shit."

Their normally even, clear skin is dark under their eyes with exhaustion, making the need for sleep evident, and their blackened brow is deeply creased with worry. After a few more clicks on their trackpad, Niles saves the file they are working on and closes the laptop.

"Are you okay?" they ask, turning to inspect my cheek.

I tip my chin away and bite down on my lip as something vile near my heart twists. My eyes flit to the bedroom door attached to the living room. My thoughts ping to the man sleeping on the other side. I can't help the flush of dread as it rolls my spine, and I avert my eyes to the ceiling as I take a breath, considering. I pull the blanket up to my chin, curling my knees into my chest as though compressing myself into a tiny ball will keep the raging torment inside me confined.

"No," I finally answer, my tone thick as tears prick my eyes. "I'm sure Yvaine told you what Lionel said."

"She did." I don't think I've ever heard their voice sound so grave.

I shrug a shoulder and turn my attention to the fire, pulling the blanket up to wipe tears away before they have a chance to fall. Niles waits for me to speak. Their silence weighs heavy between us, but I am grateful for the time they give me to try to corral my torment.

"He'll do it," I say after some time. "If he even so much as thinks I'm with Tal again, he will do it. I can't—" I stammer, the words caught behind the catch in my bleeding heart.

I don't want to say it out loud. Not now, knowing how it feels to have Tal so close. But I have to. I'm not sure where my mind is or what I am supposed to do.

"I can't stay with him. It's not safe—it never has been. I don't —Niles, I'm so scared."

Niles stretches an arm over my head and offers a hug, waiting for me to consent before dropping it around my shoulders and pulling me to their chest.

"We're not going to let that happen," they say softly. "Lionel's not the only one with some pull around here. You and Tal, you deserve to be together. To be happy." Niles blows another annoyed breath through their lips. "Honestly, your dad can go suck a giant dick if I have anything to say about it." Their tone is lighter, but I can hear the venom still brewing underneath.

Another dark laugh passes my lips as tears flow free. I settle into their side and rest my head on their shoulder.

"*He* deserves better," I sigh miserably. My heart fractures a bit further. "I can't stay. I won't put him in anymore danger. Any of you. I'm afraid none of you are safe, really."

"Cass," Niles says over a heavy sigh. It sounds like the calm before the storm. They confirm my suspicions that they are about to monologue about their feelings on the matter by kicking their feet out from under them and propping their heels on the table, taking up more space as they draw in another deep breath.

"First of all, if Lionel, or any of his fucking cronies, so much as sets foot on *any* of my properties, I'll have him arrested for trespassing. Second, Yvaine has been waiting for an excuse to punch your father for as long as I can remember, and, honestly, that's something I would pay good money to watch." They drop the humor from their tone and continue, "And I've known Talien since we were kids. *Womb to tomb friends*, we used to say. And if I know anything about him, it is that he has been crazy about you since day one. I swear, you were the only thing he talked about for the first six months after we met." Niles chuckles at the memory.

"I'm not going to tell you what to do because I know you hate it, but also because I know you will do whatever you think is best anyway. But my opinion is: I don't think you leaving is going to change anything for him this time. I think that man will chase you through lifetimes, no matter the consequences. Maybe that's hard to believe, given the past, but, Cass, I've *never* seen him like he is now. With you."

Chase me through lifetimes.

Their words settle into the cavities of my chest. I can't tell if the ache they cause is evidence that I should stay or leave, but either way, it's sharp behind my heart. I find it difficult to take a full breath as I do my best to catalog every confession.

I resonate *desperately* with their admission. I remember how significant every moment had been, every stolen glance, every secret Friday night study session. It wasn't just that I was grateful to have friends. I've always loved Niles and Yvaine, but it's *always* been more for me with Talien.

A smile twitches at the corner of my mouth as the fond memory of that first day of high school floats through my mind's eye.

It scares me to know that leaving might not keep him safe. It didn't last time. *Two weeks* in the hospital is what Lionel said.

I've been afraid to ask about that. I don't have it in me now. Nausea coils in my core.

As I contemplate, I can barely make out the tip of Niles' pointed nose flushing pink at the edge of my vision. They clear their throat, snapping me back to reality.

"Thank you," I say, setting my chin on my knee, still staring at the flickering flames, "For everything. I don't know what I would have done without you."

Niles sniffles, swiping their chunky, too-long, crimson sweater sleeve across their nose.

"You're welcome," they say, their voice cracking over the words. "God, I need to sleep. I turn into such a baby when I haven't gotten my eight to ten hours. But, you're welcome. Both of you are so fucking stubborn I'm going to go prematurely grey about it, but you'll get through this. We'll all get through this."

There's a certainty in their voice that makes me wonder what exactly it was that kept them up all night.

"Are *you* doing alright?"

"Yeah, it's been a crazy night," they chuckle, disentangling themselves from the blanket and getting to their feet. "I just need some sleep, and I'll be fine."

They lean down to plant a gentle peck of a kiss on the crown of my head.

"You should try to sleep, too," they say, yawning as they head towards their room.

I am left to turn over my many racing thoughts. I need to make a decision.

CHAPTER 32

Cassiopeia

My eyes glaze over. The longer I sit here, the further I get from even remotely being willing to tell Tal I am afraid to go on from here. The floodgate has cracked open. I can't stop the old memories as they float to the surface, replaying like an old home movie to remind me of what I would be leaving behind.

SEPTEMBER—FRESHMEN YEAR

It's my first day of high school. My first day of public school. This is supposed to be a great day. A liberating day. I finally got Mom and Dad to stop sending me to that boarding school. I should get to remember this day for the rest of my life as the first thing I got to do for myself. But no, it's been a disaster from top to bottom.

I'll never admit it to Dad.

My uniform stands out like a sore thumb. No one told me public schools didn't have a dress code. How would I know? Now, everyone thinks I'm just a freak from that all-girls catholic school. I'll never live that one down. I blame Mom, honestly. She should have told me.

I have not been able to find a single classroom the first time once. I've been late to every one so far. It's been absolutely mortifying.

227

And now it's lunchtime, and I can't get this stupid locker open. I've tried the combination at least fifty times. I'm starving and angry, and I don't want to carry these stupid books to the lunchroom where I know I'll have to eat by myself anyway, and I can't believe today is going like this.

Tears prick my eyes. Of course, I am about to start crying. I'll be the freak, private school girl who cried all day and ate her lunch with her books in the bathroom because she couldn't get her locker open.

I try to adjust my grip on my books to get a look at the combination and they topple from their precarious stack to the ground. I groan in frustration and kick at the metal as tears blur my eyes further.

"My locker seems to be giving you some trouble."

I jump in start, my anxiety spiking as I turn to find a boy leaning against the lockers a few down, watching me with a quirked brow and a crooked smile. He has bright green eyes, the brightest I've ever seen, and his dark hair is messy but somehow still neat. It falls over his forehead in that charming way I've always imagined a boy's hair to fall.

I hurry to wipe my eyes on my sleeve, silently cursing myself for crying anywhere in the vicinity of someone that cute, and turn my attention back to the note in my hand.

"I've been using this locker all day," I say, frustration still straining my voice.

The paper has my combination and the locker number.

52-13-09, locker number 213.

I look up to see the number on this locker is, regretfully, 212.

I hang my head between my shoulders and release a muttered string of curses in Spanish. I'm at least thirty percent sure he won't understand them.

"I'm sorry," I say, crouching down to scoop up my scattered books. "I'll get out of your way."

He kneels next to me, gathers the last few pages of wrinkled notes, and stacks them neatly on the pile.

"Rough first day?"

"No," I say, my tone stretched with sarcasm, "everyone has been really kind about my inability to dress myself, and being ogled all day like I'm some kind of long-lost mythical creature has been a delight. I don't know what ever would make you think that."

"I almost wore my plaid skirt and knee-highs today, too. That would have been really *embarrassing."*

A smile cracks my dismal expression, and my stomach flips at the flippant tone of his voice. I tuck some loose hair behind my ear and meet his eye, curling my books into my chest.

"What? If we matched? Yes. I'm afraid you would have had to go home and change. Only room in this school for one private school girl in these halls."

"Private school. That explains why I haven't seen you around." The boy's eyes roam my face as if to assure me that he would have remembered me.

My cheeks burn hot, and I nod.

"Unfortunately, yeah. Ever been the new kid before?"

He tips his head, and hair falls over his eyes. He brushes it aside with a smile.

"No, but I think you'll get the hang of it pretty quick, assuming you can figure out how to conquer your locker, that is."

"Well, if I get the right one next time, it should be a breeze."

The bell rings. Lunch period has started, and the halls are empty now. It's just the two of us crouched in front of the lockers.

"Oh no! Well, I guess it wouldn't be a tardy streak if I weren't also late for lunch." I stand and quickly move to my locker, double-checking to make sure it's the right one before opening it to throw my books inside.

"I won't keep you any longer. I'm sure you have friends waiting on you."

"They can wait," he says, tossing his things in his own locker

while watching me. After the door swings shut, he sets his shoulder against it and flashes another smile.

"I'm Talien," he says, extending a hand.

That name sounds familiar.

"Oh, a handshake, so formal," I tease with a wiggle of a brow before I shake his hand. I am worried he might think the gloves are weird, but if he does, it doesn't show on his face.

"Cassiopeia. Cass," I say. "Have we met?"

My attention flits to the lockers, curiosity willing me to place the familiarity. Above the number 212 is his surname. Vale.

My stomach drops. One of the founding families, the families against Dad and everything he works for. This boy is one of the people I am supposed to steer clear of. Dad would be livid if he knew I was talking to him. He'd send me back to St. Agnes tomorrow.

But why? Talien is genuinely the first person all day to offer me any amount of kindness. Maybe Dad has something mixed up.

"I'm pretty sure I'd remember if we had met," he says. "Is something wrong?"

"No," I shake my head with a smile, turning my attention back to his, "Not at all. Would you mind walking me to the cafeteria? You'd be saving me the embarrassment of getting lost for the fifteenth time today."

Talien chuckles as he pushes off the lockers and steps past me.

"I thought you had a streak to keep up? Fifteen? That's got to be a new record."

"Well, I've been known to be an overachiever," I laugh as he leads me down the empty hall.

OCTOBER—FRESHMAN YEAR

Talien is hunched over his notes, furiously scribbling something, and his knee bumps mine, pulling my attention from the history lesson. I thin my lips in frustration. I was actually interested in the topic Mr. Crowley has been going over. Tal straightens his shoulders, and

I can feel him peering at me from the corner of his eye as he slides a neatly folded note across the table between us.

I snatch it from the desk and pull it into my lap as quickly as I can to avoid being seen. Crowley will read notes aloud to the class without a second thought.

I unfold it and peer down my nose to get a look.

Hi, friendly reminder:
We're going to fail this class project.

He's decorated the border of the note with hearts and skulls with little Xs for eyes. I roll my eyes, but my heart catches in my chest.

I don't know what I am going to do about the project. We need to work on it but there is no way I can even so much as insinuate to my father that I've even come in contact with a Vale. Meeting up after school isn't an option. Being friends at lunch, between classes, and sitting next to one another in history is one thing. Anything outside of that is off the table.

As discretely as I can, I write my reply.

I told you, I'll just do it.

Talien audibly scoffs, drawing a searing look from Mr. Crowley. We have to wait a few tense minutes until he's engrossed in his lesson again before Talien can scratch out another note and slip it back to me.

Please don't make me beg to do HOMEWORK. That's humiliating.

Another note slides into view.

Sirius asked me out again. I need an excuse.

I want to meet him. Desperately, I do.

I bite down on my lip as I consider. Yvaine said she'd cover for me. Maybe, just this one time, I can get away with it.

Can we meet at your place?

Yeah, I'll text you the address.

Another note.

Guess that means I need your number

He's sketched a winky face in the corner.

I scrawl my number on one of the now four notes I have cluttering my lap.

Here. Now pay attention before Crowley embarrasses

us.

NOVEMBER—FRESHMAN YEAR

I hate this office. I hate how it smells, how the couch squeaks under me as I struggle to get comfortable. I hate the way Dad makes me sit in silence while he deals with whatever bullshit he deals with. He insists I need to prepare for this, that exposing me to this lifestyle will toughen me up enough to take over when I'm grown.

I don't want that. Dad is cruel and cold, and the people who come in here are scared of him. I don't think it's just his ability to magically manipulate people's emotions. I don't like it, and I don't want to find out for sure.

I am scared of him in here.

My phone buzzes in my pocket, and I check to make sure Dad is distracted enough with his conference call for me to take it out and see who it is. My stomach twists into knots, and my heart flutters as I read Talien's name. I hurry to unlock the screen.

I hate Dean.

I can't help the smile before it spreads, and I have to bite down on my lip to stop it. He told me he'd watch Gilmore Girls weeks ago. It's a comfort show of mine, but I didn't actually think he would.

Why?

He's a misogynistic asshole. Hang on.

I am hanging.

Some time passes with my phone face down in my lap. Which episode is he on? Because I agree and can think of at least five examples that might enrage him enough to text me out of the blue like this.

Dad asks me some mind-numbing questions about finances, and I seem to answer correctly because he's satisfied enough to take another call and let me get out my homework. I'm sitting on the floor with my calculus spread over the coffee table when my phone alerts me to another message. Excitement flares in my chest.

This is bullshit

That smile cracks my expression again. I can't control it, but Dad isn't paying attention.

> Lol. What episode?

> SHE DID NOT JUST DRESS UP AS DONNA REED FOR THIS NEANDERTHAL

I don't stop the laugh before it comes out on a muffled snort. The sound catches Dad's attention, but I offer a soft apology with a shrug. He silently scolds me to get back to my homework. I wait until he's distracted again to reply.

> LOL. Complete bullshit. Not one of her stronger moments, honestly.

I put my phone on silent and focus on my calculus. It buzzes—at least seven separate times while I am still confined to my father's office. My stomach flips every time, but I can't risk Dad taking my phone. I can't wait to get home to the safety of my bedroom to see what was so urgent for him to send so many messages in such a short amount of time.

FEBRUARY—FRESHMAN YEAR

I spend every Friday studying at Tal's. Mom and Dad think I'm with Yvaine. Sometimes I am, but it's always here. His parents are so nice. Nadia loves me. And Tal wants me to teach him Spanish. He says he wants to understand me all the time.

I think it might be the sweetest thing.

LATE AUGUST—BEFORE SOPHOMORE YEAR

I anxiously check the time on my phone, the screen lights up the night like a beacon. It's almost two in the morning. I will be so far beyond dead if Mom and Dad find out I climbed over my balcony to deface school property, no matter how just the cause.

Most of me doesn't care what Mom and Dad think, though. I want to do this, and I am angry with my father. He won't listen to me, has no respect for what I want to do with my time and my life, and Mom can't do anything about the control he has either. I don't want to be home, locked in my room like a precious doll who will break if let free for too long. I am sick of it.

The anger and defiant frustration doesn't stop my coiling nerves, though.

"You okay, Firefly?" Talien's voice pulls me from my tangle of thoughts, and I realize Niles and Yvaine are pretty far ahead of us, close to the gates to the stadium now.

I smile at the use of that nickname he gave me after the first time he saw my crest light up. It's cute.

"Yeah, just trying to determine how likely it is that I get sent back to St. Agnes if we get caught," I say as we hurry to catch up to our friends.

Niles is already in the box working to dismantle the security cameras. Yvaine waits in the shadows with our duffle bag full of spray paint.

"Oh, probably pretty high," Talien admits, casting a look of mischief my way.

"Oh, yes, that's comforting."

I huff a dark chuckle and roll my eyes as we move to stand near Yvaine. The lights flicker for a moment before going out completely with a shuddering echo of a sound.

In the darkness, Talien leans close enough for his breath to flutter over the shell of my ear.

"Don't worry," he whispers, "if you get shipped off, I'll go too. I'll

have Niles forge some papers or something. I think I could pass at St. Agnes."

A bubbling snort of a laugh breaks free, and I cover my mouth to stop the sound.

"I'd honestly pay good money to watch those nuns try to keep up with you," Yvaine says, her tone cool, but I can hear the smile there.

Niles hops down from the bleachers with a bright and proud smile on their face, their blonde hair disheveled over their family crest.

"Alright, bitches, let's light this place up," they say with notable excitement before they grab the bag from Yvaine and head out to the fifty-yard line.

Tal and I both take white, Yvaine takes blue, and Niles takes pink. We spend the next forty-five minutes while we work talking about how angry we are that Coach Smith wouldn't let Andrew try out for the team.

Andrew's transition has been a hot topic of controversy among the adults, but he is an adult, too. Still a senior, sure, but eighteen is definitely legal enough to make his own decisions about his own body, and it's bullshit to know that the genitals with which he was born are keeping him from doing something he's always wanted to do.

When we are all done painting the enormous and meticulously placed transgender flag, Talien takes the white and scrawls, "Trans Men are Men" *above the image.*

We take off into the night high on adrenaline and spend the rest of our time under the stars, sharing a snack Yvaine brought and talking about how we will stay in touch if my parents find out, and I get shipped away again.

I couldn't be more proud to call these beautiful people my friends.

SEPTEMBER—SOPHOMORE YEAR

I find my new locker, anxious to see Tal this morning. It's the first day of school, and we haven't seen each other since our late-night vandalism, but as far as I am aware, no one has any idea who did it.

I was disappointed to find that Talien wasn't in the foyer before the bell this morning. Yvaine and Niles weren't sure why he was running late, but my nerves had me thinking the worst. Did he get caught somehow?

I get my things in my locker and peer down the hall. The crowd is thinning, and only a few short minutes pass before the bell rings for first-day homeroom. I am unwilling to go find a seat without Tal, but there is still no sign of him.

Just as I am about to get my phone out to text him, he rounds the corner. My jaw drops at the sight of him as I struggled to contain my elated shock.

Talien hikes his bag over his shoulder as he trots down the hall, a dazzling smile on his face as his attention lands on me. He is wearing a crisp, wine-red button-down, a plaid skirt that falls to the middle of his thighs, and knee-high burgundy socks. It's an exact copy of the uniform I wore on my first day of school last year.

"What is this?" I ask, my tone stretched with bright admiration as I inspect his outfit.

"You like it?" he asks, giving me a little swish of his hips to make the skirt flare out around his knees.

"Yes, actually. The skirt is the perfect shape for you," I say honestly. "But why do you look like you're about to get yelled at by Sister Sarah?"

I hated that asshole nun.

Talien's face turns to a faux look of innocence. "Who me?" Before I can comment, he flashes a grin and unlocks his locker. "Honestly, I'm glad to see you. The skirt is fine, I kind of like it, but shaving was a bitch." He gags and kicks out a knee that's smooth but covered in knicks and cuts.

I throw my head back with a laugh. My chest feels bright and warm.

"Why did you do that?"

Talien shrugs, grabbing his things and closing his locker.

"I wasn't about to let you get shipped off alone, Firefly."

I have no words. I can't help but gape at him as my heart does something obscene beneath my breastbone. The bell rings, and he offers his arm with a smile. I hook my gloved hand through his elbow, and we trot off to homeroom, both lost in various bouts of giggles.

DECEMBER—JUNIOR YEAR

I am on a date with the prettiest girl in the entire school. She asked me out last week, and honestly, I have had a bit of a crush on her. Niles, Yvaine, and Tal all seemed to be wildly on board with the idea. A date with Charlotte is much better than a date with that tool of a Westfield boy.

Dad wishes I'd said yes to Bryson's offer. He'd said that his family is wealthy, and he'd make a fine addition to our family someday, but he's alright with Charlotte. She's at least one of the founding family members on Dad's side of the conflict, so he was willing to agree to a date.

But I don't want to 'add to the family.' I want to be sixteen and enjoy going to the winter festival with this amazing girl.

But that's not the extent of how I feel about it. Something is missing. Charlotte offers her gingerbread cookie, expecting me to take a bite from her hand with a flirtatious wiggle of her brow. Her navy-colored parka compliments her rich brown skin. The golden flecks in her dark eyes glimmer in the glowing street light. She's so pretty.

I offer a smile and do as she's expecting. It crumbles. She laughs and throws her head back; her curls bouncing with the movement.

I laugh, too, but I can't ignore the slight deflation of disappoint-

ment in my chest. I don't really have butterflies like the movies say I should. My heart isn't beating faster. My palms aren't sweaty.

And I can't stop my thoughts from drifting to a very particular set of emerald-green eyes, and how even just the glitter of them catches my heart in my chest.

MARCH 22ND—JUNIOR YEAR

I am laughing, my eyes are covered, and Charlotte has my gloved hands guiding me while Tal and Niles move on either side of me with Yvaine behind to ensure I don't bump anyone. They've all already wished me a dozen 'happy birthdays' today. I have no idea where they could be leading me before class starts.

I feel a gentle hand on my hip as Tal turns me. Yvaine stops, and someone stumbles. My pulse spikes and my heart flips in its cage as his voice sounds close to my ear.

"Happy birthday, Firefly," he nearly whispers as he unties the blindfold at my face.

When it falls, I find my locker decorated in bright paper flowers and balloons tied to the handle. The flowers are dahlias. The only person I've told about my obsession with the flower is Tal. In my bones I know he's the one responsible for most of these decorations.

I am stunned. Neither one of my own parents so much as acknowledged my birthday today. In fact, I was told, rather firmly, that I'd have to go with my dad on a work trip that evening, which I'd rather die about than actually have to attend.

I am so grateful.

Niles can't contain their excitement, and they throw their arms around me, nearly buckling my knees with the embrace. I catch Talien's glittering smile over their shoulder, and I don't think my heart could be any more full.

APRIL—JUNIOR YEAR

Tech week for the production of Grease *has been rough. I don't know how Niles got Yvaine and Tal to participate, but I am grateful they've both decided to work the sound and light boards. It means we all get to spend an obscene amount of time together, and my parents are none the wiser, especially since the name Vale won't show up in the playbill anywhere near mine.*

Charlotte is Sandy. Her singing voice is incredible. She's beautiful and perfect, and I am honestly proud to call myself her girlfriend.

Niles was cast as Kinicki, and I am delighted to be playing the role of Rizzo. She has my favorite song.

We're all working on the set for Greased Lightning. *Charlotte is rehearsing lines with her costar, and Niles is dancing on the hood of our unfinished car, pretending to be Danny. Well, I think they're mocking Mark's performance of Danny, but what are you going to do?*

Yvaine and I are waiting for painting supplies when Tal slides across the stage on his knees as the music picks up. He skids to a stop at my feet, holding up the paintbrush I asked him to get for me while he was in the back. I laugh brightly and pluck the brush from his fingers. Yvaine crosses her arms over her chest. He continues his charade, and Niles hops down from the car to join him. Yvaine gets coiled up in the commotion and she's swatting at Niles while trying not to smile.

Soon, I am shrieking with laughter; Yvaine is, too, and we are batting the two of them off us as they crawl across the stage, acting like the ridiculous greasers do in the overhyped choreography. I stumble, and Tal catches me. I land on his knee with an arm around his shoulder, my head back with bright laughter.

The music ends, and I lift my head to find Charlotte staring at us, a look of stilled anger on her expression. I clear my throat and slide from Tal's knee, tucking my hair behind my ear as I go back to painting the set like I was supposed to have been doing.

❄

Opening night was supposed to be fun. I've never done anything like this before, and I was so excited to get on stage and really fall into the role of Rizzo—be someone else for an evening. Instead, I am sitting in the bathroom floor, my heart cracked in two as tears ruin my carefully crafted stage makeup.

To be fair, I didn't think breaking up with Charlotte would hurt this much. Well, she broke up with me. When she cornered me and asked me about Talien, I thought I answered her questions correctly. I thought I'd done a good job of telling her I cared about her.

But when she asked if I'd be willing to stop talking to him, my answer was quick and sure.

"Absolutely not. He's my best friend."

"I'm your girlfriend," she said. "I should be more important."

I gaped at her and tried to find the words she wanted to hear, but I couldn't.

"He's too important to me," was all I managed. She threw the necklace I'd given her at me and stormed away.

Now, I am sitting here alone, and the show starts in twenty minutes.

I hear footsteps and suck in a breath as I reach up for paper towels to blot my eyes with. I don't want anyone to see me like this. I pull myself to my feet and turn to the mirror, hopeful to pass as just washing my hands so whoever it is can ignore me.

The door creaks open.

"Firefly, you in there?"

I hold my breath; my muscles stiffen as I try to categorize my emotions on the current predicament. I don't really want anyone to see me like this, but I'd be lying to myself if I hadn't been wishing Tal was here since Charlotte left me alone.

"Yeah." I try to keep my voice steady, but it cracks with tears as they spill over my cheeks.

His tousled hair comes around the corner of the door first, and his brow knits with worry.

"Hey, what happened?"

Talien steps into the room and crosses to me in a few quick strides. He lifts a hand to brush away my tears but hesitates before his skin touches mine. Instead, he covers his knuckle with his sleeve and soaks the tears with fabric.

Even that amount of consideration makes my heart lurch. No one else is ever so careful about touching me. I wear long sleeves and gloves to protect my magic from the careless, but Tal is always paying attention.

It makes me cry harder.

I know now why this hurts so much.

It's not that Charlotte broke up with me. It's that she saw through my feelings for Tal. Feelings I have been trying to bottle up for so long because they simply cannot exist. I can't even really be friends with him. My family is out there right now, and if they found me here like this, the consequences would be catastrophic.

It fills me with rage. The Vales have no grudge against me or my family, really. They don't like my dad, but he's not a nice person. I can't understand why Lionel is so hell-bent on keeping this feud alive. But I know I can't so much as ask him without risking the Vales.

"It's stupid," I say as I shake my head.

I try to suck in my breath, stiffen my spine and gather my tears, but I fear I just look like a frustrated toddler who can't get control of herself.

Talien's gaze softens.

"I guarantee it's not stupid," he chides as he scans me. "Do I need to beat someone up? Yvaine will shut down this whole production if we need to, you know."

"No," I sputter a laugh and sniffle, wiping the rest of my tears away with the paper towels. "None of that. Charlotte broke it off."

Talien's expression blanks for a second. He blinks. I swear the seconds stretch longer than usual before he speaks again.

"What?" The disbelief in his voice catches me off guard. "Why? What—I thought—Cass, I'm so sorry."

"It's fine, I'm fine."

I try my best to gather myself, tip my chin, and clear my tears as I meet his eye, but the concern I see shimmering there cracks my resolve again.

Those beautiful eyes get me every time.

My heart fissures, and my face crumples again. I can't stop the way my body folds in on itself. He's close enough to catch me, though. Tal stabilizes my frame with strong arms around my waist, and I curl my hands into my chest and bury my face in his shirt. He holds me there until the music in the pit starts. The show is about to begin. I pull away, and his arms fall.

"You need to be in the booth," I say, turning to look at myself in the mirror.

A complete disaster, but I think I can wipe the black mascara from my cheeks and get away with it until I can get to the makeup room and touch everything up. I don't give him a chance to stop me. I can't handle it. I don't have time. I squeeze his arm and offer a quick thank you before running out into the hall to take my place backstage.

NOVEMBER—SENIOR YEAR

Why are you so upset about it? It's not like he
won't be hanging out with us.

Yvaine's text makes me angrier. I feel unheard and ridiculous, and if I could explain to anyone why I am so upset, I would, but I can't, and I am furious.

> We promised the four of us would go together. It's our last winter formal and no one was supposed to have a date.

> You're going to run out of chances to tell him how you feel if you're not careful.

God damn her.

> ...Why are you like this?

> Do you want me to tell him?

> NO!

> Goodnight.

I toss the phone across my bed and flop back to stare at the ceiling. I wish I could staunch the ache in my chest, but it's been there for what feels like years, and I am not sure it's ever going to go away.

I stew in my own angst for a while before I sigh and pick up my book. Better to lose myself in someone else's romance than wallow over my lack thereof.

A couple of chapters blow by before I hear a "tink, tink, tink" against the French door over my balcony.

I sit rod straight, closing the book as I listen cautiously. Maybe I am hearing things.

But no, it happens again. This time, I see little pebbles fly over the railing and click against the glass—three in a row.

My heart lodges in my throat, and I leap from my bed to pull the doors open. I hurl my head over the stone banister, my curls rustling in the frigid wind, my brow shooting to my hairline, and my stomach twists into knots as my sights land on Talien.

He stands in the yard below my room, wearing only a heavy sweater and jeans. He blows hot air over his hands to keep them warm. As I appear, he beams up at me. The smile on his face does nothing to calm the fluttering wings around my heart. I beg the infuriating thing to take a landing. I cannot handle this.

"What in the hell are you doing?" *I hiss on as quiet a shout as I possibly can.*

My eyes scan the yard for any sign that he's been spotted. I don't hear the alarm, and all the lights in the house I can see are still off. Mom and Dad must still be sleeping, but he'll murder Tal if he finds him here. Fear coats my tongue.

"You haven't answered any of my texts," he whisper-shouts back, grinning like an idiot.

Why is he looking at me like that? It only makes me more furious.

"Because I am angry with you," I seethe. *"Oh my god, you shouldn't be here."*

Nerves twist in my core, and that heady feeling from my chest bleeds over my resolve. I feel dizzy. The flurry of emotion is almost too much for me to bear.

"Why are you angry?" he asks, cocking his head to one side.

He knows why. The quirk of his brow and the set of his smile tell me as much. I don't want to offer an explanation, but the anger and fear burn hot enough to loosen my tongue. A string of Spanish curses fly from my lips as I lean over the banister.

"If you don't know, I can't help you. Go home *before you freeze to death."*

"You're jealous." Talien takes a step forward.

A knot in my core tightens, and I cannot control my tongue as more curses, this time a mix, fly from my mouth. His brow lifts as he lets me reel, that smile still fixed on his face.

"Jealous?!"

"Jealous," he mouths, using one infuriating finger to gesture at my display while sticking his nose in the air.

I gape at him, unable to bring words of either language to my lips. He's right, of course, but I didn't expect him to be so bold about it.

Talien only gets a moment of gloating in because the sprinkler system kicks on, and a line of water knocks him right in the side of his head. I jump as he yelps and dashes for the house, tucking his head into the collar of his sweater.

Panic wells up in my throat. The sprinklers aren't on a timer this late in the year. Someone had to have turned it on.

I can't see Talien, but I know he's up against the house, probably under the balcony. I pray he's not doing something stupid.

My phone pings with a message from Mom.

Your father is asleep. Keep it down.

Thank god. Mom knows about Talien and Niles. I broke down to her a couple months ago about how I feel. She's been supportive in secret. I breathe a sigh of relief as the three dots appear, and a second message comes through.

He can't spend the night.

I scoff a laugh. As though, in any realm, that would be happening. I turn my attention back to the balcony and hang over the edge but find no sign of him.

"Talien?" I whisper as loud as I can manage.

There's a rustling below me, followed by a muffled curse, and then I see his dark hair in the mess of ivy covering the side of the house.

"¿Estás subiendo por mi pared?" My words string together on a furious hiss of frustration.

Talien grunts, and his face appears.

"I assume you're being rude again," he whisper-yells, hauling himself up another arms-length. "It's very unhelpful."

I groan miserably, though that flutter in my heart betrays the firm façade my frustration has taken on. I have to bite down on my lip to keep a smile suppressed.

Though worry coats my breastbone as I listen to him struggle with the ice-slickened vines.

"And what happens when you fall and break your neck?"

"I'm not going to fall and—" he grunts again as he gets a hand on the edge of the balcony and pulls himself up over the railing, "—break my neck."

Talien looks entirely too pleased with himself. He's soaked from the sprinklers, leaving his dark hair plastered to his forehead. Water drips down his cheeks and off his jaw, and his once white sweater is covered in twigs and leaves from his climb. He sets his hands on his hips and huffs. I cross my arms over my chest and set my expression as best as I can as I take him in.

"Why the fuck are the sprinklers on in November?"

"Mom has a sense of humor."

Talien chuckles, glancing down at the yard where the sprinklers have conveniently stopped spraying. I should invite him in. He is going to freeze, especially now that he's sopping wet. I can already see frost forming over his shoulder, and he doesn't do a very good job containing the chill that wracks his body.

But then Talien Vale would be in my bedroom.

I am suddenly vibrantly aware of the midriff tank top and shorts pajama set I am wearing under my too-big cardigan. Not because it's cold, I can't feel that over the vibrating emotions, but because it is very likely that within the next few moments, Talien Vale will be in my bedroom, and I look like this.

"What's the plan here, Tal?"

I should not have drawn his attention back to me.

"Admit it," he teases, sweeping his hair off his forehead.

"Oh, my god," I roll my eyes and turn over my shoulder back into the warmth of my room, leaving the door open for him to follow.

I beeline for the bedroom door and turn the lock with nimble fingers.

When I turn around, Talien Vale is, in fact, standing in my bedroom with one eyebrow quirked at me, eying the door.

"Mom has a sense of humor. Dad, most certainly, does not," I say.

"Ah."

Talien's attention wanders, his eyes flicking around the room.

My cheeks burn, and I pull my cardigan closed as though covering my exposed skin will also shield the very personal space within these four walls he is getting a plain view of. Never in a million years did I think this particular fantasy would come to fruition.

If I had, I would have at least cleaned up the pile of once-worn clothes over my desk chair.

I break my attention, unable to contain the nervous energy any longer and move to my closet. Before a few moments pass, I've found the oversized sweater I am looking for, and I turn to throw it in his direction. He catches it as it hits him in the chest.

"Thanks," he says, eying me with another smirk, setting the sweater on the bed.

It takes me until the second his hand reaches the bottom of his sweater to realize my mistake. In one fluid motion, Tal strips off the garment.

OhygodTalienValeisshirtlessinmyroom.

I bite down on my cheek and turn my eyes to the ceiling, though not before they get a good fill of the very surprising sculpt of muscle over his abdomen. God fucking hell.

"*What are you doing, Tal?*" *I ask, my voice stretched in a sing-song.*

I'm not doing a very good job of hiding the clear emotional turmoil I am in, but I'm not sure it matters at this point. I don't know how I got here.

"*Putting on the sweater you gave me. What are* you *doing? Is the ceiling that interesting all of a sudden?*"

"*Oh my god, I'm going to kill you,*" *I mutter.*

Talien laughs.

"*I'm decent. You can look now,*" *he assures me.*

I meet his eye again, and I'm not sure what to say. Words escape me. This was not at all how I pictured this evening. I tuck my hair behind my ears, and my cardigan falls open again, dropping over one shoulder. I pull it back up and shrug expectantly.

"*I'm* not *jealous,*" *I say, though my tone is not as convincing as I'd like it to be.*

"*Uh huh,*" *Talien snickers.*

I groan, crossing my arms over my chest again. It's clear he isn't going to say much else. He waits for me to speak with that infuriatingly playful light to his eye.

"*Fine. I'm upset because it's our last formal, and you have a date.*"

Talien peers at me from under his brow.

"*Look me in the eye and tell me that if Aiko Yagami had asked Yvaine to that dance, you wouldn't be beside yourself with excitement for her.*"

"*I—*" *I begin, but those words get stuck as well.*

I can't say that because I know as well as he does that it isn't true.

"*That's what I thought,*" *he says, looking pleased with himself.*

Irritation flares, and I am able to take a breath again.

"*And what happens if I am jealous?*" *My voice comes out with more confidence than I expected.*

"*What do you want to happen?*" *Talien asks, dropping his*

hands into his pockets and backing himself up until his knees hit the edge of my bed and he drops to a seat.

That traitorous muscle in my chest leaps to attention. Adrenaline spins my focus.

And now he's on my bed.

Oh god, how I've spent entire evenings dedicating myself to this fantasy. Except it's not a fantasy. Somehow, this is real. I can't stop my feet as they carry me to the bed after him. I am floating on a hazed, fractured, imaginary vision of this moment. I sit down, leaving some distance between us, and fix my gaze on his.

Those eyes scramble my thoughts every damn time.

"Does it matter?" *I ask, my tone hushed.*

His brow furrows and clears in a visual flurry of confusion.

"Of course, it matters," *he says, somewhat breathless.* "Why wouldn't it matter?"

My heart lurches. I can see a reflection of what I feel in his expression. I have been trying so hard to keep this at bay, convince myself that my feelings are unrequited. But this display of his is making that increasingly more difficult.

I don't know what to say. I can't track a single thought to a coherent sentence to offer.

"I'm jealous," *I finally manage with a soft shrug of one shoulder.*

My nerves are vivid, and I am gripping the edge of my cardigan with white-knuckled fists.

"I KNEW it!"

Talien shoots off the bed in a display of victory. He catches his outburst before it makes too much noise, though, and turns back to me. He flops back on the bed beside me, careful not to bump into me as he lounges on his side and sets his cheek on his hand.

I can't help but notice that the hem of the gray sweater I gave him has ridden up in his frolicking and exposed the low muscles of his abdomen.

"Now that we have that out of the way," *he chuckles.* "What. Do. You. Want?"

I can't help but laugh at how ridiculous he is being. I like how giddy he is. I am reluctant to admit it and let go of my frustration, but this mood looks good on him. As usual, I find it impossible to keep my own bliss at bay with him so near.

I want to answer him. I wish I felt even a touch as confident as he seems.

"You tell me what you want. What did you expect coming here in the middle of the night like this?"

His expression blanks for a moment. Then he shrugs.

"I don't know," he admits. "Yvaine said you weren't answering my texts because you were mad I said yes to Celena, and I just kind of...got in the car."

God damn it, Yvaine.

He thinks for a second and then sits up.

"I want you to go to the dance with me."

"What?" I gape at him.

"What do you mean 'what?' That was pretty straightforward."

"Oh my god, what is happening?" I mutter mostly to myself as I press my fingers to the bridge of my nose, "What about Celena?"

"Who?"

"Talien, your date!" I exclaim as I shove at his shoulder.

"Oh fuck, yeah." He shakes his head and looks mortified at his momentary lapse. "I'll call her on the way home," he says, waving a hand.

I'm not sure I'm ready to let the excitement free just yet. It presses against my resolve. My knee bounces against the bed.

"Just like that? You want to go to the dance with me?"

Then what?

I don't want to think about that.

"Just like that," he echoes, grinning from ear to ear.

"Okay, but like— okay, I'm afraid I'm having trouble reading your mind this evening. Go to the dance like how we were originally going to go to the dance or..."

"Or like a DATE date?"

"Yes," I say, still feeling relatively hesitant to lean into this feeling.

"Oh, date date," he confirms, bouncing his foot.

I bite down on my bottom lip, and a smile stretches free as bliss finally breaks my resolve.

"Okay," I release a breath, "a date date."

My phone buzzes in my pocket, and I pull it out to see a message from Mom.

Your father is awake.

Fear strikes a match again, and I suck in a breath through my teeth as I jump to my feet, grabbing at his sweater to haul him after me.

"You have to go. Now." My words are back to a hushed whisper.

If Dad is already out of bed to check on me, we have less than 45 seconds before he crosses the halls to my room.

"Okay, okay," he chuckles, scrambling to obey. "You're going to return my texts again now, right?"

"Yes, just move," *my strained tone is a plea as I shove him along.*

He laughs again. I am not finding anything about this funny. We're out on the balcony, and he hauls himself over, already lowering himself quietly.

"Please be careful," I whisper, peering over the edge.

His hands are still on the banister, and he hauls his weight to pop up again. It's only long enough to pull a gasp from my lungs as his lips meet mine. My eyes stretch wide, and my magic sparks to life as my crest lights, a quick response to the electricity from his kiss.

It doesn't last long before he pulls away, leaving me stunned, speechless, gaping at his giddy, crooked smile and glittering eyes.

"See you tomorrow," he whisper-yells before disappearing over the edge.

I don't have time to watch him scale the wall. I turn on my heel and close the doors as quietly as I can behind me. I sprint across the room to unlock the door as silently as I can manage before launching into my bed. There is barely enough time to open my book before the door handle turns. I am forced to hold my breath in lieu of catching it.

"Cassiopeia, it's two in the morning; why is your light still on?" Lionel asks, his tone firm but heavy with sleep.

I wiggle my book with a raised brow.

He reaches in to flip the switch on my lamp with a terse expression.

"It's time to sleep. We have a big day ahead of us."

I nod and pull the covers up, setting my book down on my nightstand. It isn't until I can no longer hear his footsteps down the hall that I finally take a breath.

My phone buzzes.

Talien:

Thanks for the sweater

It looks better on you anyway.

I curl into my pillows with a lighter heart than I expected to be possible.

That bliss-filled evening is one of the last I remember having that level of connection with Tal. Things were good for a few weeks. My mom invited him over for cookies just after that night, but I don't have a clear vision of the winter formal itself. My memory did not hold onto it well. I know I had been excited, and Tal had been....somewhere else.

Then it was never really the same. I never had the courage to ask about it; the silent rejection hurt enough. He took someone else to prom, and I got sucked into Bryson's sinkhole of domestic stress.

We stayed friends. I always thought I'd just misread something. Or maybe he just changed his mind. And I'd brushed it off because it was safer that way. He was safer. Lionel would have nothing to ruin.

We remained close even up until that night at the train station, the night Bryson lost control. I told him I didn't want to get married. It was never my choice. I thought I was doing the right thing, breaking things off civilly.

But Bryson proved to be more than I had prepared for.

I was terrified. I begged Tal to leave with me. I told him how scared I was of Bryson, my father. He barely heard me. I remember him freaking out about my face. Bryson did a number on me then, too. But I didn't care. I just wanted to leave. My mother set up an apartment under a false name in the city for me. But I couldn't leave him. On my knees, I begged. It was the desperate plea of a broken woman at the time, and I was sure he'd say no, but he agreed.

And he left me standing alone at that station, bruised and battered in more ways than one. I spent so long angry with him, but honestly, I was mostly relieved to know he was free of the danger simply being near me put him in.

Not anymore.

I don't know what Lionel did to his family, but it can't be good, and he didn't stand me up. He wanted to follow me.

He was in the hospital.

My chest hurts. Turning over those memories, walking through our entire relationship like that did nothing to sort my thoughts. It did, however, remind me of how deeply I've always felt for that man sleeping soundly in the other room. How desperately I've always needed to be near him.

God, I don't know what I am supposed to do, but I know that my life feels empty without Tal in it.

Fuck, I hope Niles knows what they're doing.

CHAPTER 33
Talien

The smell of coffee drags me out of the bedroom, leaving Cass to shower and take her time waking up. It's past noon, but I feel like I could have slept another ten hours.

As I pad across the floor, I can't help but run over the chaos of the last few days in my mind. I went from feeling like I had lost Cass all over again to soaring to heights I'd never let myself dream of to being tucked away—kidnapped for our own safety—in a cabin in the mountains. Never would I have believed *this* was how my weekend was going to go, but here we are.

Niles reclines at the little bistro table tucked into the bay window overlooking the snow-covered mountains. As I pour my coffee and turn to set a hip against the counter, they slap their newspaper down on the glass tabletop and glare at me.

Who even reads the papers anymore?

"Good morning," I offer when it becomes clear they have no intention of initiating this conversation despite the intensity of their scowl.

"You might be the stupidest person I know," Niles states.

"Wow, okay."

"Honestly, are we even friends? Do I even *know* you, Talien?" Their voice pitches.

"Of course, you know me," I assure them, feeling too severely exhausted for this. "What are you talking about?"

"*Why?*" they demand. "Why didn't you come to me? You know I could have fixed this. You know how much power there is behind my family name. Why in the fucking hell would you have chosen to let him ruin your family when *I could have done something?*"

"Niles, I—"

"You're either stupid or so fucking proud you can't get your head out of your own asshole long enough to ask your *best friend* to give your family a *place to stay* or fucking *jobs* while you get back on your feet."

I chew my cheek. They deserve to be this angry. They've been there for me through everything that I've let them be, and I should have trusted them. That mistake has weighed on me almost as heavily as letting Cass go.

"Well, which is it, Vale?" they press. "And keep in mind, I know your IQ."

"I'm sorry, Niles. You're right," I admit, letting the guilt settle heavy on my shoulders. I never wanted to hurt them. "I should have come to you. I didn't because—a lot of reasons, but none of them are good enough. I wanted to be able to fix it myself—and you had so much going on after you lost your mom—"

"Don't use that woman as an excuse. You know better."

"I do. At the time, you just had so much on your plate—" They give me another sharp look, so I hurry my point along. "I didn't want to burden you with the problems I'd made for myself."

"You didn't make shit for yourself," Niles protests, untangling their long legs to get to their feet and stride to the French doors that lead out onto the balcony.

Obediently, I trail behind them, sliding on some of the boots next to the door before stepping out into the cold.

In the frosty air, Niles' temper subsides a little, and they draw in a deep, centering breath.

"I'm livid," they inform me. "I may never forgive you, jackass, so I hope you enjoyed our friendship while it lasted."

I can't help but roll my eyes at the sarcasm dripping off their tone as I lean my elbows on the railing and gaze past the steaming rim of my coffee cup to the snow-capped treetops below.

"I understand why you thought you had to do it alone."

I'm surprised by the reflectiveness in their tone and turn to watch their ink-black brow pinch over sharp eyes.

"When Mom died, I didn't want anyone to see me as incapable. There has always been so much riding on all of our families. Sinclair, Varner, Vale—it doesn't matter, we all had the pressure of those names on our shoulders. Maybe that's why we became such good friends, huh?"

"How do you explain Yvaine?" I chuckle.

"She's a Sagittarius."

I laugh outright.

"But seriously," Niles continues, the somber tone of their voice is hushed under the blanket of the icy mountains, "I didn't ask any of you for help after Mom. Cass offered. Yvaine tried to distract me with movie nights and books. You were at my side every chance you could be, but I didn't let any of you in."

"You never have," I observe, realizing this is the most Niles has spoken about their mother's passing to me since their eulogy.

Sure, they've mentioned her now and again or commented on the things they know she'd appreciate if she were alive to see them, but they've never truly opened the door to what it felt like to lose her.

They nod, tears pricking their eyes as they tug their oversized cardigan tightly around themselves.

"Just felt like something I was supposed to be able to handle, you know?"

"You were just a kid."

They shrug. "I didn't think I was."

Ice glitters and the faint sound of snow falling out of the trees whenever a bird lands or a squirrel leaps from one branch to the other fills the silence between us for a while. My nose is cold, and my mug is barely hanging on to the heat from my coffee when Niles speaks again.

"You let me believe your dad's business just went under," they say, sounding astonished.

"I know," I groan. "I wanted to tell you."

"Oh, save it."

"No, really. Especially after we lost the house—"

"I knew something was up when your mom had to give up that house."

"Yeah…"

"You told me your dad had taken out a second mortgage on it that he bankrupted on when the business went under."

I wince. "The bones of that are true."

"Varner just forced the issue?"

"Yeah."

Another stillness settles between us, but this one doesn't drag like the last.

"Have you told her what happened?"

"Fuck," I groan. "No."

"TALIEN!"

"Listen, I know! I'm trying; she's been through a lot."

Niles rolls their eyes so dramatically I swear I can hear it.

"Did you listen to a goddamned thing I just said to you, you ignorant dipshit?"

"Yes, but thi—"

"No. This is *not* different," they snap, shoving a slender finger between my eyes. "Tell her. Sit down. And. Talk. To. Her." They punctuate every word with another prick between my eyebrows.

Sighing heavily through my nose, I let their words sink in.

"I will."

I don't want to add to her worries about her father. I know she's scared for my safety, for what Lionel might do to further drive the Vale name out of *his* city, what he might do to drive me away from Cass. But Niles is right; Cass deserved to know the truth long ago and keeping it from her is the reason we're here in the first place.

I just don't quite know how to open that door.

CHAPTER 34

Cassiopeia

"**S**top flapping your fucking arms and do *something else*," Yvaine screeches over a cacophony of joyous shouts and jibes from the rest of us.

She's reached the level of frustration that gets that vein in her forehead to stand out. Niles flails at the front of the room, trying to mime out whatever word is on their charade card.

When teams were divided, the two of them had no choice but to pair up. Seti had to go back to Newbury for work; Mr. and Mrs. Vale are an obvious duo. So are Nadia and Sophia, and Tal and I, for that matter.

I am honestly glad for it because this is hilarious.

And Tal and I are kicking ass.

The little hourglass on the coffee table is about to run out of sand, and Yvaine groans while Nadia and Tal both jeer at her, trying to keep her distracted. Vasiliki is laughing so hard her face is tomato red, she's holding on to her husband's sweater for dear life. Niles starts jumping, pulling their knees into their chest with an urgent expression on their face.

"A fighter pilot!" Yvaine finally yells.

"TIME!" Nadia shouts, scooping the hourglass off the table.

Niles and Yvaine both groan miserably, and I catch sight of

Tal's profile. His arm is draped over me, holding me close, and his expression is lifted with a kind of carefree bliss that has the ability to lift boulders from my heart.

"A FIGHTER PILOT?" Niles implores, slumping dramatically so that their too-long arms almost touch the rug. "Fighter pilot? Honestly, Yvaine?"

Niles flips their paper around to reveal the neatly printed "stork" on their card and flicks it at Yvaine's head.

"How did you not get that one, Yvaine? I thought Niles rocking like a baby was a dead giveaway."

Talien chuckles while his fingers trace little patterns on my shoulder. A shiver snakes my spine and I hum pleasantly as the sensation raises chill bumps over my arms. His touch does well to distract me from the ache still throbbing over my injured cheek. As if on instinct, I lean into him, and his cinnamon and bergamot fragrance floods my senses.

"I don't know how I am supposed to get anything if they won't change what they're doing!" Yvaine protests. "This game is infuriating."

I huff a laugh and roll my eyes as I lean forward to grab a card for my turn.

"You get mad at anything you're not immediately good at," I say with a soft shrug as I stand to take my place. "The rest of us are having fun, so suck it up, buttercup."

Tal looks at me with focus etched into his expression, his fingers steepled over his lips, a vivid smile in his eye. Nadia flips the timer. I raise my arms above my head and lift to my tiptoes.

"Ballerina," Talien says before Nadia has time to set the timer back down on the table.

"Yes," I say with a smug tip of my nose and toss the card dramatically as I spin on my heel.

"God damn it!" Yvaine shouts, "How are you two doing that?"

I offer a coy shrug and shuffle back to my seat. Talien just beams at me as he opens his arms to welcome me again.

"Don't take it too hard, darling," Vas pipes up, getting to her feet to take her turn. "They can't help it."

Talien's mom winks at me as she pulls her card. After holding it at arm's length to read it, Vasiliki nods, and the timer starts. She makes a good show of strumming a guitar and dancing to a soundless melody. Nicholas squints at his wife for a moment, clearly soaking in her free-spirited nature, before offering his guess. He's right, of course, and the play passes on to Sophia.

She and Nadia have a harder time, but not nearly as bad as Yvaine and Niles. Nadia guesses Sophia's lyrical demonstration of synchronized swimming just before the timer runs out, and we are all in tears; my stomach aches from buckling laughter.

"I'm not going," Yvaine says grumpily, crossing her arms over her chest.

Talien cackles. Niles tosses their hands up in the air and kicks up to their feet again.

"Either you go, or I do," they announce, reaching for a card.

"God, no!" Yvaine rolls her eyes with a groan. "That's worse. I'll do it."

She moves to the spotlight, looking as uncomfortable as I have ever seen her. I do appreciate what she's putting herself through. We started this game mostly to distract me from everything, and although it is impossible to let go of the dread completely, it does feel pretty far off. I am grateful for her willingness to try to play along despite her aggravated protesting.

She reads her card, and her expression twists into disgust.

Nadia flips the timer.

Yvaine sticks one arm up in the air.

That's all. She does nothing else. She doesn't so much as change her expression.

"Chimney!" Niles shouts at the top of their lungs.

She shakes her head with a tight jaw and stretches her arm higher, this time walking around in a tight circle.

I genuinely have no idea what she thinks she's doing.

"WINDMILL!" Niles cries. "PENCIL! GIRAFFE! SCUBA DIVER! Fuck! Do something different! God!"

Over the course of their screeching, Niles melts off of their chair into a pile on the floor. I don't think I've ever laughed harder in my life. I have to grip Talien's thigh to stabilize myself as I double over. He is laughing just as hard.

"TIME!" Nadia yells.

"How is that enough time?!" Yvaine shouts.

"What was it?" I manage to ask as I wipe tears from my eyes.

"An ostrich," she says, her tone terse.

"A fucking ostrich," Niles whimpers from their puddle on the floor.

"I would've guessed 'ostrich,'" Talien teases, laughing and poking the crumpled remains of Niles with his foot.

I laugh so hard I think I might throw up. Beside me, Talien is struggling to his feet, wiping tears from his eyes as he continues to fight off fits of laughter. Once he's composed himself enough to see again, he takes a card and moves to the center of the rug.

Talien giggles as he reads his card and nods. Nadia flips the timer, and he sticks both arms out to the side, sways slightly, and then pulls his arms close to his chest and makes a staccato sound in time with his pulsing arms.

"Fighter pilot!" I shout.

"Yes!" Talien beams.

"You can't make a sound!" Niles shrieks, flying to their feet again. "You cheated!"

Talien laughs, throwing up his hands.

"I would have guessed it anyway," I say, waving them off.

"That's it, we're done!" Yvaine shouts, moving to swipe the cards off the table.

"Wait, no!" I say over a laugh.

"I'll do another," Talien says. "I just got caught up in the moment."

"Does it matter? You two are ten points ahead of everyone!" Yvaine protests.

"I say you have to forfeit all your points because you cheated," Niles chimes in, looking smug.

Talien rolls his eyes. "That's a bit extreme. I made one tiny noise."

"You made a VERY accurate fighter pilot sound that was a CLEAR and BLATANT disregard for the rules. You lose your turn and forfeit your points." Niles snatches the card from Talien's stunned hand and passes the box of cards to Nicholas.

"Your turn, Mr. Vale."

"Fine," I say, swishing my hair over my shoulder. I reach out a hand for Tal, and he obliges my silent request to come sit near me again. "We'll get them back."

And we do. By the end of the game Talien and I still win with three points over his parents. Yvaine and Niles come in dead last with only three points out of what has to have been more than twenty rounds.

It's fun—so much fun, and it feels so free to be like this. I find myself melting further into Tal as the night goes on. His frame provides a stable surface to rest my weight, and he carries it well. He spends the evening offering gentle touches, keeping me close, and toying with my hair over my shoulder. I spend it soaking him in, memorizing every angle his smile can shift into. I keep a hand on his knee, drape my legs over his, anything to stay close.

After we cleanup, Yvaine asks me to help in the kitchen while she gets the cocoa ready for everyone, and Tal stays behind to talk to his parents.

"Have you talked to him?" she asks the moment the kitchen door closes behind us.

"Right for the gut punch, huh?" I ask with a miserable sigh.

To be fair, I expect that of her. I should have been more prepared for her questions. I just got so lost in the bliss.

"I'll take that as a 'no.'"

"I tried."

"Okay," she says with a note of finality.

I furrow my brow at her unusual lack of free-flowing opinion.

"Okay?"

She shrugs. "Yeah. Okay. What do you want me to say?"

"I don't know, something matter of fact and blunt, usually," I say as I take a bite of the baklava Vas brought with her. The sticky sweet coats my tongue, and I hum with approval. It's been so long since I've had Vas's signature treat.

Yvaine levels her gaze at me as she pulls mugs for everyone from the cabinet and begins to prepare the hot cocoa.

"I changed my mind."

"What?" I ask and set the sweet back down to meet her eye, my brow furrowed with confusion.

"You heard me. I changed my mind. I think you should stick it out."

"Yvaine," I say, my tone weighted with pain. I don't know how to bring words to the sting of my reality.

"No, hear me out. That man is irrevocably in love with you."

My heart aches. I wasn't prepared to hear those words out loud. I have to work quickly to staunch the free-flowing emotion before it cracks my chest.

"Lionel—"

"Lionel can eat a dick," she bites. "Don't be stupid, Cass."

"I'm not," I say, my tone more firm.

She quirks a brow and lifts the tray of now full mugs of hot chocolate. I'm not sure how she worked so quickly.

"You better be sure of that," she warns before swishing from the room to bring the comforting drink out to our companions.

Her departure leaves me with an unwelcome hole in my chest.

CHAPTER 35

Talien

I t's entirely too early for this shit.

Ahead of me, Niles is trudging through the freshly fallen snow. Their brightly colored parka is almost as offensive as the frost biting my nose and fingers. The sun isn't even up. I want to be in bed. I want to still be curled around Cass, listening to her sleepy little murmurs and the occasional snores. I want to feel her nestle into my chest as she presses her hips back into mine.

"Remind me again, why are we traipsing through the cold before I've had my coffee?" I groan.

"Because it's good for your soul," Niles pipes, their breath pluming in the morning air.

"And sunrise is the most magical time of day," Yvaine says, her tone cheerier than I have ever heard.

It spreads a warmth over my chest. She really is a morning person.

Peering over my shoulder, I catch a glimpse of Cass's bright smile as she hollers for Yvaine to come look at whatever she found in the frosty trees. She's beautiful, radiant in the pale colors of dawn, a goddess grounded to grace us with her light.

Okay, maybe the early morning hike isn't all bad.

Niles is ahead now but waits for me to catch up at the crest of the next hill, looking exhilarated from the frigid air.

"So, did you talk to her?" they ask, keeping an eye on the girls behind me.

"Not yet," I admit, adjusting the Velcro on my gloves.

Niles's face falls. "Why the fuck not?"

God, I have tried. I tried when she stumbled into the kitchen yesterday morning looking like a sleepy siren that just emerged from the sea and decided plaid jammies and fluffy socks were the ideal attire—which they *are* if you happen to be a siren hiding away in a cabin. My conversation with Niles had bolstered some of my confidence, but when she snuggled up next to me on the couch with her coffee and her sleepy voice, the amber and sage scent of her chased away every brain cell I had left.

I tried to talk to her after lunch when we happened to find ourselves alone while my parents went for a walk with Nadia and Sophia; Niles disappeared to attend some virtual meetings, and Yvaine decided to call Seti and make sure she made it home safely. It only took a flirty comment from Cass to scatter my thoughts again. We spent the entirety of Yvaine's twenty-minute call with her girlfriend, acting like teenagers making out on their parent's sofa after school.

I tried again after charades when we sat gathered around the fireplace telling stories until Cass and I were the only two who hadn't turned in for the night, but the words got stuck. They didn't feel right after such a beautiful evening full of laughter. Cass led me to bed when the embers burned low, and I tried again to get my tongue to cooperate once we were cuddled together in the dark, but she tucked her head against my chest, hummed with bliss, and drifted off to sleep almost instantly.

I shrug at Niles. "I don't know. I'm trying."

"Try harder," they grump at me. "I swear to god, if you don't tell her soon, I will. She deserves to know what he did to you—to your family."

My chest twists. I know they're right.

"Especially after what he did to her," I agree.

Niles nods as the girls get closer.

"What if I lose her?" I whisper. The words spoken aloud make me feel like the mountain is caving in under my feet.

Their eyes cut to mine, and their lips flicker in a smile. "Talien," they say, their voice full of gentle scolding, "you and Cass are soul mates. I don't think there's a power on this planet that could actually keep you two away from each other forever. And Lionel fucking Varner sure as hell can't."

"She's afraid of him," I protest.

Niles scoffs. "He's a punk-ass bitch. He'll get what's coming to him."

"I hope so," I say as Cass looks up from her boots and catches me staring.

Okay, waking before the sun *was* worth it. Niles hikes us out to an overlook where we can see the river snaking through the snow-covered mountains as the sun climbs over the peaks and bathes the white landscape in pink and orange hues. Cass nestles into my chest; her puffy coat bundles up around her chin as she glances at me with a sleepy smile.

"I honestly can't believe this is real," she sighs and reaches to brush some stray hair that has fallen over my brow.

"The view?" I ask, studying her face.

"No," she says with a smile and a scrunch of her nose. "This, you. I've spent a lot of time thinking about everything, and this just doesn't feel like it should be real."

I want to tell her now, get all the things off my chest that have been eating me away for so long. I want to pour my heart out to her. To finally let her see me wholly—like she did before everything changed.

I don't get the chance.

Something cold, firm, and wet impacts the back of my head.

Snow glitters down around us in the sunlight. A little stunned, I turn and find Niles and Yvaine standing suspiciously angled towards us instead of the beautiful sunrise, backs straight as telephone poles.

Niles's lips are folded in comically as they hold back a laugh. At the sign of my displeased scowl, they sheepishly point to Yvaine.

"Yvaine!" Cass shouts over a playful laugh.

"What? We didn't come here to play 'love birds.' Five minutes before you start making out, that's all I ask." She flits her fingers, her crest lighting a deep purple under her skin, and a creaking overhead turns our attention up to find the bough of a pine tree just above, moving with the swift kick of her magic.

Cass yelps and dives out of the way before a blanket of snow plops over our heads—or, *my* head, rather. The weight of the snow takes me to the ground. Cass's laughter blooms and my heart feels full and warm despite the snow that found its way down the collar of my coat.

"DuPont, you better start running," I call as I scramble out of the bank.

"Or what, Vale?" Yvaine taunts back as she takes a backward step.

She has a genuine smile on her face, one that reminds me of what it was like for the four of us to be like this years ago.

I dust my coat off and level a gloved finger at her.

"Run."

Niles shrieks and dives for cover behind a nearby log as I duck to scoop up a handful of snow and pack it tightly. I rear back as Yvaine takes another step away, but before I have a chance to launch the thing, another sharp sting of packed ice hits me squarely in the cheek. I whip my head to find Cass dusting white from her gloves. A bright laugh splits the air as she tilts her head back.

"You filthy little traitor!" I protest, gaping at her.

Yvaine cackles, and Cass shrugs with a wide smile.

"What are you going to do about it?" she teases. The curl of her tongue over her teeth as she quirks a brow drives a deep-rooted need through my core. I *want* to do a lot of things about it.

Since the night in my apartment, Cass and I have slept together, but only in the actual definition of those words: sleeping in the same bed. I can't deny that my desire for her has been a constant for the past few days, but with everything she's been through—everything we've all been through and being crammed in a cabin with my sister's bedroom sharing a wall and my parents in the loft overhead, it hasn't been an option.

My gaze sweeps over her, letting her see every sinful thought coiling through my mind. I want to tackle her here, bury her in the snow, and kiss her until we're both breathless. Instead, I lob a snowball at her and duck the one thrown by Yvaine, which would have been another headshot.

The snow is the perfect consistency for packing quickly, and I manage to get another ball formed and launched before I get to cover behind one of the many pine trees. Niles shouts something and hands another ball to Yvaine.

"I'm coming for you, Firefly," I call over my shoulder while packing another ball.

"You'll have to catch me first!" she yells, dashing through the trees toward Niles's fort.

Cass dives behind the log with Niles just as Yvaine launches another snowball at my head. It breaks against the tree. I return fire, hitting Yvaine in the hip before darting to another tree, closer to the three of them.

"Three-on-one? Are you still that scared? It's been, what? Seven years?"

"Not long enough!" Yvaine shouts, her tone still lifted with that air of youthful glee.

"Glad to know I left an impression!"

Another snowball breaks against the tree. I wait for a second one to hit and then take off towards their fort.

Yvaine takes another hit in the stomach, but her snowball

cracks against the hood of my coat, narrowly missing my head again.

"Why do you always aim for the head, damn it," I shout, skidding across the ice.

"Yours is thick enough to take it!" Yvaine shouts back. A branch above me creaks again as she uses her magic to interfere.

"Cheater!" I yelp, trying to dodge out of the way of the falling snow, but it topples me into a heap again.

"Nice!" Niles cheers, popping up just long enough to hand Yvaine another snowball—I'm suddenly very suspicious about who actually started this whole thing.

My arm is just free enough from the drift to launch the one remaining snowball I have at Niles' smug face. It lands.

"Gah!" they shriek, toppling backward, clutching their chest as they dramatically fall back. "I'm hit! I'm hit!"

Cass laughs brightly, pops back up from behind the makeshift fort, and jogs over. She peers down at me.

"Surrender yet?" she asks through labored breaths, warm air pluming in front of her face.

"No," I inform her, snatching her wrist and pulling her down into the snow with me.

Cass lands on top of me, giggling. I draw her closer until our noses almost touch and let her see the heat in my gaze again.

"Now what, Firefly?"

"Now that you've caught me?" She feigns thought for a moment and continues with a coy tone of voice, "You put up a valiant fight; I think a reward might be in order."

"Oh? What kind of reward?" I ask, letting my gaze drop to her lips.

My entire body heats. I am painfully aware of the thigh she has draped between my legs, and certain she can feel the effect her words have on me. Her eyes flare to indicate that that is, in fact, the case, and she tilts her chin to catch my lips with hers.

I am lost. I swear, every time this woman touches me, I fall deeper and deeper into this feeling. It's overwhelming. My mouth is hungry for hers, and I meet her passion with my own. We've shared a few brief moments stolen between distractions, a few heated kisses since that night, a small taste of the inferno raging under my skin.

My tongue begs for entrance at her lips, and she parts them for me. My hands move to find the curve of her ass.

A frigid, ice-cold blanket of thick snow lands on top of us. It bites into my cheeks.

"Cool it, you two," Yvaine shouts, and Cass yelps, laughter breaking our kiss.

"Honestly," Niles chimes in, propping an elbow on the log and grinning at us, "get a fucking room already."

"We should get back to the hike our friends so kindly planned for us," Cass says through a breathless smile.

I groan in mock frustration.

"Fine. I guess I can collect on that reward later."

Her eyes flare, but I pull myself to my knees before helping her up to follow our friends back out to the trail.

CHAPTER 36

Talien

Snow crunches under my feet as I drape the last blanket over the nook I've carved out on the top of this ridge. I'd cleared the snow under the little square of space between the trees, and, at this point, I've checked to ensure everything is set a dozen times. The battery-powered electric blanket is on to warm the pallet, the tarp seems to be doing its job of keeping any lingering snow from soaking the blankets, and the thermoses full of cocoa are neatly tucked into place. The view of the star-speckled sky is vivid from right here. There are a dozen pillows and blankets piled into a cozy, romantic-looking heap. It's perfect.

And somehow not enough all at the same time.

Tonight is the night—no more excuses. No more letting myself get tongue-tied. I *have* to talk to her. I can't lose her again because of my own stupidity. If Cass and I are going to get through this, there can't be any more secrets.

Lionel may have been against this from the beginning; he may have done everything in his power to keep us apart, but I'll be damned if I let that man make another decision for me in this life. What Cass and I could've had, what we could be now, that's up to us—no one else.

I fuss with the arrangement of the bedding for a few more

274

minutes before I decide there is nothing more I can do, and hike back to the cabin.

Between the crunch of the snow and the repetition in my brain of all the things I want to say tonight, my thoughts drift.

SEPTEMBER—FRESHMEN YEAR

It doesn't matter how much I try to make the summer days drag out; the first day of school always comes. Thankfully, Niles and I have schedules that mostly align, and several of my teachers are close family friends—I guess being one of the founding families does have its perks.

I'm on my way to drop off my notes at my locker, but someone has beaten me to it.

A head of full, brown curls drops back along her shoulders, and books clatter to the ground at her Oxford leather feet. Her amber skin and warm eyes are flushed; she looks close to tears. Even so, she's gorgeous. I swear time stands still for a moment as her full lips mutter something in Spanish.

She moves, and the spell on me is somewhat broken. Scanning her, I can't help but notice the very *pristine maroon knee-highs with little bands of white around the top and the* very *steam-press matching maroon button-down tucked into a plaid skirt.*

Well, this should be interesting.

OCTOBER—FRESHMEN YEAR

Cassiopeia Varner has spent the better part of the semester trying to convince me that she's ignoring me. She's not even very good at it. I helped her find her way around school for the first week or so, and she sits with Niles and me at lunch, but the second the bell rings, it's like I don't exist anymore.

I beat her to the cafeteria today, which is unusual, but I spot her the moment she pops around the corner. She waves to both of us and gets in line.

"*Have you asked her out yet?*" Niles asks, peering into the compact mirror they've brought with them today.

Their crest glows turquoise as they summon enough magic to shift their eye color to a soft purple. They twist the front curl around their face, and the same lavender hue bleeds into the strands.

"*No,*" I inform them.

They are always fiddling with their appearance, warping their nose to be sharper or more hooked, or raising their cheekbones. I'd be lying if I said I wasn't a bit jealous of their ability. The Vales have never had crests, even dating back to when our city was founded. The Varners and Sinclairs and every other founding family possess varying levels of magical crests and abilities, but the Vales remain barren. Dad has always said that our strength comes from our lack of more "convenient" options. I guess I can understand what he means.

Still, I wouldn't mind being able to alter my nose or cheekbones on a whim.

"*Why not?*" Niles snaps their compact closed. "*Is this too matchy?*" they ask before I can answer their first question, gesturing to their hair and eyes.

"*No, it looks good,*" I inform them. "*And* because... *it's not that simple. What if Cass only sees me as a school friend? We never hang out outside of class.*"

"*Oh, so, you both being late to history because you're too busy chatting by the lockers for the last week straight doesn't count as 'hanging out outside of class,' then?*"

I shove their shoulder, which produces a wide grin.

"*Shut up.*"

"*Ask her out.*"

"*I can't!*" I say through my teeth as Cass turns toward us with her tray of food in her hands.

She doesn't make it, but a couple of feet before, one of the meatheads from the football team backs into her. Food flies, covering Cass in a coating of macaroni and cheese and wilted lettuce leaves from her salad.

The idiot has the audacity to snap at her about getting in his way.

I'm already on my feet when Cass's face flushes, and her look of shock shifts to rage. The cafeteria fills with rapid-fire insults in both of Cass's languages, and the almost six-foot-two jock wilts like the day-old salad at their feet. By the time she's through with him, he's hunched in his seat, apologizing profusely.

With a huff, Cass storms out of the room, leaving him to cower in peace.

"Damn," Niles says over my shoulder.

Damn is right.

I return to my seat, heart thundering, and a stupid smile plastered over my whole face I can't reign in.

God, she's perfect.

JANUARY—FRESHMEN YEAR

I am laughing at the ridiculous way Niles imitates the asshole jock football players that roam the halls like they own the school. They just finished marching through the gymnasium for this pointless pep rally. We're sitting in the bleachers in a sea of students, all just glad to be out of class for a while. The marching band plays. It's too loud, and Niles turns to glare at them for interrupting their charade as though the entire marching band cares at all.

Cass sits a row down facing me, her knees tucked into her chest. Yvaine kneels beside her, weaving a braid into Cass's hair at the base of her neck. Her smile is mesmerizing. The way her nose scrunches up as she laughs at Niles' boisterous display draws all the light in the room.

My attention is centered. The buzzing of the overhead lights, the blaring tubas, and even Niles' too-loud commentary fades. It might as well be just the two of us here—Cass and me.

She pokes fun at Niles and tries to shift her weight. Her hand misses the edge of the bleacher, and she loses her balance. Yvaine yelps with a laugh as she tries to steady Cass's impending tumble. I tense and reach out to help, but Yvaine catches her with a grip on her upper arm.

Above her glove.

Cass gasps, and her eyes widen as her intricate crest flares. I've seen other crests light from magic use, but never hers. Ordinarily, it's a soft pattern of richly hued lace across the warm amber of her forehead. Now, it's a dancing display of iridescent light. It's the most beautiful thing I've ever seen.

Like a firefly in a sea of swaying grass, twinkling like the starlight overhead.

Yvaine releases her and offers a quick apology. The gentle pulse of iridescent lights flickers and fades beneath her skin, leaving the beautiful patch of swirls to drift back to their natural, umber tone.

Niles catches my eye. Their lips are spread wide in a toothless grin and pressed so high under their nose they're almost touching the tip. I run a hand over my mouth and peel my gaze away, pointedly ignoring their attention.

My gaze drifts back over Cass's crest.

Firefly.

APRIL—FRESHMEN YEAR

"Now, tell me if you don't like it. I haven't quite gotten the recipe to be like Yiayá used to make, but I think this one is pretty good," Mom says, setting a plate in front of Cass.

We've been trying to study for the past hour, but Mom can't quite help herself and keeps starting up conversations with Cass. It would probably be a more productive study session if we weren't at the dining room table, but having Cass alone in my room isn't something I've worked up the nerve to suggest.

"Mom," I groan as Cass samples the third thing Mom has brought her since she got here an hour ago.

"Sorry, Honey," Mom says with a smile. "Last one, then I'll be quiet, I swear."

Cass, of course, tells her it's fantastic, and Mom, of course, preens like a mother bird at the praise.

"I like her," Mom whispers entirely too loud in my ear as she passes me on her way to the living room.

My cheeks heat, and I can't meet Cass's gaze for longer than a second or two for the remainder of our study session.

OCTOBER—SOPHMORE YEAR

"I'm no good at this game," Nadia whines, rolling the dice.

"No one is 'good' at this game," I protest. "It's just about chance. You're not supposed to be good."

"Your luck is abysmal, honestly," Cass teases as Nadia's dice still to reveal her round.

"I know!" Nadia groans. "Niles even beats me!"

"Once," I correct her. "Niles beat you once."

"Once was enough. My name is ruined. I'll never be the same," Nadia says, moving her piece on the board and passing the dice to Cass.

Cass picks up her dice and peers at me from the corner of her eye. She eagerly rolls, and as the dice land, she shouts with glee, jumping in her seat a tad with excitement. The movement causes her to lose her balance a little tip towards me. As she comes back down, her hand finds my knee under the table.

In the year that I have known Cass, she's been incredibly particular about any amount of touch. She wears gloves all day except at lunch, never wears short sleeves, and she wears tights if her legs are ever exposed. Once, she told me it had something to do with her crest.

All I know is that Cass doesn't like to be touched, ever. So, the second her hand lands on my knee, even with the fabric between our skin, my pulse skyrockets. I can't fight the rush of nervous energy barreling through me.

Did she mean to touch me? Was it an accident? Am I just sitting too close?

My instinct is to move away so she'll feel more comfortable, but her hand stays. She doesn't pull away immediately. She lingers. She leans into me, and our arms touch, too. I am suddenly wildly aware of how close her chair has been to mine.

"Maybe I can give you some of my luck," Cass says brightly to Nadia, who is pouting miserably.

Her hand slips from my thigh as she reaches over the table to move her piece. When she sits back down, she's still close enough for me to feel her sweater sleeve brushing against mine.

"Tal? Tal? Hello?" Nadia calls, pulling me out of the haze.

I blink at her and shake my head, trying to draw some of my attention away from the gentle graze of Cass's sweater against my sleeve again.

"Sorry, what?"

"God, where did you go? It's your turn!"

"Oh, sorry."

Picking up the dice, I cast a glance at Cass, hoping the heat in my cheeks isn't obvious.

NOVEMBER—SOPHOMORE YEAR

"Charlotte asked me out!" Cass tells me, practically bouncing with excitement.

She's brilliant. The autumn sun shines through her curls and illuminates the little pops of copper she's dyed throughout it for the fall. Her cheeks are rosy from the chill, and her smile stops my heart, as usual.

But I can't breathe over those words.

I smile because I know I'm supposed to smile.

"Cass, that's amazing!" I hear myself say, but even as I glance out over the river, lit by the afternoon sun, I can't get my thoughts to catch up with me.

We'd taken a walk after school. Cass's dad is out of town, and her mom wanted help with a few of the lights for the winter festival in a few weeks, so we ended up in the town square by the river. Cass leans against the railing of the gazebo beside me.

"When did she ask you?" I manage, still forcing a smile, trying to keep the hurt in my chest from wrinkling my forehead.

"Right after school," Cass says. "You were in the bathroom."

"Ah." Damn. "That's amazing, Cass."

I shake some feeling back into my limbs, mold my features into a bright smile, and drop my hands into my pockets with a heavy sigh.

"You've wanted to go out with her for months."

"Yeah, I was surprised, honestly." She sighs, "You think it's good?"

The light catches in her honey-gold eyes, and I feel like the gazebo floor is falling out from under me.

"I think it's great."

OCTOBER—SENIOR YEAR

The pulsing beat of the music drives me outside to the bonfire. I need to clear my head. I feel like a complete idiot. My chest aches. My ears are ringing. I want to find Cass. Cass would understand. She'd have the right words to make this stop hurting so much.

But she's lost in the music, wrapped up with—what's her name? I don't know.

It doesn't matter.

The cold air helps a little. Trotting down the long stairs of Niles' family mansion, I make my way to the bonfire. Yvaine and Willow are snuggled up, holding cups of steaming cider—A vampire and her cheerleader girlfriend.

Cute.

"Wow, rough night?" Willow asks.

"You could say that," I groan, slumping to the ground beside them.

Yvaine stays quiet but offers me a sip of her beer.

"What happened?"

"Oh, my boyfriend fucked half the baseball team," I drone, lifting the bottle in cheers.

"Oh god. Keep it," Yvaine says over a heavy sigh. "I'll get another."

The vampire carefully unfolds herself from the blanket she and Willow were sharing and heads off to the house for another round.

"That's awful, Tal," Willow says, placing a hand on my forearm.

I shrug and down the rest of the bottle before lying back to gaze up at the stars.

"Fuck him," I say, but I can't deny how much my chest aches. "I fucking caught him, too."

"Shit."

"Yeah."

The sound of footsteps across the yard tells me Yvaine has returned. I hope she's brought me another beer.

Sitting up, I see she's brought something else entirely.

Cass lowers herself to the ground, letting her pirate skirt flare out around her knees; her brow is furrowed beneath a red bandana. I don't think my face could be any hotter—I'm thankful for the skull face paint covering everything to my neck.

"Hi, Yvaine tells me I have a baseball player to add to the list," she says. Her tone is level, but her eyes search my face.

The list. Our ongoing imaginary list of people we hope karma pays a visit to.

"Actually, it's four baseball players and a cellist," I correct her, dropping my head back to the ground.

"He walked in on them," Willow offers with an apologetic grimace.

"Not all of them," I protest immediately, as if it makes it any better. "He was with Carter."

"What? Where is he?" she hisses with a heat to her tone, turning her attention to Yvaine.

"I don't know, Firefly. It's fine."

"It's not fine." She snaps to her feet again. "Fuck the list. I'm going to kick his ass."

"Wait, Cass, no."

She's already halfway across the yard by the time I'm able to scramble to my feet again and catch up to her.

"Hold on, Cass," I say, coming up beside her.

"No, you should stay here. But I am not going to let him get away with this. I can't believe that asshole would treat you like that. Actually, I can. I told you orchestra boys are sneaky."

Hearing Cass so adamant about protecting me does something to me. Over the ache of heartbreak and betrayal, the pulse of that draw I have always felt toward her sparks to life. For a moment, it's exhilarating.

"Wait, Cass, just slow down," I say, breathlessly.

I can't keep up with the swirl of wild feelings cracking free again. I reach for her but pull my hand up short before I can catch her elbow.

"I don't want to slow down. I want to go talk to your shitbag boyfriend," she insists, but she turns on her heel to face me, stopping short anyway.

I can't think again. All of my protests die on my tongue. She's painted her lips a deep red, her eyes are darkened with black, and her pirate's hat is sitting crooked now. I can't breathe under the intensity of those honey and amber eyes.

I don't want to think about Stefan anymore.

My eyes flick to the beautiful, full pout of Cass's lips. She always purses them in the same way when she's angry. It's almost as beautiful as when she smiles.

I miss what we had. Things have been weird for months—since Grease. I miss her.

She must see something in my expression as I struggle for words because the intensity in her eye softens, and her shoulders loosen. She blows out a breath, and a loose curl dances with the exasperation.

"What do you need?"

You.

"I don't know," I say, shrugging. "Can we just go sit by the fire and get drunk and talk about how stupid boys are?"

She offers a soft smile and a nod before lacing her gloved fingers with mine.

"I can kick his ass tomorrow," she agrees, pulling me along to join the others.

NOVEMBER—SENIOR YEAR

The chill doesn't even touch me on the way home, despite my soaked pants and dripping hair that quickly frosts over.

Cass wants to go with me.

ME.

She's my date to the winter formal, and nothing can bring me down from this high.

DECEMBER—SENIOR YEAR

Dress shoes are entirely impractical when there's snow on the ground, but I try not to let it bother me as I get out of my car and trot up the stairs to Cass's family home. The corsage she requested is a vibrant red dahlia—just like the one I drew for her back in Junior year.

The box feels too heavy and too light all at once as I shift it in my hands and use the knocker on the door.

Mr. Varner answers.

My heart drops to the soles of my shoes—I've never officially met Cass's dad. Niles has whispered all sorts of rumors about the mysterious Lionel Varner; I've seen him at a distance at school events and plays, but never like this.

"Mr. Varner," I say, offering my hand, "I haven't had the pleasure."

"Vale? Right?" Mr. Varner asks, ignoring my hand until I awkwardly withdraw it.

"Talien Vale, yes, Sir," I confirm, feeling unusually small in front of him, even though we're easily the same height.

The look in his eye, the slant of his brow, it's very unnerving. I want to shift on my feet, but I fight the urge. However, Mr. Varner takes that choice away from me as he steps through the door onto the porch and forces me to back up a few steps to make room for him. Silently, he closes the door.

"How old are you, boy?" he demands, folding his hands behind him.

Irritation prickles along my scalp. "My name is Talien. And I'm eighteen, Sir. Same year as Cass."

"Cassiopeia," Mr. Varner corrects.

There's a tense moment between us. He wants me to repeat her full name, I can feel his unspoken expectation hanging in the air between us, but I refuse. She's not Cassiopeia to me; she's Cass, or Firefly, or Varner... never Cassiopeia.

The silence creeps on.

Mr. Varner cocks his head at me, and a plume of frosty breath billows between us.

"I'll make this simple for you," he begins. "I'm not pleased about my daughter's decision to accompany you in any fashion. I'll assume you don't need a history lesson, and I'm sure you know who, exactly, I am. So, I don't need to tell you how inappropriate it is for you to even think you have the right to speak to my Cassiopeia."

A pit has formed beneath me. My throat feels tight. My pulse races.

He adjusts his cufflinks and peers down his sharp nose at me.

"Now, it is within my better judgment to turn you away now and send a message to your family... a reminder of where we stand. But my wife has convinced me to refrain from ruining this evening for that girl in there. I care about my daughter, so I'll afford her this one night. However, if I find out you've gone anywhere near her after this evening, I'll have your family destroyed. Is that under-stood, boy?"

My jaw clenches. Some of Cass's fear of this man has bled into our lives over the years: early curfews, never going out in public—even with the entire friend group—if he was in town, and how distant she would get with me during any school event.

I understand now. Her fear makes sense. I can feel the air of authority and power rolling off of him. My hands tremble around the corsage box, but I set my jaw.

Swallowing, I tip my chin, not allowing him to see me cower.

"My name is Talien." My voice cracks over the words.

Mr. Varner's crest lights. Panic floods my veins. He leans forward, the iridescent sheen of his crest is almost blinding as he locks a hand in my collar and drags me to him until we're nose-to-nose.

"What did you say to me?"

The fear is overwhelming. The last fibers of my resolve have frayed.

"I understand," I manage to say over the rock in my throat.

"You understand what?"

"I can see her tonight." Sadness begins to saturate the fear. "Only tonight. Then I leave her alone."

Mr. Varner releases me, and the light blinks out from his crest.

"Good boy," he says, adjusting my suit jacket and laying the collar flat once more. "And if you don't?"

I'm going to be sick.

"You'll ruin my family."

"That's right," Mr. Varner says with a smile. He tips my chin to look at him, forcing me to meet his stare again.

"You will not taint my daughter; do you hear me?"

My gut twists.

"No, Sir," I confirm.

"I assume you know what I mean?"

"Yes, Sir."

"Good."

He releases my chin and claps me on the back, directing me to the door and leading me into the massive foyer of his mansion to leave me alone to wait for Cass.

. . .

I barely remember the rest of that night now. I can almost place her coming down the stairs in a deep red dress that perfectly matched the dahlia I'd brought. She laughed at the crushed box, I think, and pricked me when she was putting on my pin, but I was numb.

Cass had been in an incredible mood. The gymnasium was stunning in the dark blues and whites chosen for that year's winter formal. We danced, but I don't remember what songs played or how it felt to hold her—I just remember trying to make sure I barely touched her. Cass pulled my arms tighter once, and I tried to enjoy it, tried to keep up with her energy, but I couldn't.

The car ride home was silent and awkward. When we stopped outside her house, she turned to me. She smiled in spite of the awkward air between us. Waited.

I knew she wanted more. A good night kiss, at the very least—it certainly wouldn't have been our first.

But nothing happened. She got out. I went home.

The rest of the school year was awkward. I tried to keep my distance, Cass tried to hang on, and I let her. We still met to study. We ate lunch with our friends. I took Celena to Prom; Cass took Bryson.

I crunch up the stairs of the cabin and remove my boots just inside the door. The whole place is silent, save for the occasional snore from one of the many bedrooms. Creeping through the cabin, I make my way back into Cass's room—our room.

She's curled around the pillow, just like I left her, with the blankets snuggled under her chin. Her hair is tucked into the soft pink satin bonnet I got for her with a little bow adorning her forehead to secure it, and she couldn't be more perfect.

FIVE YEARS AGO

I don't understand how they expect you to get any sleep in hospitals, really. The beeping of the monitors makes it almost impossible to get more than a couple of seconds of shut-eye. Fortunately, the nurse gave me something to help once the scans came back.

It must have worn off, though, because I can hear the beeping again.

Groaning, I try to wiggle my hips to one side and release some tension from sitting in one position too long. It helps a little.

The squeak of shoes on the tiles alerts me to the presence of someone else. It's probably just a nurse, but curiosity gets the best of me. I pry open one very swollen eye and I swear my heart stops, though the beeping continues. Quickens.

Lionel Varner is standing at the end of my bed, arms folded behind his back, head cocked to one side, crisp suit flawless, and glasses perched on the bridge of his nose. He smiles.

Smiles.

The beeping gets faster.

"Hello, Vale," Lionel says, watching me, savoring the fear I swear he can see rolling off of me.

"Wha—" My voice cracks; my throat is too dry to speak.

"What am I doing here?" he asks, moving to stand beside me. "That's an excellent question, isn't it?"

It hurts to turn my head to look at him. My neck screams from all the bruising, but I don't want to let him out of my sight.

"Cassiopeia is missing," he informs me, watching my face. "You wouldn't know anything about that, now, would you?"

My face is too swollen to move, but I hold his gaze.

Cass isn't missing. She's running. From you.

Lionel tsks over his teeth and his crest lights. Fear floods through my system. Panic lancing every nerve.

The beeping turns frantic.

"Where is she?"

I try to focus on my breathing. Someone must be coming. My monitors are going wild.

"I told you to stay away from her, boy," Lionel growls. "I told you there would be consequences. And now, look what you've done."

Lionel strides away from me towards the window to look out at the city. With every step, the panic lessens.

"I—" I cough over the dryness in my throat and wince at the pain that rakes through my body.

"I warned you," Lionel says. "My little girl was supposed to be married today. Instead, she's vanished, the groom has a black eye, and here you are. What am I supposed to think?"

I swallow painfully as Lionel returns to the bed.

"You should have listened," he says, folding his hands. "Did you fuck her?"

"No—" Coughing cuts me off again. It hurts worse than when Bryson and his flunkies were kicking the shit out of me.

Lionel sighs heavily, almost regretfully.

"Bryson has a temper; I'll give him that, but I hardly think he'd have come after you unprovoked. Now, as a man of my word, you've left me no choice."

That pit of fear gapes wide again as Lionel brushes the hair from my forehead; his fingers against my bruised skin are painful, and I pull away.

"I'm nothing if not a man of my word, Vale. I hope you've enjoyed your comfortable life to this point. It's over now."

"Cass," I whisper, leaning down and kissing her cheek.

Her crest shimmers as she releases a sleep-ridden breath. She shifts slightly, nestling further into the bed and hums. Her eyelids flutter open, and her hazy eyes take a moment to focus.

"What's wrong?" she asks groggily.

"Nothing's wrong," I assure her. "I have something to show you."

CHAPTER 37

Talien

I swear the hike back to the blanket takes an eternity and not nearly long enough at the same time. My thoughts are still a confusing jumble, but I am determined to talk. She needs to know. I need to talk about these things.

I refuse to let Lionel Varner steal any more from us.

"It's just over here," I tell her.

I pull her closer as we crunch through the snowy path, following my footprints by the glow of my phone's flashlight.

"What is?" she asks with a tinge of a laugh.

"Your surprise."

We finally make it to the top of the hill, and the trees clear out around us enough to see the sky. In the middle of the clearing, I've arranged a pallet of all the spare blankets and pillows I could scavenge from the basement storage of the cabin. The moonlight is just bright enough to illuminate the scene as I click off my phone's light and turn to watch her expression.

"Oh, Tal," she whispers, her tone thick, her eyes welling with emotion as she fixes her gaze on the display.

"You used to say that you'd spent every night at St. Agnes gazing up at the stars—"

"Wondering if anyone was looking back at me," she finishes, her tone still hushed, her eyes still fixed ahead.

She turns to look at me, her bottom lip tucked between her teeth, her luminous eyes brimming with emotion. I reach up, tucking my hands into my sleeves before I cup her face in my palms.

"I used to sneak out my window every night and do the same thing." The words feel more significant than admitting to a little childhood mischief.

"Wasn't your room on the second floor?"

I chuckle, nodding. "Yeah, I crawled out on the roof. Mom was *pissed* when she found out."

"God," she breathes.

The way she's looking at me lifts a weight from my shoulders. Her gaze pierces mine as though she might be able to see right through to the depths of my soul.

"I never knew," she says, and it seems as though she might say something else, but her mouth snaps closed, and she leans into my touch, reaching up to hold my hand to her cheek.

"I never told you," I admit. "I haven't told you a lot of things I should have by now."

My chest aches in that same familiar way it does when Cass is too far from me. But she's right here. Staring up at me.

Can this thing between us fill the distance created by all these unspoken fears?

I search her face for a moment, trying to find the words before I remember I brought her up here for a reason.

"There's supposed to be a meteor shower tonight," I tell her, slipping my hand away from her face and motioning toward the pallet. "I thought you might not mind being woken up and dragged out into the cold for that."

"*Oh.*" She turns her attention to the sky with a gasp of excitement. "I can definitely bear the cold for a celestial event. And you brought all these blankets out here."

"I did."

She takes my hand and pulls me along, lowering to her knees, and I follow. We carefully kick off our boots and set them on the sled I left beside the pallet. I help Cass settle into the mass of blankets and tuck her into them before climbing in beside her.

"How's it so warm?" she asks as I tug her hood up over her hair.

"The hot cocoa and an electric blanket."

Her brow knits in confusion, and I laugh. I don't think I'll ever tire of how expressive she is. We've never been truly free to be ourselves; there was always something between us, and it read on her face no matter how well she tried to hide it or how often I ignored it. I can see the hesitation there now. She's freer. Brighter. Happier, despite that awful bruise that's still healing on her cheek. But even with all the walls that have been torn down, there's still something in the way.

My heart quickens, knowing I can't back down this time. I have to get through this. I have to clear the rest of the barriers between us and let her in. I want her to see me. All of me. I want her to know everything, but I'd be lying if I said it didn't terrify me.

Rummaging through the blankets, I find one of the thermoses I've buried in the depths of this blanket fort.

"You can't go stargazing in the forest in the middle of winter *without* hot cocoa," I tell her, smiling, even though my stomach is in knots. "Would you like some?"

"Yes, please," she hums pleasantly. "You thought of everything. Why are you so perfect?"

The question comes out on a soft whine, stilling some of the thundering in my heart. *I only hope she still feels that way after hearing everything I have to say.*

"Practice makes perfect?"

I fish out one of the mugs I brought and fill it for her before finding a second for myself.

"I didn't realize you had much practice in the *hopeless*

romantic department," she teases as she brings her mug to her lips. The steam wafts over her face and she sighs as her first sip hits.

"Oh, I don't," I admit, tipping my face up to scan the sky. "I have a *terrible* track record, actually. Fuckboys and assholes, mostly. Not really the 'romantic' types."

She chuckles, tips her face to the sky, and considers for a moment.

"Just a natural then. I don't want to leave this place. What are the chances Niles is okay with us just moving in permanently?"

"High. I think they secretly have always wanted a reason to loop us into their 'family business.'"

"Perfect, I'll send for my things tomorrow," she teases, shifting to tuck herself in close and rest her head over my shoulder. "But if they try to wake me up again tomorrow before six AM, I am going to *murder* them."

I laugh at the viciousness in her tone and kiss the top of her head.

"I'll let you."

Silence falls between us for a few minutes while Cass enjoys her cocoa and watches for shooting stars. My determination and the anxiety rising up my throat are at war. I'm almost halfway through my drink before I finally find the beginnings of a sentence. Just as it's forming on my tongue, Cass squeals and points. Overhead, a bright, white streak glitters and disappears against the deep blue of the winter sky.

"Did you make a wish?" I ask, swallowing hard over the words I'd tried to piece together.

"Yeah," she says on a heavy sigh, "did you?"

"Yeah."

I wished for Cass to be free; that she'd somehow, finally make it out from under her father's thumb.

"Cass," I say, bolstered by the thought of watching her thrive without Lionel there to dampen her, "I mentioned that there are things I haven't said."

"You did," she agrees, shifting her attention to me. "Are you okay?"

After a long, steadying breath and downing the rest of my cocoa, I finally find the ability to answer her.

"I will be. What you heard at Niles' party, I wasn't lying. I ran into an ex, and he threatened me—my family. I don't know if he's in your dad's pocket; I think his dad might be."

I'm getting off track.

"After you left town," I try to redirect myself. "No, before that." I blow a frustrated breath through my nose and drop back among the blanket, clamping my mouth shut for a moment to stare up at the crisp, glittering stars.

"Tal, it's okay. I'm here, take your time," she says as she reaches out to offer my hand a gentle squeeze.

Her voice calms the panic rising through my limbs. It stills. Ebbs. I can breathe again.

"Do you remember the winter formal?" I ask once my heartbeat has leveled enough for me to hear my own thoughts.

She tenses and pulls her hand away but settles in next to me.

"Yeah, I was just thinking about that the other night. Well, the night you broke into my room, actually." Her voice is still light, but there's a slight strain there now.

The tightness in my chest eases.

"Oh, fuck! I forgot I did that," I chuckle, dropping a hand over my eyes. "God, I was such a mess."

"You were cute," she smiles sheepishly with a shrug of a shoulder. "God, I was so scared you'd get caught."

"I didn't care. I was crazy about you. I still am."

I think if she asked me to climb up to the heavens and bottle a falling star for her to keep, I'd do it.

"Talien," her voice drops, a concern lingers under her tone.

I want to kiss her. To soak up this moment and only dwell on the happy memories we have of all the times over the years when our feelings for each other were so glaringly obvious and we just... missed each other. I want to focus on those happy things: the way she laughed that night as we ran away from the football field, our hands covered in paint, the fiery glint in her eye when I showed up dressed in her private school uniform, the breathless, wild way she kissed me in her parents' kitchen.

"I am. I think that's pretty obvious," I say, turning my gaze up to hers and gesturing to the blankets.

"Yeah," she breathes, "Tal, I—"

Something in her tone terrifies me. The way her brow creases, the way her eyes drop away from mine. I panic.

"Cass, wait. Let me—" Sitting up, I fold my knees to my chest and wrap my arms around them. "Please, just let me say this. I need to tell you what happened."

"Okay," she says, following me to a seat with caution in her movements.

It takes another heavy breath before I can find the beginning of my thoughts again.

"When I picked you up for the winter formal, your dad was the one that let me in. He—he had a lot to say about how he felt about me. He said he'd hurt my family if I kept seeing you, and I believed him. I can't explain it. His crest was so fucking bright, and I—I don't know. I was a kid. He scared me. So, I did what he said."

The lump growing in my throat nearly chokes me, but I force my words around it—breathe through the pinch of tears.

"I hated it. I hate that I can't even remember anything else about that night. I don't even know what songs we danced to."

She grits her teeth, and her jaw tenses as she releases a breath. Emotion churns behind her eyes, but she remains quiet.

"Celena and I got in a huge fight at prom."

That's beside the point.

I shake my head and try to find the next point I've gone over a million times in my head.

"I almost worked up the courage to ask you out again in college. But Bryson was always in the way, or I was with someone. And then—Do you remember that one party?"

I turn to watch her expression. Her brow knits, and she shifts in her seat.

"Which party?"

"Uh..." I clear my throat. There's no reason to feel embarrassed about a kiss after the things Cass and I have done now, but my heart races all the same.

"I think Bryson put something in your drink, and you ended up staying in my apartment that night."

Her eyes flare as her memory catches. "Oh god, yes. I don't remember the party. I remember the shower, though. I also remember you acting like nothing happened. For a while, I thought I'd dreamt it or gone crazy, honestly."

My cheeks feel like they're on fire.

"Yeah," I cough. "You weren't really in your right mind, and nothing *really* happened. And then you never said anything about it, so I assumed you either regretted it or didn't remember."

"I remember," she whispers, "and I never regretted it."

"That's a relief."

Chaotic flashes of Cass desperately tugging at my clothing and fitting herself against my lap as the falling water pelted down on us distract me for a moment.

God, I'd love to get her on top of me like that again.

I shake off the thought and try to forge ahead.

"We just kind of missed each other in college, huh?" Regret drips from my words.

"It doesn't sound like we missed each other at all, actually," she says, that weight still pulling at her tone.

"Then how'd you end up engaged to Bryson?"

She flinches. The words are out before I can catch them. They spill from a wound I hadn't realized was there, from the need for answers to questions I hadn't let myself ask.

I'd been desperately in love with Cass since that first day. It suffocated all reason from my brain sometimes. And yet, after all those times we got so close, nothing came from it. Sure, I'd pulled away a few times out of fear or because I thought she regretted it. I didn't exactly have a good reputation in college, so I'd written off her never bringing up that night because she wanted to ignore it.

It's a relief to know that wasn't the case.

But how did we get here?

"I was *supposed* to end up engaged to Bryson," Cass says. "I never wanted that. I thought you knew that. I thought I made my feelings clear the last time he lost his temper on my face. But I *also* thought you made *your* feelings clear."

She shifts to her knees and tucks her hair behind her ears. Her shoulders are tense, and her tone is stretched with tight emotion.

"I spent five years thinking you abandoned me. And I know now that wasn't entirely fair, but it hurt, Tal. It was the same feeling I got after you kissed me on that balcony; that night we made cookies and then you acted like I meant nothing to you, too."

It's my turn to flinch. I never wanted her to feel that way. It pains me to know how much heartache she's gone through because of me.

"And it sounds like all of it consistently revolves around my awful, horrible excuse for a father, and I don't know what we're doing here." Her words spill over her lips, her tone rising with anxiety as they fall, and by the end of her tangent, she has her fingers in her temples.

"I'm sorry, you're right." I am struggling to keep up. My pulse hitches on her words. "What do you mean you don't know what we're doing here?"

I must have misread the inflection in her voice. That defeated sigh can't mean she's talking about *us*; she has to be talking about what *all of us* are doing here, hiding in a cabin while we figure out what to do next.

Right?

She looks up at me with tears brimming over her lashes, her expression taut with emotion.

"He isn't going to stop. I thought I protected you from him. I thought—he isn't going to stop, Tal."

"I'm not afraid of him anymore, Cass."

I'm surprised to find that those words are true. *Nothing* is going to scare me away again, not now that I know she wants this. Not after all the time we've already wasted.

She levels her gaze and releases a breath as she reaches out to flutter her gloved fingers over my cheek.

"He's already hurt you. He told me he came for you, for your family. I can't let that happen again. I can't let him hurt you anymore."

"*Fuck him*," I hiss. "Cass, he only came after my family because he thought *I* was the reason you went missing. He thought I was the reason you broke off the engagement. I tried to tell him Bryson was hurting you, that *he* was hurting you by making you marry Westfield, but I—I couldn't."

My throat knots at the look in Cass's eyes. I can't help but feel like I'm making this worse somehow. I can see her pulling away. That spot in my chest, the one I know is connected to her, is aching now worse than before.

"God, I'm fucking up. Look, I know what he's capable of, okay? I've seen it first-hand, felt it." I hold her gaze. "It doesn't matter. I *want* you. I *want* this."

"And if we get back to the city and he kills you? What good will *wanting me* be to you then? God, Talien, you're all I've *ever* wanted. And I thought keeping a distance would keep you safe, but I fell for you anyway. And now, I'm hearing *that* never went anywhere because of Lionel. And I was weak *one time,* and you ended up in the hospital for *weeks.* I believe him. We can't go back to that town together. I'll let him kill me before he lays another hand on you. I can't do it, Tal. I can't—I don't know what to do."

Her words rush together in a fit of panic, rage, fear, or all three; I am not sure which is more prominent. I don't want to tip her into any of those emotions; I want to pull her back from the edge.

"He's not going to kill me, Firefly." I try to calm my voice. "He might be able to drive my family's business into the ground, disgrace my family name, and put us on the streets, but he can't kill an heir to one of the founding families without repercussions. He's not stupid enough to try that."

"What if he is? What if you're wrong? And even if you're right, what happens from here? What am *I* supposed to do, Tal? I can't stay here. Ten seconds with Lionel in the same city as me, and this is what I get?" She gestures to her face. "Everyone has been trying to pretend like that didn't happen, but it did. I left for a reason; you stayed for a reason, and now what? We can pretend everything is fine and simple in that cabin or out here in the snow, but it's not. It never has been."

My chest feels like there's a cord pulled taut between us. Angry tears prick my eyes.

"Damn it, Cass," I gasp, dropping my head back on my shoulders. "I stayed because I *had* to. Lionel bought up all of the shares he could and drove my parents out of their own business before I was out of the hospital. I had to stay. I had to help them pick up the pieces.

"I should have called. I'll probably never forgive myself for not calling you the fucking second I had the chance—but I wanted you to get away. I knew if I told you what happened after you left, you'd be on the next train back to Brunswick, and I didn't want that for you. You deserved better. You deserved to get away. You still do."

This isn't going right at all.

I thread my hands through my hair and drop my head between my knees. I'm furious. Panicked. My hands are trembling. I feel sick. Talking to her was supposed to fix things, not make them worse. I feel like I'm making things so much worse every time I open my damned mouth.

"He can't just keep getting away with this shit, Cass."

"I wish you had called me. I wish you'd been honest with me about the dance. I wish it was always going to be as easy for us as it has been these past few days. But does any of it matter? I am going back to the city, and you'll be safe."

This whole mountain might as well have crumbled out from under me.

"What?"

The pain in her eyes is only a reflection of the cavern opening in my chest. When she speaks, her tone holds a wobble of tears.

"I have to go back to the city, Tal. I can't stay here. I probably shouldn't have come home."

"You can't mean that," I croak over the pain clenching my throat.

"I have to," she whispers, her own voice thick.

"I know you have to go back, Cass."

I can't contain the tension anymore. I need to move. I push to my feet, but there's nowhere to go; we're on an island of blankets in a sea of snow. So, I just dig my hands into my hair and try to let the icy air cool the storm breaking loose inside.

"I'll go with you." My voice sounds so desperate, so weak on the frozen air. "I don't care. I haven't thought that far ahead, honestly, but it doesn't matter."

I'm still fucking this up.

I move enough to crouch beside her so our gazes meet. My heart feels like it's splintering in my chest. I hear her saying, this is too little, too late. I hear her saying she's scared. There's too much in the way. I hear how much I've fucked up, how much I've hurt her.

I want to fix it.

I'm not sure I can.

I probably shouldn't have come home.

"I'm sorry. I've done nothing but fuck this up for most of our lives, and I'm sorry." Tears threaten. My nose stings. "But, Cass, I love you. I love you more than anything, and I don't care what stands between us—or *who* stands between us—I want you. I want a life with you. I don't care where it is, as long as you're there."

My cheeks are cold in the wake of the tears, but I hold her gaze anyway. I have to get the words out.

"If that's not what you want—" My voice breaks, but I forge on. "—If you can't do this because I waited too long or hurt you too much, I will understand. I'll let you go. But I'll never stop loving you as much as I have from the moment you tried to break into my damned locker."

I can't help the bubble of heartbroken laughter that surfaces at the thought of her in that plaid skirt, books scattered on the floor. It hurts. But I won't keep hurting her. I thought there was nothing that could make me let go of her now that I finally have her. Turns out, there is *one* thing that can.

"Cass," I manage over the tears, "if you don't want me. I'll let you go. If there's too much between us, I'll let you go. But, please, don't let him decide for you."

She wipes away her free-falling tears with her gloves but doesn't break eye contact. I watch as her jaw ticks, as she releases a shuddering breath, as she bites down on the inside of her cheek, as more frozen tears stain her face.

Cass reaches out with a shaking hand to brush the hair from my brow, hers knitting together as she considers.

"Do you think your wardrobe will fit in my closet, or should I start mentally preparing to sacrifice some of my shoes?"

The ice around the ache in my chest warms, and I chuckle through my tears.

"Firefly," I breathe, tipping my head back on my shoulders in exasperation. *This woman is going to be the death of me one way or the other.* "If you're asking me to move in with you, please just fucking say it," I groan.

"Yes," she says, her tone more stable now, "I want to go back to the city with you like we were supposed to before; I want Lionel to fuck off; I never want to see Bryson's face again; I want to be allowed to love you."

My heart sputters in my chest.

"Oh god, I love you, Talien. With every fiber of my soul, I have always loved you. I am *terrified* to want those things, but I do. I want you to come with me. I want you to move in with me."

She wants me.

My heart could burst. The tension in the center of my chest releases, and the pain dissipates, leaving behind a warm, golden glow. I'm elated. I'm stunned. I can't breathe from this whirlwind of emotions. The frosty air biting at my cheeks almost hurts, but I don't care.

Cass wants *me*. Not just for a moment. Not just for a few stolen kisses and a decade of loneliness. Not just for a single passionate night and then a lifetime growing old in different cities.

I swear, in the span of minutes from hearing her regretting coming to Brunswick to this moment, I played out hundreds of lifetimes, trying to imagine what I would do without Cass.

Every one of them was empty and miserable.

But *this* life. In *this* one, she's chosen me.

It feels like my life is only just beginning.

"I love you."

It's all I can think to say. It feels so good to finally say it out loud to more than just the empty walls of my apartment. I love her. I always have.

CHAPTER 38

Cassiopeia

*T*alien loves me.

Oh, my god, I have been dreaming of hearing those words on his lips for years. And now he's crouched in front of me, tears staining his beautiful cheeks, warm breath pluming in the frigid air, waiting for me to say something.

He wants to come with me. I am scared to believe he will. I am terrified something will happen to prevent that dream from becoming a reality. But in this moment, I don't think I have it in me to care—not with the emotion I see radiating from those god blessed eyes.

He's bouncing on his heels a little; I don't know if he is aware that he's doing it. He stays still, though, keeping the distance between us firm. He's always so careful about my need for space, never wanting to touch me first. I don't want space right now, though. The air between us is wired, and a desperate need to feel him overwhelms my senses. I don't think there are words strong enough to express to him how exactly I am feeling, but I can show him.

I peel my glove from my hand, one finger at a time, and shift to my knees. I reach out to touch his cheek. I hesitate, my fingers fluttering over his skin before they make contact.

303

"May I?" I ask.

"Always," he replies breathlessly.

I press my palm to his cheek, and he leans into the touch, reaching to hold my hand to his face. My crest flares to life and its iridescent glow over his awestricken expression pulls at that spot between my breastbone. The flush of emotion I get from him is overwhelming. It takes me a significant amount of control to remain steady in the face of his unfiltered adoration. That tug beneath my ribs, the one that pulls at me when he's too far away, tightens. The tunnel between us roars to life as I allow our connection to flow freely.

My bottom lip wobbles and tears prick my eyes, but I hold firm. I release a breath and urge my own love for this man to flow through to my fingertips. My skin tingles where it meets his, a surge of electricity flowing between us, and his eyelids flutter closed.

"I love you," I manage, but the words come out on the soft beginning of a mangled sob. I've been suppressing too much for too long; it's overwhelming me. "I don't want to lose you again. I love you, please stay with me. Come to the city, we'll find you another law firm. I have a guest room; your parents can visit; please, just come with me."

Talien laughs. A true laugh that almost knocks him off balance and sprinkles my cheeks with his tears.

"Okay, okay, yes," he says, pulling me closer to kiss my forehead.

I close my eyes to savor the feeling of him so close, but he pulls back and raises a brow at me.

"But seriously, what is the closet situation?"

A bright laugh bubbles past the tears. I grip his neck with both hands, curling my chest into his, and I smother him with desperate kisses. The sudden shift in my weight knocks us off balance, but I keep moving, a desperate need to be close to him driving my muscles, and before a few heartbeats have passed, my knees are on either side of his hips, and I am doing my best to drink him in, savor the bliss rocketing through my chest.

Talien meets my desperation with his own. I can feel his emotions pulsing from his skin to mine. Bright and warm, elated and desperate. A wave of lust washes over me as his gloved hands brush over my coat to my hips, and he groans in frustration.

"I want to touch you," he murmurs against my lips.

"*Please.*" A coil of need pools deep within my core at the heat in his tone, the hunger.

The next second, Talien is tearing off a glove with his teeth, one then the other, and then his fingers are on the zipper of my coat. It's open, and his warm hands find my waist. His touch sends shivers of desire and frenzied need through me.

My crest flares, and I can't stop the gasp as his need floods my senses. Our wild emotion tangles together in a flurry, driving me to move faster, curl into him, reach for the zipper on his coat. I want to feel him. I want every inch of my flesh to be consumed by his.

Cold air flushes my midriff, where my bare skin is exposed to the frigid night. I hesitate before tearing his coat off. If I strip him bare like the feral animal of desire within me wants to, he'll freeze.

Without breaking our kiss, I fumble for the electric blanket discarded to the side and pull it over us, making some attempt to shield us from the cold. I have no intention of allowing the winter air to stop us from devouring one another.

Talien does nothing to help me in my task. His hands roam my waist, gripping at my hips, tracing over my skin like he's starved for me. He kisses my neck, cheek, the hollow behind my ear, and anywhere his lips can find purchase as I move.

I push his coat over his shoulders and sit up enough to allow him to help me remove it. I groan as his hands leave my waist, but the second I have his shirt off of him, they go right back to their exploration of my body. His touch is electric, chill bumps raise over my spine. A mangled sound of desperation passes my lips as my hands find the planes of his sculpted chest.

"God, Cass," Talien breathes against my skin. "Your touch feels amazing."

"It's the magic," I breathe, my tone a slight tease, and as if on cue, my crest flares as his fingers dig into the soft curve of my hips.

I groan, and he moves them to start at the buttons of my pajama top, tearing through them as his lips trail lower. When his face finds the swell of my breasts, his teeth nip at my skin gently, drawing little gasps from me.

"Tal..." His name is a whine, a desperate plea on my tongue, and I curl my hips against him.

His arousal meets my core, and that heat pools further; I can't stop the moan as it winds through my throat. The spike of sensation at his length against me drives me wild.

I can't believe we're here. I am lost in the vivid whirlwind of everything that consumes us. Years' worth of pining, wishing things were different between us, imagining how this would feel. There is not a single fantasy that even comes close to the reality of this. I am a raging wave curling through a depthless sea, and he is a sturdy cliffside, ready to shoulder the weight of my torrent as I crash into him. He swallows my inferno, welcomes it, begs me for more with every parting of his lips.

I give it to him. I want him to have all of me.

His lips and tongue are like fire against my nerves, and they leave ice in the wake of their absence as the icy air pricks at me. He teases relentlessly, nipping and kissing without giving me the satisfaction I crave. His lips brush past my stiffened nipples with only the barest of flutters and flicks of his tongue before he moves back to placing open-mouthed kisses along my sternum, then over the swell of my breast. It's maddening.

"Fuck, Talien," I groan against gritted teeth, grinding my hips against him.

I move my hands to tangle my fists in his hair. A throaty moan rumbles through his chest as he moves in time with me, matching my rhythm.

"What's wrong, Firefly?" I can hear the smile, feel it against my skin.

"You're a *tease*," I groan.

His tongue flicks over my peaked nipple as he chuckles under me.

"If you want something, do something about it," he purrs through more kisses.

"Done," I murmur hungrily as I pull his head up to claim his mouth again.

I move my lips to his jaw, then the curve of his neck and lower as I slide my fingers to his belt.

"Fuck," he whimpers.

I smile at how quickly he melts for me. Every fiber of that strong-willed, teasing defiance snaps as my hands make quick work of the button on his pants. I nip at his flesh with my teeth and hum pleasantly as I slip my hands beneath his boxers. I curl them around to feel the curve of his ass, and he moves his hips to give me access. I trail my kisses lower, decorating his breastbone with impressions of my lips as I slide lower along his body.

Talien shifts under me, moving to prop himself up on an elbow. One of his hands finds my hair and brushes it out of my eyes so I can see him clearly. His are wide, his lips parted in awe. It thrills me to see him so undone. The usually perfect liner around his eyes is smudged, his tousled hair is roughed and wild. The dark swirling , shadowy, feather-like lines of his tattoos over his chest and neck rise and fall with his quickened breaths.

"Cass..." My name is a sinful prayer on his lips.

I peer up at him from under my brow. The heat in my core drives me, and I continue my trail, moving slowly, lowering an inch at a time as my lips dust his flesh. I reach the line of hair below his navel, and I am breathless as I move my hands to his hips, my fingers fluttering over the deep V disappearing below the band of his boxers.

"Would you like to feel my mouth around you?" I ask as I flick my eyes back up to meet his.

"Oh god, yes," he breathes.

Heat flares in my core, and my need for him pulses between my legs. I tug at his waistband, and with a swift movement and a tilt of his hips, his cock slips free.

On the frenzied night in his apartment, I'd only gotten a glimpse of him in all his glory. Now, I take my time admiring him. The trails of his dark tattoos snake down through the closely trimmed tufts of dark hair and spiral around the length of his shaft. Already, a bead of liquid pools at the tip of his cock.

I trail a nail over the intricate pattern, feeling the beautiful veining and the silkiness of his skin. Talien shivers under my touch.

"You're gorgeous," I breathe. The words fall free before I am aware of their existence on my tongue.

I force my eyes back to his to see a look of hazed ecstasy over his expression. The moonlight cuts across his cheek with an angelic gleam. His beauty stands out against the dark. My heart swells in my chest as I take my time trying to memorize him like this—Drunk-spun on a torrent of uncontrollable desire. Above him, a star streaks the sky, a reflection of this cosmic moment between us.

I want to paint this. Talien, looking like a fallen angel against the starlit sky.

A smile quirks my lips, and I tilt my head to press them to his base, a tease as I dust my mouth over the silken flesh there.

"Fuck..."

The shaky, breathless quality of his voice lights a fresh pulse of desire through me. Even at his most wild, Talien has always been the epitome of control, flares of his rebellious spirit woven through meticulous attention to detail. I want to watch him come undone, release that control, and give himself over to this moment—to me.

He drops his hand from my hair and sets his elbow against the pillows to watch me with labored breaths. Slowly, I trail my tongue from the base to the tip, savoring the way he trembles at the contact. I watch as he unravels at the sweep of my tongue over the evidence of his sweet desire.

"Oh god, Cass," he groans, resting his head on his shoulders. "And you accused me of being a tease."

His hips lift, begging for more.

"I'm just enjoying," I croon. "Tell me what you want, sweet love."

"Your mouth. I want your mouth. Please, god, I need to feel your tongue," he says without hesitation.

I smile, satisfied with how close to completely unraveling he is, and do as he asks. He lifts his head to watch me. I keep my eyes on his as I take him to the back of my throat with ease, allowing my tongue to caress his length on the way down.

His whole body trembles. I savor the way the muscles in his abdomen contract and flex as I drag over him again.

"Fucking hell, Firefly," he groans. "That mouth of yours is heavenly."

That heat in my core spikes, and I get a flush of his desire as I open my magic to him. It's overwhelming, my vision spins, and it's all I can do to hang on to the thin veil of self-control I have. I dig my nails into his hips and offer a strangled sound of approval.

"That's my good girl. God, you look incredible."

I groan around him as his praise spikes that heat between my legs. More curses and needy whimpers drip from his lips as he rolls in time with my movements. When I come up for a breath, my lips ghost around his slick crown before letting my teeth graze over the sensitive flesh.

Talien hisses, his stomach muscles catching as his eyes flash wildly.

"Cheeky thing," he scolds, panting as he laces his fingers through my hair again.

Gently, he uses his grip to tug me up to meet his lips. With my mouth trapped against his, Talien releases his hold on my hair and slides off my coat and the top underneath.

His touch is all-consuming, and those fingers trace over my skin, trailing lower until they brush the waist of my pants.

"God, you're magnificent," he gasps against my mouth.

I arch my chest into his, desperate to feel him over every inch of me.

"I want them off," I say between kisses, a demand in my tone as his fingers curl around my waistband. I follow suit, moving my hands to the line of his pants and tug.

"Done."

Somehow, I can't feel the cold anymore. The inferno raging between us staves it off as I crash into him; over and over, I part my lips, sweep my tongue between his to claim every ounce of him, and he meets me. His tongue glides over mine, between my lips, drinking in everything I have to give him.

Talien flips me onto my back, following me with searing kisses as he rids me of my pants. I'm too lost in him to notice him removing his jeans, but there's only a brief moment of the winter chill before his warmth replaces it.

His skin is heated and soft as he presses his chest to mine. His hips settle between my legs, and I moan at the feel of him against me. Talien adjusts himself between our kisses, angling so he won't press into me, letting me grind against his length instead.

"That's it, Firefly," he groans. "Use me. Move those hips. Take what you need." His kisses sear into my neck, punctuating his words. "I'm yours. Claim me."

I do. I claim his mouth again with both fists in his hair to hold him to me as I do as he asks. I move my hips in tight circles against him. His length slides through my heat, and a pressure builds at my center. The sensation is bright and wild. The tug in my chest urges me closer to him. I am consumed by his uncontrolled desire, and I tremble against him as that pressure coils tighter.

"Oh god, Tal," I say; my words are a flutter, barely audible over my quaking need.

"Such a good little slut for me, aren't you?" Tal growls.

God, that mouth.

Even the roll of those sinful words on his lips brings me to the edge of ecstasy.

I'm close, so close, when the world tips, and we roll until Talien is under me again. I settle my knees around his hips and groan as the roiling bliss remains just out of reach. A bright smile breaks across his face as his eyes scan over me.

"God, you're so beautiful," he breathes.

"So are you," I say, moving my mouth to the line of his jaw.

I slide my hand between us as my teeth find his earlobe, and I nip gently, rolling my tongue over his flesh as my fingers find his length.

"I need you," I murmur, tracing a gentle nail over his sensitive flesh.

I suck in a sharp breath as his cock flexes in my hand, telling me just how badly he needs me, too, but the lust in his eyes clears momentarily.

"I—In my pocket, there's a—"

"I have an IUD," I say quickly, cutting off his concern with a kiss.

"Oh, good," he sighs between kisses. "Take me, Firefly. Please. I need you."

I smile as I curl my tongue over his ear. He grips my hips as though he needs the contact to stabilize himself as I position him at my entrance. I move my lips back to his and press my other palm to his cheek, locking eyes with his.

I release a tether on my magic, and my love for him bleeds through my flesh into his. His lips part slightly as the energy winds around us.

"I love you," I say with as stable a tone as I can while I move my hips to take him.

Talien's head drops back among the scattered pillows as he sinks into me and lets a low groan loose.

"God, I love you, Cass," he gasps.

His hips shift under mine, rolling so that my clit grinds against him.

"Oh god," I gasp as that pressure builds again as I move in time with him.

He splits my core, and the sensation is blinding. My tongue sweeps across his in a hungry rush of desperation, and my hands move to his chest. I push myself to a seat and look down my nose at him.

God, fuck, he's perfect. The dark lines of his tattoos bleed over the sculpted planes of his abdomen, and his hair is tousled, falling over his brow in that windswept, breathless way. His eyes are wide as he gapes up at me.

His hands glide up my thighs and over my hips. He trails his thumb over the curve of my stomach and down until he finds my clit again. The pressure of his touch pulls a gasp from my lungs, and I dig my fingers into his chest to stabilize myself.

His eyes light with mischief as his thumb trails gentle circles over the sensitive bundle of nerves. I roll my hips into him; the pressure of his length inside me in time with the explosion of sensation at his thumb is almost too much for me to bear. I lean back to give him better access and hang my head between my shoulders as I grip his thighs behind me, rocking my hips at a steady pace.

"Fucking hell," Talien groans.

Inside me, his cock pulses, flexing forward against me in a way that sends a shock of lightning through my core.

The pressure builds, and I pick up my pace. He holds me steady, his other hand firmly gripped to my thigh, and I tip my chin to look down at him again. He watches me with an astonished kind of lust I have only imagined in my dreams. I move my hands back to his chest and lean down to claim his mouth again, increasing my pace.

I try to hold on and savor the coiling ecstasy for as long as possible, but with his hand at my clit, working in time with his powerful cock, my self-control is unraveling.

"Talien, fuck. I need to cum for you," I whine.

"Are you asking for permission?" he pants back, moving his hand to palm my ass greedily.

"Yes," the word comes out breathless, a plea.

I am not normally like this with men. I like to take complete control, have them turn to a puddle at my feet. But not with Tal. Here, I want to give myself over to him, to let him see me completely. I want to show him how deep my trust for him is rooted.

I am too close; the dam is about to break.

"*Please*, Tal."

The sheen of sweat on his brow glistens in the moonlight as he gazes up at me. His admiration washes over me in waves, pushing me closer and closer.

"*Please*," I whimper again.

"Cum for me."

As though his voice is the very thing to break my resolve, the pressure spills over. I can't control my muscles as they spasm around his length. I curl over his chest, but my voice splits the night as ecstasy blurs the edges of my vision. He rocks into me as I fall over the edge, claiming me with a powerful thrust of his hips, his fingers still coaxing the bliss from my core.

"That's it," he purrs against my ear. "That's my good little slut."

His hand slips from between us to draw soothing lines down my back. The cold is suddenly a tangible thing again as it bites against my heated skin. Chill bumps prickle my flesh and graze against Talien's gentle hands for a moment, then two.

"Do you want to stop?" he asks softly, nipping at my ears as he continues his gentle strokes.

"No," I reply breathlessly as I shake my head from where it rests against his shoulder.

"Good." The smile he gives me could split my heart in two. "Cause I'm not finished with you."

In one motion, Talien flips us. The chill of the winter air

disappears in a rush of warm fleece and pillows as he rolls to place himself on top of me.

"Use that beautiful voice of yours," he tells me, trailing kisses down my chest. "I want to hear every filthy thought you have while my tongue is on you."

A finger drags up through my soaked slit, and Talien groans, sinking his teeth into the soft curve of my hip.

"You're fucking soaked," he moans, his voice heavy with need.

"Fuck, Tal. Yes, please," I gasp as my head falls back to the pillow.

His finger leaves me wanting, and I feel him move to prop his chin on his hand.

"Please, what? You're so articulate when you're not a dripping, needy little slut."

I whip my chin, and my eyes flare as a spike of adrenaline flushes my senses at the curl of his tone. I prop myself on an elbow and move my hand to his hair to thread my fingers through the thick tresses before tightening my grip to jerk his head slightly. His eyes light up and his lips part as his expression falters over molten need.

"And you're just as vocal as I expected." My tone is more stable now, a slight edge of dominance under the words. "Don't you want to clean up the mess you've made?"

"Oh god, yes," he breathes, his tone barely a whimper as his eyes flare.

"Then be a good boy and put that pretty mouth to work."

The shift in Talien's gaze from that defiant fire to a low simmer of whole-hearted submission sends another pulse of adrenaline through me.

Obediently, watching my face the entire time, he lowers his open mouth to me. The first brush of him over the sensitive bud of my clit is heavenly. He takes his time, sliding the flat of his tongue up the length of me before closing his lips around it and sucking. The sensation sends me reeling.

"Fuck yes, Tal. Like that."

He flicks against me again, sending a shock of sensation through the increasingly sensitive bud. Again and again, he repeats the motion until I'm panting, savoring the soft, beautiful press of his lips in tandem with the merciless attention of his tongue. My fist tightens in his hair, pulling a groan from him as my hips grind against him, directing his mouth lower.

Talien groans again as he marvels the evidence of my desire and dives inside. His hands lash around my thighs, pinning me to him as I rise to meet his ravenous mouth. My clit grinds against his nose as his tongue pulses into me, drinking from me. It isn't long before that blissful pressure is back, threatening to crack my resolve.

"Don't stop," I urge, hanging my head back between my shoulders.

I rock against him, the sensation building as I take my pleasure from his sinful tongue. I don't relent on my grip in his hair as I move against him. Vibrant sounds of ecstasy ricochet off the trees. It builds until I cannot breathe, and it's all I can do to keep watching him as I am pushed up against the edge.

"Tal, I'm there, fuck, don't stop," I demand, though the words are a plea.

He groans with approval and tightens his grip on my thighs. The bright pressure splits, and I am screaming into the night. My hold on his hair tightens, and my thighs clamp around his head as I lose control of my limbs. I curl over onto my side, and my core lurches as my vision turns white at the edges. It's a few strained moments of roiling pleasure before I am able to relax enough to release him.

Talien comes up for breath with a wide smile as I roll over on my side, and my chest heaves, trying to catch my breath.

"Holy shit," he pants, crawling up to curl himself around me. He tugs the blankets up over us and kisses my cheek as he wraps his arms around my middle.

"You are incredible," he whispers against my bare shoulder.

My body melts into his, and I do my best to bring words to the surface, but I can't. I am still trying to catch my breath, but I manage to turn over, arching my chest into his and catching his lips with mine again.

Talien's lips part for me and welcome my tongue. His hands trace over me until they find my face and cup it tenderly. When I pull back enough to gasp for air, he meets my gaze with a wild heat in his eyes.

"Are you still feeling needy, Firefly?" he asks, his tone teasing, eager, but gentle. "Was two not enough for you?"

"God, more than enough. You're incredible. But I want you to come undone for me," I say, reaching up to touch his cheek, trailing my nail along his jaw.

His beautiful green eyes widen, and a smile curls his lips.

"Pleasing you is enough for me. I am content if you need to stop," he says, kissing me. "But I am yours, Cass. I want everything you are willing to give me. So, use me, tease me, make me scream your name until I can't remember my own, or let me hold you until the sun comes up. Whatever you want. I'm yours. I always have been."

"God, all of it," I breathe, running my hand through his disheveled hair, "I want all of you."

I shift and pull him to a seat, draping my legs on either hip, and he supports his weight on one hand, and the other finds its grip on my ass. I position him at my entrance and nip at his bottom lip, pulling it between my teeth to flick my tongue along its length. Slowly, I lower myself to a seat until he splits my core; the pressure of him pulls a gasp from my lungs. I tip my hips, rolling them against him.

"Unravel for me, sweet love."

"God, you feel incredible," he groans.

His fingers dig into my skin, rocking me against him in time with his own movements. I capture every sweet moan that spills from his lips with my kisses as I draw him closer and closer to the edge. Each grind of my hips is met with his own. We lose ourselves in each other. Talien's mouth begs at my own, his pleas growing more and more frantic between our kisses until he's breathless.

The second I break from his lips, he drops his mouth to my nipple. Any moment he isn't using that tongue to kiss me or please me, sinful words and lustful sounds pour out.

"Fuck me, Cass."

"Yes, god, like that."

"Fucking hell, you're dripping."

"God, you fuck me so well."

It's an endless stream of desperate, filthy praise as he nears the edge. I can feel him stiffening inside me, feel the powerful pulse of his cock flexing against me as his breathing turns to stifled groans.

"Cass..."

"Yes, do it, Tal. Cum for me," I demand, keeping up my furious pace.

My words are his undoing. He comes apart for me. His cries pierce the dark sky as he buries his face in the crook of my neck, linking his strong arms around my waist to hold me to his chest. He trembles and shakes, driving into me again and again as his climax courses through him.

As his breathing settles, his thrusting slows to a gentle roll and then to a softening of his arms around my waist. I hold him, my fingers coming through his hair, murmuring affirmations and praise as he comes down. It's only a few moments before he shifts under me and pulls us to the makeshift bed. I curl into his embrace as he tugs the electric blanket over our shoulders. I tip my chin to press my lips to his, a tender kiss in the wake of the wild display of our devotion to one another.

"I love you," he whispers against my lips.

His fingers brush the damp hair off my brow tenderly and trace every line down to my cheek—being sure to avoid the tender skin before trailing down to my jaw and settling his palm against my neck.

"I love you, Talien," I murmur.

The words settle into place between us as my eyelids flutter, heavy with blissful exhaustion. If I never had to move from my spot within this man's arms again, I'd die happy.

CHAPTER 39

Cassiopeia

Waking up in Talien's arms wrapped up in the mess of our blankets still staring up at the dawn dusted sky is a memory I want carved out of time, set in stone to look at for the rest of this mortal existence. I want to take it with me to the next life to remind myself of what it feels like to be close to him like this.

He pulls me from sleep with soft kisses to the temple, tracing intricate patterns over my spine with gentle fingers. We take our time greeting the day, enjoying the comfort of unfiltered bliss before getting our clothes on to head back to the cabin for breakfast. Tal insists he'll go back out later to clear everything up after his coffee has a chance to set in.

It's still early when we get back to the cabin, but I can smell the bright aroma of breakfast on the stove. The fragrance wafts over my senses and instills a sense of comfort within me. It's familiar and not at all similar to the bacon and coffee scent that filled the cabin yesterday.

Tal opens the door, letting me inside and I find the living area devoid of life, though I can hear voices from the kitchen. They float back and forth on a vehement kind of cadence, and I furrow my brow as I try to place them.

Just before I open the kitchen door, my heart spikes in its cage.

"You *better* find them. If I have to be the one to go out there in the snow, you'll be sorry, mark my words," my mother's voice, thickened with frustration and worry, floats through the door.

I furrow my brow and trot the rest of the way through to the kitchen, busting the door open to find everyone huddled around the bar top. My mom, in an apron, is angrily waving a spatula at Niles, who looks very shaken.

"Mija!" she exclaims, running around the counter to greet me. She folds me into a quick embrace before pulling away to slap at my upper arm with the kitchen utensil.

"Ouch!"

"*¡Me tuviste preocupada como nunca! ¿Qué te pasó?*" she exclaims, clear worry and frustration under her tone.

"*I'm sorry*, Mami," I shrug and rub at the welt on my arm. "I didn't have my phone."

"For two days you didn't have your phone?" she scolds, looking between me and Tal. "A text, a call, nothing! I have to hear from your friend where you are. And I get here, and no one knows. What is the matter with you two?"

She slaps Talien on the arm as well, for good measure.

"*Mami!*" I protest.

"*Hola,* Mrs. Ramos-Varner," Tal says, his cheeks flushing a bright pink as his eyes dart to mine with a look of comical horror.

She levels a glare hot as brimstone at him.

"You are lucky my daughter is back in one piece." She waves the spatula in his face and turns over her shoulder, muttering something under her breath as she returns to the pan, which I can now see is full of fried plantains.

"It was a relatively inconvenient time for the two of you to take off in the middle of the night," Yvaine says from her stool at the bar. She takes a bite of the food my mom has prepared for breakfast from a display plate and wiggles her brow at me. "Did you have fun?"

"No—yes—shut up. What's going on? Why is everyone up so early?"

Talien backs a step away from my mother, inching towards the door to the hallway.

"Where do you think you're going?" Niles asks, eyeing him sharply.

"Bathroom," Tal answers, thumbing over his shoulder. "Swear I'll be right back, and then you can yell at me all you want."

"No, wait, don't you dare—" Niles calls after him as he escapes from the room, completely ignoring their plight. "Ohmygod, he's infuriating."

The sliding door to the deck out back opens, and a striking woman steps inside. Her rich, brown skin is complimented beautifully by the deep red hijab wrapped around her head and neck. She's followed by a stocky, muscular masc with a neat bun and a sharp fade up the sides of their head. The tall woman is dressed in a burgundy-toned tailored suit and perfectly pointed heels, while her companion wears a simple, dark button-down tucked into dark-wash jeans and practical boots. The woman's heels click across the wooden floorboards to join us, slipping her phone into a pocket along the way.

"You must be Cassiopeia," the tall woman says, offering her hand to me.

"I am. You are?" I ask with a furrowed brow and a cautious tone.

No one seems to be alarmed by the presence of these strange people, but my nerves are set on edge anyway.

"Marguerite Nakab," she says, displaying a hand towards her companion. "This is Detective Holmes."

They move to extend their hand to me. "Detective Sierra Holmes, she/her. It's good to finally meet you, Ms. Varner. Ms. Nakab and I have been working with your mother on this case for some time now."

Her tone is serious and her light eyes match the timber; the icy blue stands out against her pale skin and dark hair. She looks severe—the perfect picture of a detective, honestly.

"Marguerite!" Talien's voice is pitched with surprise as he comes back into the room. His face looks freshly washed, and his hair is damp and slicked back from his brow.

"What are you doing here? Did Crystal not get my message to you? If you send all my files here, I can keep working—"

Marguerite cuts him off with a wave of her hand.

"That won't be necessary, actually. I'm here because I believe we finally have almost everything we need to make a case against Lionel Varner."

"*You what?*" I ask, exasperated surprise lifting my tone as I shoot my attention back to Mom.

"You've been gone a long time, Mija. Life did not stop because you left, and neither did your father's reckless behavior. I've been working with Ms. Nakab and Detective Holmes for quite some time."

"I don't understand," I shake my head with disbelief.

A sickly sense of dread crawls up my throat as I shift to move closer to Talien. The need to find comfort in his presence is a silent tug on my core as my nerves wind themselves tighter. As if sensing my discomfort, Talien moves to my side and wraps an arm around my waist.

"With your mother's help, Ms. Varner," the detective begins, "we've been compiling documentation on Lionel Varner's dealings for the past five years. There's a *long* list of things we will go over momentarily. Mx. Sinclair, would you like to take it from here?"

Talien's fingers tighten around my waist as we turn to Niles.

"Maybe we should sit," I mutter, my knees are wobbling under me.

Tal walks with me to the bar top, and Yvaine moves to stand so I can take a seat. Talien remains standing beside me, brushing comforting strokes up and down my back as our attention pins to Niles.

"Thank you, Detective," they say, nodding. "As most of you know, the Varner's blatant disregard for the treaty formed centuries ago between the founding families at Brunswick's beginning has been a problem for decades. Repeated offenses of utilizing magic to manipulate those around them for political or financial gain have been difficult to prove. However, when I found out what he had done to the Vale family, I did some digging. It turns out that my mother had been keeping tabs on Lionel Varner since he took over. Her file on him helped put some of the pieces together."

"What really helped," the detective interjects, "was the video footage we have of him threatening Mr. Vale after Ms. Varner skipped town."

"Video footage?" Talien's hand on my back stills.

"Yes. As it turns out, the hospital had been experiencing an unusual number of thefts around that time, especially in rooms with patients on narcotics. Mr. Vale's room was being monitored for similar activity and caught Mr. Varner's visit."

Mrs. Vale gasps softly, drawing my attention. Her eyes glisten.

"You didn't tell me that man came to visit you after we left."

Talien opens his mouth to speak, but Niles cuts him off. "Oh, don't worry, Mrs. Vale. Talien has been annoyingly tight-lipped with all of us, it turns out. We could have put this all to rest quite some time ago. If we'd known about the threats Lionel made on-camera sooner, this would have been a lot simpler."

Talien's chest inflates, but he stays quiet.

"Thankfully," Marguerite interjects, raising a brow at Niles, "after Mx. Sinclair learned about the encounter with Mr. Varner a week ago, they were able to go back through some of the documented encounters from the late ItMiss Sinclair's files and track down some similar instances of Lionel using not only his power and influence to force businesses and families under his thumb but further indications of illegal use of his magic, as well."

"The encounter with Mr. Vale is the most obvious and

blatant evidence we have of him using his magic for coercion and threats," Detective Holmes adds.

"Why did no one know Lionel threatened Tal?" Yvaine asks, a crease of worry between her brows. "I mean, aside from how *stupid* it was of you to keep something like that to yourself. If that room was being monitored, where did that footage go five years ago?"

Again, Talien opens his mouth to reply, and again, he is cut off.

"Unfortunately," the detective continues with a sigh, "we believe whoever was in charge of checking the recordings for that night was either bribed or—"

"Incompetent," Niles finishes for her. "The tapes for that night specifically were never reviewed. They've just been sitting in fucking storage files at the dumbass security agency that set up the system in the first place. The cameras were taken down a couple of days later, so whoever was in charge of monitoring shit just fucking pissed off about it."

Marguerite rolls her lips through her teeth to hide the humor. The expression pulls at the corners of her mouth at Niles' heated and very animated rant.

"So," Talien finally speaks up, "Where does that leave us?"

"Unfortunately—" the detective begins again.

"If the next thing out of your mouth isn't 'Lionel Varner is already in custody, and all of you can go home to sleep in your own beds,' I don't want to hear it," Yvaine interrupts with a terse tone and a lifted brow.

Detective Holmes narrows her vibrant blue eyes at Yvaine and offers her a charming smile.

"Then you may want to leave the room, Miss DuPont."

Yvaine groans.

"I believe we have a case against him for money laundering, bribery, and a few other charges," Marguerite says. "But, if I'm being honest, I want to put that bastard away for as long as we can."

"And what does that entail?" Tal asks, his hand settling on my hip.

Marguerite glances at Detective Holmes, then Niles, before taking a breath and folding her hands neatly in front of her. Something vile at the edges of my intuition twists. I don't like the way her expression has shifted; it rattles my nerves.

"We need Mr. Vale to bait him into making good on his more violent threats."

CHAPTER 40

Cassiopeia

"**A**bso-fucking-lutely not," I hiss with a vile kind of venom laced through my words as they fly for Niles. "You've got to be out of your god damned mind."

It's just the four of us now. Mom, Tal's boss, and the detective are talking to Tal's family, trying to fill in the blanks and answer questions. Yvaine and Niles followed me and Tal to the living room after I nearly blacked out, pitched a mammoth of a fit, and had to be escorted from the kitchen to *cool off*.

There will be no cooling. I will burst into flames and burn down the entire Varner empire before I even so much as begin to entertain this half-baked death sentence of a plan.

"Listen," Niles is saying, "I don't like it any more than you do, but—"

"But if it gets him away from you once and for all, I don't care." Tal's jaw is set. His brow stern.

A string of heated curses fly from my mouth on a torrent of twisted rage and fear.

"*I care*," I seethe at him through gritted teeth before turning on Niles again, frantic desperation fluttering in my chest. "Send me. I can get him to lose his temper. I can get you what you need, and he won't kill me."

326

"Like hell," Tal snaps, a similar fire lighting behind his eyes. "I'm not letting that man lay another finger on you."

I whirl on him. The terror coating my heart is only eclipsed by this adrenaline-fueled rage.

"And I will not allow you to walk freely into an execution!" I turn my heat back to Niles, my finger in their chest before I have a chance to gather my free-flowing thoughts. "You said you were going to protect him. Is that what you think this is?"

"I *am*, Cass. Just *listen* to me!" Niles snaps back.

"Cass, maybe we should take a walk," Yvaine says, her tone level as she reaches out for my arm.

I bat her away with another string of curses, turning on my heel to pace the confined space.

"Firefly." The plea in Tal's voice tugs at my heart.

I turn on him, my spine straight and my jaw set, but the expression on his face, the way his gaze captures mine, falters my resolve, and skids some of my fiery rage to a halt.

"You can't go." I have full intentions of delivering the words on a pillar of strength, but instead, my tone wobbles and my eyes burn, traitorous tears pressing their way past the quickly crumbling façade of rage.

Before the first of those tears can trace my cheek, he closes the distance between us. His hand is already covered by his sleeves when it reaches my cheeks, still so careful not to touch my skin, to pull at my magic without my consent.

"That man is not going to take me from you," he says, his tone sure. Strong.

He can't promise that, though. Not when it comes to Lionel.

"You heard Detective Holmes," Niles chimes in, their voice resigned. "She wouldn't have suggested it if she wasn't confident she could get him out. Her team has never failed a sting. They're waiting for the go-ahead now to prep the apartment."

God, it's too late. This fit is pointless. They've already set the plan in motion. The feeling of helplessness sends my mind reeling, and my knees weaken as I lose control. I tangle my fists in his shirt and pull him closer; his hand finds the back of my neck as he touches his forehead to mine. A wave of his confidence, his love for me, floods my veins.

I groan miserably and close my eyes against the flowing tears.

"I swear to god, if anything happens to you, I will follow you to the afterlife, kick your ass, and drag you back. You *do not* get to leave me here."

Tal's chest inflates against mine, and he blows a heavy breath out through his nose.

"What if I ask really, *really* nicely?" he groans through his teeth.

"*Talien*," I scold.

I want to ask him to run away with me. Right now. I want to get in the car, drive to the city, start over tomorrow, and pretend Lionel Varner never existed. But something catches in my throat. I'm not the only one fighting to free myself from Lionel's grip. My mom is out there. I left her behind once, and she's been fighting for her life since. And Tal's whole family. They've been through hell. I know him better than to think he would ever leave his family to fight on their own. I can't ask him to do that.

Talien sighs heavily and kisses the top of my head. His hand cups my face, and I tip my gaze to meet his.

"Hi, was that a yes or no? Detective wants an answer," Niles says.

Dread coats my resolve. I can't stop this, but maybe I can still protect him. Maybe there is still something I can do.

"We'll go together," I relent, my gaze locked on Tal's. "He needs to see I didn't listen, right? This is about me, so let me bait him. Let me go with you."

He opens his mouth to speak, his brow pulled together with clear concern, but before he has a chance to offer any kind of protest, Niles interjects.

"Excellent compromise, children. Now, let's get this son of a bitch."

CHAPTER 41

Talien

In all the chaos, I'd somehow managed to ignore the feeling of falling through an endless voice into that familiar nothingness. However, the silence on the drive back to Brunswick was the perfect place for it to fester into a solid stream of panic pumping through my veins. Thick and suffocating.

But it was worth it. This was going to work. Cass was going to be free of him. Of them.

We stopped outside of town to meet with Detective Holmes' team. The detective, under Yvaine's opinionated supervision, personally handled getting Cass wired up while one of the officers helped me. Niles explained the plan, in detail, to my parents a few times over. When Cass returned with the detective, we were given minuscule earpieces—I didn't even know they made them that small. Detective Holmes showed us the location of the cameras in my apartment.

I don't remember most of their instructions now as I unlock the door to my apartment and lead Cass inside. We don't know how long it will take, which is the worst part, but Cass is certain Lionel will make good on his threat tonight. The deadline he gave her to turn herself over to him has passed.

In her defense, Cass wasn't the only one who fervently

329

opposed this idea. Mom and Nadia had been equally in favor of trying to take him out with the money laundering and vague ties to the drug rings in Brunswick. Maybe that was the smarter option. But I wasn't willing to wait the years it would take to get him put away—if he would even end up behind bars—to make something of what I had with Cass.

No. I wanted him out of our lives. Tonight.

A large part of me doesn't believe he'll go through with it, anyway. He might be a violent man, but killing one of the members of a founding family—no matter how disgraced that family may be—is a line I can't quite picture him crossing.

So why are my hands shaking?

Cass moves awkwardly around the apartment, unable to find a way to get comfortable—I can't blame her. It's like we're waiting for someone to pull the pin, knowing we'll only have seconds to deal with the grenade.

"God, I want this over with," she groans as she fiddles with the mic secured under her shirt.

"Don't mess with that," I say, moving to gently take her hands. I kiss her knuckles and rub her arms tenderly. "I want it over with, too. Just—"

"There's movement in the parking lot," the detective says over the earpiece. "One suspect. Heading to you."

Cass's eyes widen in fear, her fingers tighten around mine.

"Breathe," I say softly. "We're going to get through this."

A knock sounds at the door—two sharp raps, then silence. Cass moves between me and the door, her eyes stretched wide and fixed ahead.

"Tal," she says, her tone lifted with tight worry.

"Looks like it's Westfield," the detective says. "Can't be sure. His hood's up."

"Breathe," I say again, moving her hand to rest briefly against the center of my chest.

He knocks again. Louder.

"I'm coming," I call, moving past Cass to answer the door.

It takes far less time than I would like to get across my small apartment. I'm to the door before I have the chance to think everything through for the thousandth time.

It doesn't matter, though. We're out of time.

I toss a glance over my shoulder to make sure I know where Cass is in the room, then unlock the door and open it as casually as I can manage.

Bryson Westfield's face is enough to sober me up a little. Westfield has always been one of those little men—an alpha. Always overinflating his ego and puffing himself up by kissing the asses of anyone bigger than him. In high school, Bryson used to brag about his father taking him to lunches with Lionel; how big of a privilege that was.

I shouldn't have been surprised five years ago when my encounter with him set Lionel off, but even now, staring at his perfectly reconstructed nose and cocky grin, I can't help but think just how satisfying it would be to break it again.

"Sorry," I say, leaning a shoulder on the doorframe. "We didn't order pizza."

Westfield scoffs, puffing his chest out as disgust solidifies his expression. His attention doesn't linger on me long, though, as his gaze snags on Cass over my shoulder.

"You've got to be joking. Just as big of a *whore* as I always imagined you to be, I see," he spits.

Rage lights under my skin, but I can't lose it. I can't throw the first punch. Not this time. Instead, I shift my hip, leaning into Bryson's gaze and cutting off his view of Cass.

Keeping my tone, I raise a suggestive brow at him, as much as it pains me to do so, and try to bait him.

"Listen, if you're going to call me a whore, the least you can do is fucking choke me. Be a gentleman."

Bryson seethes.

"Tal," Cass's tone wobbles, a timber of cautioned worry there.

I don't have time to react as the fragile resolve Bryson wields fractures. His hands grip my shirt collar with ferocity as he shoves me back into the apartment. The door hangs open as he throws his weight into the attack. I expect his fist, so I manage to deflect the first blow he aims at my face. His momentum drives us backward until my legs crash against the small table in the hall by the door.

My head impacts the wall, and Cass shouts. The blow knocks one of the paintings to the floor, but I expected that, too, and keep my wits enough to deflect another blow to my ribs.

So fucking predictable.

For once, I'm grateful Westfield lacks even the barest drop of creativity. Sure, last time, I threw the first punch, but as he releases my collar to try and get his arm cocked to elbow me in the head, just like last time, I'm ready.

He swings, and I duck, taking him around the waist and kicking off the wall to take us both to the floor. It takes me no time to get Bryson on his back, but he locks his thighs around my waist and swings again.

That one hits. The world spins for a second, and my cheek burns.

"*Talien!*" Cass shrieks, her tone stretched thin with panic.

"Wait for Lionel," Detective Holmes rings in my ear.

I catch Bryson's fist this time and pin it above him. He may have been able to get the better of me five years ago, but not anymore. Not after Niles and I trained for hours every week to ensure this motherfucker couldn't get the best of shit if he chose to pick a fight with me again.

"See, I'm not into hitting," I groan, still reeling from the blow.

He tries to yank his hand free and fails, so his other hand strikes at my ribs again. I brace and take it.

"I think we need some ground rules here," I growl. "A safe word, maybe?"

That one hurt.

"God damn it, *stop.*" Cass is closer than I expect, and panic flares as she deflects Bryson's next blow. Both her hands catch Bryson's forearm as she tries to knock it out of its path. The disruption causes him to swing wildly, clipping my shoulder instead.

"Cass, don't!"

It doesn't matter. Bryson's next blow is aimed at her. I try to roll him before he can make contact, but he's too fast this time, and his fist cracks against her cheek.

"Fuck!"

Westfield's pristine nose crumbles again under my fist. It's not nearly as satisfying as I had hoped it would be. In the chaos, I'm able to roll him, which brings the little hall table crashing down around us. Unfortunately, Bryson weighs at least twice as much as Niles, and though I've practiced with a number of the Sinclair personal detail who are similar in build to Westfield, the man has some *heft* to him. In the cramped foyer of my apartment, I can't get back on top of him, and I'm forced to try and grapple his arms to keep him from swinging again.

"Cass, try—stay out—the way," the detective's voice crackles in my ear, it comes through choppy and broken.

"Fuck that," she hisses before the ceramic vase from my counter shatters over Bryson's head.

Westfield shouts in pain. It isn't enough to knock him out, but it is enough for me to break the hold his legs still have on my waist. While he's stunned, I buck him off of me, practically sending him out onto my front step through the open door.

I scramble to my feet at the same time Bryson does, snagging my hand on a shard of ceramic on the way up.

Sorry, Nadia. She'd gifted me that vase during a brief moment of insanity in high school when she thought she was into pottery. Thank god she always made her pieces too thick and heavy.

"Movement—unmarked vehicle—Varner—one unidentified —" Holmes stutters through the earpiece.

"Fucking finally," I groan.

Before Bryson can make another move, Cass steps outside and manages to place herself between us. A look of blistering anger twists Bryson's expression. I reach for Cass, my fingers just catching the sleeve of her sweater as I come up beside her.

"That's enough, Westfield. I can take it from here," Lionel's voice croons lazily before he saunters from the shadows into the dim light illuminating the heavy night. "Cassiopeia, I am wildly disappointed in your behavior. Can't say I am surprised, though."

We're too exposed here for him to try anything. A part of me is relieved. But we need him to *do* something.

Bryson is glaring daggers as I slip my good hand into Cass's, holding the other against my chest and clutching my fingers against the blood pooling in my palm from the cut. Cass's grip is iron-clad, and she stands rigid against me. I'm not even sure she's breathing.

"Don't you have anything to say for yourself?" His tone is more firm now. There is a dangerous flare to his expression, like an ember of rage sparks a flame at her refusal to engage. "Silence is unbecoming on you, my little spitfire."

"*¡Vete al carajo!*" she spits. There is a venom under her tone as she tenses, and it spikes my adrenaline.

He tuts her, the perfect picture of a disapproving father. Anger flares through me, and Cass's grip on my hand tightens.

"No need for that kind of language." He turns his vile attention to me. "We can handle this like men, don't you think, Vale, Westfield? I'd prefer not to discuss this matter on the street, if the two of you don't mind."

"No—don't like it—Stay—the open," Niles barks over the earpiece.

"—move the detail—soon as—inside," the detective counters.

Everything is moving in slow motion. Bryson was close enough to me during our brawl that I was able to feel the combat knife sheathed at his side. I count myself lucky it hasn't made an appearance yet. Lionel, on the other hand, is hidden beneath his trench coat. I can't tell what he may be concealing.

Lionel shifts on his feet. I can tell he's losing his patience.

"Of course," I say, motioning towards the still-open door.

Cass grips my arm, her fingers a vice. Her feet remain planted. "Tal, no," she protests.

"If you cannot handle the business of men, Cassiopeia, then step aside. Or I can have you removed."

My fist clenches over the cut in my palm.

"Brutus would be glad to escort you back to my vehicle," Lionel explains, gesturing to the black SUV behind him as a large, scarred man gets out.

Lionel's tone is calm and level as he slips a hand into a perfectly pressed pocket.

"Cass, Tal's mic—damaged—isn't picking—up.—stay close," The detective rings in our earpieces.

"It's okay, Cass," I say, eyeing the three men as I step towards the door. "I'm sure your father just wants to talk."

I'd be lying if I said my heart isn't racing. Westfield is one thing, but if that giant of a man gets his hands on either one of us, I can't say I'd put my money on Detective Holmes' team.

"—right behind you.—at the door—for our move," Holmes assures.

Cass releases a tense breath and does not relax her grip, but she shifts slightly to allow me to step back through the threshold. It's a tense few moments—surreal—as Westfield follows us back into my small apartment. Lionel Varner steps in behind him, examining everything with a sneer, curling his lip—the brute is last, dwarfing the space. As the door closes behind him, my pulse increases.

Silence bleeds between us as Lionel strolls around my apartment, observing. He turns his nose up at the choice of art over my bed and the scuffed leather of my couch.

"Did you come here to judge my interior decorating, or should we 'discuss business?'" I ask, keeping my tone even.

He tips his chin, thinning his lips as he unbuttons his jacket. As he pushes the lapels back to reveal the harness over his shoulders and the two pistols secured at his ribs, my blood stills.

"You don't need guns to talk," Cass hisses. Her fear-tinged anger is tangible as she shifts beside me.

"Cass," I protest as the muscle moves to flank us.

"Child," Lionel says, his tone condescending, condemning, "I warned you, did I not? What your reckless actions would lead to."

Bryson folds his arms over his chest, a sickeningly smug look over his expression.

"*Pedazo de mierda.*"

He sighs and looks down on her disapprovingly.

"See, that language again. I regret letting you spend so much time with your mother. She's always been...*difficult* to corral as well. Step aside, sweetheart. We have business to attend to."

She tips her chin defiantly.

"I will not."

"So be it."

He doesn't give us any more time to consider. In a lightning-quick movement, Lionel shifts. His hands are on his guns, and he has both unholstered before I can blink. Cass screams. Her reflexes are quicker than mine. A skull-shattering *crack* echoes through the studio. My thoughts splinter as my eardrums reverberate against the sound. Her shoulder is in my side, knocking me off balance.

Taking my place.

Horror lances my chest as I realize what she's done, but it's all happening so quickly. Her scream is cut off, replaced with a gut-wrenching groan of pain. As I gather my balance, Cass stumbles backward until she falls limply to the ground, a bullet hole in the sternum of her sweater.

I don't feel myself move, but my knees bite into the floor, and her head is pulled into my lap. My chest is caving in. My hands are shaking uncontrollably.

The door crashes open, and there is shouting. I can't hear. The words echoed through their demanding tones reach my ears in muffled bursts.

Nothing matters. Nothing except this woman in my lap. This

woman I've loved desperately for so long. I've wasted so much precious time trying to stay away to protect her. I was done wasting time. I was prepared to die tonight for the hope that I would get to love her completely. Freely.

I wasn't prepared to lose her.

Oh god, I am going to lose her.

She's moving. Breathing, barely. Her chest heaves like she can't get enough air. She's staring up at me. But I can't stop the tears. I can't hear my own voice pleading with her to stay with me. I can't lose her now. Not when we've just found each other. Not when we've just figured out what this can look like between us.

"Firefly..."

<h1 style="text-align:center">CHAPTER 42</h1>

<h1 style="text-align:center">Cassiopeia</h1>

I can't breathe. The air has been entirely stripped from my lungs. The pain in my chest is unbearable, and there is a ringing in my ears that scatters my thoughts. The overhead light is too bright, but I can't close my eyes.

Tal is over me. My head is in his lap. He's panicking. His hands flutter over me and his lips are quivering. His eyes are swimming, stretched wide, and he has tears streaming his cheeks.

I try to speak, croak words into existence, but nothing comes from my throat. I am still struggling to replace the air in my lungs.

I reach for his hand, mine shaking as I struggle to maintain control and guide it to the collar of my sweater with my eyes locked on his. He follows my lead, his fingers fluttering helplessly with despair, and he allows me to urge his touch beneath the garment. Confusion pinches his brow for a moment, but as he finds the stiff material protecting my chest, realization dawns, cracking a fraction of his horror.

Kevlar.

I am wearing a bulletproof vest, courtesy of a plan crafted entirely by the bickering of Niles and Yvaine.

I'm still gasping for air. I want to explain, but all I manage is a pained groan as I roll over in his lap; he curls his arms around me, I feel a need in him to keep me close.

"Cass," Niles' voice is the first sound to pierce the din of stiffened silence, the ringing in my ear, and they are on their knees beside us.

They bat Tal's hands away gently, and they help me out of my sweater, then the vest, as Tal sits in stunned silence, watching us with a gaping expression. Guilt gnaws at me. I wanted to tell him. I knew if it came to this, it would affect him like this, but I couldn't. He would have stopped me. The second Niles peels free the vest, leaving me in a tight-fitted crop top, Tal claims me again, wrapping his arms around me with an iron-tight grip as his chest wracks with a sob.

"I thought I lost you," he weeps into my hair.

I groan as I struggle to wrap my arms around his waist, shifting in his lap. Moving hurts. There is a blinding pain in my side. It stretches my focus, spins my awareness.

"Nope," I manage. "I do think I might have some broken ribs though. Oh my god."

Niles calls for the EMT. Tal loosens his grip around me and moves to take my face between his palms instead.

"*Never* do anything like that again, Varner. Do you hear me?" he demands, his tone still firm and surprisingly steady despite the tears still falling over his cheeks.

My heart pinches. I didn't want to make him feel this way. I'd hoped things would go smoother. That Lionel would say something incriminating enough to force the team in. But I know my father. He's not one to talk about his actions before he inflicts them. It gives his victims too much time to react, too much of a chance to fight him off.

I was right. And I'm glad I had been ready to protect him, but I can't help the guilt I feel as my mind works to burn his pained expression into my memory. I soften my features and try to offer an explanation, an apology, but I can't over the waves of despair I am getting from his contact. It tangles with mine in a gut-wrenching torrent of agony.

The EMT arrives and separates the two of us, much to Tal's disapproval, so they can inspect the damage done to my ribs. I haven't had the focus to gather what happened to Lionel or Bryson, but as I lift my arm to allow the medic to work, my attention snags on the officers wrangling the handcuffed men out the door. Lionel is staring at me, a vicious, red-tinged look of rage boiling beneath his expression. I meet his gaze without so much as a flicker of remorse.

Relief settles over my nerves as he disappears from view.

It's over.

Niles takes a deep breath and gets to their feet. Tal looks up at them.

"You told me the detective had never failed a sting," he shoots, his tone holds a bite of betrayal.

They nod after the men who have just been escorted from the apartment.

"She hasn't." Their tone is level, calm.

"Cass could have been killed." Tal's is not; his voice shakes with rage.

"Honestly, both of you could have been killed," Niles counters, still sounding sure.

"You're not helping," Tal says.

Niles tips their head in understanding and adjusts the lapels of their coat.

"It was originally my idea to put both of you in vests," they begin. "But Yvaine pointed out that Bryson would probably pick a fight. We decided it was safest to put it on Cass and keep her between the two of you."

Tal seethes. I don't think I have ever seen him this angry. I reach over and gingerly take his hand in mine, offering him a gentle squeeze.

"Hey," I call his attention back to me, "I'm okay. Everything is okay."

He considers me for a moment, his jaw ticking as warmth flushes his cheeks. My heart clenches in my chest as I wait for his response, and eventually, he swallows and releases a heavy breath.

"Don't scare me like that again, Firefly," he says finally, his voice cracking over the words.

"I'm sorry. I would have told you, but you would have stopped me," I say, my tone thick with regret, and I wince as the woman at my side checks my ribs. "He's hurt, too." I direct the EMT's attention to Tal.

Bryson beat him to shit, and his hand is bleeding.

The EMT finishes her assessment, then moves to Tal. He tries to brush her off, but I insist, so does Niles.

After she does some prodding, she insists we move to the ambulance. She asks if we need a stretcher, and I tell her no, but it's more difficult to stand than I'd like it to be. Tal helps me to my feet and supports my weight as we make our way outside.

Yvaine is waiting impatiently with her arms crossed over her chest, biting down on a nail. She waits with Tal's family and my mom, who all look equally concerned. Mom breaks from the crowd and sprints to close the rest of the distance, scooping me away from Tal into an embrace that makes me cry out in pain.

"Mami, stop, oh god," I groan.

"I'm so sorry." She pulls back and smooths my hair back with tears in her eyes, looking at me with a pained, glittering expression over her features. "I'm so sorry, Mija. I never wanted you tangled up in all this mess."

From the corner of my eye, I see Vasiliki showering Tal's face in kisses while Nadia cries into her father's shoulder. Tal winces as she cups his face in her hands and softly scolds him, but the EMT is quick to break up the aftermath and usher Talien and myself into the vehicle.

Tal moves to sit next to me. We must look awful. My face is throbbing from Bryson's blow to my already injured cheek, and Talien sports a matching lump that's starting to swell one of his eyes closed. He, very gingerly, puts an arm around my shoulder, and I glance out at the faces of my family and friends gathered around. Over the tops of their heads, past tear-streaked faces, Detective Holmes is directing my father into the backseat of the cruiser. He casts a withering look our way.

Still draped around my shoulder, Talien's wrist twists just enough to very pointedly raise his middle finger at the man. I huff a dark chuckle and turn to pull Talien into a kiss. Thankful for the bliss that blooms freely in my chest.

We're free. Talien is alive, and my father will never be able to take this. He cannot destroy this us. His power is gone.

Talien winces as I break from him but tightens his grip around my shoulder.

"So, I've been thinking," Talien says as we watch the cruiser pull away.

"Oh yeah? What about?"

"I think I can work with a 60/40 situation."

I furrow my brow and look up at him with confusion. "What are you—Are you talking about the damn closets?"

That bright smile breaks across his features before he leans down to steal a kiss.

"You might have to sacrifice some shoes."

CHAPTER 43

Cassiopeia

ONE YEAR LATER

"That's my good little slut, staying so quiet for me." Talien's voice rumbles, his lips grazing my ear as his seduction-dipped tone urges a deep groan free of my throat.

I clench my teeth and let my head fall back to the wall, digging my nails into his shoulder as he continues his torturous rhythm with his hips. He nips at the crook of my neck as he adjusts his grip on my thighs, leaning into me to use the wall as an aid in supporting my weight.

He grinds against me, and I reach up to grip the coat rack above us. A few hangers clamber to the ground, their falling coats adding to the mess we've already made of this closet at our feet.

He's teasing me. The slow circle of his hips builds the pressure deep within me. It's a maddening contrast to the ravenous, heated, lust-fueled fit we found ourselves in the moment the door closed.

This pace is going to drive me wild.

"Fuck, Tal," I groan through gritted teeth. "Harder. *Please.*"

"Aw, Firefly," Talien purrs, his lips against my ear, "begging so soon?"

343

He rolls his hips again, flexing inside me in that delicious way that makes that coil deep within my core threaten to spring free.

"Yes," I breathe, tipping my chin to nip his earlobe between my teeth. "God, yes, please. Make me come apart for you, sweet love."

Talien's pace turns vicious. Another batch of coats tumbles to the floor as he drives into me. We slide along the wall until I'm wedged into the corner, and I can get a grip on the shelf overhead. Somewhere in the haze of ecstasy, Tal's phone is buzzing again. He doesn't seem to hear it as his kisses become ravenous.

"Tal," I gasp between thrusts. "Your phone."

"Fuck my phone."

I agree.

Nothing could be more important than this. I breathe through a mischievous laugh. I clench my thighs around his waist and tip my hips into him, doing my very best to keep the sound rolling from my throat to a minimum volume.

His phone rings again. It vibrates from his pocket against my thigh. We ignore it, and I keep drinking from him, absorbing every ounce of him he is willing to give me.

The buzzing stops, and this time, it starts again almost immediately.

"Tal," I say between the ravenous parting of lips, "What if something is wrong?"

"Unless the building is on fire—I do not care."

He trails kisses down my neck. He continues to the swell of my breasts in the tight bodice of this dress. Little nips and flicks of his tongue drive me wild. A lust-heated breath deflates my lungs, and my head falls back again as that coil winds tighter, the pressure at my core brought to a head.

"God, fuck, me either. Fuck me, Tal."

"Gladly."

Talien pulls from me unexpectedly, but I hardly have time to groan in complaint before he drops me to my feet and twists me around. With a hand on the back of my neck, Talien pushes me against the wall and flips my skirt up around my waist before driving into me mercilessly again.

His free hand drops to grip my thigh and lifts it, giving himself a deeper angle. I moan with pleasure, arching into him as his hand drifts from the back of my neck to close around my mouth.

"I thought we agreed you only get to come if you can be a good, *quiet* slut," he croons against the shell of my ear.

Despite his scolding, Tal continues to drive into me harder and harder.

"It's a good thing I'm feeling generous."

His hand stays firmly over my lips, keeping me quiet as he winds me tighter and tighter.

"Gods, you're close, aren't you." The growl in his voice is almost my undoing. "Touch yourself, Firefly."

I obey. My hand moves between my legs and finds my clit almost before he is through speaking.

"Good girl."

I whimper against his hand. I'm close. So close. I need this. I need him. I need to come undone for him.

"Cum for me, Firefly," he groans, his voice taut in that way that tells me he's on the precipice, too.

His demand, his lips against my ear, tip me over the edge. The heat in my core fractures and my entire body is unraveling, only supported by his strength as a shudder wracks through coils of taught bliss. I am hurdled through ecstasy. My vision splinters, and I cannot stop the strangled groan only muffled by his hand, still firmly clamped over my mouth.

Tal's forehead braces against my shoulder as he rides the waves of his own release. His moans drown out any sounds that might have slipped free from me as he loses himself in the moment. Once his hips have stopped pumping into me, and his groans have faded into heavy pants and scattered kisses, he releases my mouth.

His phone rings again. Or maybe it never stopped. I can't remember anymore.

Talien chuckles against my back as sweat from his brow kisses the curve of my shoulder.

"Okay. Okay. God," Talien complains, awkwardly fishing his phone from his pocket while keeping me pinned and panting.

"Yes? What?" His voice is thick with the evidence of what we've just done.

The unmistakable timber of Yvaine's livid rage hollers back. I release a low chuckle with my cheek resting against the wall. Tal is still firmly seated inside me. I work to catch my breath, my lungs still heated with the embers of desire.

In retrospect, it maybe wasn't the *most* responsible thing to sneak away from Niles' holiday ball to fuck in the coat closet.

It was really fucking hot, though.

"Please don't do any of that," Talien says, sounding only mildly annoyed and mostly pleased with himself. "We'll be down in a minute."

He hangs up without waiting for Yvaine's response and kisses up the side of my neck.

"Yvaine's pissed."

"We can't have been gone *that* long," I say through a sigh, arching back into his chest as his lips send waves of pleasure over my skin.

"Forty-five minutes," Tal informs me. "Niles has already started their speech."

"Fuck," I say, the word falling over a hazy laugh. "We need to go, Love. Yvaine is going to kill us."

Tal moves to let me down.

"She threatened to personally castrate me," he informs me while carefully cleaning himself up and discarding the condom in the small trashcan by the door. "She also threatened to send my mother up here to fetch us—I haven't decided which threat I'm more horrified by, honestly."

I laugh and sift through the fallen coats for my lost underwear crouched on the toe of my stilettos, but I can't find them.

"Oh my god, brightly colored underwear *only*," I mutter. "Niles is going to be pissed about this mess."

"I'll slip up here while they are making their rounds with the guests and clean it up. Looking for these?"

Tal asks, pulling my lacey black underwear from his back pocket and dangling them in front of me on a finger.

"Yes!" I pop to my feet and try to snatch them, but he pulls them out of reach. "Tal! We're late!"

"You don't *really* need them," Tal protests. His gaze softens, his dominant air pulling back as he dips to steal a kiss. "I think I deserve a prize."

"Hm," I melt into the contact, tugging on his lapels to bring him closer. I tip my chin and brush my nose to his. "You fucked me *so* well. But I am still a mess for you, Sweet Love. *Dripping*."

"Fuck."

Tal swallows as if his mouth has gone dry and I can tell the next words out of his mouth will be to offer a solution to that problem that will absolutely keep us here for another twenty minutes.

"Hold that thought." I press a kiss to his nose. "I am not done with you. But we have to go. I don't want to find out how serious Yvaine is about that threat."

"Fuck," Tal says again, much less enthusiastically this time. "Okay."

It takes another minute of both of us trying to right ourselves before we stumble out of the closet. I have his hand in mine as I do my best to jog through the halls, laughing and dragging him along as I work to keep my skirt where it belongs at my thighs.

It doesn't take us long to make our way down the spiral staircase and hurdle ourselves into the ballroom, where Niles is on the stage speaking to their audience. Tal winds us easily through the crowd to Yvaine, who is steaming as we come up beside her. Vasiliki, on the other hand, offers a small wave and a warm smile with a scrunch of her nose. I smile and wave back.

"Sorry," Tal mouths to Yvaine.

"Of all things to be late to," she mutters angrily. "Fix your damn hair. Both of you."

I offer her a sheepish shrug and quickly run my fingers through my curls to right them while Tal runs a hand through his.

"—Couldn't be more grateful for the community that came together to make this happen," Niles says. They glance our way, clearly checking in with Yvaine, and catch sight of the two of us. A flare of relief and a red flush of annoyance filters over their face. I mouth a sorry to them, a heat creeping up my neck.

"Oh, thank god," they say, not quite under their breath. "Okay, enough of my chattering. Talien?"

Confusion grips me, and my thoughts clear as a second spotlight clicks to life, highlighting myself and Tal at the head of the crowd. My stomach twists as Talien releases my hand. He offers a smile, his cheeks flush red, and he jogs up the few stairs to meet Niles, who hands him the microphone and steps back.

"Thank you. Ah..." Talien turns and flashes a smile at the ballroom. For once, he seems a little stunned for words.

The light washes over him, and even in my stunned and confused state, I take a moment to admire the fit of the leather pants against his sculpted legs and the way the ruby-toned top he's wearing glitters under the lights. The full blacked-out sleeve of his tattoo is on display under the studded side of his blouse. It's a beautiful compliment to asymmetry with the soft velvet of the long sleeve on the other side. The buckled harness over his chest is askew. My pulse spikes again.

I could have sworn we had fixed that.

"Can we get another round of applause for Niles Sinclair?" he continues.

The crowd responds with cacophonous applause. Though my skin isn't touching his, I swear I can feel the uncharacteristically nervous energy rolling off him in waves. This isn't like him. He's usually so collected, stable. My heart flutters in my chest, and the light on my skin makes it crawl.

When the cheers subside, Tal's bright eyes land on me. He

pins me with that gaze. I suck in a breath, bringing a hand to my chest as I furrow my brow at him.

"About a year ago," Talien begins, "Cassiopeia Varner texted me in the middle of the night. I won't get into the details of how crazy the next two weeks were, but since then…"

His eyes glimmer in the lights. His throat bobs as he gathers his words. My heart beats between my ears. My mind has not quite caught up to my body's reaction to his words.

"Cass, before you came back, I was lost. I was drowning or trying to. No matter what I did, no matter how long we spent apart or how infrequent the texts got, the ache of missing you stayed."

Oh my god.

Tal's hand moves to press against the spot on his chest, the same spot my hand now rests on my own, over that warm pulse thriving between us. The connection throbs against my breastbone; it begs me to be near him.

"I have loved you for as long as I can remember, Firefly. Since the moment I saw you, and I know how idiotic that sounds, but it's true. I used to get up so early just to get to school so I could see you before the bell."

His eyes glisten, and he chuckles. I have tears streaming my cheeks. I don't know when they started, but I bubble up a laugh despite their weight.

"I *hate* mornings."

Yvaine chimes in with disapproving confirmation—clearly still bitter about Tal oversleeping during our weekend trip to the beach this summer. He missed the most beautiful sunrise she and I had ever seen.

"But it didn't matter because I wanted to spend every moment I could with you."

Tal moves down one of the stairs and motions for me, extending a hand. My feet are frozen; I can't move. Yvaine and Vasiliki push me forward. I turn over my shoulder to find my mom standing near, holding a tear-stained handkerchief to her eyes as she waves me on. I climb the couple of stairs until my hand is in Tal's, and his nervous energy rushes through the touch.

I wish I could offer a flow of comfort, but my own emotions are a roiling torrent of chaos.

"Almost fifteen years later," he says, "I *still* want to spend every moment with you. I've wasted a lot of time. Made a lot of decisions I wish I could go back and change. And as much as I have been standing up here talking about the past, I don't want to think about the past or the regrets. I don't ever want to be in that place again. I want to focus on now and tomorrow and the day after that."

As I stand before him, gaze locked on his, the crowd fades away. It's just me and him, the din of chaos in my chest slows as those two pools of green radiate his love for me. I can't breathe.

Tal digs a hand in his pocket and drops down to one knee before me. His eyes flash with mischief, even as the edges shine with the build of tears. I bring a trembling hand to my mouth.

"Firefly, I love you. I always have, and I never want to know what it's like to miss you again. Will you marry me?"

All I can manage is a nod as tears fall freely. The crowd erupts into applause, jarring me back to reality as I take his face in my hands, pulling him from his knees to claim his mouth. His arms are around me, holding me close as we pour into one another.

A crack bellows through the air, and I jump in start, pulling away in time to see the billowing curtain of colorful confetti as it showers the crowd. Our families are on the stairs below us. Yvaine and Mom are holding one another, both crying, waiting for a chance to steal me from Tal. Nadia, Vas, and Nicholas stand near as well. Nadia is bouncing on the balls of her feet like she's made of excitement.

Talien takes my hand, pulling my focus back to him. He slides a swirling silver band with tendrils like branches twining up to encase a bright sapphire. It's a blue as deep as the night sky from that night under the meteor shower an entire year ago. I can still see the stars shooting overhead in my mind's eye. Just over the main setting in the ring sits a small diamond. It's set off to one side with a trail of glittering silver. A shooting star. It's breathtaking.

Niles has the microphone again.

"It's about damn time," Niles breathes into the mic as they come to stand beside us. "I won't take any more of your time. Feel free to greet the happy couple throughout the night, but for right now, you'll have to excuse the future groom because I need to scold his ass for almost missing his entire proposal."

A laugh cracks my chest. The bliss rocketing through my chest is unimaginable. Despite the withering scowl, Niles shoots Talien's direction, the joy on their face is unmistakable.

I turn my attention back to Tal and stretch on my toes to offer another kiss. He pulls away and rests his forehead against mine.

"I love you," he breathes.

A year ago, I wasn't sure we could even exist in the same space. Now, I can't imagine a space without him. My heart glows, adrenaline courses through my veins.

"Oh, my god, I am so in love with you."

We don't get another chance to express our love to one another before we are tackled with embraces from all of our loved ones. Vas and Mom are asking to look at the ring, Yvaine is holding me, and Tal is fielding the affections of his family.

The music resumes, and the crowd below turns back to their dancing as the spotlights fade. I meet Tal's eye over the commotion. The love in his expression is overwhelming.

I can't wait to see where the rest of this life takes us.

Also by Hannah Danielle

THE SHATTERED SOURCE SERIES

Born of Flame and Fury

Venom and Vengeance

The Fated and Fallen

Also By K.F. Starfell

WYVEREALM CHRONICLES

Realm of Shadows and Demons

Kingdom of Wings and Scales